WHATEVER
LOVE MEANS

Also by David Baddiel:

Time For Bed

WHATEVER
LOVE MEANS

DAVID BADDIEL

LITTLE, BROWN AND COMPANY

A *Little, Brown* Book

First published in Great Britain in 1999
by Little, Brown and Company

Copyright © David Baddiel 1999

The moral right of the author has been asserted.

The author gratefully acknowledges permission to
quote from the following: (*You Make Me Feel Like) A Natural Woman* Words
and music by Carole King, Gerry Goffin and Jerry Wexler © 1967 Screen
Gems-EMI Music Inc. Reproduced by permission of Screen Gems-EMI Music
Ltd, London, WC2H 0EA. *Evergreen* Words and music by Barbra Streisand
and Paul Williams © 1976 First Artists Music Co and WB Music Corp., USA.
Warner/Chappell Music Ltd, London W6 8BS. Reproduced by permission of
IMP Ltd. *Teenage Kicks* (O'Neill) © 1980 Reproduced by permission of MCA
Music Ltd. *Monogamy* by Adam Phillips © 1996, Adam Phillips. Reprinted
by permission of Faber and Faber. *The Ego And The Id* by Sigmund Freud,
translated by James Strachey. Translation copyright © 1960 by James Strachey,
renewed 1988 by Alix Strachey. Reprinted by permission of W.W. Norton &
Company, Inc.
Every effort has been made to trace the copyright holders and to clear reprint
permissions for the following: *Maurice* by E. M. Forster

*All characters in this publication other than those clearly in the public domain
are fictitious and any resemblance to real persons, living or dead, is purely
coincidental.*

A CIP catalogue record for this book
is available from the British Library.

Hardback ISBN 0 316 64857 4
C Format ISBN 0 316 85267 8

Typeset in Sabon by
Palimpsest Book Production Limited,
Polmont, Stirlingshire
Printed and bound in Great Britain by
Clays Ltd, St Ives plc.

Little, Brown and Company (UK)
Brettenham House
Lancaster Place
London WC2E 7EN

For Suz Gautier-Smith, Ruth Picardie and Simon Lazarus

If it is true, that Fechner's principle of constancy governs life, which thus consists of a continuous descent towards death, it is the claims of Eros, of the sexual instincts, which, in the form of instinctual needs, hold up the falling level and introduce fresh tensions . . . This accounts for the likeness of the condition that follows complete sexual satisfaction to dying, and for the fact that death coincides with the act of copulation in some of the lower animals.

Sigmund Freud, The Ego and The Id

PROLOGUE

I used to tell this story.

In the early part of 1990, I went with Adam, a friend of mine from college, to see *Henry: Portrait of A Serial Killer* at the Phoenix Cinema in East Finchley. It wasn't just showing straight: the London listings magazine, *Time Out*, was doing a special screening, followed by a discussion, led by a panel made up of a couple of censorship/anti-censorship types and the *Time Out* journalist who had reviewed the film in the first place. The place was packed, and, after the film, emotions were running high: the 1980s were only just over, and the politics of culture still counted. Then, suddenly, a woman in a purple woolly hat a couple of rows in front of us stood up and, her voice trembling with anger, began berating the *Time Out* journalist. His review, she said, had given no indication of how violent the film was going to be. She had read it, come along, and now felt shocked, soiled even, at the graphic depictions of killing and maiming she'd had to witness. 'You should have given us *much* greater warning,' she'd just started saying, when a man at the back shouted, 'For fuck's sake, what did you expect: it's not called *Henry the Elephant*, is it?'

Everyone laughed. I mean, really; it got a big laugh, a big

boofo woof. Even the woman, through her wool-capped earnest-ness, half smiled. But me, I couldn't stop laughing; fifteen minutes later, when everyone else had settled back into po-faced point-making about the power balance between viewer and *auteur*, I was still giggling, holding my breath and looking down into the butt and popcorn purple floor. I owe that man a great debt, I think; I think it was at that point that the eighties fell away for me, or at least, that *seriousness* fell away for me, seriousness as in that adolescent, or post-adolescent, concern about everything. I was never going to be intense again.

Anyway, recently I saw Adam, and this memory came up, and he told me that the man, the one who'd shouted 'It's not called *Henry the Elephant*', had died. Turned out he was a friend of a friend, and Adam had just happened to hear in passing that he'd died, he didn't know what of.

And now I can't tell that story any more. Or at least, not quite the same way. Seriousness, it seems, has a second wave.

D.B., 1999

PART ONE

Summer–Autumn, 1997

When love flies it is remembered not as love but
as something else.

E.M. Forster, *Maurice*

VIC

Vic fucked her first the day Princess Diana died. He'd thought of the sympathy scenario before, of course, some heavy issue she might come to him with that he could turn round, problems with Joe, her mother's illness going terminal, whatever. But Emma, round about then, she was a problem-free zone; even given her mother's condition, you could bank on her chipperness, always opening the door looking like she'd just been laughing, her face still crinkled with pleasure at some joke now gone into the untellable ether. So he thought of it, that transmission, such a short move, the conciliatory arm over the shoulder going down a touch, to touch, or better still, a hug, which when you move apart from, your faces are close enough . . . he thought of it, but it was never top of his list of probables, because she was never sad.

And then: Sunday, 31 August 1997. At 8. 30, Tess woke him up, calling from Paris. She'd been on the night-time train from Marseille, getting back from a tasting – this shipment, she'd said, was going to crack the market, she'd found some nondescript vineyard in the South where the bottles were like Lafite, only one-tenth of the cost – when a gendarme, a proper Peter Sellers, give his hat a neck-hanky and he's in the Foreign Legion, 'tache and everything, raps smartly, raps like in a film, on the *compartement* door. Bleary-eyed, probably hungover, Vic's girlfriend rolled over, and, without getting off her top couchette, slid the glass to the left: a tumble-haired, elongated woman in an XXL T-shirt saying DEATH TO THE PIXIES, probably not the image the gendarme had in his mind when he made the decision to alert the English passengers to the terrible news.

'Vous-êtes anglais?' he said, urgently, his voice snapping with import.

'Oui . . .' said Tess, squinting against the white backlighting him against the carriage window.

A pause; a dramatic one. He took a breath. 'Lady Diana . . .' (so many people said that: *Lady* Diana; so ingrained, whatever you are first called) '. . . elle est *morte*!'

Another pause, but this time filled with nothing, a not know-ing what to say or do. They looked at each other for a while, and then Tess told Vic she said: 'Um . . . *Merci*.' And slid back the glass door.

They laughed, at the gendarme, at the idea of him standing crestfallen outside the door, maybe staying there for a while uncertainly, before pulling himself together and moving on to the next *compartement*, in the hope of the news being taken by those passengers with a greater sense of historical moment. And then Tess said she'd decided to stay in Paris for a few days because England was going to go crazy.

Vic spent that Sunday doing what you did. He watched TV all day, looking, looking: for increasing moistness in Martyn Lewis's eyes, for evidence of conspiracy, for more news when there was none. He sat in the one big chair in his small flat, high above Sydenham Hill, and overdosed on the death of Di. He wasn't thinking about Emma at all, except maybe to ring and talk to her or Joe about it – that'd be a new vein to puncture in the feeding of this novel craving – and then the phone went and it was her.

'Hi,' she said, and straight away he could hear the struggle, the getting through the lump it took even to say that small syllable.

'Hi. You OK?'

'Uh . . . not really. Can I come round?'

Funny, but he didn't think why she might be upset. He didn't know then that people, actual people, would be devastated, that all their griefs were going to get parcelled up in this one big one; and so he just thought 'what's wrong?' but didn't say it, because already his possibility fire had been lit.

'Yeah, sure. I'm going to be in all day.'

Vic liked it when you knew that about days.

When Vic opened the door, and saw her looking all snuffly and red-eyed and definitely not crinkled up from some recent Joe joke, she said to him,

'God, Vic – have you been crying?'

He hadn't, not at all. One or two of the hastily put together montages to music, yes, he'd let them through, more to feel something different, to shift the cold fascination to something else: pity, maybe. But crying, no.

What he did have was hay fever. It lasted really long that summer, starting in May, the first phase, the ticklish feeling just behind the face, controllable with antihistamines, and then round about mid-June the second phase, a whole new set of pollens blown in from the fields, turning his skull to water, that no pill or spray or potentially lethal injection can stem. By September, though, the dandelion clouds are normally on their way, and if the streets are full in an Indian summer, it's liable to be hay feverites, trying desperately to enjoy the weather the one time they can. But that year, for some reason, maybe because summer came not at all in July and only haltingly in August, the pollen hung in there, and there were still days in September when Vic's nose was a snot volcano. On 31 August, though, it was mainly his eyes, so itchy his index fingers were in a permanent crook ready for the next rub.

Now, Vic had had hay fever since before he knew what it

was, and he hated it, he hated it with menaces and outrage, this recurring inner rash; he'd never forgiven it for forcing Pathology – the shoegazing band to which he had devoted most of the late eighties – to cancel a potentially breakthrough showcase gig at the Garage in 1990 because he simply couldn't play guitar for sneezing. Hay fever had no up-side, no redeeming features whatsoever, not like some allergies (yeast: good for dieting; antibiotics: good for forcing doctors to give you unusual drugs; onions: McDonald's have to hand-cook your burgers – how special, Vic thought, must that make you feel) but suddenly, for the first time in thirty-one years, he saw a way of turning it to his advantage.

'Might have been,' he said, with an approximation of a watery smile.

'Oh *Vic*,' she said, and crumpled, like the zones of that car, into him.

Straight afterwards, lying in bed with her head full of sleep trusting on his chest, his first fear was how to keep up the tearful aspect, the crying eyes, what with the fading bloom of summer and all: he'd want it to last as long as the desire did. But then God smiled in Vic's direction, oh what a big Teletubbies sun-baby grin it was, and covered London for him in a carpet of flowers.

*   *   *

He never fancied her much, though. No, not Emma, Vic always fancied her, obviously: Diana. He was never that much fussed about that kind of look, the Selina Scott big-featured pretty-horse-faced six-footer. He'd even written a somewhat disrespectful song about her whilst still in Pathology, called 'Shop Girl Queen', which he was glad now they hadn't recorded – someone, somewhere, might have dug it out and he'd be lynched.

Elegant, that's the word for that sort, he thought, isn't it, *elegant* – not sexy, not cute, not lovely. Vic had never been turned on by elegant; he couldn't be excited by someone who only looked good in Versace.

His affair flourished in the warmed (as by a fever) bedfolds of fascism. England, England so tolerant, so diverse of thought, such a rainbow of opinion always, suddenly, there was only one thought, and one way of thinking it, and the single-thought police were everywhere, on the TV, in the papers, surrounded, besieged, England was, by Princess propaganda. And the biggest propagandists of all were the People themselves – as they would be, of course, being the very object of her princessliness – thrust continually into shot that week, reporters prompting them like Pavlov with fat microphones under their noses to speak again and again their radically unoriginal thoughts: 'Well, the thing is, I think she was like the Queen of People's Hearts.' *I* think: like it was an independent conclusion. The People spent the whole week mistaking the word 'I' for the word 'we' – the fundamental error of fascism. Not just the People who read the *People*, but all People, the sushi as well as the spam, him with the ghetto-blaster and her with the Prada bag, they all blubbed together as Elton sang his telly bye-bye to England's Rose.

But say what you like about fascism – it intensifies the old emotions. This one more than most, because the fascism in Diana's Death Week was emotional fascism, that's what the one thought was: *you are very emotional.* England was moved, and the People spread their hearts like meat paste on their skin. Good that, Vic realised, if it's the week you end up having an affair. Sunday: Di dies, Monday, Emma's on his sofa, in a mist of grief and lust, and *Richard and Judy*'s on. (From Vic's point of view, *Richard and Judy* was just fabulous that week. Everyone has a secret book in their soul, and this week Vic's was open; it was open and taking bets on when exactly in *This Morning* Judy Finnegan was going to cry. Some days, the signs were so clear he was getting it right to the *second*. After the montage, back to the studio, double beat, close-up, whack: her friendly teacherface crumples. By Tuesday he was extending it to spread bets on how often.) Two minutes gone, the first Diana sequence cascades in, and, forgetting himself, Vic was about to turn to Emma and say 'Christ, how much of this are we going to have to put up with?' when he saw her lip trembling again. So instead he put his mouth to her cheek and she bent her face into it, and then the pattern ran basically . . .

ON THE TV	ON THE COUCH
Diana getting married, happy, hopeful	Vic unbuttoning Emma's dungarees, frantically
Diana on a walkabout with Charles: the first signs of tension	Emma turned around, reaching behind her to unbutton Vic's fly
Diana shows baby William to a cheering public	Fellatio
Diana alone at the Taj Mahal	Continuing fellatio
Diana's sparse kiss with Charles, turning her face to use her jaw as a weapon	Continuing fellatio + (following quite a complex bit of contortionism) cunnilingus
Diana arriving in *that* dress to a function on the same day as Charles' first public date with Camilla	Intercourse (fumbled missionary)
Diana at Alton Towers on a water slide with the kids, laughing, the only image where she seemed completely natural	Intercourse, more successful from behind, making good use of the sofa's left arm
Diana visiting an AIDS victim	Emma on top, a stupid move on a two-seater, the primary issue in Vic's mind not the pulpy hold

Diana in her riot police
gear, walking through
land-mines, the one that
surprisingly no journo ever
talked of as a crass allegory
of her life

of her vagina on his penis
but how to stop the entire
thing toppling over

As before, but much too fast,
that point in sex where
your desire starts to insist
on a speed of movement
beyond physics

Diana on a boat with Dodi,
the sea bathed in pink light
from the moneyed shore

Orgasm

Diana's face in close-up,
surrounded by VT-
soft mist

Falling away, breathing,
slight embarrassment,
cuddling

. . . their sobs of ecstasy chiming in a strange harmony with Judy
Finnegan's of grief.

At first Vic thought he was just exploiting one individual's
grief, but then he realised he was exploiting the whole nation's
– disturbing, even for a conscienceless fellow like Vic. Because
maybe, under normal circumstances, Emma would've been fine
after a day or two, and that might've been that, considering
how he'd ridden so into her heart on the back of this particular
sadness, but (the great thing was) this sadness – she wouldn't
let go of it, she was like a dog with a favourite bone, growling,
chomping and refusing to drop it, and why should she, when
every time she turned the TV on all she saw was her own
sadness mirrored and magnified in ten-mile-long queues of
condolence. Which was great for Vic: after one particularly
inspired afternoon, he considered going himself to join one of
those queues, standing there for ten to twelve hours in the quiet
hum of mourning London, to write not condolence in those fat
leather-bound books sitting open in those silent chambers but
thanks. 'Dear (Vic didn't know who you actually addressed these

messages to. Earl Spencer? The Royal Family? God?) To Whom
It May Concern – Cheers.'

It was glorious, those first few days. In between getting
Jackson looked after, explaining absences to Joe, and taking
flowers to Kensington Gardens, Emma somehow found time
to come round a lot, almost as much as his desire could stand.
All his session work was cancelled – only soft-pedalling piano
players seemed to be wanted suddenly – and he felt curiously
that the mood around him was not of mourning, but of national
holiday: scootering around the littered-with-people streets on
his 1959 Lambretta, he felt like each day was a bank holiday.
Vic wanted to say so, to Emma, at times, but realised it wasn't
quite right, that even in the midst of rapture they had to retain
a modicum of dignified grief. So he kept quiet about it, but he
felt glorious; happy and glorious.

JOE

Joe was the sort of man who struggled against becoming progressively more right-wing. Having been brought up in a socialist household, there were certain things that his first instinct was always to despise: private medicine, private education, tax breaks for the rich, etc., etc. And yet, as he grew older, he found more and more that this first instinct was just that: an *instinct*, an animal impulsive dislike, which, when he concentrated long enough on the subject, cleared, leaving him with opinions often coldly incongruous with his initial rush of antipathy.

It wasn't that Joe's own financial situation had become such that, as with many of his generation, a sense of his own increasing comfortableness had rendered radical left-leaning sentiments hypocritical: he managed a biochemical laboratory for Friedner, a German-based multinational drugs company, twelve years of which work had brought him, on a small but ever-increasing pay ladder, to the unprincely salary of £36,000 per annum – enough to survive, certainly, and to ensure the survival of his wife, Emma, and child, Jackson, but not enough to disturb an intrinsically socialist *Weltanschauung*. In fact, working for Friedner, if anything, tended to warm up what studenty, rebellious leftovers were still lying around in the sink of his spirit: in particular the way the promotional hierarchy

operated, tending over the years to steer employees like Joe –
an intellectual, certainly, with a published Ph.D. from Warwick
University on the relationship between nucleic and amino acids
– away from theoretical and practical research towards admin-
istration and middle management. So far, in fact, Joe had
successfully avoided that particular dry fate, staying more or
less hands on amongst the test tubes and the microscopes;
nonetheless, the fact of its presence overhanging his career
would engender in him, occasionally, a standard resentment
at the soul-destroying nature of corporate capitalism. But if
it did engender such a thing, it would be only for a moment,
and Joe, more self-aware than most, would soon recognise it
as a piece of personally motivated spite, rather than any kind
of objective critique.

Also, he noticed, his heart had ceased to soar.

Emma and Joe didn't watch the funeral together. The tension
between them had been too evident during the other big TV
moment of the week, the Queen's address to the nation. They
watched it with Emma's mother, Sylvia – or Mrs O' Connell as
Joe was forced to call her now: her dignity, a central character in
the tragicomedy of her Alzheimer's, did not stretch to accepting
why a hard-faced blue-eyed man she didn't seem to know should
be calling her by her first name. Later, Joe would drive her back
to her tiny flat in Woolwich.

At Christmas, Joe had always hated the Queen's Speech. His
real father, a dentist much older than his mother, died when he
was four; when his mother married again two years later, it was
to a Czechoslovakian immigrant called Patrick, a pipe-smoking
disciplinarian she was so insistent the children accept as a father
that she changed the family name by deed poll to his name –
Serena – relieving Joe of his flat Anglo-Saxon surname, Lodge.
Patrick was something of a contradiction: despite politically
retaining the Marxist-Leninist leanings predictable in someone
from 1960s Eastern Europe, culturally, he thought that arrival

on these shores necessitated becoming more English-than-thou – every day, he would buy the *Daily Express* because of the little man with the Cross of St George on his shield – and thus would force the entire family to gather round the TV sharp at three o'clock every Christmas Day and collectively pretend to be enjoying the monarch's endless platitudes about the Commonwealth.

But this time, Joe felt a weird sense of sympathy for Elizabeth II, as she sat backed by the blue summer sky above Buckingham Palace, a sky that said *It's not Christmas*; below her words you could hear the constant to-and-fro shuffling of flower-bearers to her gates. He felt, for the first time, that the Queen's detachment and distance was – exactly as it should be – appropriate, in the sense of acting with propriety; in tune, even as the country was so out of tune. Joe felt at one with the Queen: alienated, displaced, forced into contrivance. He felt like a member of the Resistance watching a coded message from his leader.

Since last Sunday's dreadful news . . .

'She doesn't mean it,' said Emma. Her gaze was fixed on the screen, and she was frowning hard – a fact not easily detectable from her eyebrows, which although knitted, were downy to the point of invisible, but from the unusually deep lines appearing on her forehead, tracks in her skin virgin there like snow. 'Look at her eyes. So cold.'

'Frightened, they look to me,' said Joe.

Emma tutted, and turned away. They were sitting on the sofa she had designed herself, in the days before Jackson, when she had worked for Chaise, a bohemian furniture shop in Clapham; she at the end with the high curved back, and he at the one with the single wrought-iron arm. Sylvia sat between them, the top of her liver-spotted hand constantly stroked by her daughter. In the corner of his eye, Joe could see the flesh layering with each upward stroke.

So what I say to you now, as your Queen and as a grand-mother, I say from the heart.

15

'Yeah right . . .' said Emma. Joe looked down, embarrassed by Emma's sneering, an act so out of her natural repertoire that her stab at it seemed awkward and contrived, like a bad actress trying to 'do' sneering. He felt hot, like you sometimes do when you take on all the embarrassment for someone else, and his hand felt instinctively for his right ear. Joe's features were generally regular – regular in the fast-food sense, that is, neither large nor small (although his nose was flatter and wider at the tip than a view of his bridge would seem to suggest, something he was self-conscious about, as it gave him, he thought, the air of a pugilist) – except for his earlobes, which were virtually non-existent: Joe's ears looked as if the lobes had been sliced off in some bizarre industrial accident. During adolescence, when, of course, the earlobe becomes an important B area of erogenous activity, Joe had become perturbed by his lack in this department – an early girlfriend actually chucked him because of it – and had taken to rubbing and pulling at them in an attempt at extension. The habit persisted today; the motivation, in general, had faded, although every so often he would still look in the mirror and wonder if old age, where it would bring all other men great flapping pensioner lugs, would bring him the gift of normal-size earlobes.

She was an exceptional and gifted woman . . .

'Oh for God's sake. Speak with a bit of passion for once!'

'What do you expect her to say? That's the only way she knows how to express herself.'

'Well, this is her chance to change all that! To connect!'

Joe's heart sank. She seemed no longer the person he knew, placid, sweet-natured, generous of heart. She sounded, to him, like all those lunatics vox-popped every day by the TV. They always looked so broken, those people, so like the products of bullying. He'd read some columnist somewhere in the forests of articles, saying that the people coming out to mourn publicly were the people who connected most with Diana: the marginalised, the dispossessed. Joe knew, though, that it wasn't her they connected with, but hysteria – the clamour of it, chiming with their own needs, saying to them what they most wanted to hear, come, here is identity.

'I know that woman,' said Sylvia. She took her blue glasses off, and pointed one of the arms at the screen.

'Do you, Mum?' said Emma, turning to her with a sense of hope.

'Yes,' said Sylvia firmly. 'It's Mrs Irving from the bakery.'

. . . never lost her capacity to smile and laugh . . .

'No, Mum – you remember' . . . and here she sang 'God save our Gracious Queen, long live our noble Queen . . .'

'God save our gracious Queen, long live our noble Queen . . .' sang Sylvia immediately back to her. Emma nodded, the slow nod of the schoolteacher to the young child who has finally got something right, and then together they sang: 'God save the Queen.'

Sylvia, in her day, had been a sometime singer, mainly of Irish folk songs, in the clubs and pubs of County Cork, and a peculiar facet of her Alzheimer's was that it had not destroyed her musical memory. This is not uncommon: there is a famous medical case of a Cambridge organist whose short-term memory has been wiped completely from the hard-disk of his brain, who can yet play *Toccata and Fugue* from start to finish. Music, like smell, operates on the memory in a way not entirely understood by science, an abstract, mystical way. The capability most lost by Alzheimer's sufferers is narrative; and yet that's all music is – a narrative, a series of notes one after another, like words in a story. But if Emma asked her mother to tell a story, or to repeat a story, her face would only set into a lost look; as indeed, in fact, it would if she *asked* her to sing a song. What Emma had learnt to do – and did often, now, it being the last genuine method of communication left open between them – was just to begin singing a song: her mother would join in, confidently, unhesitantly. Sometimes Emma would phone her and all she would do was sing; Joe

17

would hear her from wherever he was in the house, and know that her mum would be giving it her all on the other end of the line. Emma could even sing a song to her she didn't know, and Sylvia would repeat it back to her exactly as her daughter sang it, although she would forget the new song soon afterwards.

They finished singing, and looked back to the screen. 'Yes,' said Sylvia. 'It's definitely Mrs Irving.'

No one who knew Diana will ever forget her. Millions of others who never met her, but felt they knew her, will remember her.

Both Emma and Joe were silenced for a second by this crystal drop of simplicity in the midst of the monarch's portentousness. Whatever their positions, neither could find anything to quarrel with in that basic statement. In the pause, Joe considered he might temper his attitude somewhat; he knew that the emotional downward spiral their relationship had got into was now focused on their differing responses to this event.

I share in your determination to cherish her memory.

Emma snorted and picked up the remote control, aiming at the wide screen.

'Don't,' said Joe. His voice felt alien, unused to sounding absolute.

'Why not?'

'Oh for God's sake, Emma. I've wanted to turn the TV off a hundred times this week. And you wouldn't let me. And I *do* want to watch this. At least it's not another . . .' he hesitated, wanting to say 'fucking', but the presence of Sylvia held him back, though why he didn't know, as she would most probably not hear it, and certainly not remember it, '. . . review of her life and works, or another loony on the street supposedly representing "our" feelings.'

'OK, Joe,' said Emma, getting up. 'I know how you feel about it.'

'Well . . . I'm not trying to be heartless. And you know I like sentimentality. I love a good cry. When it's Spielberg or someone making me. I just can't stand bloody – ' he waved an impatient hand towards the TV – 'Peter Sissons doing it.' He was annoyed now. He had wanted to hear the Queen, and now they were having another argument, and he was missing it.

'Yes, we've talked about it enough now. It's fine. It's fine for us to think differently about some things,' replied Emma, trying to sound tired rather than testy.

'Is it?'

'Of course.'

'No, I mean . . . I know obviously it's all right for us to think differently about some things. But I don't know if you really think it's all right for us to think differently about *this*.'

These acts of kindness have been a huge source of help and comfort.

Emma moved away, towards the kitchen. Joe felt a childish urge to at least dent the shield she was putting up towards him.

'I don't know why you're so bothered about it all anyway. I mean . . .' and here he turned to look at Sylvia, who was resolutely facing the screen; an onlooker may have thought she was pretending not to notice her daughter and son in law's argument, but there was no element of pretence about it, 'you're not even *British*.'

Emma stared at him and opened her mouth, but then shook her head, as if such a banal point was not worth answering. She turned to go into the kitchen. They owned a house, decorated by Emma herself in shades of blue and red – a small terraced cottage in the slightly less respectable part of Greenwich, overlooked by the flickering pyramid of Canary Wharf; it had always spoken somehow of Emma and Joe's premature – at least by the standards of everyone else in their circle – embracing of domesticity, their apparently happy early resignation into contentment, that they had bought a house, and not a flat.

19

A house is a narrative; a flat, spatially, expresses only the present.

Joe got up quickly and held her arm, restraining, no more than that – he would never have done more than that; but still, when she turned, her speckled green eyes flashed with that mixture of fear and defiance learnt from domestic violence dramas.

'Em . . .'

'Really, Joe, it's *OK*,' she said, her voice struggling to achieve firmness. They looked into each other's eyes, with the consciousness of significance and moment which always accompanies that action. *How did we get here?* thought Joe.

'I—' began Emma, guilt making her features melt. She wasn't going to tell him anything; she didn't know what she was about to say, but the bitterness of secrecy festers alternately inwards and outwards, and she felt moved to make some sort of amends. And then, from the bookshelves on the far wall, a faint bubbling like someone gently drowning: they turned to face the accusatory white grille of the baby monitor, a radio permanently stuck on the same station.

'I'll go,' said Joe, and turned away from her and went out the other door. Emma watched his stocky back retreat, slightly slumping; she felt herself relax a little once he was gone, a not unfamiliar feeling in recent days.

May those who died rest in peace, and may we, each and every one of us, thank God for someone who made many, many people happy.

'What's she doing on the telly?' said Sylvia.

On the day of the funeral itself, then, Joe just went out for a walk. He went out into London to *avoid* the funeral. He walked along the river, coming off the towpath from time to time to venture into the streets, all the way from the Millennium Dome – looking more and more, he thought, with its new points sticking up in the air, like a huge bald head given a very poor hair transplant – to Tower Bridge and back again. As he walked, he thought how, in years to come, he would possibly be the only person who knew what London actually felt like on that day; because everyone else – *everyone* else – was either at home watching the TV or lining the route. It felt like a place on which a neutron bomb – not talked about much these days, the capitalist bomb, which destroyed people, but preserved property – had dropped: a *Marie Celeste* of a city. No people were on the pavements, no cars were on the roads, no shops were open; Blackheath empty, Bermondsey shut, Wapping closed down. The only creatures he saw were birds circling in the high blue air, and cats sunning themselves on front garden walls. Every so often a dog would bark, but always in the distance; the *only* sounds were distant ones, far-off planes and far-off cortèges, and underneath it all the combined hum of ten million TV sets tuned to the same event. Normally, he thought, televisions would be tuned too diversely to register, but today they were all blaring out the same clanging bells, the same clip-clops, the same lone wailing, the same incongruous applause, the same poetry, the same singing, the same speeches. Only the commentators might be different in different homes, but you wouldn't know it, speaking as they were in the same hushed, reverent tone. Joe tried to imagine how it would sound, the combined commentary, the strange loudness of ten million whispers.

Coming back through Greenwich Village, as it is confusingly called, seeming to have nicked the name from the place named after it, he passed one other person, a man in a trench-coat, odd for this vehemently hot day, but somehow congruous, in Joe's mind, with their undercover status, their joint defiance of this national curfew. He thought about perhaps exchanging a few words with him, maybe apposite ones, about how absurd it all was, or maybe just to ask him if he had seen anywhere that was open to buy a drink, as his throat was arid with walking so far in such heat. But the man looked down as he approached, and Joe thought it best not to, thinking – jokingly, but still thinking it – that he might be some form of secret policeman.

21

Before going back home, he turned into Greenwich Park, and walked up the hill towards the Observatory, the spot where, in a couple of years, new time would begin. Often, when contemplating the next century, Joe would remember that as a child, he'd once calculated how old he would be at the year 2000 – thirty-five – and found such an age impossible to imagine. But today, his thoughts were less personal. Looking out over the vast view of London the top of the hill affords, he felt the city stretching, stretching itself and this event it had so made its own. From here, he could almost hear it calling, calling to the Observatory, to mark Diana's death, and all its attendant business, as the last great historical event of this millennium. It was a palpable sound, he thought, the sound of significance demanded.

And then at twelve o' clock he felt the appreciable dip, from this silence to another. It was a silence he recognised from before occasional sporting events, spread across stadiums, but rarely heard city-wide, *country*-wide. Two minutes, as well, not one: a marathon of silence. As it went on, he realised, moreover, that this was a deeper silence than ever experienced pre- a sporting event, because there it is forever broken by mobile phone rings (followed immediately by the embarrassed scrabbling of plastic into pocket), and distant oblivious building work. But today, for two minutes, even that was stopped: all mobile phones were off; all building ceased. Standing at Greenwich Observatory, he felt a terrible and uncharacteristic urge to cry out, something banal, something obscene, like you want to at a wedding during the 'if any man here' wait. *Cunt*, he considered mainly – although *bollocks* crossed his mind too – a long whoop, extending the *u* for ages, all the way to the end of the two minutes before coming down hard on the *nt*, a lone voice echoing across the skyscape, *cuuuuuuuuuuuuuu*; but before he had a chance to start – and actually Joe, although he felt urges, rarely acted on them; that was far more his friend Vic's provenance – the silence ended: he could make it out, pick-ups of sound here and there, a city shuffling, creaking and coughing held-in coughs, like an enormous audience between movements of a symphony. He put the urge away, setting off back towards his house where his wife would be sitting in tears – tears that he knew would be turned angrily on him for his absence – and left London behind, London, with its circus at Oxford, its circus at Piccadilly.

Joe had fallen in love with Emma so hard. That was his way: he found casual sex problematic, because he felt so indebted, so ridiculously grateful, that he always kept in contact, and even the most ludicrously inappropriate drunken mistakes would end up as, at least mini, relationships. And, at some very deep level, he couldn't bear disapproval, or rather, he couldn't bear easy negative categorisation – that post-post-coital moment, when he was at the door, and through the curtained dawn light the woman would look at him *expecting* no swapping of numbers, no promises. Joe felt such a pressure to defy that expectation; perhaps what he was frightened of, more than anything else, was cliché.

He had, moreover, taken a long time to join the dance, not losing his virginity until he was at university, to a mature student called Andrea. Predictably he stayed with Andrea throughout his entire course, thus setting into place for the future a constant underlying concern that he hadn't exploited his sexual opportunities to the full at the time when most people were supposed to: a concern that only consolidated the same feeling he had about his teenage years, when shyness had similarly prevented any such exploitation.

Andrea left Joe, eventually, for her tutor, the biochemical scholar Dr Henry Monroe, with whom it transpired she'd been having an affair for most of their three years together. Joe felt he should be devastated, and for a short time was, but soon realised that he would never have broken it up with Andrea, and came to see Dr Monroe as a kind of saviour. Immediately following graduation, he resolved to embark on a Viking-like promiscuous rampage, making up for lost time, but then discovered the one-night-stand wall, and retreated into serial monogamy. Until Emma, who felt as if she could not be anything but the last in the series.

He met her in Chaise, just before Christmas 1989. He was visiting the shop to look for furniture for the flat that he was intending to share with Deborah, his girlfriend at the time, a sharp-eyed woman with a convinced air, convinced most of all that Joe was going to be with her for ever. Let's begin the new decade by making a commitment to each other, she had said when broaching the living together subject, and Joe, as he did when women took the initiative, had said yes, let's.

'Sorry, I don't work here,' said Emma, looking up from a large sheet of A5. Unable to find an assistant out front, Joe had poked his head through an archway in the back of the shop and intruded upon a warehouse space not big enough to hold the multitude of legs, table-tops, fabric and tools strewn apparently randomly around; it looked like a giant fractious child had broken all his toys and refused to clear up the mess. 'Well . . . obviously, I do work here. Just not selling the stuff. I design it. Some of it.'

Joe considered her features again: the sheeny white skin, lightly freckled, the touch of – inherited, rather than dieted for – gauntness in the cheekbones, the green eyes, freckled themselves to match her skin – and processed them into her rolling, stroking accent: Irish. Her nose was straight and a little thin, but her nostrils, which can so make or break a face, were perfect ovals.

'So . . . you're not actually allowed to tell me the price of anything you've designed?' he said, and was surprised by the slight lilt of his tone to discover himself flirting, an activity he wasn't given to even in his short periods of singleness, and had never practised whilst attached, unfaithfulness not being in his lexicon.

Emma smiled, her unpainted lips parting to reveal unaggressively

24

even teeth, human teeth; Deborah's overlapping hard tiny pyramids, Joe always thought, had just a tiny element of wolf. It was a generous action for such a light joke, and, he noticed, her eyes went with the smile instead of staying detached from it, the way people who are only politely smiling smile.

'I don't think I actually know,' she said, looking towards the archway, the line of her profile fluid like a brushstroke. 'Paul. Paul!' The archway remained empty. 'Sorry,' she said, smiling again, this time apologetically, 'he's always pissing off without telling anyone.' She shifted off her high stool, away from the diagonal of her drawing desk. 'What was it you were interested in?'

Together they began picking their way through the furniture detritus towards the front of shop. Emma was wearing dungarees, something Joe had initially read as conventional feminist bohemia, but now, moving in front of him, her body in them seemed the opposite, the sexiest juxtaposition of soft and rough, of shape in shapelessness.

'That sofa in the window. The one with the single arm . . .'

'Ah . . . good taste, then.' Although she said it in standard ironic inverted commas, Emma twisted her neck around to catch his eye with appreciation; her hair, moving from the sepia gloom of the workshop into the glassier light of the front of shop, became its colour, ash blonde. It was strewn like raffia on top of her head, blonde criss-crosses pinched together by black spangly hairgrips in the shape of butterflies; her fringe fell across her face in strands.

'One of yours?'

'My finest work.'

Joe stood behind the sofa, surveying its red velvet lines and deliberately quirky ironwork. He crouched down for a closer look, not knowing why, but because that's what people did when buying big objects, like when men examined second-hand cars. He was aware of her looking at him, and hoped that his mousy brown hair, recently cut to a strict shortness, was not thinning as much on top as he was frightened it might be. Through the window, shoppers passed, above the line of the sofa's back; from his point of view, the tableau was like one of those children's books where the top half picture and the bottom half picture can be changed, to comic effect. A silence set in, a silence he felt was somewhat charged, but he couldn't work out whether the tension was sexual or economic.

'Um ... I can't really judge unless I sit on it,' he said eventually, aware of the banality of this observation but not really knowing how to achieve greater sophistication in the arena of sofa-purchasing.

Emma looked down at him, ever so slightly smirking. 'Go on then.'

'. . . What?'

'Help yourself. Sit.'

There was a short pause, during which Joe uncrouched, and steadied himself for a second statement of the obvious.

'It's in the window.'

'Yes?'

'Well, I'll have to sit in the window. People'll think I'm some sort of display dummy.'

Emma laughed and frowned at the same time. 'How long do you plan to sit on it?'

Joe rolled his head from side to side, with cod thoughtfulness.

'I don't know. It's not worth doing unless I can relax into it, and I don't know how long it'll take me to relax in public like that. My buttocks might stiffen up.' Emma laughed again. He had never spoken this easily with a woman he didn't know before; he wasn't sure he'd spoken this easily with women he *did* know before, including all the ones he'd gone out with.

'OK,' he said, sighing, and stepped on to the window display area. He stopped and looked round. 'You're sure you haven't got another one somewhere else in the shop I could test-drive more discreetly?'

'How dare you,' said Emma. 'Who do you think we are, Habitat?' She raised an arm, bare except for two silver bangles, balletically indicating the leopard-print chairs, the fluffy blue dustbins, the transparent plastic standard lamps. 'Every item in here is unique. You'll never find anything else exactly like this.'

'I think I'm beginning to understand why you work in design and not in sales,' he said, continuing the fighty-flirty discourse, but sensing somewhere inside an extra resonance to her words. He turned, feeling her eyes on his back; he felt wide and bulky here amongst these delicate carved things, as if at any moment he might turn and knock something over. Already, a white-haired couple with a Yorkshire terrier had stopped and were watching him.

He sat, feeling very self-conscious; he felt as if he should have tails to sweep up and away like an Edwardian gentleman. He had to hold his right wrist with his left hand to stop it wandering to his ear. A young skateboarding boy moved through his frame of vision and then into it again, backwards. Joe felt keenly the disjunction between the public act of display and the private act of getting comfortable, like being caught between two worlds, inner and outer.

'What do you think?' said Emma. 'How's your buttocks?'

'Clenched,' said Joe, without turning round. The white-haired couple moved off with an air of disappointment, as if they had expected at least a puppet show. And then Joe said it. Normally, something like this, he would've prepared it in his mind, he would've rehearsed it, tried it out in front of the mirror and most probably given up; but this time, he just said it. It took him by surprise.

'I don't think I can judge sitting by myself anyway. I think you can't judge a sofa unless you're sitting on it with some-one.'

Emma paused before answering. 'Well, do you want me to get one of your audience to come in and sit with you?' The skateboarding boy had been joined by a small gang of friends,

27

who had begun making faces at Joe. One of them had turned round and was threatening to drop his trousers.

'No, I was thinking . . .'

'OK, OK.' He heard the wood of the display area creak behind him. 'I should be prepared to publicly endorse my own creations, I suppose.'

She came round the side of the sofa and, with considerably less obvious stiffness than Joe, sat down; he felt her presence on the other cushion like the moon feels the earth, like gravity. In Clapham High Street, the watching crowd swelled to include a wild-eyed tramp, two sneering schoolgirls, a policeman, and three people lured away from a busker on the other side of the street. Simultaneously, Emma and Joe turned to each other and burst out laughing.

'Are we in the red light district in Amsterdam?' said Emma.

'Yeah. We're in the nice sit down, watch a bit of telly brothel.'

'So what else do you want from me?'

'Sorry?'

'To judge the sofa. Do I need to do anything else? Or just sit here?'

'Um . . . well . . . you need to be like . . . like someone who I might be sitting on a sofa with?' His pale blue eyes, not naturally playful, narrowed in mock-seriousness.

'Ye-es?'

'Like someone I might be sitting at home with, comfortably, watching TV, night after night . . .'

'Like . . . a girlfriend?'

'That kind of person.'

Emma drew her knees up on to the cushion, and rested her chin on her thumb. Joe noticed how the laces in her trainers were far too long, necessitating four enormous bows. 'OK,' she said, gesturing towards the window. 'What else is on?'

'Uh?'

'I don't want to watch this. I hate these ordinary people documentaries.'

'Oh, right. Well . . .' said Joe, rather woodenly, amazed at finding himself in this situation, but carried through by the momentum of it all, '. . . er . . . where's the remote control?'

'I don't know. Don't ask me before you've even looked for it yourself.'

Joe smiled. 'Have you lived with a man already, by any chance?'

'Don't come out of character,' whispered Emma; then, louder: 'What do you want for dinner? I could do some pasta, or we could get a takeaway . . .'

'Oh . . . well . . . maybe I'll go down to the Chinese in a little bit.'

'OK.'

A silence set in again. Joe felt a small panic inside, knowing he never had the stamina to keep up this kind of improvisation. He looked somewhat helplessly to Emma, who blinked at him, neutrally.

'Leave your ear alone,' she said, whispering again. Joe brought his hand down, reddening.

'We seem to have skipped something,' she continued, after a thoughtful pause.

'Um . . . ?'

'I mean – are we going straight into domesticity? We're going to cut straight into the night after night, comfortable stuff? What about the three months of careless unbridled passion?'

Joe felt as if he was falling, down through the cushions. 'Just to test out the sofa?'

Emma looked at him sternly. 'I'm a method performer.' Then she glanced at the window; the busker, a bearded rangy guitarist in combat gear and a beret, was slouching over the road, looking depressed.

'And besides, how else are we going to close the show?' she said, and leant over to kiss him on the lips, her mouth opening slightly to allow him access to those vivaciously human teeth. Immediately, the crowd outside burst into spontaneous applause; through the amazed register-centres of his brain, Joe thought he could make out a muted shout of 'Go on my son!' He closed his eyes, trying to swim for ever in the dark lake of her kiss; but then a bell sounded, spelling, like bells do, the end of playtime.

'Em! What the fuck?'

Emma pulled slowly away from Joe, ignoring Paul, Chaise's owner, who had just walked through the clanging shop door, ignoring the crowd, still clapping and laughing, ignoring everything except her husband-to-be's intensely focused-on-her eyes. She could see two tiny images of her face reflected in his bursting pupils, and they were smiling.

'You'd better bloody buy it now,' she said.

TESS

_____

Tess sometimes felt she was a man born inside a woman's body. Not in the standard, gender-bending, sexually ambiguous way, not at all – as far as genital interest went, she had always been clearly attracted to, somewhat fascinated by, in fact, the male set. But, at the risk of sounding like Kenny Rogers, there's more to being a man and being a woman than that.

It was a humour thing. This is not a small issue, now. Now, humour is the *modus operandi* of all human communication, the primary medium through which we make, keep and bond with friends: all judgement of others starts with – and then continues to operate by – their compatibility with our own sense of humour. In previous times this role would have been taken by money, or status, or dress, or bearing, or even, heaven forbid, moral conduct, but now all these are as nothing compared to humour. These days, it is the Fool who is King, whereas shit anecdotes or flat-falling witticisms are more likely to lead to social exclusion than leprosy. It *is* rank.

And Tess was a female born with a male sense of humour. She had a hardness, an unflinching brutal edge to her sense of humour, which she could only find really locked into, at a deep level, men.

Which is why Tess didn't really have female friends. The

notional idea of women being funny together – so prized by *Marie Claire* culture – on the odd exceptional occasion Tess found herself within any kind of objective correlative of it, a hen night, a pyjama party, she always felt alienated, adrift amidst a sea of shrieks and giggles and sighing jokes about men and what they were like.

It didn't really bother Tess, her lack of female friends. But at times it pissed her off, primarily when she sensed amongst the girlfriends of her male friends an antipathy, and with that antipathy an easy accommodation of herself in *their* minds as one of those women who can only function in terms of male approval, or who find other women sexually threatening. On these occasions, she found herself wondering if perhaps she should have striven harder to find friends amongst her own gender; that what she had mistaken for women was a *Girlie Show* myth of women, or at least of women together, and that, although a potent myth, one that when very many groups of women were together they did self-consciously per-petuate, there did exist numerous other women with a similar sense of humour to Tess, but they existed, as it were, in a diaspora, scattered throughout womanhood, unaware, through post-feminist propaganda, of the existence of each other. Tess felt, sometimes, that it was her mission to find and unite this diaspora.

One of these times was when she came back to England on the Eurostar in mid-September 1997. She had phoned Vic on her mobile to tell him what time she was getting in, and they'd started talking about other things, and then, in passing, neutrally, he'd mentioned that he'd seen Emma. In most cases such a nondescript mention of another woman by a man might have engendered some kind of disturbance in the mind of his partner, but Joe and Emma were, in her social mythology, so much an unbreakable unit, that Tess didn't even begin the process of suspicion. Instead, once she clicked off her mobile and put it away in her attaché case, she began to muse again on how she'd never really become friends with Emma, who she really liked on one level – she was clearly a *good person*, and far from humourless – but there was a point beyond which, Tess knew, she could not go with her, remarks she might make which would occasion, not censure – Emma was too unaggressive for that – but blankness: Tess could already see presented to her Emma's pure, easy features frozen in the friendly frown of polite incomprehension.

During the journey, Tess had every so often glanced across the Formica table at her travelling companions. One of them, visible from a proudly sported lapel name tag, was a minor Eurostar executive, standardly red-faced and blue-suited, but marked out from the rest of that type in the carriage by his barely submerged pride in the everyday workings of the journey. Every time the refreshments trolley passed by their table, he seemed to beam, to – to use a Yiddish word reserved normally for the action Jewish mothers do when seeing their children succeed – to *qvell*; at one point he took nearly four minutes over a choice of sandwich (egg and cress), deliberating out loud and rolling the names of other flavours questioningly around on his tongue, as if to demonstrate the impossibility of selection when faced with such a smorgasbord of the finest delicacies in Christendom. Tess internally tried to record the most laughable of his characteristics, to tell Vic about when she got home.

The other, a woman in her early thirties, gave her more pause. Short-haired, with an intelligently angular face, although with just an undertone of anorexia in the concavity of her cheekbones, she was reading the *Observer*; now and again she appeared to raise a quizzical eyebrow at some of the more intense eulogies contained within. Tess watched her for some time, gradually becoming more and more convinced that she could well be of the many lost in the diaspora. When the woman appeared to snort in derision at her paper, Tess decided to chance her arm.

'You think that's bad. Have you seen this?' Tess said across the table, getting out of her bag a copy of the *Star*, which she had found left on a seat by an English passenger as she had entered the train at the Gare du Nord. The front page had been completely given over to a photograph of an enormous cloud, halo-ed around its left-hand corner by the light of the sun behind. Tess had glanced down from putting her suitcase up on the luggage rack and seen it, scrunched up on the seat with two other tabloids, a riot of red and letters; she had undergone a moment of disbelief, and then stuffed it in her shoulder bag, thinking that Vic, whose tabloid of choice was the *Mirror*, was unlikely to have seen it.

Tess held up the paper on her side of the table. The woman looked up from the *Observer*, slightly shaking her head, as if uncertain if it was herself being addressed; the Eurostar executive glanced round from one of his many lovingly rotating overviews of the carriage environment. They had just come through the tunnel, on to English soil.

The front page – a shot of the sky taken purportedly on the day of her funeral – was captioned DI IN THE SKY. The cloud was in the shape of Diana's face. It was, as well, once you looked at it; there it was, her bulky-nosed elegant profile, framed in the light-bursting blue. Yea, very like Diana's face.

'Look!' said Tess, smiling. 'She's alive! *In droplet form!*'

The woman continued to stare, but in the mirror of her face Tess saw no reflection of her own smile. The Eurostar executive's eyes, so full of self-satisfaction up to this point, started to dart from side to side, as if he was nervous they were being watched.

'I'm sorry,' the woman said, eventually, as Tess's stomach started to give, like a child's who, having imagined that they've said something really clever to some adults, begins to understand that in fact they've said something really bad, really really bad, a swear-word they didn't know was a swear-word, a question about the whereabouts of an uncle who's run off with a younger

34

woman but no one explained it to the child. 'Are you talking to me?'

The woman's voice was somewhat strangled, partly out of shock, but partly for a more unfortunate reason, which, as soon as she had begun to speak, became clear to Tess: she had, while reading her paper, been trying not to cry. What Tess had mistaken for a snort of derision had in fact been an attempt to clear a tight and lumpy throat, a drawing up of tears away from the eyes via the nose.

'Yes. I . . .' said Tess, considered apologising, and then, realising that, like Macbeth, she was already in blood stepp'd in so far that returning were as tedious as go o'er, pointed directly at the centre of the picture. 'I mean, how *medieval* can you get?' The question – a good one – remained unanswered. 'What is she now, in heaven? What deity does she represent?' she continued, holding up this icon, this tabloid Turin Shroud. 'The Goddess of Eighties Hairstyles? Of Being Photographed Leaving a Health Club? Of Shagging Chinless Twats?'

Time didn't seem to stand still, so much as melt: all clocks went soft. And then all hell – all *hell* – was let loose.

'I don't know how you can – are you trying to be – what do you mean by – I don't even know you . . .' The woman with the angular face seemed to be saying all these things, and every other trope in the lexicon of outrage. The Eurostar executive had gone very red, and started consolidating the implication created by his darting eyes – that these were words that should not be spoken in public, dangerous words, words that might be overheard – with a dramatic twisting and turning of the neck. Along the carriage, various other passengers could be heard harrumphing and puffing with negativity. H.M. Bateman would've turned in his grave to think he'd missed the chance of caricaturing it. The sound of the train itself along the rails became a series of tuts.

Tess looked on with amazement. She had, of course, told Vic that she was going to be staying in France, because England was going to go crazy; but not, she thought, this crazy. The fact is, when a country is in the grip of a phenomenon, any phenomenon, you simply can't register its intensity from abroad, not actually, not viscerally. She'd seen pictures on French TV, and sat through the endless vox-pops, but had assumed that these were exaggerations, highlights, individuals whose own neuroses had generated dramatically heightened reactions to Diana's death, specifically chosen to make the best television. The French themselves had not taken the death of Diana with levity either. Rather, as an English person in France at that time, she had felt all around her, in hushed tones and dipped eyes, that aura of polite concern extended to the recently bereaved by people who did not themselves directly know the recently dead. She had interpreted this taking-no-chances approach as a result of the French being at one remove, and that once she got back to Britain she would find, away from the predictable outpouring of plebeian grief, that most people thought like her, and that she could easily chime with her own kind by being funny about it all.

How wrong she was. Tess felt trapped, as the non-stop train hurtled further and further into England, towards London. A minute ago her journey was a coming-home, with all the comfort and reassurance that implies; now, without warning, it had taken on the quality of nightmare, one of those where you're on the wrong train to the wrong station, but you don't know how it's happened, or how to right your wrong: in fact, the only thing you do know is that there's no getting off. She considered immediately throwing herself out of the train window and running back through the tunnel, through darkness into light, into sanity. But, as the angular woman burst into tears, great body-shaking sobs held back throughout the journey, Tess simply folded away the paper, and put it back in her bag. *She's alive*, Tess thought again, as the cloud-face crumpled. *She's alive*: the people so wanted the stars to say it, but had to settle, as ever, for the *Star* saying it.

VIC

When Vic was younger, he liked to think that he had some diseases. Some diseases, he used to think, were really cool. Old ones, he thought, they were cool – scurvy, rickets, scrofula, tuberculosis – he liked the sound of them, with their palpable, clunky, sixteenth-century consonants; having one of them had a kind of highbrow, sepia ring, *and* granted instant cred because it meant you didn't eat much healthy food. He flirted with the idea of some of the more obscure biggies, particularly the long-drawn-out but not *obviously* terminal ones – multiple sclerosis, that was pretty sexy, what with Richard Pryor endorsing it, although not as sexy as motor neurone disease, a disease that sounded like a fucking Ferrari. He really fancied motor neurone disease: to be like Stephen Hawking, an archetypal, poetic contrast of psychical power and physical impoverishment, and you got one of those brilliant voiceboxes as well.

Epilepsy, that was pretty cool (even in ancient times: Hippocrates had called it 'the sacred disease'). Kind of druggy – a doomed rock star's disease, Jim Morrison had it, and Ian Curtis (Ian Curtis danced to it); and – *top* sexy points – epilepsy brought with it more than a hint of demonic possession. Anything twitchy and fitty was good, although Vic's more perverse side tended to prefer more obscure variants, St Vitus' dance in particular, which he once spent a whole day working on pretending to have, on the basis that it would allow him to hit people apparently by accident. And because he thought it would give him a great trump card to play at parties, when faced with someone going on and on about one of those modish, abstract and definitely uncool diseases.

'. . . yes, it's been a terrible year really – the ME just makes me so tired all the time – you've never had it, I presume?'

'No. I've got' (SHOUTED) 'St Vitus' dance!!'

'Ow. Yes. So I see.'

But his attraction to St Vitus' dance was completely superseded on the day, in mid-1990, when he saw *John's Not Mad*, a repeat of a TV documentary about John Davidson, a young kid from Galashiels with Tourette's Syndrome. *John's Not Mad* was a *QED* that was first broadcast in the early eighties on BBC2, and is perhaps the premier documentary of its type: that is, one of those which you watch for the first five minutes with a serious face, and an internal mood pitched somewhere between sympathy and horror, and then give up and piss yourself laughing. Its only serious contender is a documentary called *The Jarrow Elvis*, about a troupe of mentally handicapped Elvis impersonators who perform every Monday night in a pub in the North of England.

Vic, however, watched it in a slightly different way (he wouldn't have bothered anyway with those first five minutes of attempted seriousness). He watched it and fell in love. Not with John Davidson, although he could feel his awe and admiration going up a notch every time the poor confused young man called his mother a whore in Sainsbury's, or spat on his sister's birthday cake; with the disease. It had all the tics and tacs of St Vitus' dance anyway, but added this fantastic bonus – it allowed you to swear, shout and generally do in public whatever would cause maximum offence. When he read up about it – which he did as soon as possible, off down the road at ten o' clock the next morning to Sydenham local library, every so often spastically twitching his arms and shouting the word *arse* – he was delighted to discover that the symptoms can include spontaneous genital exhibitionism.

Vic was not, it should be clear, a hypochondriac. He was not frightened of disease, he lusted after it (which, admittedly, hypochondriacs may be doing, but not consciously); nor did he sit at home obsessively spotting symptoms. He did, however, start to believe he might have Tourette's Syndrome – in a way.

'Everyone's got it!' he told Joe, as he spooned out the last steaming lumps of Chicken Dhansak from its silver boat on to his own plate. They were meeting, as they still did then, every Thursday night, in the Spice of Sydenham.

'How has *everybody* got it?' replied Joe, carefully arranging Aloo Gobi and Muttar Paneer in distinct sections around his plate in order to avoid the whole thing just melting into a spicy vegetable stew. Under the hum of conversation, an Indian version of 'Down Under' by Men At Work played.

'Look. You saw the programme, right?'

'Yeah . . . ?'

'Well, that stuff the kid did. We all want to do that.'

'Do we?'

'Of course.'

Joe finished his food-arranging and looked up at his friend, noticing, not for the first time, how the colour of Vic's hair and eyes – that point of dark brown practically indistinguishable from black – matched perfectly. It was especially noticeable now, since Vic's pupils were dilated like a cat's in the dark – whether through excitement at his theorem or by some more chemical inducement, Joe couldn't tell – and the border between pupil and iris had become indistinct. When he goes grey, thought Joe, something more than usual will be lost.

'We all, at all times, feel inside us urges to do the most . . .' Vic struggled for a moment.

'Terrible?' suggested Joe, glancing at his watch. Nearly eleven, he thought.

'Outrageous things.' Vic chewed as he spoke. 'The most outrageous thing at that moment. Our brain has a natural impulse for it.'

'Like what?'

Vic picked up his knife. It was an unusual move, as he didn't tend to use knives much, even with food that wasn't already cut up, preferring instead to fork-lift the steak or piece of fish or potato or whatever and bite through it.

'I can't hold a knife without wanting to stab someone,' he said calmly. 'For example.'

'Well, I really must be going,' said Joe, pushing his chair backwards to follow through his joke.

'No, you cunt. I'm not going to stab you. I'm never going to stab anyone. But I recognise the urge. I don't deny its existence. Similarly, whenever someone hands me a cup of tea, my first instinct is to throw it in their face.'

Joe smiled, strangely as it might seem, with fondness. What he most liked about Vic was his compulsive honesty, his relentless confessional drive, the way he poured out of himself with no attempt at self-censorship, like a boiling pot of personality. Joe, undemonstrative in the extreme, had been amazed and then attracted by Vic's X-ray presentations of self, when he'd first met him at Warwick. He remembered their first conversation. He'd just come out of an event at the Students' Union, at which Steven Huxtable, one of those young people who make themselves twenty years older by thinking, as only middle-aged people do, that parliamentary politics lies at the centre of the universe, had given a talk called Whither the Centre Ground? On leaving the lecture hall, well before the end, Joe had heard a voice spitting with rage behind one of the elephantine concrete pillars that held up the buildings of the Central Site. It was a tone he was used to hearing at the university, a combination of angry and assured, with just a hint of cockney thrown in.

'Fucking Huxtable. What a fucking idiot.'

Joe looked round to see a man, dressed fairly orthodoxly for a mid-eighties' student – that is, huge backcombed spiky Goth hair and long black Oxfam overcoat, although his nose ring took him a bit beyond that which the rebellious middle-class young were normally prepared to go – talking, in between sucks on a roll-up, to a curly-haired flat-faced woman in an army jacket, who was nodding enthusiastically.

'He so *loves* getting on his high horse. Any chance of moral superiority, he loves it.'

Joe, unusually for him, decided to join in this conversation, less because he wanted to make friends with this bloke, who looked a bit too, well, *studenty* to be honest, than because he also felt the need to relieve himself of annoyance at what he'd just stupidly decided to sit through.

'But it's so clichéd, his morality,' said Joe. Vic looked up, and straight away Joe could tell he was being assessed. He blushed a little, and half wished he'd not worn his denim jacket – it made him look a bit heavy metal. 'Don't you think?' he added nervously.

Vic looked at him for a second longer; then smiled, and said, with a sweeping arm gesture and a yee-hah cowboy accent to match: 'Of course. He rides his moral high horse across the canyon of unoriginal thought.'

The curly-haired woman laughed uproariously, a hooting owl-like sound that rather ruined the moment, but Joe was still impressed: he'd never heard anyone talk with such confidence before. In the weeks following, he made an effort to become friends with Vic. As a biochemist, practically a natural scientist, Joe represented the lowest of the low for the arty crowd, but – in stark contrast to almost everyone else who dressed like him – Vic turned out not to be intellectually or socially elitist, and seemed to quite like having Joe around. Why was not entirely clear to Joe; but he was glad of it. Vic provided him with all sorts of vicarious pleasures.

The only point that troubled Joe, distantly, was a sense that recently – certainly, in the four years since leaving university – Vic had tended to forgo any kind of qualm about his opinions and confessions. Time was, when he would mix them up with at least a soupçon of guilt, or, if not guilt, at least of uncertainty – uncertainty about whether it really was OK to say these things. Now, though, it seemed that everything – every desire, every lust, every moral ambiguity – was mitigated in the saying, in the process of utterance: as if candour itself cleansed.

'How's the band going?' said Joe, feeling a need to return to familiar ground.

'Crap. Virgin aren't picking up the option on a second album, and I don't think I can stand working with Jake anymore anyway. His voice sounds kind of out of date to me now.'

'So what are you going to do?'

'I dunno. I can't go on for ever. I like playing the guitar but the music business is *so* full of arseholes. Besides, I'm getting to the age where being in a band's just a bit embarrassing.'

'You're only twenty-six!'

'Well – that means soon I'll be thirty. Perhaps it'd be different if we were going to be big . . . but we're not.' He said it with a light, unresentful definitiveness. 'I thought I might just go into session work. Adverts, that kind of stuff. You can make a fortune.'

Joe frowned; he didn't like the idea that Vic had this talent and was prepared to waste it. Vic, however, was all about high-grade wasting.

'What about you,' said Vic. 'How's Wellcome?'

He shook his head. 'I think I'm going to take the job at Friedner. I think they'll let me work more on finding a cure.'

Vic tutted. 'Why are you so bothered about AIDS?'

'I'm not *so* bothered about it. I just have a few theories about the way the immune system works which I'd like to follow up.'

'You know of course that it's a gay plague.'

'Fuck off.' Joe sighed a bit inside. Vic was determined

tonight to wind him up.

'It is. Well. I don't mean it's God's revenge or any of that bollocks. I mean only gays, bisexuals, and women who sleep with bisexuals, can get it really. I don't know why you lot don't just admit it.'

Joe nodded, sarcastically. 'My lot. Yes. We control all the information.'

'Well, the AIDS lobby. It's just *propaganda* to suggest that everyone's equally at risk. Look. Correct me if I'm wrong, Mr King of Biochemistry, but you can only get it through transmission of bodily fluids. Yes?'

'And intravenously.'

'Yeah, never mind about that. Now. How are bodily fluids going to get transmitted into me?'

'From a vagina?'

Vic curled a lip. 'Pretty tough. It doesn't exactly shoot its fluids around like some organs, does it? Basically, to get it, you've got to have a penis inside you. Which leaves heterosexual men out of the equation.'

'Vic. Trust me. It's really more complicated than you're saying.'

Vic shrugged, too lazy to contradict. He was more interested in making a point than proving it.

'Besides, there's too much effort made in our culture to stop people dying early. Dying early's glamorous.'

'I don't think you'd say that if you'd seen some of the things I have.' Vic didn't respond, as he never did when Joe got genuinely serious. 'How is it glamorous?'

'They know things we don't. The dying.'

'Isn't that the dead?'

Vic shook his head. 'The dead know nothing. Anyway,' he continued, returning to his central theme, 'the Tourette thing. I can feel it now.' He leaned across the candle-heated grill in between them and lowered his voice. 'Do you know what I want to shout out now?' Joe shook his head, leaning in too, conspiratorially.

'Paki cunts!' said Vic, in a hard heavy whisper.

'*Vic . . .*' Joe withdrew, his prepared smile fading. The AIDS speech had been difficult enough for him, but this was much worse. At Warwick, he had been very PC: *right-on*, they used to call it in those days, and there wasn't, as in our postmodern age, any shame in being so. Rather the opposite – being right-on was an entry level attribute for credibility, then. At this point, at the beginning of the new decade, Joe was just starting, as many of his generation were – Vic, clearly, quicker than most – to reassess some of these beliefs; the boundaries of what he considered acceptable vocabulary were just starting to loosen. He still wasn't very happy with the word 'cunt', but was prepared to let it go, aware that the status of the word was shifting; but 'Paki' would always, he hoped, be for him beyond the socio-political pale. The shock of the new word broke his entrancement with Vic's energy and made him notice that it was now getting on for 11.15.

'Oh don't get sanctimonious,' said Vic, leaning back and raising his voice to a normal level. 'I'm not a racist. You know that. I despise all that. But that's my point. You don't *want*, concretely – you don't objectively want to do this stuff. In the sense of "things I really must get done today: (1) stab my friend, (2) pour some hot tea in someone's face, (3) upset the waiters at the Spice of Sydenham."' He paused, to finish the rest of his pint of Kingfisher. 'It's just the first computation the brain makes, in any situation, is "what's the worst thing I can do now?" In fact, it doesn't even ask the question; it just comes up with the answer, and sticks it in the front of your head.'

'Well—'

'Look. Haven't you ever been on the top of a cliff, and straight away felt an urge to throw yourself off?'

'Yes.' Joe wasn't sure he really wanted to carry on with this conversation. His right hand swung from his right ear.

Vic shrugged. 'Well that's it, then. Same thing.'

'Do you want anything else, sirs?' The chubby waiter with the bouffant dyed black hair had begun collecting their plates. Joe

44

looked at the dessert menu: five photographs of various-flavour sorbets inside carved-out cases of their matching fruits. 'No thanks.'

'So my point is,' said Vic, obliviously, 'Tourette's Syndrome doesn't *give* you these urges. It just knocks out the part of the brain that controls them. People with Tourette's Syndrome just can't stop themselves doing what we all want to do all the time.' He removed one of the steaming white towels, provided seamlessly by the waiter, from its plastic wrapper. He felt it at the edges, trying to gauge the split-second, that tiny window of opportunity, during which the flannel is no longer absurdly hot but not yet gone damp and cold, when he should do that thing that only men do, reflexively, without ever considering that these are meant to be hand-towels – melt his face into it, like a soft death mask. He looked up to see Vic already removing his one, whiteness sliding off over his dark shiny features. 'Might wrap this round my head in a minute and shout "Oy! Like me turban?"'

The door to the Spice opened; Joe's senses lifted at the tinkle of small Keralan bells, and a current of cold air dispersed the curry haze. He turned quickly, and his face melted with warm recognition. Vic's face, turning slower, caught in his jokey grimace, did not change. Why should it? The woman taking her coat off had ash-blonde hair and speckled green eyes, and a pleasing symmetry of feature, but seemed otherwise unremarkable, attested to perhaps by her decision to dress in dungarees. Looked at for a little longer, though – she seemed to be smiling directly at Joe, although that wasn't very likely – her hair *was* piled up on her head, and falling across her face in strands; her skin looked touchable, made for male hands to glide across; and there seemed about her a warmth, a glow that called to Vic's mind the aura that used to surround children in the Ready Brek advert, one of very few memories he seemed to have of his childhood – but perhaps it was just the reddish light of the restaurant.

'Vic?' said Joe, breaking his reverie, a state of mind Vic only recognised as such when it broke, 'this is Emma.'

JOE

In the first days, Joe and Emma went away as much as they could. Joe at the time was living in Surrey Quays, having come off considerably worse from his split with Deborah – the only time in his life he had ever initiated the end of a relationship. Joe had dealt with the terrible guilt it occasioned by offering her the flat they had been about to share, and – when this failed to turn back the waves of her tears – 98 per cent of his possessions. Mr Hamdad, a property developer from Jordan, had converted every room in Joe's Victorian redbrick building, situated on the mainest of main roads, into what the estate agents referred to as 'one-bedroom studios' – bedsits, obviously, but *so* archetypal, *so* squalid and cramped – so *brown* – as to be virtually sets for 1960s films.

Emma, meanwhile, was sharing a large house in Bow with about twelve other young people, and so, as far as quality time went, let alone romance, the new couple faced a stark choice between freezing beside the two-bar electric fire in Surrey Quays or constant interruptions from Steve, Sal, Dave, Ryan, Jackie, Jackie's dog, and all the pikies in the basement who didn't actually seem to *have* names.

So they went away a lot. Joe could afford it, because straight out of college he had walked into a job researching AZT for

46

Wellcome. He had, in fact, enough money, or certainly potential income, to move in somewhere much more comfortable, but was caught between secretly hoping to do that with Emma, and not wanting to do it too soon because of the upset it would cause Deborah: thus, for the moment – indecision causing, as it does, practical as well as spiritual hardship – he stayed in the bedsit, the consolation being that the rent, though exorbitant for what it was, left him a surplus at the end of the month large enough for the odd weekend for two at a hotel in the country.

On one of these weekends – the weekend beginning 17 April 1991, to be exact, a date that was to become significant for them – Joe, who by then had left Wellcome to take the job Friedner had been courting him with for some time, found himself suddenly with enough disposable income to hire a car as well, and so, as a surprise, turned up at Emma's house on the Friday in a cherry-red Golf convertible. Emma screamed when she saw it, and seemed to be embarrassed in front of her housemates by this classifiable-as-yuppie demonstration of wealth, but still wouldn't let go of his mouth with her own all the way down the Bow road. The sky wasn't to be moved by their love a spectral fibre away from its standard English grey, but nonetheless they drove with the roof down all the way to Southwold on the Suffolk coast.

Joe was already madly in love with Emma. But on these weekends he could find himself more than madly in love. At least in the normal run of his love, he could sense himself playing some kind of active role in its dynamic, but on these weekends, love seemed to take him and twist him violently up and around like a ghost in a hurricane, and when he looked at Emma in the framed country light, sleeping or not sleeping in the wider, cleaner beds than either of them had ever known, he felt his heart caught in its endless rushing spiral.

Their happiness was always uppermost on arrival at whichever hotel Joe had carefully selected from his *Ideal Breaks* brochure. It seemed to them both then that the weekend was

47

so long, that they had so much time – the landscape of shared joy spread out so far into the distance, when viewed from the perspective of Friday. It was almost as if the present, however enjoyable, was not as enjoyable as the prospect of the immediate future; they would get into the room and lie on the bed together, silently savouring the two days ahead, days before they would have to go back to London and work and separateness, as the most delicious buffer.

This, of course, would not last. And Joe, in particular, would find himself getting depressed, often as early as Saturday afternoon, at the thought of having to go back – to the point where depression at the thought of going back would disable the possibility of enjoyment while they were still there.

On this weekend, though, something – perhaps the misty air itself, lying diffusely on Suffolk's monochrome beaches – held time in suspension, and Joe remained uniquely oblivious to its passing, even until late on Sunday afternoon. They were in the car, driving back along country lanes to their hotel and listening to *Tapestry* by Carole King – a cassette that, on the way from London, they had bought from a service station rack ironically, and ended up listening to compulsively during the entire weekend.

> *Looking out into the morning rain*
> *I used to feel so uninspired . . .*

Joe reached down and turned the volume dial up. Once a song had become a song that moved him, he always wanted to listen to it as loudly as possible, to have his soul swamped by it.

'I didn't even know this was by her,' said Emma. Joe stirred out of the trance of music and road. 'I'd only ever heard the Aretha Franklin version.'

Joe nodded. He too had only ever been aware of that version, and although he felt that it was probably definitive, something about King's plaintive white voice chimed to a yearning within him. Emma began to sing along; she had a good voice, something Joe did not. His voice, in all its aspects, was a locus of embarrassment: singing, shouting, doing accents – attempting any of these would make him flush to the red.

> *Your love is the key to my peace of mind . . .*

Joe was always a bit unhappy about that – 'your love is the key to my peace of mind' – he preferred Aretha's elision, 'you're the key to my peace of mind', thinking it scanned better. But he let it pass, this time. As Emma sang, the sun, as if charmed, burnt through the ever-present cloud on its way down below the flat horizon.

'Fucking hell,' said Joe, pressing a button on the dash. 'A genuine excuse!' The leather roof of the convertible accordioned backwards, exposing their faces to the wind and the cold, but they didn't mind: the song was building to its chorus.

> *'Cos you make me feel,*
> *Yeah, you make me feel . . .*

Emma, her fringe blowing in wisps across her eyes, was singing loudly now, turning to him and smiling. He knew what was wanted, by her, by him and by culture – and, once again, he felt the ropes of shyness that normally bound him bitten through by her teeth. He joined in, at the top of his voice.

> *Like a natural woman . . .*

By the repeat chorus, he was belting it out, practically shouting; and laughing at the same time, half at his own terrible vocals and half at the absurdity of the lyric heard enunciated in a booming male voice. It was the purest, most delightful loss of self, all these sounds pouring out of him. A phrase came into his head from his childhood: *music and laughter to help you on your way*, and thankfully he couldn't remember where it was from, although it remained, in its own way, appropriate.

They were still singing when they passed three kids walking along the lane in the opposite direction, one of them pushing a bike; their faces turned to watch Joe and Emma's little musical speed past them like some sort of strange float.

'If that was me, when I was a kid, seeing us,' said Emma, above the continuing song, 'I'd *so* want to grow up. I'd be *so* jealous of adults.'

Joe looked at her, her eyes so full of the moment, so full of now. He'd never felt this precisely that he didn't want to be anywhere else.

If I can make you happy then I don't need to do more . . .

Joe pulled over to the side of the lane and asked Emma to marry him.

TESS

_____

Tess threw her bag on to the sofa, and headed straight for the drinks cabinet.

'Yeah, that doesn't surprise me,' said Vic, after he'd asked her how her journey had been. 'The whole country's gone fucking mental.'

'I should've stayed in France,' she said, pouring herself a large tumbler of Jim Beam: the intrinsic maleness of her tongue extended to her taste buds. 'Or maybe gone somewhere else.' She drank, quickly, like a cowboy who has picked up his slid-along-the-bar glass. 'I don't know where, though. Where in the world could you go to get away from this?'

Vic came over and put his hands on Tess's shoulders. He had intended just to remove her coat, but her shoulders raised under his hands like a pianist reaching a particularly moving passage of music, and he realised that she was expecting massage.

Vic lifted up her hair. Tess had long black hair: she was of the opinion that short hair was something women could have when young or when old, but not in between. He lifted it up and away from the back of her neck, which tilted to the left in expectation of touch; with his other hand, he gently probed the bone in the back with his thumb. Tess dropped her shoulders and breathed in deeply, signifying relaxation. Vic was good at massage – he had, in his repertoire, the variety of pressure of a musician's fingers; and something about providing pleasure through touch was synchronous with his amoral instincts. His wiry hands bent backwards at the tip of the fingers like a Balinese dancer's.

He pressed slightly harder, both thumbs now, moving in a circular motion around a pressure point on the nape. He was glad he had cut his nails this afternoon, it made touch easier. All his extremities – his nails and his hair – grew as hard as they grew strong; he could never use clippers, only big paper scissors like secateurs. When dead, he imagined, his corpse would soon look like a skeletal Struwwelpeter.

His fingers stretched across either side of her neck, the tips of his indexes meeting on the dual bumps of her collar-bone; his Tourette voice called out the word 'strangle' to him.

'Venus,' said Vic. 'You'd have to go to Venus.'

Tess's head fell forward. 'Isn't that where she's gone?'

'Maybe.' His hands moved upwards, travelling lightly across her face like a blind man feeling his way towards physiognomy. He pressed into her cheekbones, and rotated the skin, imagining it wrinkling slightly around his fingers.

'Hmm,' said Tess. 'You sound . . .'

His fingers stopped. 'What?'

'Almost sad.' Vic moved his hands further up her face, and rested his forehead on her crown; his breath swirled through the small hairs on the back of her neck. 'Don't tell me that even you—'

'Don't be absurd,' said Vic. His fingers closed her eyes, trickling along the lashes. 'I never even fancied the horsy old Sloane.'

She moved her face forward, out of his hands. The back of her head was framed by the window: a view of still keening London. Vic's eyes, she noticed, were red and streaming.

'Oh – how's the hay fever?' she said.

'Bad,' he replied. 'Really bad, this year.'

'Aren't your antihistamines working?'

'No. Well, a bit. I keep on forgetting to take them.'

Tess put her hands out towards his face, each of her ten fingers slightly outstretched, and then, very gently, placed them on his skin. This, a different massage – just the holding of his face in her hands – had worked for him before. Somehow, the mere act of being touched could soothe like an unguent his flaming face. It worked again: he felt, for a second at least, calm and sanity returning to his sinuses. Through a small gap in his eyes held gently closed by her long white fingers, he saw Tess's face, smiling with fondness and familiarity.

'Oh, I've missed you,' she said.

'I've missed you too,' said Vic, and meant it.

Tess and Vic were not an apparently perfect couple. Tess – the kind of woman who tends to be described as 'handsome', which means her features, although not ugly, gravitate towards hard – was, in the early part of their relationship, constantly having to stave off anti-Vic advice from friends convinced of his unsuitability: he was too lazy for her, too offensive in his opinions, too liable to have a roving eye, too dangerous.

They met, in the summer of 1995, at a wine-tasting in a vintner's under the arches at the South Bank. Tess, at the time, had been buying for a small chain of arty off-licences called Glug. Four of her wines – two French and two Spanish, all red – were on show at this tasting. Vic, meanwhile, having just played on a radio advert for Glug, had blagged a ticket for the tasting off Ivan, Glug's PR, who turned out to have been, in his twenties, a closet fan of Pathology's.

'. . . and "Cold as Stone", what about that?' Ivan was saying in between swigs of an Australian Sauvignon. He and Vic had been paying little attention to the spit-out buckets for the last hour. '"Standing in the rain it is so cold/You auctioneer, you bought and then you sold!!"' he sang, or rather barked, tunelessly. His rather spindly goatee, clearly an attempt to disguise a growing double chin, gyrated to the lyrics.

'Yeah,' said Vic nodding. He sipped his wine, a Chilean Merlot, and began to come to the conclusion that none of the wines at this tasting were worth having to put up with Ivan. He was going to have to get drunker.

'"Brave New World", that was brilliant! "And the brave new wo-rld/Has completely returned!"'

'Ivan.'

'What?'

'Who's that woman?'

Ivan turned; or rather, lurched his head violently around with his mouth open.

'Who?'

'The tall one, in the suit. With the dark hair.'

Ivan squinted. 'Tess? What about her?'

'Who is she?'

'She's a freelance buyer. Goes all over the place looking for little independent vineyards, then sets up deals with off-licences and supermarkets here.' Ivan lurched back round, and attempted a knowing smile. 'Why? You fancy her, do you? Eh? Doesn't surprise me. What's that one – "Feeling like I'm gonna blow/So many women out there on show!"'

'Ivan,' Vic said, walking away, 'that's by fucking Aerosmith.'

'What wine is this?'

Tess turned, glad to have an excuse to leave her conversation with James Foy, a seventy-two-year-old master of wine who always turned up at tastings, and who always sought her out, under the assumption that enough invitations to share classic bottles of Mouton Rothschild and Pétrus in his private cellar would eventually swing Tess's affections his way. She hadn't seen the man asking the question at a tasting before; in fact, she hadn't seen a *type* like him at a tasting before – wine people don't generally wear old suit trousers, Duffer of St George T-shirts, or – if she wasn't mistaking the smudge of blue perceptible under the left arm of his T-shirt – have tattoos; and they generally don't have a thick shock of all-directions dark hair, with eyes to match. What's more he was tall – perhaps to the point of lanky, somewhat gangling – but Tess was always interested in tall, as she hated bending down to kiss.

'It comes from a small vineyard in northern Spain. It's basically a Rioja, but they've used a blend of Merlot, Tempranillo and Garnacha, and aged it slightly longer than usual in oak, so it's quite spicy, like a Rhône Hermitage . . .'

Vic sipped from his glass, and swallowed. 'I haven't got a fucking clue what you're talking about,' he said.

'It's a *nice drink*,' said Tess, meeting his eyes, in which there was a dark flirtatious smile, though his face was deadpan.

'I must say,' said James Foy, 'I agree. The qualities of this wine remind my palate, if anything, of Paul Jaboulet's 1972 Aine Hermitage, a fantastic port-like claret—'

'Do you have any white?' said Vic. James Foy blinked over and over, like a stuck machine.

'No. I don't do white,' said Tess.

'Why not?'

'I don't like it. Well, I like the odd one. I like them if they've got some body, some depth and some intensity to the finish – basically if they approach the condition of red.'

'Aha!' said James Foy. 'Now I think the white you should try – and I've told you this before, Tess – is a 1986 Gewürztraminer—'

'Would you like to go somewhere else?' said Vic. James Foy began to cough, quite violently.

'For what?' said Tess.

Vic's lower lip pushed his chin upwards, as if pondering. 'A drink,' he said. And then to James Foy: 'I was thinking I might plump for – perhaps – the John Smith's. 1995.'

Tess laughed. 'The Case Is Altered.'

'Is it?'

'It's a pub on the corner of this street. I'll see you there soon as I've packed up. Fifteen minutes?'

*   *   *

Until the day Princess Diana died, Vic remained faithful to Tess. This was no small achievement for him, since, for Vic, sex was not something to be thought about every fifteen seconds or whatever the tired statistic is. He hardly *thought* about it at all. He *felt* it, at all times, as a physical sensation, entirely locatable at a specific point in his body – halfway up the perineum, an unscratchable itch, lodged there like a tiny piece of radioactive grit. Fingers could not be got to this itch – only flooding by orgasm could satiate it, and then only for a moment. Desire did not come upon him; it was existential.

For Vic was an evacuee. Not, obviously, a small child in a paisley wool tank-top and enormous grey shorts on a steam train to Swansea during the Blitz: no. He was an evacuee in the sense that he was in need of constant evacuation. Always, at his front, he could hear, like Chinese water torture, the dripdripdrip of fluid into his tree-like veiny testicles. He fantasised, sometimes, about attaching an enormous hypodermic syringe to the underside of his scrotum, constantly draining him, free (as Gala would have it) from desire.

Sex, though, was only the most obvious symptom of Vic's evacuative pressure. All urges had to be dealt with immediately. He couldn't bear a cc of liquid in his bladder, a molecule of solid in his bowels. He once read in a medical page in the *TV Times* – his memory told him the advice was Katie Boyle's, but with hindsight, this seemed unlikely – that in order to avoid haemorrhoids, bowel movements should never be forced; rather, the turd should be long baked until ready to ease itself out unforced. Vic tried but found it impossible. He couldn't imagine how to exist carrying excess baggage; how you could go about your life undistracted by the presence – even the tiniest presence – of impulse.

Likewise with thought: Vic never actually spent any time thinking – not, at least, as Rodin's *The Thinker* thinks, archetypally, on his own, in silence. Which is not to say he was not, in his own way, cerebral. It was just that for him, thoughts were things that could not be contained in the head – thoughts were urgent things, things that needed to be said, out loud, now: things that needed to be expelled. Vic only thought as he was speaking; sometimes, when unable to sleep, he would speak out loud in bed, trying to push out into the dark his overcrowded consciousness. Vic did not talk in his sleep; he talked his unsleep.

But despite the febrile nature of his urges and impulses, infidelity did not occur to Vic while he was with Tess. It had always occurred to him in the relationships he had been through in the past. He was one of those men who never swallowed the monogamy lie. He believed desire to be driven by novelty; by *revelation*. 'The really exciting thing about sex,' he once, on a Spice night, explained to Joe, who tended to be the listener once the conversation got round to this subject, 'is discovering what someone else looks and feels like naked, and this, I'm afraid, is only a *discovery* for a limited period. The man you want to be to make sex last for ever with one person, I've worked out, is Don Powell.'

'Don Powell?'

'The drummer of Slade. He's got a rare form of amnesia and wakes up every morning having completely forgotten everything up to that point.'

'Hm. I'm not sure sex lasting for ever is worth eternally having to relearn the drum part to "Cum On Feel the Noize",' said Joe.

Vic felt that the long-term relationship was irreligious. He felt it because he worked out that, paradoxically, the human relationship is the opposite of its own archetype, Adam and Eve, who when they were *first* together had no sense of each other's nakedness, and then *later* felt shame: we *first* feel shame – and with it, excitement, lust, titillation, fear and everything else that makes up good sex – and then *later* have no sense of each other's nakedness. Later, we become over-comfortable with each other's bodies, and what they have to do. Vic once wondered what this would be like if it happened early in a relationship, and so rang Emily, a somewhat prim PR woman who he'd gone out with twice before, and asked her, for their next date, if she fancied coming round and cleaning her teeth while he had a dump. Through the following unbroken dial tone, he considered that he'd probably been thinking about ending it anyway.

Excuses are generally made for men who consistently wander: they have a longing to humiliate woman, or to prove themselves, or whatever. But Vic had none of these longings; he had a simple, unalloyed, look-no-deeper-than-this longing for – to use a phrase that, say, Eddie Murphy might prefer – new pussy.

Before Tess, Vic lived for new pussy. Now, obviously, if you live for new pussy, at some point you are going to end up upsetting or humiliating – um – old pussy. But this was not – although many of Tess's friends tried to suggest that his past track record proved that it was – Vic's motive; the damage done to old pussy was, in Vic's mind, purely an unfortunate by-product of the search for the new.

It wasn't helped by the speed at which, for him, new pussy turned old. Pussy, for Vic, really did seem to live in cat years: a month in human terms was about a year in pussy terms. Pussy had that disease that Robin Williams has in *Jack*.

He always knew the exact point too, at which new became old; he knew it – as men do – through masturbation. Vic was very committed to masturbation; sometimes, the main reason he wanted to have sex with someone would be to provide himself with fresh images for a future wank. Again, this had led to some confusion as to his psychological make-up. After a first sexual episode with a woman, Vic, like a standard patriarchal villain, wanted her to leave immediately, or, if the episode had happened elsewhere, he wanted to go home immediately. This wasn't, though, because he was repulsed by her as soon as his desire was quenched or any such misogynistic nonsense; rather, it was because he wanted to have a wank. And not just for the sake of having a wank (although that was undeniably in there);

it was because he wanted to replay the sexual images from the night before in his head as soon as possible, whilst still fresh, because that was a way of committing them to memory. For Vic, a wank in the hand was a wank in the bank.

But how long do such memories remain fresh? Vic found, more and more, that they went off like the milk in his irregularly powered fridge: i.e. after about three days. So he would often return to the same woman, attempting to renew the memory; but then a second type of degeneration would set in, when any memory of sex with this particular woman was no longer exciting, no matter how recent the sexual experience was. There was always a point, in masturbation, when the woman Vic was presently fucking would exit from the stage in his head. He might try to bring her back, with all sorts of *dei ex machinae*, but basically, her body in whatever contortions he might place it, was no longer wank-fodder; *that*, to conclude, was the point at which, for Vic Mullan, new pussy became old pussy.

Which is not to say that Vic was not emotionally involved with any of the women he slept with. He considered, in his own mind, that he was; indeed, one, a modern hippie from Brighton called Janis, he claimed very forcefully to be in love with.

'So, if you're in love with Janis,' said Joe, between mouthfuls of Chana Dosa on another Spice night, 'how come you're shagging Emily?'

'And Sacha.'

'You're shagging *Sacha*!?'

'I *am* in love with Janis,' said Vic, emphatically. 'It's just there's two and a half billion other women in the world who I really have to see naked.'

That would have been enough for him, too, he thought sometimes. If they just came into your room, one by one, took off their clothes, allowed you a view (front and back) and then left. That would do for him – that, and the acquisition of a photographic memory.

But with Tess, he remained faithful. Maybe it was because

sex seemed to remain novel and fresh with her for much longer than with anyone else (Vic characterised her, in his own mind, as *recyclable* pussy). As something of a male herself, she too was easily sexually bored, and keen to make it new as much as possible; but more importantly because Vic had never really been mates with a girlfriend before. He had always been on good terms with girlfriends, always found them good company, always been friends: but not mates.

He first noticed this distinction one evening while they were watching Gaby Roslin on the television. Something had always bothered Vic about Gaby Roslin. He wasn't sure what it was: she was, without doubt, an attractive woman, who normally he might have fancied, but every time she appeared, something about her turned him off. He was just about to articulate this when Tess said:

'Don't you just hate women who wear trousers with high heels?' at which point Vic underwent something of an epiphany: in fact, four epiphanies – one, that Gaby Roslin always wore trousers with high heels; two, that that was what he didn't like about her; three, that he never liked women who wore trousers with high heels, especially trouser *suits* with high heels; and four, that Tess was the only woman he'd ever been with who would've said something like that so directly and so brutally – and so in tune with his own instincts.

So Vic remained faithful to Tess. Not because he wouldn't do the dirty on a mate. He would. What he discovered, though, is that being mates with a girlfriend is a great way of dispersing the sexual frustrations of monogamy, of releasing the pressure of desire, because you can talk about it; you can talk about other people you fancy, something Vic and Tess did all the time.

The one person he never told Tess he fancied – a lot – was Emma.

SONIA AND MICHELLE

Sonia and Michelle were two solicitors who had set up their own partnership together after having met at Foster, Lewis & Benbury, a firm in Clerkenwell. This is not important information for this story, but there's something funny about the names of accountancy and legal partnerships; something to do with the stupid *adultness* of a blank row of surnames, or the sense, because only the surnames are given, that really you should know who these people are. Before Foster, Lewis & Benbury, Sonia had worked at Klein, Garr, Wegg & Head (who *so* needed someone with a polysyllabic surname to join them), whilst Michelle had done articles at the daringly &-missing Freedman Prosser Cohen of, perhaps unsurprisingly, St John's Wood. Sonia was a pseudo-aristocrat from Edinburgh with an air of dignified intelligence not actually justified by anything she said, and a boyfriend who played rugby; Michelle was a lesbian, with the looks – and something of the no-nonsense humourlessness – of Lara Croft.

'I really don't know why we're going,' said Tess, on the way to the party, a celebration of Sonia and Michelle's business venture, being held at Michelle's flat in Camberwell. She was sitting in the back of Emma's Renault Clio, alongside Vic; Joe was driving, Emma was in the passenger seat. The presence of the child seat in the back made things a bit cramped: they had been going to take Joe's car, an old Volvo, but Vic had made a lot of fuss about not wanting to be seen turning up at a party looking like he was being driven by his dad. It was the first time all four of them had been together since before Diana died.

'Sonia, in particular, is just a twat.'

'In what way is she a twat?' said Joe. He often felt the need to defend people when Tess was like this, more to dilute her sharpness than because he felt particularly supportive of the object of her attack.

'That voice. That fucking posh Scottish voice. "Well, heallooo everybody, I sound a bit like Kirsty Young."' Everyone laughed at the accuracy of the impression, even Joe. 'She speaks like she's got a boiled egg lodged in her mouth.'

'That's really true, she does,' said Emma.

'Tess hates parvenus, don't you darling?' said Vic, reflexively ironising the final word.

'Hates what?' said Emma.

'*Nouveaux riches* pretenders. Social climbers. It's because she's proper posh. She keeps it under her hat, but she's got some genuine aristo blood in her.'

'Yes, that's right. I keep it under my Gertrude Shilling monstrosity that I bring out every Ascot.'

'Have you really?' said Joe.

'No of course I fucking haven't.'

'You have,' said Vic, pushing it. 'What's your middle name?'

'I'm not disclosing that.'

'Oh, come on Tess, what is it?' said Emma, looking back at her, girlishly.

'It's Sharon.'

'No it isn't,' said Vic, laughing. 'Tell them what it is.'

Tess looked at him, mild daggers; then tutted, and raised her eyes to heaven. 'Octavia,' she said, wearily, turning to the window.

Joe snorted a little. Emma flicked a hand at him. 'I think that's a lovely name,' she said, sincerely.

'But undoubtedly posh,' said Vic.

'It was my grandma's name, OK?'

'So she was posh, then. Which means you must be.'

Tess adopted a familiar attitude, halfway between amusement and ennui.

'All right Vic, I give in. You're right. I can trace my line back to Ethelred The Unusually Fat. My father owns the Duchy of Hendon. My great-grandmother on my mother's side was the mistress of the Earl of Bollocksville. And that liquid they use on tampon adverts?'

'The blue stuff?'

'That's from my family's personal blood bank.' The car laughed as one. 'But despite all that,' she continued, 'I still don't sound as if I've got a fucking boiled egg lodged in my mouth.'

'And just that – that one idiosyncrasy – probably not her fault—'

'Yeah, it's probably a speech impediment, Joe, and not at all an affectation.'

' – just that is enough to make her a twat?'

'No,' said Tess. 'There's also everything else about her.'

Emma laughed, rather too furiously for Vic's liking.

At the party, the talk was all of conspiracy.

'MI5. They did it. Definitely,' Neil, a simian telesales king with shades on his forelock, was saying, above 'Never Ever' by All Saints.

'What do you mean definitely? What do you know about it?' his girlfriend Kate countered; her tone was contemptuous, but whether this was of Neil's opinion or just of Neil was unclear.

'Look. A woman like her doesn't just *die*.'

'Oh. Was she invulnerable?'

'Like Asterix and Obelix,' said Douglas, a City boy who

liked to pretend he wasn't, by using what he considered to be unexpected cultural reference.

'Only after they had drunk their magic potion,' said Emma.

'What?'

'They weren't always invulnerable. They had to drink a shot of magic potion from their gourds.'

'The Royal Family have got loads of friends in MI5.' Neil was ploughing on, between swigs of Budvar. 'And they were very unhappy about her getting involved with an Arab.'

'Not just any Arab,' said Douglas, coming out of a short sulk over the Asterix and Obelix incident. 'Son of a very rich and powerful Arab.'

'Oh don't talk shite,' said Joe, finally moved to speak. He'd been tired when they had arrived at the party, and the endless chatter of spurious invention was making him more tired. 'It was an accident. No one was behind it.' All eyes turned to him, but he could feel only Emma's, untrusting, flinching these days, whenever this topic was around. 'It's always the same when any big death happens. People have to suggest some conspiracy behind it. Because it's more reassuring – more comforting – to think that some government or crime syndicate or whatever must be behind it than to face the fact that death is just random.' He paused, wanting to wind up, uncomfortable with the spotlight; he was aware of his fingers, worrying at his earlobe. 'It reassures people at the same time as allowing them to seem anti-establishment and a bit dangerous.'

'Look, it's simple,' said Michelle. 'Like Hannibal Lecter says in *Silence of the Lambs*. First principles. You've got to go back to first principles.'

'"Of each particular thing, ask what is it in itself,"' quoted Tess. '"What does he *do* this man you want?"'

'Yeah—'

'He's quoting Marcus Aurelius.'

'Yeah, all right, Tess. So, applying the same principle: what do you have to be *doing* to be in a car going at 122 miles an hour through Parisian subways without a seat belt and not worrying about it – *not* screaming "Stop! Slow down, for God's sake!"'

The group, crowded around the magnolia fireplace, looked at her blankly. Leaning on her shoulder, dipping a stick of celery into a mayonnaise dip on the mantelpiece, was Nichole, who had only come out last week, much to the horror of her boyfriend Daniel. Daniel had chosen not to come tonight.

'Coke,' said Michelle definitively. 'That's what you have to be doing.' There was a pause as they all took this in. 'It's true. What other drug would have that effect?'

'Speed?' suggested Vic.

'Oh fuck off. Like a member of the Royal Family'd be taking *speed*. I suppose she was into sniffing glue as well?'

'I'm not sure that was your question—'

'*He* was a well-known cokehead, as well,' proffered Nichole, supportively.

'Yeah. And you're not going to tell me *she*'d never come across the stuff.'

'Who would offer it to her?' said Emma.

Joe looked across at Emma, whose face had fixed on the floor. He had felt her mood humming within him throughout this conversation; initially breezy, happy with it, prepared to give the sacred some slack – but now, he knew, they had gone too far. He saw her hand move to her crown and pull at the hair on top of her head (her less crazy hair now, worn in something of a bob) – an action he knew she did only when under pressure, the equivalent of his own earlobe touching; he moved his eyes away, unable to bear her intensity, and let them alight on Vic, who was watching her too.

'As Nichole just said,' said Michelle, with a hint of a sneer, 'he was a cokehead.'

Emma's face remained fixed down. Her fingers twirled above her crown. 'I'm not saying no one she ever met would take coke. I'm saying who would've dared to offer her it?' She finally looked up. 'She was a *princess*.'

There was a silence, as the party-goers communally weighed up this statement, considered the possibility that it was somehow postmodern or ironic, realised – from the commitment in Emma's eyes – that it wasn't, and shuffled through a range of reactions, from embarrassment to hauteur.

'I met her once, you know,' said Sonia, barging in on the circle, her wide-as-a-fridge boyfriend in tow. 'At a charity dinner.'

Emma moved away, with a small excusatory cough, followed quickly by Joe.

'What's up with her?' said Tess, under her breath, to Vic.

'And obviously I was a bit stuck for what to say,' Sonia was continuing, her purring Morningside vowels coating every word with an amused aristocratic smirk.

'Oh, she's quite upset about Diana.' He could feel his eyes turning to neutral.

'*Really?*'

'So I asked her the only question I could think of, which was . . . is there anyone left in the world you'd really like to meet?'

'Yeah, something about it really got to her.' Vic felt displaced, pulled in different directions; a new feeling, a redrawing of perspective seemed to be happening within him. He wanted to go and comfort Emma.

'And do you know who she said?'

'Actually,' said Tess, 'something about that fits.'

'She's not stupid,' said Vic, quickly, surprising himself.

'Noel Edmonds.'

The circle of friends laughed as one.

'Noel bloody Edmonds!'

'I never said she was,' said Tess, squinting at her boyfriend inquiringly.

'You know, not only does that show a terrible lack of imagination, it shows a terrible lack of organisational ability! I mean, did she not *have* a PA?!'

'I meant, she's always . . . overempathising. She's like . . . got one skin too few.' Tess looked at Vic, waiting for a response, but he only nodded distractedly. She looked around at the grinning London monkeys. 'Let's get them and get out of here.'

'OK.'

Turning into the hallway, Tess looked back and said: 'If you had to sleep with either Sonia or Michelle, which would you prefer?'

This was a game they played often. Vic would normally have an instant response – he knew his desires so well, such questions could be answered without thought – but he was looking up the stairs for Joe and Emma, and had to turn back to look through to the living-room where he could survey the two candidates.

'Um – I dunno. Michelle, I think.'

'Yes. I think . . .' said Tess reflectively, 'if I were a bloke, I'd prefer to fuck Michelle.' Vic nodded. 'But I think I'd prefer to come in Sonia's mouth.'

Vic looked at his girlfriend; he was used to her masculine imagination, but this level of detailed understanding was almost frightening. Tess turned to him, her mouth curved at one side in a thoughtful smile.

'But then, I do like some salt on my boiled egg.'

Emma and Joe appeared at the top of the stairs, with their coats on: Emma looked almost as red-faced and crumpled as she had on that first day. Vic tried to catch her eye and communicate some message of secret sympathy, but his face was cracked and malformed because he was still laughing.

JOE

'It's a strange thing, isn't it, marriage? Why do people do it, exactly?' Joe remembered Vic saying, at the Spice of Sydenham, the evening he'd first told him that Emma had accepted his proposal. He had been expecting a slightly more personable response, but could see that his friend was in speechifying mode.

'Because they're in love?'

'Right. And of course *unmarried* couples aren't?'

Their plates had long gone. They were sitting there, Vic with the remains of a bottle of Bulgarian red wine, Joe with a sweet lassi, ignoring the tired looks from the two hovering waiters. Joe had waited until the end of the meal to tell him, somehow knowing that he would disapprove: a month had already gone by since the weekend in Suffolk. Outside, rain polished the roads black.

'No. It's got to be more than that. In the past, this wasn't an issue. People got married to have sex. Or to pay off a debt of three chickens.'

'I think they still do that in Somerset.'

'Maybe. But now people don't have to get married to have sex. In fact . . .' and his dark eyes grinned a little at the cleverness of his own formulation, 'quite the opposite: the

68

vast majority of people have to have sex now in order to get married.'

'Excuse me? Where? In tribes with some sort of initiation rite?'

'No, it's true. I mean, imagine if someone you were seeing, but not sleeping with, suggested marriage. You'd leave skidmarks.' Vic paused, looking his patiently smiling friend up and down. 'Well, actually, *you* probably wouldn't. *You* might even say yes, for the sake of politeness.'

'Yes, I am that shit.'

'Yes.' He looked at the pile of After Eights on top of the bill on the plate in front of them; they were such regulars at the Spice that the restaurant always gave them practically the whole box. 'I think this is it. Imagine relationships as rounds of poker, with the chips being declarations of love.' He picked up the plate, tilting it towards him; the After Eights fell off in a heap in front of him. 'At the start, you're cautious, right? You make small bets.' He slid a single chocolate gambler-like into the centre of the table, just behind the four silver salvers of chutney, saying, at the same time, with clear inverted commas attached, googling his eyes and over-softening his voice, '"You know, you're not like anyone else I've ever met."' He looked up at Joe to see if his point had registered; then he slid another, saying, '"God, I didn't think I'd ever be with anyone so on my wavelength."'

'I think I understand the analogy,' said Joe, wondering how long Vic was going to go on; Emma had said she'd come round later.

'Then,' said Vic, 'as more begins to depend on it, you have to use more chips.' He put in two After Eights.

'"I really, really like you, y'know."'

Two more.

'"I've always avoided commitment in the past, but now I'm not so sure . . ."'

Then three.

'"Mum. Dad. This is Sally."' He drank the last dregs of wine in his glass. 'OK? And then, finally, you see each other.' He slid the five remaining chocolates into the middle of the table. Joe looked at him, waiting.

'"I love you,"' said Vic.

'You show the hand in your heart,' replied Joe, calmly.

'That's right!' said Vic, smiling. 'The trouble is, though, poker may end there, but in love you've got to keep raising the stakes.'

'Do you?'

'Yeah! "I love you" is subject to the law of diminishing returns; like . . .' he nodded jauntily downwards, 'one or two other critical elements of a relationship, it loses a bit of thrill-value every time you get it out.'

Joe laughed, but felt a little alienated, as he sometimes did when Vic got like this, like his friend wasn't really talking to him at all; he was just a sounding-board for whichever taboo-breaking opinion formed the centre of tonight's Vic Mullan Manifesto.

'That's what happens with "I love you", continued Vic, his hands jutting about in time with his points. 'That same phrase that you once shouted Hollywood- or Heathcliff-like in the lashing rain, now – now you're saying it dumbly at the end of every phone conversation, a follow-on from "I'll be back for dinner". Once it came out in a spontaneous rush, it *forced* itself out; now it's a reflex.'

He paused, smiling to himself. 'That, of course, isn't good enough for love; so you have to go further. And there's only one phrase that tops "I love you" in Passion's Premiership . . .'

'Will sirs be wanting anything else?'

They looked up. The bouffant-haired waiter was trying to do his special grin, reserved for regulars, but his eyes were exhausted.

'Yes,' said Vic, holding up an After Eight. 'Have you got the box?'

'Sir?' The waiter did that extraordinary rubbernecked head waggle that only Indians can do.

'Just to make a point.' The waiter repeated the waggle, but went off, coming back a second later with a whole new box of After Eights, the cellophane still on.

'Perfect,' said Vic, taking it from the proffered silver plate and plonking it down melodramatically into the centre of the table. '"Will you marry me?"'

They never got treated quite the same at the Spice of Sydenham after that.

For Joe, this conversation, previously held in his memory as a light anecdote, had been resonating in his head lately, or at least since his marriage had gone into decline. A man whose methodicalness increased as he got older, he found himself spending many hours thinking – on the verge of getting out a notepad and jotting down ideas – about what might have gone wrong. Eventually, as a result of considering the time-period over which the decline had occurred, he was forced inextricably to link it to the birth of Jackson. He hated doing this, partly because he loved his child, and partly, again, because it seemed to him a cliché, a marriage foundering on the rock of a first child. But it wasn't so simple anyway; he knew that their relationship had not crumbled, as so many do, under standard new parental strains – lack of sleep and constant nappy-changing and the sudden disappearance of sex. All *that* they could cope with; in fact, the suffering element of having a baby only had a bonding effect, and Emma had been fine about giving up her job at Chaise and designing from home. It was more to do with magic.

They were, in their first years, one of those couples who, having found each other, end curiosity there, and seal themselves off; Tess, soon after meeting them, once remarked that she felt that Joe and Emma – although with great politeness – saw Vic and her somewhat on sufferance. 'There's always that tiny feeling that seeing us is something they have to do before they

71

can get back to being with each other,' said Tess. And, to a large extent, their relationship had been based exactly on this sense of hermetic enclosure: sometimes they would lie in bed and look at each other for hours, and feel that all each needed was the total presence of the other.

When Emma became pregnant, then, it seemed as if the baby could only be an expression of this totality – and while he was in her stomach, he seemed indeed thus, lying between them like a joint organ of Siamese twins. But when he was born, something shattered. It was nothing to do with Jackson himself – he was a lovely baby, a perfect cross between the two, Emma's green eyes in Joe's rather frowny forehead, although he did have, just underneath the right side of his mouth, a purple birthmark, which doctors had been telling them for some time now would eventually vanish. It had to do with structure: the horizontal lines of connection between Emma and Joe turned right angles towards him. Their relationship had relied on there being only two of them, and perfect and satisfied and replete as such; three disturbed the chemistry – it defocused their love. Maybe they loved each other as much as it is possible to love; and so, in order to love someone else, they had to siphon some of this off.

Joe remembered, as well, that one of the first times he noticed real tension between them was about two weeks before Jackson was born. They had had a dinner party – because of Emma's condition, he had done all the cooking – and afterwards they were sitting around, with Vic, who had stayed after all the other guests had left. Tess was away – not on wine business this time, just seeing her family in Devon; and anyway, it was early enough in Vic's relationship with her for her absence not to be especially felt: Joe, Emma and Vic functioned easily as a threesome.

'God,' said Emma, holding her stomach, 'he's really grouchy tonight.'

Joe, sitting next to her on the sofa, put his hand on her convex bump; it was always harder than he expected it was going to be. She was right – he only had to wait a second before a kick strong enough to knock his hand upwards came from within.

'Blimey,' he said. 'What can we do about that?'

'I know,' said Vic, and from the corner of the room he picked up Joe's old six-string guitar. He came back and sat cross-legged in front of the sofa, and started playing a version of 'Lady Grinning Soul' by David Bowie, augmented with his own improvisations to give it a classical, Spanish air.

'I read somewhere – *Elle*, I think it was – that playing music to unborn children has some sort of good effect on them,' he said, as his fingers blurred.

'God, Vic,' said Joe, stunned, as ever, by Vic's ability, 'you're such a brilliant guitarist. Why are you fucking wasting it on Findus?'

Vic shrugged – his last job had been on an advert for curry pancakes – and carried on playing, without bitterness.

'Is it having any effect?' said Joe.

'You know, I think it is . . .' said Emma, drumming her fingers on her navel. She looked admiringly at Vic; he smiled, and, still playing, held the guitar out towards her stomach. 'Perhaps you should come and play when I have him. It might calm me down too.'

'Oh darling, it'll be all right,' said Joe.

'*You* say.' She grimaced. 'It probably will be for you.'

'Are you frightened?' said Vic, rather innocently.

Emma laughed, like she sometimes did, a throaty, guttural, Irish laugh that seemed to come from a much older woman.

'Only bloody shitting myself.'

Vic looked to Joe: now it was his turn to shrug.

'Yes, well – there comes a point where men have got no advice to give, really . . .'

'I dunno,' said Vic. 'Why don't you try projecting the pain on to someone else?'

Emma sat up a little. 'How do you mean?'

He propped the guitar against the sofa. 'When I was

twelve, I was playing football at school. And I dislocated my shoulder.'

'Oh God,' said Joe. 'It's not the Graham Whale story?'

'Shut up. You never know, it might help. Anyway, I was in floods of tears, sprawling around on our crap all-weather pitch, and our PE teacher, who was also the ref – Mr Branston—'

'As in "Bring out the"?' said Emma.

'Yes, as in "Bring out the" – he crouched down to me and whispered "I'm going to snap your shoulder back into place. It's really going to hurt. Now, who do you hate most on the pitch?" And I said, through my tears, "Graham Whale. He knocked me over."' Vic did a brief impression of himself as a small crying boy; Emma laughed. 'And Mr Branston whispered back, "OK, this isn't happening to you, it's happening to Graham Whale. You're just a voodoo doll for Graham Whale." So I did. I really concentrated on it. I pretended I fucking *was* Graham Whale – with his eggy smell and his weed-in trousers and his haircut that his mum had clearly done with a bowl. And then Mr Branston snapped my shoulder back into place.'

'God,' said Emma. 'Did it hurt less?'

'It hurt like fuck.' Emma and Joe laughed together at this. 'But maybe it would've hurt more.'

'Did Graham Whale look in pain at any stage?' said Joe.

'Not that I noticed.' Vic took a small silver casket out of his pocket, along with some Rizlas and a packet of cigarettes: underneath all this, he slid an available CD, *The Bends* by Radiohead.

'Vic . . .' said Joe, wearily, gesturing at the tobacco. 'Not a fortnight before it's due.'

'Oh sorry . . .'

'Oh forget it, Joe,' said Emma. Joe frowned; Vic held the CD, with his stash still piled upon it, in mid-air, and looked between them, as if waiting for a decision. 'Honestly, darling . . .' she continued, reaching out a hand to Joe's shoulder, trying to stroke him out of his perturbed expression, 'one passive joint's not going to do anything to him. Except maybe make him come out smiling and asking for Mars bars.'

Vic laughed, and put the CD back down in front of him. Joe shrugged, holding an earlobe between thumb and forefinger, but felt uneasy, partly at the potential damage being done to his unborn child, and partly at being positioned in the role of wet blanket.

'But I still do it now, sometimes,' said Vic, resetting his things.

'What?'

'What Mr Branston taught me. If I've got a really bad thing coming up, I just imagine it's happening to someone else. Someone I don't like.'

'Bit cruel, don't you think?' said Joe.

Vic shrugged again. 'It's not actually going to happen to them, is it?'

'Were you Mr Branston's teacher's pet, then?' said Emma, smiling.

'I dunno,' said Vic, grinning. His hands expertly crumbled the brown lump he'd taken from the casket on to a Rizla paper. 'I don't think he was so keen on me after he met my dad at a parent–teacher meeting.'

'Why not?'

He licked the paper along one edge. 'Mr Branston said, I like to think I get on well with my pupils. They call me Pickley. Because of my name, you see? And my dad said: Right. So it must be another Mr Branston that my son calls Mr *Embryo-Head*.'

Emma really laughed at this, uncontrollably, almost as if she'd had some of the joint that Vic went on to light and take a draught from through his fist. Joe laughed too, but stopped soon, having heard the story before, and, as he looked at his wife still laughing five minutes on, felt a little excluded. Later that night, they had one of their first proper rows.

Joe was, however, a man prepared to do what he could to

improve his marital situation. Conversant enough in Men-Are-From-Mars, Women-Are-From-Venus-speak, he had concluded that, now, exactly opposite to their earlier life, things tended to be better between Emma and himself when they *had* some sort of other focus: now, shared concentration on the welfare of a third party could bring them, at least, some relief, could, for a little while, divert their mutual gaze from the widening gulf between them. So it was, on the weekend following Sonia and Michelle's party, that he offered to come with Emma on a visit to see her mother.

'But what about Jackson?' she said, putting on her blue Diesel anorak: like many of her coats, it was slightly too big for her, and her smallness inside it made Joe's heart ache a touch. 'It's too late to call a babysitter.'

'Let's take him!'

'Oh Joe . . . I'm tired,' she said, and he felt his insides tighten, sensing incoming criticism. She spread her hand around her neck. 'My glands are up again.'

Joe tutted, sympathetically, unsure whether to raise a comforting hand of his own. 'Are they?' Emma was one of those people whom stress and tiredness seemed to affect mainly in the throat; she was given to infections there, and swollen glands.

'And you know how difficult it is for me to cope if Mum's . . .' she struggled for the word, '. . . *bad*.'

'Look, it'll be fine. Let Jacks be my responsibility. I'll make sure he doesn't get under your feet.'

A corner of her mouth pursed, but her face was not unsoft; she could see he was trying.

'OK. On your own head be it,' she said, her accent coming through stronger, as it always did when she said something folksy.

Outside, Joe strapped Jackson into the padded child seat in the back of the Clio; as usual, he tried to undo himself immediately, but couldn't, his tiny hands still reserving most of their power for grip rather than pull. Emma had already turned the engine on, so Joe ran round the other side and hopped in.

'Hello?' he said, when she didn't pull away.

'It's no good just doing *him* up,' she said, pointing at Joe's unbelted belly. 'No good if he survives a crash but his daddy's gone through the window . . .'

'Right,' said Joe, slotting the metal clips together. *She never used to tell me off this much* came riding into his head, but he put a lid on the thought, reminding himself how this was an old issue between them. She had always despaired of Joe's tendency to do up his seat belt as he drove off, or when stopped at the first traffic light: he thought it saved time. Feeling somewhat safe in the confines of familiar argument, he pointed to her section of car floor, and said, 'I'm not sure kicking your shoes off to drive is especially high on the list of road-safety tips, though, is it?'

She looked down; her trainers lay with their block soles upwards, missing her feet in their grey woolly men's socks resting on the pedals. With another little ache, Joe noticed that the laces on these ones were too long, as they had been on the day they met.

'Oh we are Sir Robert Mark today . . .' she said, with friendly sarcasm. Joe was grateful for her good mood. She fiddled with the radio, pressing the pre-sets absently, searching for any good song.

'Why do you always do that?'

'I don't always do that, as well you know. I do it when I'm wearing these trainers. The soles are too big to feel the pedals properly.' Joe looked at her, and waited; he knew from her tone that there was another, sillier, reason, and luxuriated in the knowledge. No matter how bad things got, he would always at least know her this well.

'And . . .' she said, eventually, her eyes catching his in a quick sideways move, '. . . I like the feel of the . . . what are they called? Tessellations?'

'What?'

'The things on the pedals. The curly bits. I like the feel of them on my feet.' She turned to him, and smiled. 'OK?'

He smiled back, but with some strain; they had wandered, he felt, into bad waters. Emma loved having her feet stroked; a touch that others might have found torturously ticklish, she craved, often telling Joe it was where she most liked to be touched. Some men may have been unhappy with this information, preferring her to say other places, but Joe wasn't, knowing that one of the rarely sung joys of being in a relation-ship is the access it gives you to *non*-sexual touching – to lying around, having your neck stroked, your hair played with, your forearms caressed, your shoulders massaged, your hand held. Emma's reference to her feet brought home to him the recent absence of this type of touching between them, feeling that his hands had been replaced by the weird Celtic circles on their car's brake, their car's accelerator. He went quiet for the rest of the journey.

After an hour or so at Sylvia's, Joe was fairly pleased when Jackson crapped himself. He was a naturally patient man, but after he'd explained who he was for the seventh time, it was a relief to smell the homely, reassuring stench and know he could excuse himself into the bathroom with the baby for ten minutes. He picked up his child, saying, 'Oops, I think it's time to change somebody's nappy', something a darker-minded man might have considered not saying until they were certain the smell was coming from Jackson.

The cramped bathroom was scrupulously clean – she's prob-ably cleaned it about twenty times today, he thought – but so old and austerity-years redolent that it felt unhealthy: the bath had one of those yellow trails from tap to plughole built up from years of reaction between soft water and hard enamel that no amount of Jif will deal with. For no apparent reason, there was a white footstool topped by a padded powder-blue cushion in the corner opposite the toilet: he rested Jackson's pygmy body on top of this, and began unfastening his little dungarees, followed by his Pamper. Jackson looked up at him, his green eyes exactly like Emma's, except possessed of that particular vacuity which always accompanied him shitting himself, as – Joe noticed, looking down at the spreading brown stream – he was still doing. It reminded Joe of the expression in Boris's eyes – Boris being Sylvia's ancient boxer dog – when he was resolutely crouched over the pavement: absolute blankness, emptied of all awareness of what it is he is doing. Joe wasn't overly fond of Boris; when they had arrived, as ever, he had gone into barking and growling overdrive, which pissed Joe off, partly because he thought it might frighten Jackson, but mainly because he always felt there was an element of showboating to it.

Love . . . soft as an easy chair . . . ?

He looked up. Emma's voice, echoey and muffled through the wall, went up expectantly on the last note, different from Barbra Streisand's phrasing, but for a reason: she was leading.

Love . . . fresh as the morning air . . .

Sylvia's answer was a little cracked, but underneath still held the vibrato of the cod professional. Then together:

Onnnnne . . . love that is shared by two . . .

Joe wrapped the soiled nappy up in its plastic bag and dropped it in the bathroom flip-bin. He was careful to avoid getting mess anywhere else; he didn't want Emma to have a reason to find fault with him.

I have found with you.

He was just holding Jackson's legs up to wet-wipe around

79

his buttocks when Emma poked her head through the bath-room door.

'I'm just going to take Mum out for a little walk. Do you want to come?'

'No, it's OK. I haven't finished changing him yet. Where are you going?'

'Just down to the shops. We were going to go out on the common with Boris, but he's gone into hiding somewhere. Seems to have become the only dog in canine history not to like walks.' She shrugged. 'Be about twenty minutes.'

'Fine,' said Joe, looking back down to the baby, glad of this breeziness between them, even if it felt a little forced. Emma came over and bent down, face close to the naked boy, his arms and legs reaching up in a backwards all-fours, the only creases in his skin the ones at the points where his body joined.

'All clean now, little man? Aren't we? Eh?' Jackson's eyes went live, and his chublet face smiled, the on-the-way-to-trying-out-the-next-expression smile of the thirteen-month-old, made slightly lopsided by the continuing presence of his birthmark. Emma and Joe's hearts, bonded still over this, melted; is there any gesture in which the gap is greater between what is intended and what is taken than a baby's smile? She looked up, her lily-white face a mix of sadness and gratitude, and for a moment both felt that maybe here, hovering over the boy, was a place they could still go back to, even if it was the same place where they had originally parted: perhaps it was the best place to pick up the thread. They could have kissed then, their backs, their faces, and their baby forming a perfect triangle, when Sylvia's voice cried: 'Now what on earth am I doing standing here with my coat on?' and Emma's eyes blinked away from reconciliation, back to their undertow of stress and irritation, although not without a transitory moment that looked to Joe like apology. Then she was off, and he could hear her helping her mother back on with her coat and reminding her that she had just been really looking forward to a walk.

The door slammed. Joe finished wiping Jackson, and fastened the new nappy, white and bundled like scrunched-up tracing paper, around his belly button, the out-of-proportion belly button, big with its recently finished purpose. As he lifted him up and made for the door, he heard a small growl from down the hall. He stopped, and put the baby back down; once again, a threatening rrrrrrrrrr . . . Oh, he thought, Boris thinks everybody's gone out; now he's heard a noise. Joe wasn't frightened of Boris, and was about to go and deal with him, when he had a thought: I wonder what kind of guard dog he really is, then? Here was his opportunity to find out if the old mutt was a showboater after all. He remembered reading once that dogs and cats recognise their owners, and anyone else they might be familiar with, only from their faces; and so, in a rare moment of fancifulness, he pulled his black French Connection sweatshirt up over his head, and went out into the hall. As soon as he appeared, blindly facing the front door, he heard the dog make the same growl once more, but only for a split second, before it mutated into a yelp, and then, basically a dog-scream: rrrrwwwwwwaaahhhh!! He pulled the neck of his sweatshirt down, just in time to catch sight of Boris, fear rent into every cell of his bleary purple-lidded eyes, powering as fast as he could back down the hallway and, following a skid and a scuttle that took his legs in all directions at once, right into Sylvia's bedroom, shit spurting out of his arse like water from a fireman's hose. Once he came down from immediate shock and twenty seconds of uncontrollable laughter, Joe realised that, on one side of the hall, the area between the skirting-board and the picture rail was completely spattered, pebble-dashed by dogshit. A picture of Emma's father, stout and unsmiling in a wing collar and evening suit, was totally obscured.

He didn't even have time to check what damage had been done in the bedroom, from where he could hear manic panting as Boris hid, he presumed, under Sylvia's fat quilted divan, before the front door opened, and Emma and her mother reappeared.

'Wouldn't you believe it—' she began, about to tell him of the sudden onset of rain when her hand went to her nose, leaving her eyes visible in wide-open horror and disgust. Sylvia wandered past her, and looked at the hallway wall with interest, as if she'd never noticed this pattern before. Joe opened his mouth to speak, but then realised there wasn't a straightforward explanation, so he hung like that for a few seconds, stroking his earlobe silently.

'Nappy-change go a bit wrong?' said Emma, from under her hand.

Returning home, Joe suggested they drop in at Vic's: it was on the way, he said, and he needed to pick up a book he'd lent him.

'Oh Joe,' said Emma, from her leaning position over the back of the passenger seat; Jackson had somehow managed to perform a feat of escapology from the binds of the child seat. 'I said I was tired. Jacks is tired.'

'Oh come on Em. Just for five minutes.'

She sat back down again, and drew her own belt across her shoulder.

'You just want to tell him what happened. At Mum's.' She looked at him; he kept his face to the road, but could not contain a half-smirk. 'Don't you?'

'Well . . . maybe.' He chanced a look at her, he hoped a winning one. 'It *is* a funny story.'

Emma opened her mouth to speak, but then shut it again, and looked out of the window.

'Blokes,' she said. 'Can't wait to make each other laugh . . .'

Joe took this as assent, and turned right, for Sydenham.

'Hello . . .' said Tess, as Joe and Emma came through into Vic's living-room. She was lying along the entire length of his sofa, her feet dangling from its arm, herself and the room strewn with all manner of Sunday supplements and style sections.

'Tess! Sorry, we were just passing and—'

'No, that's fine,' she said, getting up, subconsciously moving another section of the paper over the one with the five different images of Diana on the cover. 'I'll stick the kettle on. I think we've got some bagels left from this morning as well . . .'

'It's OK, we're not going to be long,' said Emma, a little coldly. Joe looked at her, and felt the panic of domestic wrongdoing; something seemed to have dipped her mood suddenly.

'Tea, at least, though . . .' shouted Vic, who had gone into the kitchen, more of a kitchenette in truth, off the living-room.

'Have you lost weight, Joe?' said Tess.

'No . . . don't think so . . .' he said, and felt a small sinking inside. This was something he noticed that people said to him more and more these days, and he took it to mean that they had a memory of him as basically fatter than he was.

'It is OK, us coming round?' he said. 'You weren't in the middle of something?'

'No,' said Tess, 'in fact, we were just talking about what to do with the rest of the day . . .'

'God,' he said, turning to Emma, with ham-fisted jocularity, '. . . those were the days.'

'Sorry?' said Tess.

'You'll understand when you have a baby.'

'*When* I . . . ?' replied Tess, mock-archly.

Emma and Joe exchanged glances. Neither of them knew Tess well enough to know her feelings on this matter; nor indeed whether or not this might be an off-limits subject for health reasons.

'Sorry, I just meant . . .' Joe continued, reddening as he spoke, 'if you *have* got a baby, days when you just sit around lazily wondering what to do seem to go completely off the agenda.'

'It's all right, Joe,' said Tess, laughing. 'Don't look so embarrassed. I can have them. I just don't fancy the idea much.' She put both her arms out in the direction of the baby sling around

Emma's neck. 'Doesn't mean I don't like giving other people's the occasional hug . . .'

Emma looked a little taken aback, but then smiled, and lifted the boy by his underarms out of the sling. She came across and handed him to Tess, who made a face comically indicative of the trepidation of the non-baby handler, but managed to lay him easily enough across the upper part of her chest, his face looking blankly out over her shoulder towards the kitchenette where he could see his father going in to talk to his friend.

Emma sat down on the sofa, her face at the same level as the belt of Tess's jeans. She sat down too, putting Jackson on her lap, laying him back to cup his head with her hand.

'He's a bit old for that,' said Emma, leaning over to pull him upright before his Plasticene face morphed into crying mode. 'Sorry, I—'

'No, it's fine. What do I know? Still, I can see what you mean, he's really grown since I saw him last.'

Emma nodded, and smiled again. A slightly awkward silence set in, broken by the sound of Joe telling his anecdote in the kitchen, and Vic laughing.

'Do you really not want to have one?' said Emma, eventually. Her voice was quiet, like a child's first question after digesting some hard fact of real life. Tess pushed her lower lip out, and shook her head slowly.

'Sorry.'

'No, I don't mean—'

'Really, I'm used to apologising for it. A woman in her mid-thirties who doesn't want children? What kind of unnatural monstrosity am I?'

Emma put her head down, reaching up a finger to pull at a single hair in her crown. Sometimes, she would pull the hair out, and stretch it like a cat's cradle across her fingers.

'You don't have to apologise to me. I don't think that women *have* to have children.'

Tess, realising that she was hurt, put a hand on Emma's knee, before passing Jackson back to her.

'I *should* apologise, though. I don't not want to have children for any good reasons; because . . .' she opened her palms, guessing, 'I'm a feminist, or I'm trying to be unconventional, or whatever.' She shook her head again. 'No. It's fear. Let's see . . .' She raised a splayed right hand, fingers at the ready, the index of her left already wrapped around at the little one at the tip. 'Fear of feeling sick for nine months. Fear of having my vagina torn apart. Fear of being left on my own with the kid when the father decides to piss off with someone who looks less like they've been through the mill.' Emma nodded, trying to look receptive, but struggling against the bleakness of Tess's tirade, her tendency to look things too full in the face; it was making her feel dizzy, or like she wanted to hold her breath. 'Anything else? Oh yeah. Fear of having a mong.' She scratched her ski-jump nose. 'Always a worry once you're past thirty-five.'

'Yes, well . . .' said Emma, somewhat reactively, '. . . defending the idea of having kids to someone who thinks like you is always difficult. You always end up saying things that sound like clichés. Even if they're true.' Jackson screwed up his face; then returned to vacancy; then screwed up his face again. 'Like . . . *you feel different when you have one. Or . . .*' and here, just a trace of wickedness crept into her eyes, which she kept down, '. . . *maybe you just haven't met the right man.*'

As if on cue, Vic and Joe came back from the kitchen, laughing. Vic handed Emma a cup of tea. She looked up and smiled at him, but revealed nothing, her teeth a shield.

'On the contrary,' said Tess, breezily, 'considering how I feel about children, I think I've met *exactly* the right man.'

Vic gave her a questioning look, and was about to demand an explanation when, with a belch guttural enough to have come from a seventy-six-year-old brown-ale drinker, a splat of bright reddish liquid flew out of Jackson's mouth, and on to Tess's 501'd lap.

'Oh I'm so sorry—'

'Really, it's fine,' said Tess, grinning. 'He's probably understood every word.'

'Joe, have you got a tissue or something?'

'It's all right, I've got one.'

Tess took a packet of tissues out of her pocket, and plucked one out; she wiped away the baby vomit – so smooth, so unchunky with solids, almost blended – from her lap.

'Joe,' said Emma, looking round for somewhere to put her tea, 'could you get something to wipe his mouth with?'

'Don't worry, I'll do it,' said Tess. She got out another tissue for the purpose; and then had some sort of blackout. Not a real shutdown, get-her-to-a-life-support-machine blackout; more just a moment when her normal appreciation of immediate reality, and with it her faculties of judgement, shifted tinily, but fatally, awry. She didn't realise it at first. Tess in fact thought she was doing a good turn, making amends maybe for being a bit too hard-faced in her rendition of the anti-kids speech; and it was only when she looked up from the baby and saw the look of incomprehension on Vic's face, and that of horror on Emma and Joe's, that she realised – looking back down to the position of her hand – that she had been wiping, vigorously and for some time now, not at the side of Jackson's mouth where a trail of spew ran in a neat line down to his chin, but on the side disfigured by the purple birthmark.

VIC

Of course, now that Tess had come back, and would therefore periodically (and unpredictably) be round at his flat, Vic and Emma were having an affair. While she'd been in France, their liaison had had a nameless quality – neither of them would have called it an affair; but with her return, the sheer fact of having nowhere easy to go made it inescapable. Nothing brings home the reality of having an affair better than geography.

Vic had never had an affair before. He preferred random infidelity, chance meetings, sudden changes of fortune. An affair might be just the job for him in some respects – mainly the sexual variety respect – but they do so require a lot of organisation. A random infidelity just happens, but an affair, he realised, you have to plan, suddenly you're into times and places and codewords and remembering which woman you've told which anecdote to – and Vic just couldn't be bothered. Not being bothered – except to enjoy and express himself – was, essentially, Vic's calling in life. He was possessed of a fundamental, hard-core laziness. He would slouch not only when he walked but also when he ran, an activity he hadn't actually done since . . . he couldn't be bothered to work it out.

Vic tried to convince Emma to continue coming to his flat, but Tess's attitude at the weekend – comfortable, installed –

convinced her that as a couple, Vic and Tess had gone past the
stage when Tess's appearance would always be presaged by a
phone call. Vic thought he could detect a certain resentment in
Emma's consequent refusal to come round any more, but he
let it pass: otherwise, he knew, they would be into the sticky
question of exactly how serious his relationship with Tess was
– the answer to which was, as it happens, that they had recently
discussed the idea of living together. They had discussed it as
recently as the week before Princess Diana's death.

They could theoretically have met at Emma and Joe's during
the day, while Joe was at work, but the presence of Jackson
was a problem: for Emma a moral one, and for Vic, a sexual
one (he found that his lusts required a mental blocking of
Emma's maternal status). Then, while Vic was at Rock Stop
in Herne Hill looking for a new wah-wah pedal, Francis, the
shop's pony-tailed manager, asked him if he knew anyone who
wanted to rent a flat.

'Don't think so. Why?' said Vic.

'There's a couple of rooms upstairs where we keep some of
the gear. I thought I could move it and then rent them out.
It's a bit of an old bedsit, but . . . oi!' He turned to face the
lank-haired teenager who had been playing the opening riff
from 'Spirit of Radio' by Rush on a Squire Fender Telecaster
for fifteen minutes. 'Are you going to buy that or what?'

'Actually,' said Vic, 'I might know someone.'

'Joe,' said Emma, looking up from her book.

'Hm?'

'I wouldn't mind giving Toni a bit more to do.'

Joe looked round from his kneeling position by the fireplace.
It was mid-October, and he'd decided that this winter they
were going to use the fireplaces. Working fireplaces had been
a priority for them as house-buyers, but the first year they lived
there, they hadn't realised the chimneys needed sweeping: their
first attempt at a romantic night on the hearthrug had gone

up in a cloud of soot and smoke. Since then, Joe had had to spend a whole Saturday with two enormous Scotsmen and their industrial vacuum hose – despite everything he knew, he had still been half expecting a small black-faced boy in a raggedy waistcoat with a long brush to turn up – and he was going to feel the benefit. Perhaps, also, he thought that real fires were what was needed to stem the drain of cosiness from their house.

'Like what?' he said, dusting coal off his palms.

'Oh, nothing in particular. Just basically use her more.' Joe turned back to the grate, carefully sliding the last couple of waxy white firelighters underneath an elaborately constructed pyramid of coal, twigs and paper twirls. 'If we can afford it . . .'

'Well, she doesn't come cheap. And I sometimes wonder if her mind's totally on the job of looking after Jackson anyway . . .'

'I think it'd be good for me to be able to get out more during the day,' said Emma, a little steadfastly. Joe lit a match, but found that the way he'd built the fire meant that he couldn't actually bring it into direct contact with any of the firelighters. 'I can get a bit stir crazy here sometimes.'

He tried dropping it through a crack in some twigs, but it just burnt itself out, rising on one side as its end went black: it reminded him of a trick with matches a schoolfriend had once showed him called Dead Man's Erection. He lit another one. 'Yeah, no, that's understandable. Why don't we get her to do a whole day at least once a week?' Carefully, he edged this match underneath the twigs and let it fall; it fizzed on contact with the white cube underneath. Flame slowly unfolded from it, crackling at the thinnest wood above. He felt Emma's lips on his cheek and, startled, turned; she was crouching beside him.

'Thank you,' she said, and, for a moment, he thought he saw some sadness in her eyes, and couldn't imagine why; surely he'd only scored a little Brownie point in the table of their relationship. But then the fire took, in a sudden mini-roar, and they both turned to it, and then back to each other, and she was smiling, her face full of wonder: just at this, this tiny achievement. Maybe fire is the answer, thought Joe.

If Vic had been in love with anything before, it was guitars. When he was thirteen he had gorged himself on two types of pornography: pornography, and guitar pornography. Guitar pornography – muso magazines, trade papers, catalogues – was the simpler of the two; he didn't have to pretend to be older than he was to buy it, and his mother didn't scream the house down when she found it in his bedroom. The only drawback, really, was that you couldn't wank to it, although, in Vic's case, not for want of trying.

He would spend hours in his bedroom staring dreamily at the feminine shapes, rows upon rows of Stratocasters and Telecasters and Flying Vs and Les Pauls in a multitude of different shades and sunbursts, waxed reflective in the photography-studio light. Sometimes, his mind would stray to an acoustic, the rolling-hill curve of a 12-string Martin, or the bulbous back of an Ovation. But the focal point of his desire was the semi-acoustics: on seeing pictures of a Gretsch Country Gentleman or a Gibson 335 he could feel, like hunger, like a button pressed, his want instantaneously – that same direct unencumbered line between object and desire that he felt on seeing a vagina.

His first guitar was a Columbus Stratocaster copy. It cost him £70, second-hand from *Exchange and Mart*; £70 which he had to delicately lift from his Aunt Marion's purse and for which he had to suffer endless accusations and not a small amount of belting from his father who was determined to extract a confession; £70 which he handed over to a man with a hacking cough who claimed to have played with Jeff Beck and who wouldn't let him leave his squalid flat in Bexleyheath – not for any darker reason than that he didn't have anyone else to tell his sad stories to. But it was worth it. He had an electric guitar; such a prize possession, so much a symbol of another, more glamorous, unreachable world, that the other kids at school scoffed at him when he talked about it, refusing to believe that anyone they knew could possibly have one.

Even now – now that Vic had been through the flattening reality of being in a band that hadn't made it, and ended up playing for jingles and boy bands – he hadn't completely fallen out of love with the instrument. And so, for him, in his own way, there was something romantic about the flat above Rock Stop. It was a drizzling Tuesday – the day Emma and Joe had decided to make the nanny's full day – when he first let her in. He turned the light on and she burst out laughing – whether from horror or joy, he couldn't fathom – and then, after an 180-degree head-sweep, taking in the space, danced, in a crazy, four-year-old's jig, through the two adjoining rooms – bedroom and kitchen – zigzagging her way between the black flight cases.

'I thought you said the owner was going to move all this stuff out to the back!' she said, in a sing-song rhythm, timed to her dance.

'Yeah,' he said, appearing from behind her, and stopping her movement, 'but when I saw what was in them I changed my mind.' He reached round in front of her and fiddled with the lock on the case immediately in front; its door sprung open to reveal, cosseted in purple fur, a sunburst Gibson Howard Roberts Fusion, the guitar Django Reinhardt played, fat with musical potential.

'God. It's beautiful,' said Emma softly, her head turning; her lips touched his neck.

Vic nodded, released his hands from her waist, and began moving around from case to case, opening buckles: in this corner, a turquoise Guild Starfire, in that a silver Beck Pedal Steel, propped up by the mouldy sink a glistening Bossa 6-string bass, blocking the stuck-open sash window overlooking Dulwich Road a black Rickenbacker 335, like the one played by the young Pete Townshend. And lastly, in a case lying free-standing just off the centre of the room, a Gretsch Hollow Body 1600, the semi-acoustic Chet Atkins gave his name to, its polished maple body *glistening* its colour, its deep Rothko red.

'This is the one,' said Vic, kneeling as if in genuflection before it. 'This is mine.'

'How do you mean *yours*?' said Emma, laughing.

'Well . . .' he said, locking the case, 'I can't quite afford the two and a half thousand Francis wants just at the moment. But he's promised to hold on to it for me until I can. Which – ' he smiled at her ' – of course, could just be for ever.'

'Why should he do that?' said Emma, innocently.

'It's one of the very few good things that come my way as a result of having at one time been an extremely minor rock star – people like Francis still wanting to do me favours.'

She looked at him, smiling fondly at his little-boy pleasure in this small piece of power. The room seemed starlit, pinpoints thrown around it by the guitars' combined reflection of its single naked light-bulb. They kissed and, standing, fell into the other room; moving an electric mandolin, they made love languorously on the nylon sheets of the sofa-bed, the luxuriousness of the surrounding instruments compensating for the squalid furnishings.

'Why'd you get an angel?' said Emma, afterwards, tracing with her fingernail the tattoo that ran down his bicep from his left shoulder: it was an androgynous figure in dark blue robes, with closed wings and a gold face, more like a medieval icon than a soft-rock record cover, cold and not a little extra-terrestrial.

'I've told you.'

'I've forgotten. I think my mind was on other things when you first took your top off.'

He smiled, flattered. 'Because I got it in San Francisco, on our one and only US tour. In a gay shop.'

'How gay?'

'Only in Albania could you have seen so many bushy moustaches in the same surface area.' He stroked his chin, musingly.

'So it was the angel or . . . well, basically, every other tattoo design the bloke there did looked like something by Tom of Finland.'

'Did it hurt?'

'Yeah. I think. I was a bit out of it at the time.' He grinned, slightly apologetically; she, eyebrows raised, did the sarcastic nod of no surprise. 'But afterwards it did. Sometimes it still does; or at least it itches now and again – in the summer especially . . . ow!' He turned from looking upwards at cracks spidering across the ceiling, to face her. She was squeezing his upper arm between her hands, pinching the flesh together. 'What are you doing?'

'Trying to make it fly.' She took her hands away. 'You should have got something that moved when you do. My Uncle Jerry used to have two men shovelling coal on either cheek of his bottom.'

He looked into her eyes, happy with the moment, and with the memory. 'Did the Cork Constabulary know about Uncle Jerry showing you his bottom?'

'Never mind about that. The point is, around the hole itself – '

'Oh please – make me visualise it.'

' – there was a ring of fire. And when he walked, it looked like the two men were actually stoking a fire in his arse.'

Vic moved his head slightly away from hers, his face a mask of affectionate disbelief. 'You make your own entertainment in Ireland, don't you?' She laughed: he adopted a diddley-dee accent. 'What shall we do tonight, Seamus? I know! Jerry, man – drop your trousers and pants and walk across the village square for us again! That'll be a fantastic crack. At least, Jerry's will.'

She laughed again; so did he. Then, coming down from it, she asked, stroking his arm once more, 'Which angel is it?'

'Sorry?'

'There are four of them aren't there . . . Gabriel, Raphael, Michael . . . and one other. I can't remember. They're the named ones. The archangels.'

He shrugged, shaking his head. 'Dunno. She's the angel of torch songs, probably, considering where I got it. Poppers. The angel of watching TV and saying, "Course, he's one."'

Emma smiled and kissed him there, on his shoulder, which meant that she kissed the angel at the same time, on its inscrutable face; then she sat up, looking around her and through to the other room where the guitar case stood still open.

'Of course, I first fancied you when you played the guitar once . . .' she said. Her back was propped against the wall and her knees were drawn up to her chest. She was shivering slightly, despite the efforts of the 1960s gas fire facing the bed – although to be fair to the fire, Emma often seemed to be cold, even when her skin felt warm to Vic's touch; even in the summer she would crave blankets, hot-water bottles, rugs. Perhaps warmth for her was not simply a matter of temperature.

Beyond her profile, Vic, face flat against a bobbly foam pillow, could see on the MFI bedside table a beige dial-phone, presumably disconnected; and beyond that, the always depressing sight of a bedroom sink. 'Which time was that?'

'Just before Jackson was born. That time me and Joe came round and you went on about music supposedly being good for the foetus.'

'Oh yeah.' He remembered it clearly. 'Just a way of getting to a position where I might be able to impress you.'

She smiled. They were having a lovers' conversation, one of those where the honesty levee breaks and each partner joys in telling the other about secret desires and motivations past.

'That's nice.'

'It still surprises me . . .'

'What does?'

Vic hesitated; he wanted to say this, but felt it might blow his entire cover, although he was no longer sure if he was working undercover.

'That you fancied me at all. I always thought you and Joe were such a rock.' He felt his face go modest. 'I always thought you thought I was too . . . irresponsible.' A phrase Joe had once used to describe him came into his mind: *a man whose sense of social responsibility is exhausted by pulling over to let an ambulance by.*

'Too much of a sleazebag, you mean?' said Emma, in her most Irish voice. Vic punched her on the shoulder. She stroked his hair. 'I don't know. I think I just fancied you. And then when you played the guitar to the baby that time, I started to wonder if you weren't such a sleazebag as you pretend to be. That underneath all that hard sex machine front you weren't really just another desperate romantic.'

Vic smiled, and nodded, as if it were true; he was starting to wonder if perhaps it was.

'And then,' she continued, 'when I came round on the day of Diana's death and saw all those tears in your eyes, I knew I was right.'

He looked at her; she was half smiling – it was long enough ago now for them both to be ironic about it – but not smiling enough to risk telling her the truth. He kissed her on her softly giving cheek.

'And then you said that thing about Graham Whale,' she said.

'What?' he said, pulling away, smiling and frowning.

'After you played the guitar to my stomach.'

He laughed. 'Yeah. I remember.'

Emma's face became more serious. 'I took your advice, you know,' she said, softly.

'How? When?'

'When I gave birth to Jackson. I projected the pain on to someone else.' Her eyes looked slightly away from his, as if she were ashamed. 'I think it helped, a bit.'

Vic nodded. 'Who?'

'What?'

'Who did you project the pain on to?'

Again, the slightly shamed look, but more coyly this time. 'That's my secret,' she said, and hopped out of bed, wandering back towards the other room. Vic watched her idly, interested in the sensation of being able to see the curves of her buttocks, moving under the lip of her grey T-shirt, and appreciate them, as it were, in tranquillity. He reached over to the floor and picked up a Gibson J-200 acoustic. His fingers ran easily over the fretboard, playing nothing in particular, just expressing his skill, the speed of his fingers; for a second, he thought about playing 'Shop Girl Queen', but was distracted by what sounded a little like a harpsichord in the next room. He put the guitar down, wrapped the sheet around himself, and went to investigate.

In the middle of the other room Emma sat on a large box, her knees bisected by something Vic had only ever seen before on the side of a pint of Guinness: a Gaelic harp. Her eyes were shut and her hands were resting on either side of the strings, palms outstretched, waiting for the reverberation of the last note to end; and then they began again, plucking at the strings like synchronised spiders, their slow walking over the gut of the harp producing a dancing mournfulness which he located as some sort of Irish folk music – not his area of expertise. He was, though, transported somewhat by the beauty of her playing, and again felt strange, like he had done at the party.

With a long, sweeping chord, Emma finished and opened her eyes; Vic, somewhat self-consciously, aware of the cliché, applauded. She looked up at him, her face moving from con-centration to warmth.

'I didn't know you could do that,' he said.

'Hm . . . don't I have to say, "There are loads of things you didn't know I could do" now?'

He smiled, and came round to sit behind her, snaking his arms around her back to put his hands on the strings. For a second he felt her back stiffen, as if something about this position discomforted her

'Do men always ask you to play the harp for them?' said Joe, not wanting to play the also-ran.

'No,' she said. 'Sometimes. Usually I won't, even if they ask.'

Joe, pleased, a child with a gold star, put his arms around her waist from behind, her arms still around the harp.

'So *why the exception?*'

'*You are an exception, Joe,*' she said, *and his heart soared even more.*

'*What sort of song was that?*'

'*It was a syngoch. There are three types. A syngoch, a nongoch, and a jigoch. Syn means cry, so it's a lament; non is sleep – a lullaby; and jigoch is a song of joy.*'

Play me no jigochs, thought Joe, who asked only to be moved

but then she relaxed into him, her body moulding like liquid against his.

'Herne Hill,' said Emma, her eyes towards the window, with its view of other windows. 'I always thought it was by the sea.'

'That's Herne Bay.' He kissed her, like a partner rather than an illicit lover, on the shoulder. 'There's a clue in the name.'

She tutted, play-scornfully. 'Yes, I know. But I used to get them confused. Where is Herne Bay?'

Vic shrugged, lifting her slightly with him. 'Geography's not my strong point. Devon?'

'No, Kent, I think. Not even that far from here.' She sighed, slightly. 'I wish it *was* Herne Bay.'

'Thanks.'

She turned her face three-quarters back towards him. 'No, I don't mean – it's lovely, Vic. But the sea makes me happy. The sound and smell of it. It's so much more relaxing than—'

'The sound and smell of Dulwich Road?'

Emma turned back, smiling, but her eyes had some longing in them. 'It washes over your senses. If we were by the sea . . . how lovely would it be to spend a night together listening to the sea?' Her question remained unanswered; she trailed her hand over the harp. The open strings chimed like plainsong.

'Did you even know this was here?' she said.

'No. I didn't bother to open the non-guitar-shaped cases.' He plucked at the strings of the harp, dissonantly. 'I think there's an electric piano over there as well . . .'

'It's a lovely one. Half the size of a classical.' She put her fingers through his, making them touch individual strings in time, guiding him towards a simple melody. 'My father taught me to play. I think it was his way of instilling a bit of the old country in me.'

'It works. What you were playing made me think of Ireland.'

She laughed, again turning her face halfway back towards him. 'No, it didn't. It made you think of Murphy's adverts.'

Vic laughed too, but pulled away slightly, surprised that Emma had within her the potential to be cynical. As he did so, she caught his right hand, and held it, upturned in hers.

'How did you get this?' she said, the tips of her fingers trailing over a thin cut, grazed white at the edges, at the side of his wrist.

'Trying to kill myself out of longing for you.'

'Oh, of course. Silly of me.'

'I got it jump-starting the bike this morning. My trusty old faithful decided to konk out in the middle of Sydenham High Road.'

She bent her neck forwards and kissed the cut, still semi-fresh; he felt the impress of her lips around it. He imagined the cut as an opening, through which her breath was filtering into his body. He could feel the heat of it diffusing, underneath his skin.

'Let me go and see if there's a Band-aid somewhere . . .'

His biceps gripped her round the waist, holding her. 'Don't worry. I like it anyway. With a bit of work, it'll develop into a tasty scab.'

'You're disgusting.'

'No, honestly,' he said. 'Scabs, gnat bites, verrucas – they're all really worth having. I love itch-making things. Such heaven when you scratch them.' She edged herself all the way round, to end up astride his lap facing him, and let her tongue fall out of her mouth in a vomit mime; he placed his own –

long and pointed, one of those tongues that can appear like an alien creature in the mouth – on her taste bud area and licked upwards, making her withdraw, screwing up her nose and laughing. 'You know what I really dream of? Eczema.'

'Oh please . . .'

'Or even better – psoriasis. Psoriasis and some kind of servant employed, twenty-four hours to scratch me. What bliss! A total body-itch, constantly relieved.'

She shook her head. 'I don't think I'd fancy you anymore if you looked like that bloke out of *The Singing Detective*.'

Vic tutted, camply, raising his eyes to heaven. 'Oh! How shallow and body-fascistic can you get?'

'Ah,' she said softly. 'I don't think *I'm* the one obsessed with the body . . .'

His internal alarm bells rang a little at this, but then, in her focused eyes, trained fondly on him, he saw how her image of him was clearer than he supposed, and, at the same time, more accepting. Vic smiled, and felt the airy freedom of displacement, of not being in control. He brought his mouth to her ear.

'Play me something else,' he whispered.

JOE

Marian Foster placed the syringe in front of her face and squeezed the plunger: a short jet of fluid – a so far unnamed CD4 protein disabler – shot out from the needle. Although there were good reasons for doing this – there is always the possibility of air bubbles remaining within the body of the syringe – Marian always felt a bit of a charlatan doing it: it felt too much like the sort of thing doctors do on telly, and she wasn't even a doctor. She little needed reminding of this, as the injection she was about to perform was not a healing one. The rat inside the cage looked up at her and twitched its nose expectantly. This was quite a friendly rat, much more so than the last one which, apparently aware of the danger it was in, had had a habit of throwing itself, all four limbs forward, at the bars of the cage and clinging on, its mouth stuck wide open in a hate-filled rictus.

From the other side of the glass that served as both window and partition to his office, Joe looked on, uncomfortably. CD4 is one of two protein structures on the surface of a cell that allows HIV to attach, enter and thus infect. The disabler component, which Joe's laboratory had been working on for the last seven months, destroys the protein – which is beneficial in that it reduces the possibility of HIV transmission, but less beneficial in

100

relation to CD4's more mundane role as an accessory molecule, forming part of larger structures through which the body's most protective agents, T-cells, signal to other cells. So far, Joe's laboratory had found no way of disabling the protein without drastically damaging the immune system; and in his heart, he felt the quest to do so was probably fruitless.

The telephone on his desk rang; he knew who it was from the flashing Line 1 light.

'Hello Jerry.'

'Joe. I wonder if you could come up and see me.'

'Now?'

A pause, a clicking of the tongue. 'Unless you're *extremely* busy . . .'

'No. Now's fine.'

Closing the door to his office, Joe caught Marian's eye as she turned away from the cage; probably, it was just that she hadn't been expecting him to come out, but for a second she looked guilty and innocent at the same time, like a child caught out.

The Friedner Pharmaceuticals Research Building is a white, T-shaped, three-storey building situated in three acres of country-side in that part of the South-East dominated by the M25. On this side of the city, at least, London does seem to end: it ends at the great circular border of the motorway, in contrast to the north where now there is no palpable point at which London stops and the country begins, but only a gradual osmosis of the capital into its grey surburban satellites.

Level C, at the top of which lay Jerry Bloom's office, had pre-viously been devoted to clinical trials, but since 1996 had been converted into an administrative centre, the point of contact between the Research Building and Friedner's corporate centres in London and Frankfurt. The top floor was vigorously open plan, designed by someone who had seen too many films about American newspaper offices; as Joe walked across its charcoal carpet he felt, as he always did, that many of the bureaucrats

101

working there would look better in green see-through hat-shades and calling for hot coffee and donuts.

He reached Jerry's office, the only glass box on the floor not to be see-through; it was still a glass box, but the use of glass bricks on three sides kept the goings-on inside hidden. Immediately outside, at a desk that appeared to be just placed there, with no partitioned space to call its own, sat Valerie, Bloom's secretary, a woman who had undergone such extensive HRT that Joe thought she could be on the brink of a second pubescence, possibly this time into a monkey.

'Hello Mr Serena,' she said. 'Go right in.'

Joe opened the door. Jerry was on the phone, but he beckoned him in.

'Ja. Das ist richtig. Nein. Was du willst . . . ja.'

Joe sat on a black leather chair opposite Jerry's desk. There was a lot of black leather in Jerry Bloom's office furnishings: that, and the consistent use of blue lighting, combined to give the room a level of eightiesness not normally seen outside the worlds of professional figure skating and German rock music. To his right, a wall-to-wall window gave out a view of open countryside no one would choose to walk on, a sunlit land of science parks and silicon estates.

'OK, OK. Ja. Auf wiederhören.' Jerry put the phone down. 'Sorry, Joe. The Frankfurt office . . .' He waved a hand in the air, as if explaining: then his gaze snagged on him. 'Hey! Have you lost weight?'

'No . . .' said Joe, sighing.

Jerry moved the hand down towards the intercom on his desk, poising an index finger above it. 'Coffee?'

Joe shook his head: he felt the tiredness coming on again, and couldn't be bothered to indulge in any pleasantries with Jerry. Silence would force him to the point.

'Well . . .' said Jerry, settling back into his reclining chair, the greater part of his stomach coming forward as he did so, 'how's things on your level?'

Joe blinked. Jerry's old-gold hair was frizzing out today very much to one side of his bulky, jowly features: he looked like Billy Whizz gone very badly to seed. 'Coming along. We still haven't found a way round the side-effects of the CD4 disabler. We're going to try it in combination with some of the protease inhibitors, and intravenously administered Cidofovir – it may work in cocktail, I don't know.'

'Hm . . .' Jerry didn't really seem to be listening. 'The thing is . . . we could do with a big development.'

There was a pause. 'When you say "we", Jerry, do you mean "we" – the human race – or "we" – Friedner Pharmaceuticals Incorporated?'

Jerry smiled. 'Well, both, obviously, Joe. Both. But in the short term . . . mainly the latter.' With a puff and a sigh, he got up and walked towards the window; the trousers of his blue double-breasted suit were ruffled and saggy at the back. 'The point is, as you know, there's only so much money we get here for research. We can't afford to invest money in continual research to fight specific diseases if there's no evidence that a useful drug is eventually going to be produced.' Jerry waited for a response, but Joe said nothing. 'Your lab has been devoted to HIV research for the past five years.'

'With some success.'

'Yes. Some. Cocktails. Inhibitors. Possible extended survival rates. But frankly—'

'Friedner want a big fuck-off *cure*.'

Jerry Bloom looked at him sharply; he was at an age when swearing was still something you didn't do in front of your boss, unless you work for Gene Hackman. Joe coloured, surprised at himself, and at his level of tiredness.

'Charmingly put, Joe. But yes. Anything less is becoming financially untenable.'

Now, Joe looked out of the window. In the distance he could see the motorway continuing its siege of London, the barricade of cars. Above them, a plane climbed, leaving a long white trail in the sky like a huge sperm searching out the giant yolk of the sun.

'Oh, Jerry. You know it's a tough one, HIV. The virus mutates. It's elusive.' Jerry nodded; at some level, he was still a scientist. 'But it's not just the slowness of the research, is it?' Joe continued. 'It's fashion. In the eighties, AIDS was fashionable. A chance for rock stars to look deep and serious and go about challenging prejudices on big worthy TV events. But it was *too* associated with fashion; and so now it's out of fashion. I can see it when I tell people I'm working on AIDS research. Once they were frightened, like I might infect them or something; then, for a little while, they were excited, or admiring; and now – well – they just look a bit bored. AIDS, now, is a bit . . .' he looked around the room slightly nervously '. . . it's a bit *eighties*.'

'Despite infection rates in the Indian subcontinent having just reached over 30 per cent.'

'Despite that, yes. Since when did events in the third world have any impact on people's thinking in the West? And besides, who's arguing for what now?'

The phone rang again. Joe gestured as if to give Jerry the opportunity to pick it up, but he shook his head.

'You're right, of course. A lot of the money for research into HIV that was around ten years ago just isn't there any more, and that's nothing to do with lower levels of infection. The point is – Friedner don't want to carry on with the research budget your level operates on at the moment.'

'But we need more money, not less—'

'I know. But this is a commercial pharmaceutical company. We have to think about the financial return.'

Joe looked down; he fiddled with his ear. 'I can't believe we're having this conversation,' he said. The phone stopped ringing. Joe felt Jerry Bloom's hand on his shoulder, and looked round. Below the knuckles, the skin was lightly shaded with the beginnings of liver spots.

'Ah, Joe. You'd have been so much happier working in a hospital or a university, wouldn't you?'

Joe ignored the maudlin imprecation; he wasn't going to place his hand on Jerry's. 'Why now?' he said. 'What's brought this on?'

Jerry shrugged. 'I don't know, exactly. Maybe – I think – Diana's death.'

Joe's mouth fell open. '*What?*'

'We co-sponsor two of the AIDS charities she used to patronise. Or rather we used to. Frankfurt think that perhaps now we might pull out.'

Joe laughed, rather bitterly, a sound that didn't suit him. 'Right.'

'And maybe you're right. About the whole . . . brand image of the disease. It's changed. It hasn't got the same place in the – what do newspaper columnists call it? – yes, the *Zeitgeist*. She was part of all that: redefining attitudes, etc., etc. Seems to me her death is some kind of watershed there. Some kind of an end.'

'Yes, you're right,' said Joe, getting up. 'She of course was a bit eighties too.'

Back in his laboratory, Marian was taking a blood sample from the rat. It would already, Joe knew, show signs of T-cell diminishment. He nodded at her as he returned to his own office, still too angry at Jerry Bloom to speak. He went over to the water tower in the corner and held a small paper cone under the tap; it felt thin in his hands, like a membrane about to burst. Looking back out at Marian at work, a phrase broke into his head, shocking him: *beneath the rat, the Jew*. Joe's sense of self misgave at the thought that such words could ever seem appropriate – that even his subconscious should find them apposite; he felt dizzy, displaced. It was from a poem, he knew that, misremembered lines, but the sentiment was right – and then it came back to him: T.S. Eliot's *Burbank With*

105

A *Baedaker*, which he had read as a teenager in English class and been startled and deeply disturbed by the idea that a great poet could be a racist. He couldn't deal with the contradiction – how on one level Eliot's appreciation could be so perfect, and on another, so misguided. The confusion was great enough to put him off arts subjects, at which he had been showing considerable promise, for good; instead he chose the clear-cut lines – and freedom from moral confusion – of scientific understanding. But today, science didn't seem like that at all.

VIC

Vic didn't really like sleeping with women. He was never, he would freely admit, much good at it. He did, however, as we have seen, like having sex with women, very much. It was just the sleeping part.

Vic was a good sleeper, on his own. On his own, he could decide to partake in a triple espresso for a night-cap, and still awake in the morning after a solid eight hours, his head blank of dreams. But put someone else in the bed alongside him and his night would become sandblasted with insomnia. He could feel their every move, hear their every breath (once he tried to counter this by synchronising his breathing exactly with a woman, but it was no good, sleep kept on changing her rhythm). And, try as he might, he could not make himself fit round their sleeping form. Every position, every cradling of her, would follow the same narrative: a couple of minutes of initial comfort, during which the woman would invariably fall asleep, followed quickly by a draining of blood from whichever of Vic's arms was most under her weight. If Vic was ever able to ignore the resulting excruciating tingling – and he was not a man who easily ignored the whispers of his body, let alone its shouts and screams – he would soon be defeated by the continual tickling of her hair on his face, which would force his head back away from

107

hers, his neck perfectly angled to produce the sharpest crick. Even with Tess, whom at all other times he felt as comfortable with as he was on his own; as a result, she tended not to sleep the whole night at Vic's, knowing that she would eventually be forced into the spare room by his frantic sleeplessness. It was always the same.

Until he slept with Emma.

At some point in an affair, one of the partners starts to talk about what a shame it is not being able to spend the whole night together; and it is almost always one of the points most dreaded by the other partner. In Vic and Emma's case, it was Emma who started talking about it, and Vic who dreaded it, although his dread was less to do with standard concerns about time, place and excuses than simply about sleeping.

'Where would we do it?'

'Here.'

'*Here?* But we've never actually got into these sheets.' It was true: they had always made love on top of the bed in the flat above Rock Stop. Vic moved his hand away from her head on his chest and picked at the nylon sheet, folded back over a sky blue blanket. 'I'm not sure we should. Moving about in them might get us electrocuted.'

Emma laughed, but said: 'I'm serious, Vic. I want to spend the night with you. I want to wake up and you be here. I'm getting depressed about just coming here on Tuesdays.'

Vic nodded, and felt another new feeling: fear – a fear that Emma might get too depressed, and start thinking that their affair was not worth continuing. He was beginning to get destabilised by the onrush of all these new feelings tumbling over one another as they entered his heart.

Trying to wrench the conversation back to his home ground – the purely physical – he laid his head between her shoulder blades and ran his hand down her back, moving the sheet down with it. She shivered slightly.

'Do you still go to that tanning place?'

When Vic first met Emma, she had been going through a phase of challenging her skin's genetic destiny, by visiting a health parlour with sunray booths.

'Haven't been for ages. Carcinogenic, I read somewhere. Why?'

'I'd like it if you had a tan. But not an all-over tan.'

'Why?' She submitted for a moment to this digression, hypnotised by the stroke of his hand across her back. Her skin, quickly reactive to being uncovered, felt cold and glassy; Vic felt momentarily like he was rippling the surface of still water.

'I don't know why women always insist on trying to get an all-over tan. It's much sexier if you can see the outline of bra and pants.'

'Bra and pants?'

'Well, you know. Bikini marks.' He paused, his hand going down to her buttocks, allowing his fingers to remind him again – like a blind man reading his favourite bit of braille over and over – of their delicious W. Around her orifices he could feel heat, the slow constant release of it from her body. 'I like it when you can see those on a woman. The reminder of clothes. It's like – it's like they're wearing a strip-tease.'

He looked at her face, on its side against the pillow with her eyes shut, a little nervously. He felt maybe he'd let a bit too much of himself out with this piece of sexual proselytising; that, even given the greater level of honesty they were now operating on, he'd unpinched the fingers holding the tip of his balloon of self too quickly. He remembered how, the second day she'd come round to his flat, she'd said, pulling him by the neck of his T-shirt towards the bed, 'Make love to me'; and he, never fond of the phrase, had said, with unnecessary firmness, 'Don't say that. Say what you mean.'

She made her head shake tinily back and forth, and framed her smiling face to a question mark.

109

'Fuck me,' said Vic, explaining, and as her smile became somewhat brave, knew it was too much too early; even though the sex they were having *was* often raw and clutching, she had surrounded it with a certain ethereality, and his words punctured the bubble – they broke the suspension of disbelief.

They had gone on, though, falling together into bed, the physical strength of their drive towards one another too powerful to be stopped in its tracks by a moment of disjunction. But he'd marked it – be careful – and, for a moment, he thought he might have done it again. He was still learning it, the strange chess of relationships. But she just smiled and said, through closed eyes, 'Tess is going away next weekend, isn't she?'

Vic sat up.

'Yes. Barcelona.'

Emma opened her eyes, and twisted herself up against the bare wall behind the bed.

'OK. I've told Joe I'm going to stay at my mother's Saturday night.'

Vic felt a little dry in the mouth, taken aback by Emma's determination, her production of a *fait accompli*.

'Right. How is she?'

'No better. We're going to a meeting with the council people tomorrow about the possibility of placing her in care.' Emma's eyes pulled focus into a stare, and her face hardened into a wall, the wall she had to put up to this possibility. 'She can't remember who I am now. Or rather ... she can, a bit. That's the problem, that's where she gets frustrated. She can remember that I'm someone she *ought* to remember.' Her hand drifted towards the top of her head. 'That's one of the most terrible things about Alzheimer's. It doesn't *quite* wipe out the memory. It'd be better in a way if it did. When Mum asks me what's for lunch for the hundredth time, it's not just that she's forgotten what's for lunch – it's also that she has a tiny memory – like a trace – of wanting to know what's for lunch.'

Vic nodded, and looked sympathetic, but didn't quite know how to respond; he wasn't even sure if he was meant to. Alzheimer's was not one of the diseases he used to fantasise about; it had zero cool, because it wiped out the possibility, always there with the other terminals, of grim wit. In fact, it wiped out wit. What is a wit without quick recall, especially in our ultra-referential culture? You were fine enough being a wit and a bit Alzheimery in Dr Johnson's day, he thought, when all you had to do was make the odd epigram about Life. But these days, Vic knew, that wasn't enough: you need to be able to name-check, to bounce-refer your wit across the pop culture spectrum from Evel Knievel to Barbapapa, and if the names are hidden behind the dry stone wall of nomemory, then the timing's gone, the moment's lost.

Emma lay back down again, snuggling into his shoulder. Her head moved up and down for a while on the wave of his breathing.

'What if Joe phones you there?' he said, eventually. She blinked, and moved slightly away.

'Well, I'm going to go there, Vic. I'm going to see my mum,' she said, a little fiercely, as if accused of using her mother's illness for her own ends, which Vic wasn't doing: the accusation was coming from inside her. 'But she goes to bed quite early now, about nine o'clock. Once she's away, and fine, I'll phone Joe, tell him everything's all right, and then . . .' she hesitated, and then went on with it, tied to pragmatism, '. . . come here. About ten.'

When Vic didn't say anything, Emma looked up at him.

'He doesn't suspect anything, Vic.' Her tone became softer. 'He doesn't really *have* suspicion. It's not one of his emotions.'

Vic looked back at her, aware that he might look chinny from her angle. 'You sound sad,' he said. 'You always sound sad when you talk about him.'

111

'When do I talk about him?'

Vic took this on board. 'Not often. Maybe because it makes you feel sad.'

Emma levered herself off him and sat on the edge of the bed, looking out towards the window; the off-white light of late afternoon was already turning dark.

'I love – I used to love Joe very much,' she said.

Vic sat up on his elbow. 'And . . . ?'

She kept looking out. Her hand went again to the top of her hair. 'And then something went wrong. I don't know what exactly. Sometimes relationships go wrong. And the reasons aren't clear, they're lost.' He listened, appreciatively. At another time, to another person, he might have said that that was because the whole idea of *relationships* was wrong – the whole stupid idea that love can last forever; but he felt no urge to say it now. He could no longer find that certain doubt. 'But that doesn't mean I don't feel anything for him.'

Vic gently removed her hand from her crown. He watched the single hair fall like ticker-tape from its pulled-taut line.

'You shouldn't do that all the time . . .' he said, softly.

Emma smiled ruefully. 'I know. I don't even realise I'm doing it sometimes.'

'Doesn't it hurt?'

'No. There's something delicious about the moment you pull one out.' She put her hand back to the top of her head, but playfully this time, plucking at it with a finger like it was one of the strings of the harp. 'I think it's actually recognised as a minor medical disorder.'

'Pulling your own hair out?'

'Yes. It's got a name and everything.' Her diaphanous eyebrows knitted together. 'I can't remember it – it's a really long name.' She shook her head. 'It's gone. Joe . . .' She hesitated at this new mention of him. '. . . Joe always remembers it.'

'Does he.'

'*Vic . . .*' She moved her hand to his hair, so thick that it was

112

impossible to ruffle; her fingers stuck fast in it. 'Don't sulk.' She paused. 'I don't complain about Tess. And you're still sleeping with her. Me and Joe haven't . . .' she trailed off. 'Well, not for ages.'

Vic returned her look. 'But I don't go on about her.'

Emma adopted a mock-aghast expression. 'When do I *go on* about Joe?'

'Just now. You said you still loved him.'

'I didn't say that. I said I can't say that I don't feel anything for him.'

'Even when you're with me?'

Vic said this unsure of his own tone. Before, when she first came to him, he had been acting, being the person she wanted him to be; now, the things he heard himself saying, they were, he knew, still what was expected of a lover in this situation, but he *felt* them viscerally as well: he wanted to know the answers to these questions.

She kissed him, her lips like butter on his.

'No. Not when I'm with you.' Her face withdrew a touch. 'But I live with Joe. I'm constantly reminded of the memory of our love.'

Vic met her eyes; he nodded, letting it go. He kissed her back, then said:

'Why *don't* you complain about Tess?'

She looked at him, her eyes narrowing a little, as if wondering why Vic should want to go into this territory.

'Because I know it's no use. You're not going to split up with her for me.'

Vic felt his features rise in surprise at this proclamation. He couldn't believe it was what Emma thought. It was, rather, exactly what *he* would always have thought about *her* with regard to Joe, and wondered if she was saying it in order to provoke a contradiction. And yet he felt an odd incapability of denying it, stemming from a place inside him somewhere between his sense, inculcated through years of promiscuity, that promises were dangerous, and – a site on his inner map that he hardly knew was there, but seemed suddenly pinpointed by Emma's remark – his well of loyalty and fondness for Tess, a well that he had not drunk from recently. Instead he said: 'OK. I'll meet you here on Saturday night.'

JOE

There are better places in the world to be than the Woolwich and District Community Services Residential Care Unit Assessment Office. In fact, it is possible, thought Joe, taking in the wall-to-wall filing cabinets – how do their corners get so *scrunched*? he wondered – the smeary double-glazing, the thin-as-can-be grey carpet, not quite fitted properly so the edges lay ragged against the skirting-board, the Formica table he was facing, an Olympics symbol of coffee-cup marks in its centre, the light, somehow angled to throw a wash of shadows over every face in the room, making everyone look even more drawn and stressed than they already were, the odd, apparently randomised information leaflets on the wall, drawing attention only to the most depressing things in life (*Where to Start with Cancer, South London Guide to Hostels for the Homeless, Coping with Disability*) . . . it is possible that anywhere else in the world – starting with Rwanda – would be preferable.

The purpose of this office – to interview pensioners with a view to discovering just how fucked either their brains, by Alzheimer's, or their bodies, by whichever one of the thousand natural shocks their flesh was heir to, had become, and therefore what level of care they should be placed in – harmonised perfectly with its appearance. Ms Andrews and Mr Panjiit were,

115

to be fair to them, making the best of it. Their tone remained gently buoyant, and their questions – easy topical queries – patient, however frustrating and sad Sylvia's answers.

Emma and Joe had been forced to bring her, having reached the point of despair. Two weeks previously, they had gone round to her flat to discover Boris lying on her bed, dressed in three of Sylvia's hand-knitted jumpers, a pair of her tights, four odd socks on his paws, and one on his tail. Around his head was one of those plastic rain-hats only old ladies own. 'He was cold!' protested Sylvia. He wasn't; it took perhaps the tiniest fraction of Joe's biochemical knowledge to work out that he was dead. Emma gingerly explained this to her mother, who burst into tears. Joe thought it was kind of her to leave out of her explanation the most obvious cause of death, which would appear to be starvation.

After a difficult funeral – difficult for Sylvia, at least; Joe had never really forgiven Boris for the hallway-spraying incident, and Emma seemed only distracted – they had assumed that that was the end of it. However, the next day Joe had to rush home from work in the middle of the day after a distraught phone call from Emma, saying that her mother had gone missing. Joe drove the twenty-three miles back to south-east London, to discover her walking up Pepys Road, looking all around her as she went. When he got out and asked her what she was doing, she said, 'Looking for my dog. I can't find him anywhere.' Finally convincing Sylvia to come home with him – 'But I don't *know* you!' – Emma was then forced to explain to her again that Boris was dead, at which point she burst into tears.

A version of this event had now been going on every day for the last week and a half. They had got to the point where, somewhat cutting through her original sensitivity, Emma had put up a large sign in Sylvia's room saying THE DOG IS DEAD. Unfortunately, this only reminded her in the morning, and she was still tending to wander out in the late afternoons to shout 'Boris!' all over the Woolwich area. There was some consolation in this, in that at least she kept the dog's name firmly in her memory, not confusing him with the dog she'd had as a child, a dark brown retriever called Nigger.

It had been a tough decision, but Joe had convinced Emma it had to be taken, as much for Sylvia's sake as for their own; Emma could not look after her mother and her baby simultaneously, however much of a familial node she was.

'So . . . just a few more questions, Mrs O' Connell,' said Ms Andrews, a pale woman with a couple of unfortunately placed moles, specifically one between her nose and her upper lip. 'I wonder if you could tell me . . . who the Prime Minister is?'

Sylvia frowned, and leant forward on her stacking chair, placing her hands on her knees.

'Oo. I should know this one. I really should. Don't tell me . . . ?'

No one did tell her. A silence set in.

'O . . . K,' said Mr Panjiit, his voice rising on the 'K', to suggest *no matter*, 'what about . . . let's see. Yes. A member of the Royal Family died tragically recently, in a car crash. Do you know who that was?'

Sylvia frowned again. She scratched her head.

'King Edward?'

'No . . .'

She tutted. 'Of course not! He's not dead, is he? He's just *abdicated*.' She laughed. 'I don't know what's wrong with me.'

Mr Panjiit smiled, condescendingly of course, but there comes a point where condescension is no longer optional, and no fault can be ascribed to it. His voice went down a gear. 'Now then, Mrs O' Connell. What year is it?'

'Oh. Yes. Now this I know. 19 . . . something, isn't it?'

'Yes . . .'

Joe looked at Sylvia's concentrating profile. Something still beautiful about her, he thought. At times the Alzheimer's, creating as it does a second innocence, makes her look young.

117

Mr Panjiit's face, open behind a heavy black pair of glasses, remained encouraging.

'No, it's gone.'

Mr Panjitt nodded sagely. '1997, Mrs O' Connell,' he said, helpfully.

'Of course it is!'

'I see you've got a brother still alive, Mrs O' Connell?' said Ms Andrews.

'Jerry! Oo yes. Healthy as a pair of old gumboots!'

Joe leant over to the desk; the interviewers bent their heads. 'Died in 1983. The living one's called Denis . . .' he whispered. Ms Andrews grunted, then turned back to Sylvia.

'Good, good. Um . . . let's see . . .' She checked her files. 'Your dog. How's he doing?'

'Oh I don't know. Boris! *Boris!*'

'Right, fine, I think that'll do.'

Mr Panjiit scribbled down a few notes. A sense of closure, of business finished, began to set in.

'So . . .' said Emma, who was looking down, 'what kind of place do you think my mum should be . . . in?'

He stopped scribbling, and offered a weak smile of reassurance. 'Well, that depends. We need to send in our report, and then there'll be an assessment, and in ten days or so . . .' he flipped a calendar pad on the table in front of him '. . . yes, round about the 18th or 19th of December we should be able to recommend somewhere suitable.'

'Maybe *she* should have a say in it,' said Emma, looking up, a little defiantly.

Mr Panjiit hesitated. 'How do you mean?'

'I mean – why shouldn't my mother tell you what kind of place she'd like to spend . . .' and here she faltered '. . . the next few years living in.'

Mr Panjiit and Ms Andrews exchanged glances.

'Yes. Why not,' Ms Andrews said eventually. 'I quite agree.' She adjusted her face and tone. 'Mrs O' Connell.'

Sylvia's eyes came back from whichever nowhere they had been seeing. She smiled politely.

'Is there any particular type of residential care that you would like to be placed in?'

Sylvia put a finger to her mouth.

'I mean . . .' continued Ms Andrews, 'any special requirements, any specific activities, that sort of thing?'

'I'd very much like to go somewhere . . .' said Sylvia at last, still with her finger on her mouth; then, pointing it sharply forward, 'where they put on a lot of quizzes.'

VIC

_____

That weekend, Vic did something he'd never really done before: he made an effort. He went out on his scooter and bought a series of throws and drapes and nailed them up around the flat. He bought some nightlight candles for the bedroom, and some Christmas fairy lights for the main room, which he strung across a series of guitars to create a small circle of light and music, in the centre of which he placed the flat's only table, covered with a red cloth. He stuck a candle in a bottle, wondered for a short time if he should've burnt a few candles in it already to create that dripping fountain of wax effect they get in bistros, put out knives and forks, and ordered some take-away Chinese food to arrive at ten. Of course, the one thing he really should've done – bought some new cotton sheets for the bed – didn't occur to him, but luckily it did to Emma, who threw them up in the air on seeing the fairy lights come on: white folded in plastic rained down on them as they kissed.

They went to bed soon after dinner, and made love, although not functionally, certainly more quickly than usual, as if eager to maximise the time spent sleeping, or rather dozing dreamily in each other's arms: that, rather than sex, was now the illicit act, the thing they weren't normally allowed to do, the site of treat. But, before the moment of post-coital melt, Vic got up, saying:

'Oh! I nearly forgot!'

He walked over to a carrier bag lying in the corner of the room. Again, he felt a new sensation: self-consciousness at his own nakedness, a sense of Emma's eyes on him as he crouched over the bag, afraid, perhaps, of spots on his back, or the ape-like squat of his buttocks. He turned around and came back to the bed, holding something.

'What is it?' said Emma, sitting up, the bedclothes clutched to her chest.

'The sea,' replied Vic, handing her a CD. She held it up to the flickering light of one of the bedside candles. On the cover was a seascape, realistically but not very well painted: a beach rippled by a calm sea, under a pink and orange sky, and below this, the legend *Relax with Nature, Vol.1 – Ocean Waves at Sunset.*

'I got it from that new age shop across the road,' he said, plucking it out of her hands. From one of the many boxes by the side of the bed, he lifted out a Technics portable stereo, which he removed from its polystyrene vice and placed on the floor; he pressed a button on the remote control, and the oval top whirred up, invitingly. He placed the CD inside, pressed another button, and got back into bed.

For a few seconds they lay with their backs propped up against the wall, two thin pillows the only buffer between their skin and the cracked plaster, looking at each other. Emma's eyes, Vic noticed, were violet in the half-light; the gaunter edges of her face, too, were softened by its chiaroscuro. The sound of the portable stereo began slowly to filter into the room, one wave after another, building from a watery whisper to a small calm crash, as of sea against sand rather than rock: and then the melting hiss, the shh of withdrawal. Still without saying anything, Emma turned and blew out the candle, and they slid down together into the sheets into the darkness, like children, when underneath the bedclothes can be anywhere.

'Are we in Herne Bay, darling?' she said.

Vic felt his chin on her forehead as he nodded, astonished at

121

how comfortable he was with an unironic use of the word 'darling'. Rocked by the sound, the regularity of its repetition as hypnotic as any lullaby, he felt himself swirled into sleep, his body curling effortlessly around hers like the sea around a sand-castle.

'You're so lovely,' she said, in a just-before-sleep mumble, and for a second Vic believed her, and felt convinced that he had performed an action of pure goodness, generated only by his sense of *her* pure goodness; and still he believed it as he fell asleep, although his conviction dimmed slightly as his over-musical ear became aware of a tiny edge of tinniness – just a minor hint of compression – in the sound of the waves.

PART TWO

Winter–Spring, 1998

One is unavoidably faithful to the dead body growing inside one.

Adam Phillips, *Monogamy*

JOE

Joe stretched across the wide expanse of bed and touched her on the shoulder; cupped her whole shoulder bone, in fact, in his right hand, one of the many gestures that by a slight readjustment of shape and angle alters entirely in significance – the one, a tap on the shoulder, the other an entreaty, a first move, a hopeful preliminary.

In the litany of marriage, there are a thousand different ways the process of initiating lovemaking can go. It is unlike the process of initiating it before marriage, or at least in the early stages of a relationship. All things come back to the first time, but often become simply an imitation of the first time, a kind of post-ironic recapitulation of it. For some, the fact of marriage, or of time, guarantees licence, and therefore the process of sexual entreaty becomes stripped down and demystified – what had been a series of codes and diversions and body linguistic suggestions becomes 'Shall we go to bed?' or even 'Do you want to have sex?' For others, though, those for whom marriage or long-term involvement goes the other way, the way of complication, the process of initiating sex becomes *more* tortuous, *more* twisting, than for nervous first-timers. Notably, if sex has stalled, then you are into that terrible cycle of self-consciousness – where every fuck counts, either in itself or in its weight of history – and then suddenly there seems no freedom or lightness to the act, and no way back to them either: spontaneity cannot be chased.

This was the place, the bad place, the desert, where Emma and Joe found themselves. Joe held his hand on her shoulder for some small time, waiting for the moment when it might be gently – and, as it always seems to men, although never intended by women, *patronisingly* – lifted off. That movement not forthcoming, however, Joe felt the first quiet twinklings of hope, and moved his hand to and fro – although not directly down, as there would have to remain in his movement a pathetic sense of the possibility that sex was not his intention, an insurance against complete humiliation. Emma did not move, or clutch at his hand; but as, with misgiving, her husband did at last stretch his hand a little towards her breast, she said in the darkness, 'Not tonight, darling, I've got a headache.'

This was something they used to say in the rapturous days, a little ironic inverted-commas statement, a bas-relief against the amount of sex they *were* having: only heard on the very rare occasions when, spent and/or exhausted, either of their bodies would react against the possibility of, say, a tenth attempt in two days. They were a couple who used to indulge in a lot of private language, a whole lexicon of pet names and little babyish words for the stuff of their personal universe; now, bits and pieces of this language still survived in their landscape like half-standing houses in a bombed city.

'That's not funny,' said Joe, the hurt in his voice painting a picture to Emma, even in the dark, of the grim set of his face. He turned over, tugging sharply at the duvet as he did so, creating a separate space, force-fielded with resentment, within the shared bed. Emma listened to his breathing, each inhalation and exhalation heavy with blame, the wordless air of reproach. She heard him reach out to drink from the glass of water always by his side of the bed – three-quarters still, one-quarter sparkling: Joe so liked to customise everything –

before settling back in, an aggressive settling, his face pushed deep into the pillow, his body a bristling foetus. She considered reaching over and stroking his back in sympathy, in sorriness, but then turned over herself, angry at being made to feel guilty. After all, it was true: she *did* have a headache.

TONI

Toni couldn't understand what had got into Jackson today. Normally, she looked forward to her Tuesdays at Winsley Road. The house, even though it was decorated a bit too colourfully for her taste, was lovely – so different from all those places in Camberwell and Brixton where she had to work most of the week. She was sure, as well, that Molly, the Wendells' kid, was being mistreated in some way, having grown in the last three months from being a sunny, open three-year-old with a penchant for nonsense singing, into a withdrawn, tense ball of leave-me-aloneness. Toni had no idea what to do about it – going to the social services, if she was wrong, would definitely lose her the job, and probably most of her other work once the news got round. It made her want so much to be back in the Mumbles, where someone would look after *her* again.

But Tuesdays, normally, were different. It was the nearest Toni got to her idea of what being a nanny was meant to be like – the idea of it she used to have before she came to London. Nice (a very underrated word, Toni always thought), that's what it was at Winsley Road: nice house, nice parents, nice food in the fridge (which she was always careful not to help herself to overmuch – she didn't want to take advantage, and besides, it was nearly March now, and she still hadn't lost that stone she'd

128

promised herself she would before Christmas), and nice, really nice, kid. When Toni first saw Jackson, she thought: 'That's the sort of baby I'd like to have', he looked so pretty, apart from the birthmark of course, and – although you couldn't tell, obviously, yet – so intelligent. And normally he was a dream to look after – asleep most of the time and, when awake, happy to feed and, up until today, virtually uncrying; or at least, no more than odd yelps and gurgles, certainly not the present unbroken howl.

'Jackson, Jackson,' she said, patting his back for the hundredth time, as she walked round and round the living-room, like an animal in a too-small cage. She pulled him away from her chest, holding him at arm's length, and feeling, not for the first time that day, a twinge of sympathy for Louise Woodward. The noise appeared not to be coming any more just from the livid circle of the baby's mouth, but from all parts of his purple bulging face, contorted in unthinking intensity; his face was so purple, in fact, that his birthmark had vanished, blending in invisibly with the rest of him. 'You're changed, you're fed – what's the matter?'

Toni walked over to the corner of the bedroom and laid Jackson down in his cot. She felt keenly the helplessness of the nanny in this situation, where all that seems to be left to do is continually pick the baby up and put it down again. She checked the time on her Baby-G, a present from Val, her boyfriend. Toni didn't really like the Baby-G – even though it was pink, it looked to her, with all its buttons and controls, like a boy's watch – but knew that it was part and parcel of Val's attempt to trendify her, which she felt she should go along with. Mrs Serena – Emma as Mrs Serena insisted she call her, although Toni was generally confused about her name, having once heard her on the telephone call herself Emma O' Connell – was now an hour and a half late; if she didn't come home soon, Toni was going to have to phone Val and cancel going with him to that club in Clerkenwell – what was it called? Zion, that was it.

Self-pity in Toni began to spill over into rage: this was the fourth time Mrs Serena had been late in the last two months, part and parcel of a general change in her attitude since the New Year, and the injustices were piling up inside her. 'For fuck's sake, where is she?' Toni said out loud, and then blushed a little, as she didn't tend to swear in front of children she looked after, even ones as young as Jackson (especially ones as young as Jackson – Toni always remembered a local story that the first word said by the youngest child of the Lanes, a posh family from Swansea nannied briefly by slaggy Susan Crane, was 'cunt'). Still, he probably couldn't have heard her over his screaming anyway.

In the Serenas' living-room, Toni sat on the Chaise sofa and picked up the phone. Emma and Joe's main phone was an old black one they had bought at Greenwich Market, refurbished to work on a modern line. Toni wondered what it was made of – the receiver felt like ivory, although she wasn't sure what that was supposed to feel like – and what the letters were that surrounded each number like a little triptych. She had just begun to dial, when she heard the door slam; a second later – Emma and Joe didn't have much of a hallway – Emma was in the living-room.

Her hair and clothes were wet and her eyes were blazing. 'What are you doing?' she shouted.

'I – I'm phoning—'

Emma virtually leapt across the room, and snatched the receiver from Toni's hand.

'I'm only a bit late!' she said. Toni felt she could hear, in her screaming, a version of what Jackson had been doing all day. 'God! A little bit late, and you've got to get on the phone to Joe!'

'I wasn't—'

'You'll get him all worried, and worked up about me! He's got work to do! He's working late at the moment because he's under a lot of pressure there and the last thing he needs is stroppy phone calls from the nanny—'

'Mrs Serena,' said Toni, shakily, trying to make a stand. 'I wasn't phoning your husband.' Emma blinked at her; the idea was so clearly rooted in her mind that it took a moment for reality to adjust itself. 'I was phoning Val – my boyfriend—' It was all she could say before collapsing into tears; it had been a long, difficult day, and now she didn't even have an excuse not to go to Zion.

'Oh God, Toni, I'm so sorry,' said Emma, sitting down beside her on the sofa and putting an arm around her. She stroked her minutely shaking head, and felt how little difference, really, there was between her and Toni, how small was the gap between them, even though the roles *wife, mother, employer* were all on her side of the equation – all forcing her into the big role *adult*.

'And you're not a *little* bit late, anyway!' said Toni, petulantly now, tears forcing her small outrage forward. 'You're nearly *two hours* late!'

'Yes – I know,' said Emma, quiet now, in the way the shouter gets when they become the shouted at.

'Where *were* you?'

'I – I don't know.'

Toni looked round, her face red and wet as Jackson's. 'Pardon?' she said.

'I don't know where I was,' said Emma. 'I got lost.'

'Oh,' said Toni. Calm and a little awkwardness spread between them. Toni coughed. 'Were you coming from somewhere you'd never been before?'

Emma shook her head, and then said, as if to herself, 'No.' She looked up and smiled, trying to frame her features to friendly. 'No. It's odd. I just kept on looking at the streets and . . . I knew them. I knew each one. I just couldn't see how they . . . worked together. You know. To make . . . the journey.'

Toni nodded, but felt a little embarrassed at Mrs Serena going all weird on her. 'Jackson's not had a good time either,' she said, trying to rein the conversation back to safe ground. 'I've never seen him like it. Crying at the top of his little lungs he's been.'

'Really?' Emma, having spent the last few hours so concerned about herself – about both her moral and physical safety, in her lateness and lostness – felt the perverse relief that comes with worrying about someone else.

'Yes.' Toni frowned, then her face cleared, as a thought took shape in her head. 'Maybe it's because you were late.' Emma tilted her head politely, not understanding. 'You've never been this late before. Babies get a bit like that. They like routine. Maybe he knew something was wrong, when you didn't come back.'

'Maybe . . .'

'Although,' said Toni, getting up, 'listen to him.' The muffled sound of crying could be heard from upstairs, loud enough to render the baby monitor obsolete. 'He hasn't worked out that everything's fine again now, has he?' She smiled, and smoothed herself down a bit before exiting from the room, with a sense of getting back to the job. *No he hasn't*, thought Emma.

VIC

Vic was lying in bed, late on a Monday night, or rather, early on a Tuesday morning, when he got the call. He was awake anyway, having woken needing to go for a piss. He had been lying there for some time, as one of the things he hated most was getting out of bed in the middle of the night for a piss. He had thought long and hard about how this could be avoided. A potty was the obvious solution, but that still involved getting out of bed. The best way round this, Vic thought – and in his head, he actually saw the technical drawing – would be to carve some sort of small door (possibly cylindrical?) into both the bed frame and the mattress, which could be opened at the touch of a button, allowing immediate access between potty and urinating penis. Another possibility was to wear a specially customised condom in bed – customised by puncturing a hole in the tip and then attaching it by a series of straws to the pot, or, if he could find enough straws, all the way to the toilet.

'Vic here . . .' he said, having scrabbled at the floor by the side of the bed to pick up the phone. It was his standard phone greeting. He felt his heart beating with bad news fear.

'Darling?'

'Em?' He heard the croak in his voice and glanced at the illuminated red numbers on his digital alarm clock, which he never set to go off. 3:12.

'Were you asleep? Sorry, stupid question—'

'No, I wasn't, actually.' He wondered whether he should have told her that Tess rarely spent the night. Occasionally, she still did, and tonight could have been one of those occasions. 'Are you OK?'

'Yes. Well. I don't know.'

'Where are you?'

'Downstairs.'

Her voice was a little above a whisper. Vic had an image of Joe, upstairs, asleep, the space next to him a ruffle of sheets.

'Jackson wake you up?'

'No. Although I'll say he did if Joe wakes up; I'm holding him now.' Vic felt a slight discomfort, as ever, with Emma putting on the hard hat of affair management. 'Listen, I'm sorry to call so late, but I didn't know when I might be able to otherwise.' She took a sharp intake of breath, as if dragging viciously on a cigarette. 'I – I don't think I can make it tomorrow.'

Vic relaxed a little, through his stab of disappointment. 'Oh, fine. It's not like a permanent arrangement.'

'No, it's not, is it? Permanent . . .'

Vic waited, and looked into the darkness. His whole flat, despite Tess's protestations, remained exactly the same as when he moved in: white walls, grey carpet, IKEA furnishings. The bedroom walls were the only ones he ever considered painting, because their white, as now, meant the room was never, even in the blackest of Sydenham nights, that dark, and Vic sometimes felt the need for darkness at night. He felt it now, a little, as for the first time he had a sense of the problematic nature of the future, of their future; he felt he would rather be looking into a warm coating of black than into something in which shapes and objects and tones were gradually becoming distinguishable.

'My GP's fixed me up to see a specialist,' said Emma. 'At the Royal Brompton Hospital.'

His stomach fell. 'What's wrong?'

'Oh, I don't know. I've been feeling a bit under the weather for a while. My glands are up, my throat hurts.'

'For how long?'

She paused. 'Since the New Year.'

Vic felt his forehead tighten.

'What? You've been feeling ill for two and a half months?'

'Not *very* ill. Just a bit under the weather. I thought it might just be the stress of y'know ... everything. And I'm used to throat problems, I often get them.' She paused again. 'But then I started getting these headaches. And – I didn't tell you – a few weeks ago, on my way back ...'

'Yes?'

'I got lost.'

'Lost?'

'Yes. It took me nearly two hours to get home. Eventually, I had to stop and ask someone the way. I had – Vic, I had to pretend to this man on the street that I didn't know where my road was ...'

'I'm sure it's nothing,' said Vic, quickly.

'Yes. Probably. Oh God, I hate being ill. I hate bothering everyone with it. That's why I haven't told you before.'

'You're not ill.'

'These headaches are quite bad, though. They're not really a head-*ache* at all. More like a shooting pain, which starts at the back of the neck and then goes up into the skull and then just – explodes.'

Vic said nothing; time was when he would have been interested in the details of any symptoms of any illness, but not this time.

'I've got one now ... *and* my neck hurts.'

135

'Poor darling . . .' he said, feeling again that peculiar contiguity, of knowing, self-consciously, what was expected of him, and yet still instinctively wanting to say it.

'Poor me.' Her voice became a little distant. 'Maybe it's just the way I'm holding the phone.'

'Huh?'

'I'm holding it with my neck. I need a hands-free baby. One moment, caller.'

Vic heard a shuffling and a small sleepy gurgle, as Emma readjusted the phone to her other ear.

'I don't know, darling, I'm sure it *is* nothing,' she said.

'Have you told Joe?'

'. . . but with Mum like she is I always get freaked out by the idea of anything bad happening to my head.'

'Emma? Have you told Joe?'

'Darling? Vic?'

'Yeah, I'm here.'

Nothing. Then: 'Vic? Oh for God's sake, now the line's gone dead.'

'No it hasn't, I'm here. Em—'

He was interrupted by the unbroken burr of the dialling tone. Vic put the phone down and went into that mental vacuity, that dead time, of waiting for the other person to call back. He was just starting to wonder about calling her back, but then remembered Joe, asleep, when the phone went.

'Darling?'

'Hello?'

'Sorry. The line went dead, and I thought I'd put Jackson back in his cot.'

'Yeah. It was fine at this end, though. I could hear you perfectly.'

'Was it? Oh well. I should go back to bed really – heavy day tomorrow.'

'What time's the appointment?'

'2.30. Wouldn't you believe it – right in the middle of our

136

day.' She sighed. 'Our wonderful Tuesdays . . . and here's the worst thing. I've got to go back *next* Tuesday to pick up the results.'

'Oh for fuck's sake!' A thought crossed his mind, a partner's thought. 'Should you be going there on your own – I mean, do you want me to come with you?'

He felt he could hear in her next words a sad smile. 'Vic. I wish. But I don't think that'd be a very good idea.'

'Will Joe go with you?'

She hesitated. 'I haven't told him yet.' The line crackled between them. 'I'd rather not, while I don't know if anything's wrong. He'll only get too worried.'

'Right . . .' Vic said, wondering why she had chosen to tell *him* – to ignore *his* worry. The colder part of him, subdued often when talking to Emma, but still there, told him that she wanted to see how he would react: how he would react to her in jeopardy.

'Where's the Royal Brompton?' he said.

'Chelsea.'

'You're not going to get lost getting there . . . ?' he said.

'No,' she laughed. 'I know where it is. I remember seeing it that time I went to Kensington Gardens.' There was a pause, during which both of them felt the impact of recent memory, like nostalgia experienced too soon; electric though their affair still was, the passion of that week would perhaps never be topped. As if to complement this, Emma continued: 'It's funny, now, thinking about that time. I was so caught up with it. It felt so real. Now I feel – I feel a tiny bit embarrassed about it all.'

'Sorry,' said Vic. 'Are you talking about us, or . . . ?'

She laughed again. 'No, darling. Not us.' He heard her breathe in. 'I'll prove it to you. I really don't think I can make it tomorrow, but *next* Tuesday – I know Chelsea's a long way from Herne Hill, but I'm sure I could still get there for maybe an hour or two afterwards. If. . .' she paused, changing gear, 'that is, you'd still find me sexy with a brain tumour.'

'Emma!' said Vic. He was shocked. Vic was unused to that. He was normally the sayer of the shocking thing. And, beneath the shock, a worrying prickle. *Brain tumour*. He remembered something about brain tumours. 'Don't say that. Please don't say that. I couldn't bear . . .'

'I'm joking, darling. Don't worry,' she said, and he thought he could hear just a tiny trace of satisfaction in her voice, or rather, relaxation; those had been the words she wanted to hear. 'It's good to joke about illness sometimes. You know Iris Murdoch?'

'Not personally . . .'

'*Duh*. You know she's got Alzheimer's?'

'Yes.'

'Apparently, all she watches now is the Teletubbies. She really likes it.'

'Right . . .'

'You know why that is, don't you?'

'The quality of the writing?'

Emma laughed. 'No. What word do they use most? The Teletubbies.'

'Em, I know I hang about watching TV all day but I'm not that well versed in the Teletubbies. It's on a bit early for me, for a start.'

'*Again*. That's the word they use most often. The whole programme's based on repetition. That's why kids love it. *And* why someone with Alzheimer's would like it. Shh, darling, shh.' In the background, Vic heard the opening note of Jackson's cry die away, as if he felt he should really be crying but couldn't actually be bothered. 'Anyway, the first time I thought of this, I tried to tell Joe, but I just ended up really laughing at the thought of this grand old lady of English letters being really into Tinky Winky and Po and the big bunnies. And you know how he gets, a bit pompous at times – he came over all horrified. But I'm so used to Mum's illness now, I sometimes think the best thing to do is laugh. What other defence have we got against illness and death, except laughter?'

Vic said nothing. Not because he had drifted off in the face of someone else expanding an idea, as he sometimes did; nor because he could hear in Emma's tone – *you know how he gets, a bit pompous at times* – more than a little remnant of affection for her husband.

'Anyway, darling, don't worry. I'm sure I'm fine really.'

He said nothing, because he'd read a lot about diseases, especially about their symptoms. He said nothing, because he was thinking – not about himself, and the cold goosepimples of realisation, rising on his flesh, or even about Emma, still talking, moving the subject on to other, less bleak, subjects, or about Joe, upstairs, unknowing, or about Tess, in her own flat five miles north, having made the weary journey back from Vic's flat earlier that night – he was thinking about Jackson, laid out quiet in his cot, a little line, a smear of life and reliance. He said nothing because he knew that one symptom of a brain tumour is deafness in one ear.

JOE

Sitting down on the sofa after making coffee on Sunday morning, Joe was startled by a dream-memory. Various fragments of the night's imaginings had been swimming around in his head since he'd got up, but none of these were resonant, none *epiphanic*: just the bits and pieces that swim around in your head for twenty minutes before you wake properly. But once this particular memory hit him, he realised, as one often does, that something had been bugging him all morning, something had been lying in wait in his consciousness: a feeling similar to the realisation that he'd forgotten something. As with that feeling, he was able to back-date the sensation – the feeling of the brain nagging at itself – to *before* the dream-memory came to him.

This was it. Joe suddenly remembered kissing a woman in a jewellery shop. The image made him shiver so much that he chased it; he chased the dream in his head. Going back and forth, he recalled – in that vague, uncertain way that memories of dreams are, already degraded so soon after they've happened, the brain treating them like ultra-quick versions of real memories – that he and Emma had been on holiday in some uncertain destination with a large group of people; and that one of the women in the group was called Liz. In the course of the dream, which had stretched, somehow, in the five or six minutes of sleep that had constituted it, over three or four days, he had become very friendly with Liz. And in the early part of the dream he had been happy with this; he was pleased just to find a new friend. But then, abruptly, in this jewellery shop, he had been overwhelmed by a desire to kiss her; and in fact he had been harbouring this desire all along, or at least ever since her personable qualities had warmed him to her.

'Liz . . .' he had said, and kissed her passionately, desperately. They parted, and looked at each other in the harsh strip lighting of the shop, where amulets and embroidered stones lay displayed on velvet cushions under glass on every side. She turned away.

'Oh, OK,' said Liz, somewhat sadly. 'Now it starts going really fast.'

Now it starts going really fast. This, he realised, was the high-water mark of the dream, the very point of epiphany. He knew exactly what she meant: that what could have been a long and fruitful friendship was now going to become a short, intense and soon-to-end affair; that the slow, relaxed train of companionship in which they had been travelling together had become the out-of-control Mercedes of lust.

He looked up from the sofa, towards the stairs. Emma was still in bed. It was his turn to look after Jackson this morning, and he knew he was putting it off. He felt keenly the fragmentation of their lives, into turns, taking turns where once they might have done everything together. Dreams, in particular, they used to share, as if their apartness in sleep could be eradicated – successfully, it seemed: at one point, they had told each other so much about their dreams that one morning they woke up having had exactly the same dream.

But he would not tell her about this dream. He was somewhat shocked by it. He had never been unfaithful, except with Emma while he was with Deborah, and that had involved little more than the kiss in Chaise. The idea of extramarital involvement, even in a dream, troubled him – in a way, troubled him *more* in a dream, because it suggested desires and yearnings in his subconscious which he wasn't aware of, and couldn't control. Despite everything Vic had told him in a hundred Spice of Sydenham nights, Joe thought it natural that if you were monogamous – if you were in love – you never desired anyone else; it never occurred to him that love might be a dynamic, a struggle, in which the desire for otherness is a given.

The baby monitor gave out its distress signal; Joe picked up his coffee cup. On his way up the stairs towards Jackson's room he glanced out of the window. Outside the deli on the other side of the road, a warmly dressed couple was just exiting, their arms loaded with Sunday papers and bagel bags. The woman was laughing; Joe could see steam coming out of her mouth in bursts. Looks like a scene from a film set in New England, thought Joe, who often thought about New England. He had never been, but he liked the idea of it – the idea of a new England, a fresh, crisp, new England, fresh and crisp as the snow that he always imagined lined the streets there, as opposed to Old England, or rather, Modern England, New and Nearly New England, Grant and Phil Mitchells' England.

The baby monitor sounded again. He blinked, and realised he had been standing there for some time, long enough for his coffee, hot when he last noticed it, to have gone cold.

VIC

Tess was drinking. This was something she rarely did at home, because of the amount of drinking she did whilst abroad. She had always been of the opinion that the standard tasting-action, settling the wine on the tongue, breathing in to release the flavour, swilling it round and then spitting it out, was, as she once told James Foy, 'bollocks'. Tess felt this method never allowed you to experience the wine fully; for her, the effects of consumption – the *taste* effects (the throat-warming, the echo on the tongue, the difference between first and second gulp) not the mood-altering ones – were integral to a wine's identity. She was the only professional buyer of any repute who routinely swallowed wines at tastings. She was also the only professional buyer of any repute who *could* swallow wines at tastings, as Tess had an extraordinary capacity for wine, able to drink magnums, jeroboams – *crates* she could drink – without losing her ability to minutely judge the next glass.

Which is why, tonight, in The Case Is Altered, she was drinking tequila. Tess wanted to get drunk. She wanted to get hard drunk, which is why she was drinking tequila, as opposed to whisky, or gin or vodka, all of which would have done the trick, as far as getting drunk was concerned, but wouldn't have had the spin that tequila has. Tequila, in its effects – very much

143

its mood-altering ones – is the most druggy of drinks, the only drink which takes you to an altered state rather than a ruined one. Tess didn't take drugs, but she did, at times, crave that altered state, and tequila was the most familiar route there.

Vic wasn't sure why Tess was so determined to get drunk tonight, but he knew the state she was heading towards. He was at the bar, about to buy Tess her sixth shot of tequila and wondering whether to get drunk himself. Vic didn't often get drunk. He didn't mind being drunk, but he didn't much like drink. Vic was a man of fairly immediate instincts and responses. Essentially, these had not changed much since he was a child: as a child, he had tasted alcohol – a pale ale, force-fed to him by his father – and thought 'urrgh'. Vic didn't quite understand how it was that, as you grew up, you were supposed to develop a different response – your taste buds don't change, he thought.

But he wouldn't have minded getting drunk tonight. He didn't often get drunk, and he generally didn't need to: he was someone who, as a condition of being, was sort of out of it. He had a sleepiness, born of distance, that meant he could travel through the world unaffected, untouched, unbothered. And yet, now, he was bothered. He could feel under all his thoughts – and still when he wasn't thinking, when his mind was just a vacuum, sponging up stimuli without subtext – *anxiety*, drawing everything to it like a magnet in his head. He wasn't used to it, and his surface self fought it, framing the thought that if he'd known this was going to happen, he'd never have fucked her in the first place.

'Mullan!' came a voice to his left. Vic looked up. The queue to the bar was three rows deep, as it always was on Friday nights, and coming out of it carrying three pints of various lagers was Chris Moore, a music journalist who had once interviewed him for the *NME*.

'Hello, Chris,' said Vic.

'Long time no see,' said Chris Moore. His breath smelt like he wasn't carrying the first round of the night, and his eyes were so bloodshot and red Vic almost wanted to look round for a man taking a flash photograph.

'How's things?'

'OK,' said Vic, but felt a sudden urge to tell this bloke who he hardly knew, and who he had to say 'OK' to when asked how things were, that things weren't OK, that his secret lover might have cancer. He was pleased, at least, to have this distraction from waiting at the bar. Since Emma's phone call he had found himself disturbed by the act of waiting, triply impatient in traffic or queues – yesterday he had even lost his rag on the toilet, having taken five minutes to find the first tear on a new piece of roll – as if he knew that time had suddenly become a diminishing return. He had felt something like it before, driving towards Rock Stop on Tuesdays, the constantly narrowing time that is snatched time, every little hold-up amplified and contorted. 'What about you? Still at the paper?'

'Not really. I'm a features editor at *Jack*.' That figures, thought Vic. *Jack* was a late addition to the *FHM, Loaded, Maxim*, aren't-we-the-naughty-ones magazine market; it specialised in covering topics too shallow for its competitors. On the odd occasion Vic had read one of them (not often: Vic hated stuff that aspired to, but wasn't, pornography), he'd recognised more than one byline from his days of contact with the music press, men who in their twenties would've been politically correct to be rebellious, and who now had to be politically incorrect to be rebellious, instead of realising that the dignified thing to do is stop being rebellious. 'Although I still do odd bits and pieces for them. Can I help it if I still bloody love rock and roll?'

It was at that point that Vic remembered just how cunty Chris Moore was. He wasn't just a cunt. He was off the cuntometer.

'I do, y'know. I even thought about buying an electric guitar myself the other day . . .'

'Well anyway,' said Vic, 'I've got to get to the bar.'

'Sure, man,' said Chris Moore. 'Oh! *Afore ye go* . . .'

'What?'

145

'I've got a little something on me,' he said, and winked. He actually winked, thought Vic, staring at his forty-something shaved-to-mitigate-baldness head. 'I'm just off to the Gents to avail myself of it, if you're interested . . .'

Vic's heart sank a little, partly out of a sense of how sad Chris Moore was, still desperate to take drugs with rock stars, even ones who had never properly made it and last played guitar professionally on a jingle for Talk Radio. But also partly because he knew he was going to say yes.

'Hold on, I'll just get this drink in for my girlfriend and—'

'I'll meet you at the jukebox in five,' said Chris Moore, and left, with all the speed of someone who feels they've said a really cool thing and now must cap it with a slick exit.

Tess hardly noticed Vic handing her the tequila, because she was looking all around her manically noticing everything else, as she tended to while drunk.

'Um . . . just going to the toi—'

'Look at this,' she said, pointing to a flyer on the wall next to their corner table. It was a white photocopied sheet, with the words POETRY NIGHT stencilled across it, above a jocular cartoon of a man with a large book and a quill. *Every Tuesday, admission £3.00*, he was writing. 'What a shit idea! Sorry, is it 1982 in here? What the fuck!'

'Yeah. Anyway, I'm just—'

'Like, isn't this just the perfect place for fostering the poetic instinct!? Yeah, you can just imagine Sylvia Plath over there on that crappy stage, reading out extracts from *Ariel*, can't you? Above people shouting out "and a packet of KPs"? She'd be straight into the kitchen, chucking the meat pies out of the oven to make room for her head. Which reminds me – '

There was no alternative for Vic but to sit down for the moment.

' – what I've never understood about all that, right, is that everyone goes on about Sylvia Plath. OK – but then Ted Hughes married again, didn't he – and his second wife killed herself. In exactly the same way!'

'Did she?' Vic didn't know this and even though he could see Chris Moore already making his way to the jukebox, thought it was interesting.

'Yeah. I mean – what must he have thought, the day he came down and wifey number two's lying with her head in the oven.'

'I really must get an *electric* cooker next time?'

Tess laughed, loudly. 'Yeah. I bet Ted hated it when British Gas came up with that slogan: *cook, cook, cook, cookability that's the beauty of gas.*' Her voice, always quite resonant, was booming now with tequila; a woman wearing a purple woolly hat, sitting on her own at a table opposite, was frowning at her, frowning at her *actively*, frowning at her in an 'I'm *frowning*!' sort of way, but Tess was running with it now. 'You don't think they ever asked him to be one of the celebrities who did the thumbs-up thing in the adverts?'

'Yes, I think they did.' Vic stuck his thumb up. 'Only Ted's thumb didn't have a little flame coming out of it, just a seeping noise and a weird smell. And people around him shouting, "For God's sake, don't switch any lights on!"'

Tess laughed even louder, a big drunk *hahaha*.

'Do you mind!' said a voice in front of her. Tess stopped laughing. Through the mist of drunken vision and pub smoke she could just make out a woman, a woman the colour of whose face was practically indistinguishable from that of her hat.

'Sorry?' said Tess.

'Do you mind not shouting offensive – really offensive . . .' and here the purple-hatted woman struggled for a collective noun, '. . . *stuff* like that out loud!'

Tess blinked at her. 'Why are you talking to me?' she said, with genuine innocence.

'Not that it matters to you – not that I should think you give a monkey's – ' the woman was continuing, 'but Sylvia Plath was

147

– Sylvia Plath *is* – a heroine of mine.' Around the edges of her eyes, crow's feet gathered, emphasising her bleak, dry anger.

'OK,' said Tess, 'but why are you talking to me?'

The woman shook – not a great movement, slight and contained, but containing an enormous rage. 'Why are you asking me that? It's obvious!' She raised her voice, already querulous, to a higher pitch. 'You were making offensive remarks about her!'

'I wasn't,' said Tess, raising a correcting finger, with something of the calm of the drunk, but with something of her own personal calm too. 'I was making offensive remarks about *Ted Hughes*. Something I should think you – and what with being such a big fan of Sylvia's, you must fucking *hate* Ted Hughes – would enjoy.'

The purple-hatted woman took a sharp breath in for a reply, and then, in lieu of any words coming to her, just held it for a bit, before exhaling.

'And also,' said Tess, 'I hardly said anything. OK, I started the subject, but I would say if anyone was really making offensive remarks,' she angled her correcting finger down towards Vic, shutting one eye like a sniper, 'it would be him.' Her sights moved back round to the purple-hatted woman. 'So why didn't you tell him off?'

The woman looked round at Vic, who was smirking (but a little uncomfortably, and if you're going to smirk you really have to do it comfortably). The answer to Tess's question which she would've liked to give – *because you're a woman. That kind of stuff is all you'd expect from men, but for a woman to come out with it, for a woman to condone it, for a woman to deride a feminist heroine so – why, it's treason!!* – even through all the armour provided by her purple hat, the woman knew the time had come and gone when she could have said such things. With as withering a look as she could muster, she left, her attitude attempting to paint in the air the words: I'm not even going to dignify that with a reply.

'You're right,' said Vic, getting up, 'it clearly *is* 1982 in here.'

'Yeah,' said Tess, staring into her shot glass, 'but I sort of didn't want her to walk away. I sort of wanted her to tell you off.' Vic stopped, and frowned at her quizzically; eventually Tess looked up and met his eyes. 'Someone needs to, don't they?' she said.

In the toilet, three men were pissing, and four others were waiting. There was only one cubicle. The sharp smell of urine mingled, as ever, with faint cross-currents of homophobic suspicion. Vic remembered something that Joe used to go on about, how he hated pissing in a public toilet, especially a crowded one, because the pressure he felt to finish and leave the urinal for the next person was so intense he normally couldn't even get started. Vic, always ready to evacuate, at the time couldn't understand the problem, but his currently destabilised condition made him feel more uneasy in this arena than ever before: the Gents is designed for the radically unselfconscious.

He was standing, with Chris Moore, waiting for the cubicle door to open. The already not all that attractive prospect of sniffing cocaine off the top of the toilet was steadily becoming less so, as the noises from the man at present inside escalated into an ever more unusual series of bursts and moans. What had Tess meant? wondered Vic. He had asked her, but she had changed the subject, off on another rant, this time about Greeks. Was it a reference to his infidelity, and if so, how did she know? How much should he push it? And then Vic stopped wondering, because he had come to a point he had reached before, a point where he couldn't be bothered to emotionally aggravate himself any further; a point where all he could be bothered to deal with was the matter in hand, which in this instance was quite aggravating enough.

'I never like this bit,' Chris Moore whispered in a remarkable moment of honesty: he was the sort of person who could find glamour in the most mundane sordidness. 'I always think everyone knows what we're going to do.'

'Maybe we should start kissing,' whispered Vic back.

'Eh?' Chris Moore seemed, for an instant, terrified.

Vic looked around him, and then back. 'Confuse the issue . . .' he said.

Chris Moore's face moved out of terrified, went through uncertainty, and was just about to break into a sycophantic smile when the door opened and out lumbered a bald man fat enough to ask Cyril Smith if he called that a cummerbund. His girth turned out, however, to be a blessing, in that it allowed Vic and Chris Moore to nip behind him together into the cubicle in an almost unseen way, like some sort of rather skanky magic trick.

Ignoring the animal smell, Chris Moore instantly crouched over the stopcock lid with a wrap retrieved from his pocket, his hands performing the furtive origami of cocaine. Vic caught sight of the powder, white against newsprint, and felt bored and excited at the same time, like when you make love to a very familiar partner.

Just as he was shutting the cubicle door, however, a figure glided slinkily through the small gap to join them. Vic continued his instinctive shutting movement, so the door was locked before the figure spoke:

'All right, Victor!! You wouldn't be . . . "*Flying on an angel's wings/To a place where your soul sings!*" . . . by any chance?'

Vic stared at Ivan with disbelief; his goatee was even thinner than he remembered, an adjective which could not be used to describe his chin, or indeed, chins. 'What the fuck are you doing here?'

'I always drink here!'

'Do you? What, specifically in *here*, from the bowl, like a cat?'

'Oh. No, I just saw you going into the cubicle as I came in. Thought I'd invite myself to the party.'

Vic looked at him; the smallness of the cubicle – not, after all, designed for three – was forcing Ivan's stomach against his.

'Chris, this is Ivan,' he said wearily, his introduction sounding absurdly formal in these circumstances.

'Hi,' said Chris Moore, and carried on chopping, realigning and chopping again, drugs protocol insisting on the complete acceptance of a stranger in the cubicle.

'Hi. Hey Vic. I know what I wanted to ask you. What was that song . . . on the second EP, the one with the wah-wah pedal?' Vic looked blank; he was trying to look deadpan, but to Ivan it came across simply as blank. 'You know – dum, da-da-da, dumdumdum! Badoom! Dum—'

'Da-da-da, dumdumdum, Badoom!' joined in Chris Moore.

'Yeah!' said Ivan. His fingers trilled: 'Diddly, diddly, diddly – something about – *floating in space/ready to crash . . .*'

'Oh God, don't tell me . . .'

Vic looked at his hands, and cursed them for having locked himself into this tight little cross-section of hell. Tess, he realised, would, even through her drunkenness, be wondering where he was.

'Hey Vic,' said Ivan, when he realised that Vic wasn't going to answer their pop trivia problem, 'how'd you get on with that bird?'

'What bird?'

'The one you went off to talk to at the wine-tasting last time I saw you.' He clicked his fingers. 'Tess!'

'Oh. Yeah. I did OK. She's my girlfriend.'

'Really! Cool!'

Vic nodded; his eyes went a bit sleepy as he tried to check his soul out of the situation.

'Wine-tasting . . . ?' said Chris Moore.

'That's what she does. She buys and sells wine.'

He looked round.

'Hmm. I wouldn't mind having a chat with her. I've really got into wine in a big way recently.'

Vic felt his insides droop, both at the thought of having to introduce Chris Moore to Tess, and the consequent extension of time with him that would entail, and at the thought of him *getting into wine*, endlessly expanding his tired self-pleasuring know-how.

'Not tonight, Chris.' He couldn't be bothered to explain himself. 'In a bit of a funny mood . . .'

Chris Moore, though, was not a man to take hints. Turning back to the task in hand, he said, cheerfully, 'Just a chat. You know, establish contact . . .'

Jesus, thought Vic, before suddenly seeing a way out. He fished in his coat pocket and, sorting through a small pyramid of tube tickets, receipts, tissues and condoms, brought out a business card.

'Here . . .' he said, handing it to Chris Moore over his shoulder. His over-ringed hand took it and held it up, as if gauging it principally for cocaine-chopping utility: centred, a bunch of red grapes, in a black outlined square, and underneath Tess's name, address and phone number. 'Give her a call, or write to her . . . another day.'

'OK . . .' he said, shrugging.

'Still, you want to be careful taking coke, then,' said Ivan, who had spent the last minute staring steadfastly at a biro doodle of an enormous spurting phallus, underneath which a different phone number had been written, accompanied by the words I WILL SUCK YOU OFF: another type of business card. 'If you're with your girlfriend.'

'Because . . . ?'

'Because it fucks you up for sex. Can't get a hard-on. Last time I pulled on coke I was nowhere. Couldn't get wood. For ages. Luckily, she let me fuck her up the arse.'

'To fuck someone up the arse, in my experience, requires a wood of antique restoration furniture proportions,' said Chris Moore, without turning round. The smugness of his tone reminded Vic of the dull, deliberate political incorrectness of most of the writing in *Jack*. It made him hate, as he sometimes did now, his own younger self.

'True,' said Ivan. 'But I managed it. Through the coke. It sort of hardened in her arse.'

Vic stared at both of them.

'You know, that conversation has impressed me more than any work either of you have ever done,' he said. Then specifically to Chris Moore: 'How long are you going to be sorting out those lines?'

'Uh . . . thing is,' he said, half looking round, 'the top of the toilet was a bit . . . damp.'

'. . . yes?'

'And so now the coke's got a bit damp.'

Vic and Ivan came over to have a look. The drug lay on the china in three flat sticky lumps; it looked like a scale model of some islands in the Antarctic.

'So what do we do now?' said Vic.

Ivan shrugged. 'Wait till it dries out,' he said.

When they finally left the cubicle, a crowd of men, all of whom appeared to have only legal reasons for wanting to get in, were waiting outside. The looks of resentment on the part of those men who could easily guess what activity Ivan, Vic and Chris Moore had just indulged in were matched only by the look of horror from an elderly man at the end of the queue, who could not.

'Easy . . .' whispered Chris Moore out of the corner of his mouth to Vic, as they worked their way through the bodies, the three of them like some downcast conga. As they opened the Gents door, Vic breathed in the smoky, old sofa air of the saloon bar with some relief. He could feel the tart wash of the drug sluicing around his head. It make him feel up, ready to deal with the world, with Tess, with Emma, with whatever news he was going to have to hear at Rock Stop next Tuesday.

'OK, Vic,' said Chris Moore. 'Good to see you again.'

'Yeah, you too,' said Vic, kind of meaning it, insofar as he was so pleased that Chris Moore was now going to go away that he liked him, felt, in fact, a burst of love for him. Looking around, he noticed that Ivan, too, had vanished into the pub throng. Things were definitely on the up, he thought: as long as the paranoia doesn't kick in.

JOE

In the circle of the microscope lens, Joe could see the cell structure clearly. This was his favourite microscope. People don't imagine scientists have favourite instruments, Joe knew: part and parcel of their alienation, their hived-offness from ordinary society. But they do – they have a relationship with their scopes. Doctors have favourite stethoscopes – physicists their favourite gyroscopes – cosmologists see particular telescopes and fall in love – and Joe, a biochemist, found a special satisfaction and harmony with this microscope. It was an AO Microtome 820, in grey and black, with trinocular head, and 100x magnification eyepieces, a heavy circular base for Petri dishes, and dual pincers for slides; made in the early seventies, it shouldn't really still have a place in a modern research lab, but Joe had customised it by attaching a microcamera system, a series of heat filters, and an ultraviolet illuminator, thus saving it from the science bin. It had a name, from a time when things like microscopes had names: the *Grey Lady*, it was called, and Joe always felt at peace looking into it, slowly rotating its tungsten wheels. Things came into focus under the *Grey Lady* gradually but absolutely; a point of focus could always be reached with it that felt perfect – you could feel it, as well as see it, that point where a ratchet more or a ratchet less would be wrong: that optimum.

155

It was good for Joe that the pure operation of the *Grey Lady* gave him such satisfaction, as what he was actually doing did not. He was performing a biopsy. The commercial constraints that Jerry Bloom had been threatening to impose on his laboratory had, to some extent, come into force, and, although Joe's HIV research had not been terminated, it had been curtailed. Instead – and Joe felt that this was clearly an interim measure, and he knew what normally followed interim measures – the lab had been forced to devote the first two days of its working week to endeavours that were primarily money-making: cosmetics research, upgraded analgesics, new antihistamines, and this – blood and tissue testing, lucratively subcontracted out to companies such as Friedner by the NHS in an effort to deal with its own vast overload of information finding and carrying: they now dealt with up to 30 per cent of all biopsies for hospitals in the South-East. Of all the new work Joe was expected to do, he was least happy with this, partly because it reminded him most keenly of the research he wanted to be getting on with, but also because of a residual guilt he felt at being a collaborator in the *upgrading, modernising, streamlining* and all the other buzz-words he felt – in his gut, if not his head – shouldn't really be applied to the National Health Service.

He was testing a tissue culture, a cross-section of a lymph node, excised from a patient's throat by syringe aspiration at the Royal Brompton Hospital, last Tuesday, 24 March 1998. He felt sorry for this patient, whoever he or she was, because as he peered into the heart of the culture, there was no mistaking the virulence of this particular tumour. The normal architecture of the lymph node had completely broken down, replaced by a clumped scab, a dark mass like a bad planet; on deeper magnification he could see that individual cells had lost all their identifiably nodal characteristics, as happens in cancer – cells, like the people they form the basis of, lose all sense of themselves, of what they're supposed to do, of their function in life. Joe knew, too, that finding such a growth in a secondary site like a lymph node implied the probable presence of a primary tumour in a much more critical area of the body – the breast, or, possibly, the brain. He had a vision of this cancer, released from the fixture of the paraffin slide on which he was viewing it, live in the body of the patient; he saw it spreading rapidly, its cells dividing and subdividing at super-speed, lustfully, rampantly giving birth to hundreds and thousands of new cells in its own negative – negative like a camera negative – version of life. As he peered deeper into the microscope, Joe began to wonder about this lymphoma – something about its remarkable ugliness rekindled his researching instinct, dispelling his normally somewhat sulky attitude to such biopsies: he would have liked to know more about this case, primarily whether or not there was something in the lifestyle of this patient that would have promoted such a carcinoma.

'Have you finished with those samples?' said Marian, approaching with a black clipboard.

'Yes,' said Joe, looking up. His eyes screwed up reflexively, readjusting to the tubular white light of the lab; he had been looking into the *Grey Lady* for longer than usual at this one.

She handed him the clipboard, on which rested a piece of paper with a series of boxes for him to tick referring to each tissue sample he had tested that afternoon. The boxes described the medical identity of each sample in detail, but ended baldly with two boxes, one marked 'malignant' and one marked 'benign'. All the samples Joe had worked on in this session were benign apart from the last, and he felt uncomfortable, as he had done before, ticking the 'malignant' box, feeling the incongruity of using a tick, this little jaunty hieroglyphic that says 'well done', for such a bad result. He could, of course, have used a cross, but he found that a tick focused the mind more, and avoided the horrendous possibility of absent-mindedly making a mistake on the results sheet.

Before he handed the clipboard back, his eye moved from his tick in the malignant box back along the line to the other axis, where the identities of the patients from whom the samples had been taken were grouped, one on top of another, as a series of numbers: codes. The bottom one, this one, read G3489/Z14. G3489/Z14. He repeated it to himself, as you sometimes do when trying to remember a phone number when you haven't got a pen.

'Joe?' said Marian.

He glanced up from the clipboard; Marian had her palm offered up quizzically. Her face had adopted a patient and slightly fond expression, signalling her familiarity with Joe's occasional distractedness.

'The results need to go back today . . .' she said. Joe shook his head from side to side quickly, as if waking up, and smiled.

'Sorry . . .' he said, handing it over. Marian smiled back, took the clipboard, and began to walk away. Joe watched her from behind, and wondered if she was perhaps the woman represented in his dream, the woman he was friendly with who secretly he desired. He wondered too if his sexual horizons had always been limited by science – by an environment in which all the women he ever met wore shapeless white coats. And he wondered something else.

'Marian?' he said.

She looked round. Her hair – curly almost to the point of ringlets – was, of course, tied up, as long hair must be in a lab, but Joe found an image scooting across his head of how it might have fallen across her shoulders had it been untied.

'If I wanted to trace one of these samples, how would I do it?'

'Trace?'

Joe's face set a little; he tugged at his earlobe. 'If I wanted to find out a bit more about the patient.'

Marian stared at him. They both knew this wasn't ethical. She frowned: but then she looked down at the clipboard, making, in so doing, her frown one of thoughtfulness rather than disapproval.

'Um . . .' she said, walking back over, 'you could run the code through Medisearch.'

'Would that work?'

'Possibly. Which one is it?'

Joe pointed; she looked down. He caught a slight smell, the tiniest hint of perfume. God knows what it is, he thought. What a long way I am from the type of man who can identify particular perfumes.

'Hmm,' said Marian. 'Royal Brompton. Yes. I think we'll be fine with that. Our network has access to their mainframe, for support services.'

She swivelled round and typed a command into the keyboard resting on the table to their left. A graphic came up on the monitor: the words MEDISEARCH™ bold against a yellow background. Driving across the bottom of the graphic was a tiny cartoon ambulance, its blue flashing light illuminating sections of the background as it went. Jocularity in everything, thought Joe.

Marian typed in more commands, swiftly. Joe felt a pang, a feeling-old pang, knowing that he'd never quite got his head round computers: his was a generation in biochemistry – quite possibly the last – for whom the microscope, rather than the computer, was still the central tool. A dialog box appeared on the screen. Marian typed in an access code, and pressed RETURN. The computer clicked and whirred, grumblingly: then a chime, a chord, a cyber-welcome.

'We're in,' she said, with a little nod of self-satisfaction. 'What was the sample code again?'

Joe looked back down at the clipboard. 'G3489 . . .' he said, intoning carefully, before pausing. Marian touched five keys.

'. . . stroke. Z14.'

She touched the other keys, and once again pressed RETURN. Her fingers, Joe saw, were topped by long nails, painted that shade of dark red that is nearly brown; an indication of her other self, of what she might look like away from the lab. Everything else about Marian's looks – hair, make-up, clothes – could be changed easily to and from here, he thought, but her nails – she's not going to redo them every night.

'What do you want to know?' said Marian, as they waited for the computer to process their request.

'Oh, I dunno. Any other information. It's a very virulent sample. The structure of the cross-section implies the presence of a type of cellular growth I've only seen occasionally before.'

Marian looked up at him; she was ever-so-slightly smiling.

'So . . .' continued Joe, knowing that her expression was essentially questioning, 'I'd be interested in knowing more about this case for our research. We are still doing our research here, y'know . . .'

He was interrupted by a ting from the computer. Their faces turned. A table had appeared on the screen. On its left-hand side, running down, was a series of codes; on the right-hand side was listed the series of tests undergone so far, and results obtained. Ten spaces down, near the base of the screen, was the row beginning G3489/Z14: Marian highlighted it.

'Blood, unconfirmed,' she said, reading. 'Lymph node, unconfirmed.'

'Not after today.'

'No. RNA brain scan . . .' she scrolled the cursor down, '. . . growth indicated, frontal lobe.'

'Hmm. Yeah, that's what I thought.' He looked down at Marian, noticing the tiny hairs that fell forward from her pulled-back hairline, lighter than the others. 'Anything else?'

She raised both her eyebrows questioningly, but her fingers flurried on the keyboard and clicked on the mouse. The computer whirred, and a new box of information appeared.

'OK,' she said, folding her arms and leaning back. 'Now you know her name and her age.' She looked back up at her boss, who was staring at the screen. 'What are you going to do? Trace her, so that you can – are you all right?'

160

Marian had a postgraduate degree in biochemistry from York University, and she knew how the body works – she could, in other words, normally trace any physical effect back to its biological cause; but looking at Joe now she had no idea at all what had made his face go so white.

VIC

Vic's scooter was a 1959 Lambretta LD. It was what in the trade is known as a character vehicle: it had two seats, rather than the modern long single cushion, a green leather case attached to the inside front panel, only three gears, and various insignia all over it, including the original registration certificate from France on the back side panel, and, below the headlight, a metallic badge in red and silver saying *Seine Paris Sepsex*, whatever that meant. Close up, without doubt, it looked cool, although from a distance it had a tendency to look like the sort of motorbike an out-of-control Norman Wisdom should be crashing through hung-out-to-dry laundry on.

Vic had a soft spot for the Lambretta. His attitude towards cars and bikes – old cars and bikes – was similar, in one respect, to his attitude towards guitars, although different in another. The difference was his ability. His ability to play and understand guitars inspired him actively towards them: he was in a *relationship* with guitars. The similarity lay in his enthralment to the aesthetic – the pure, passive adoration of curve and lustre and colour. He could feel that pure, passive adoration well up within him when looking at classic vehicles, and felt almost guilty about it (as he never would with women), as if his interest in them was somehow a betrayal of guitars. He

162

had bought the Lambretta as a sort of compromise, feeling that guitars would be not quite as upset by having to share his life with a motorbike, as they would be by a car.

He was not in a relationship with the Lambretta; he, essentially, had no call on the Lambretta, no say in what it decided to do and when it decided to do it. And so when it decided to break down, as it did often, he usually accepted it with good grace, realising that such bikes were meant to be owned by people who knew about them, who for God only knows what reason liked *tinkering* with them on a Sunday morning, and so – usually – Vic would feel no inner rage with the bike, no desire to kick it or smash it up. Usually, he would just phone the AA, wait the within-the-hour wait, greet the mechanic – more often than not a familiar face – warmly, and then, once it was fixed, calmly ride the bike back home, resigned to the hassle, accepting it as simply the down-side of the bargain he had made with God when he bought the Lambretta.

Today, though – standing on the corner of Dulwich Road and Railton Road, twenty yards from Rock Stop, late on this Tuesday afternoon – Vic didn't feel like that. He wanted to destroy the bike. He wanted to take it apart with his bare hands. Pour petrol on it and set it aflame. Bite its fucking complacent face off. All around him, South London rush-hour traffic crawled past; men perched high above in juggernaut-cabins glanced down curiously at his despair as they passed. Please work, thought Vic. *Please.* I've been so patient with you. Don't I deserve something?

He kicked the starter pedal again, and pulled on the throttle again. Nothing: not even the coughing and clanking of a few minutes earlier. As more cars went past, he felt desperate to share in their movement, in their movement away. Normally, a breakdown like this one – when you're trying to leave somewhere, rather than get somewhere – should be unproblematic; that sort of breakdown merely involves going back in to where you've just been, and waiting around. It could even be a good thing, an extension of fun. But he couldn't do that this time: he couldn't go back inside.

He felt vulnerable standing in the road, in the limbo just below the kerb, the no man's land between pedestrian and vehestrian. He heaved the bike, heavy with neglect, off its stand, and pushed it a little, gradually getting faster; then, when he was at some small speed, he let out the clutch. The engine puttered slightly. He gave it some throttle: suddenly, the bike flared into life before he had a chance to jump on, pulling his right arm almost out of its socket. Next thing Vic knew, he was lying on his back on the pavement, and the bike, its wheels turning furiously like the legs of a dying insect, was on its side, blocking the progress of the Dulwich Road traffic.

'What the fuck are you playing at, you stupid cunt!' shouted a red-faced man out of the window of his black Volkswagen Golf. Vic, picking himself up, ignored him easily; his other-planetness kicked in quickly when faced with aggression. He could feel tiny nicks and grazes on his legs and elbows. Quickly, he bent down to the bike, trying to get it up before it died – but then the wheels stopped turning, and with them, the engine.

He grabbed the bike with both hands and, straining, raised it back up again. Trying to kick the starter pedal, he noticed it had been bent by the fall, backwards under the footplate.

'Shit!' he cried. 'Shitshitshitshitshit!'

'Excuse me,' said a voice. Vic looked up: a dark-skinned woman, her face wrapped tightly in one of those wrap-around furry Camden hats, was standing on the pavement staring at him.

'Yes?'

'Is that an LD?'

Vic looked at the object of his hatred. 'Yes.'

'How old is it?'

'How old? 1959.'

'Right . . .' she said, and circled round the front, surveying it with a knowledgeable eye. 'I've got an LC 1957.'

Vic, startled, came out of his enclosed ball of anger and looked at her properly. Interesting, he thought. And not bad: something of Natalie Wood about her. Maybe I should carry on this conversation, pretend to be keener on bikes than I am . . . and then he stopped himself short, surprised – even he was surprised – at how quickly he'd reverted.

'Do you wanna push?' she said. 'Mine sometimes starts better with a push.'

'Um . . . yeah.' He got on, tying his helmet under his chin. Vic wore an old-style white peaked helmet, with no visor.

'Try it in second . . .' she said.

'OK.' She went round behind him and gripped the back bar with gloved hands.

'Er . . . before you start,' said Vic, turning round, 'this is very nice of you.'

'Thanks,' said the woman, nonchalantly.

'Only I won't be able to thank you afterwards. If it starts, I can't really turn round. In case it stalls. I've got to keep—'

'It's fine. Wave.'

Vic smiled and nodded. The woman looked round: there was a small gap in the traffic. She began pushing; the bike started to make a regular clanking noise, getting faster as she speeded up. Vic took a deep breath and let the clutch out. The engine gave a little, and the biting-in of the gear forced the bike to start backwards slightly, making it more of an effort to push. The woman doubled her effort, and they speeded up again – and then Vic heard it just about begin to tick over, very very slowly, so slowly the word 'tick' was appropriate, more like the rhythm of a grandfather clock than an internal combustion engine. Desperately, he opened the throttle as far as it would go. Please, he thought again, please: I've got to get away, far, far away, speed me anywhere but here – and then, with a great rasp, the engine burst into life and he was off, and, in that moment the acceleration of his Lambretta LD felt huge, it had G-force effects, he was an astronaut in a taking-off space shuttle.

As promised, he waved; from the woman's point of view, much smoke, a retreating back, and a raised fist. Vic was so pleased to be moving he thought he would look back at her, after all. She was standing with her arms folded, smiling; on seeing him turn, she put a hand out and did a thumbs-up. Vic smiled back, and returned the thumbs-up. At that point, he saw behind her what he didn't want to see, what he'd been trying to avoid seeing: Emma, still even from that distance visibly in tears, leaving from the side door next to Rock Stop. Quickly, he turned back round to face the road ahead, and hoped – for the only time in his life, he prayed – that she hadn't seen him. Please, he said to himself for the third time, but this time: Please God – don't let her have seen me. Don't let her have seen me smiling, doing a thumbs-up.

TESS

Tess lived in a small flat opposite Lambeth North tube station. As she walked back to it now across Westminster Bridge, she mused to herself how much more her property would be worth – five times as much? ten? – if it was positioned exactly the same distance away from Parliament Square, but to the north. Amazing what a stretch of water can do, she thought.

The lights lining the walkways around the south bank of the Thames were just coming on. London was doing that thing it only does if seen at this particular place and time – one of the central river bridges at dusk – of looking suddenly exotic: of looking, to those who have lived there for ever, and are aware of the city, if at all, only as the enormous urban blanket in which they are wrapped, suddenly like somewhere they might want to *visit* one day. She stopped in the middle of the bridge, and looked out; underneath her a tug passed, sweeping the river away in two currents from either side of its bows, like curtains lifting from a watery stage. All around her the gentle murmur of grief, audible throughout the city since the death of its Queen of Hearts, lowered another notch.

Tess looked at her watch: 6.20. Vic was meant to be coming round at half-past. She took a last look at the scene, breathing it in, and moved on, past Waterloo roundabout and down

Westminster Bridge Road, feeling the deflation, the hurt almost, at how quickly London goes back to being prosaic.

Back in her flat, she went straight into the shower. Vic, she knew, would be at least twenty minutes late. She had time. She put her head under the scalding water. Through the pain, she considered trying to lower the temperature, but knew it wasn't worth it, the point of equilibrium between hot and cold on her shower knob being so evanescent as to hardly exist at all; the tiniest movement towards blue, she knew, could trigger a rush of ice.

Stepping out, she reached for her white robe hanging on the shower door. A lethargy had set in with Tess over the more mundane businesses of living these days: more and more, for example, she couldn't be doing with towelling herself dry from the shower, but instead would just wrap herself in her robe while still soaking. It was, after all, made of towelling, she reckoned; it did the same job.

About to do up the tie round her waist, she caught sight of herself in the bathroom mirror; or rather, of bits and pieces, fragments of herself, visible in the unfinished jigsaw of steamed glass. She let the two halves of her robe fall, and surveyed herself. I get away with a lot through being tall, Tess had often thought. Tall, she had worked out, was a looks con, but a good one, one that the whole world seemed to have swallowed. All the supposedly 'beautiful' women in the world are over six foot, she'd calculated. Imagine any of them a foot, a foot and a half smaller. Same face, same statistics: just smaller. Suddenly, they wouldn't be in the super-beautiful league any more. She didn't know why tall should count for so much, but she was happy to go along with it.

She looked at her body and wondered what was wrong: what was wrong between her and Vic. She felt somehow, subterraneously, that he might be having an affair, but she didn't know how to tell. All the normal clues didn't really work with Vic. He hadn't lost interest in sex, but then, he couldn't really, it would be too obvious a change: interest in sex wasn't just a component of his, imagining him without it was like trying to imagine a completely different person. He was distracted, of course, but he had always been distracted, always apparently half-thinking either about something else or, deeply, about nothing.

She hated thinking like this. Obviously, partly, because she didn't like the idea of Vic having an affair, but also for other reasons: because she could anticipate the smugness of all those people who had tried to warn her off him when they first started seeing each other; because she was a creature of action, and action requires certainty; and also because – she had to admit it to herself – it was so fucking *womanly*. This, too, was the reason why she hadn't challenged Vic on the subject. What more clichéd question can a woman ask, she wondered – with the possible exceptions of 'What are you thinking about?' and 'Shall I pop that spot for you?' – than 'Are you having an affair?' And what more tired response when the question is answered with 'No. Why should you think that?' than 'It's just a feeling I've got . . .'

She looked more closely at herself. Even given the tall con, though, she looked all right, she thought. Her thinking about herself, physically, was generally positive, instinctively avoiding the self-deprecating, the victimised. But, as she looked, the mirror began to clear: more and more of herself appeared in it, hard and precise in the flat bathroom light, and, as the steam dissipated, so, for the first time, did Tess's confidence. No, she thought, I don't look all right: I look old; I, childless, have the breasts of an African mother of ten; my skin is falling. She fought it, she fought it hard, these negative impulses, but as the bathroom fan sucked and the condensation disappeared entirely, Tess felt that the way she had been looking at herself earlier had been a cheat; had been, literally, in soft focus.

She looked at her watch resting on the sink, with a certain amount of anger: anger at time itself, and anger at the time.

169

7.15. He was later than usual. Why? She tried again to stop thinking this way, but couldn't help it – what was he doing? where was he? If he doesn't arrive in a minute, I'll be sure he *is* – and then the doorbell rang.

Tess realised in an instant that she had not really been expecting him to turn up at all: why otherwise had she been standing here for so long, instead of finishing getting ready? Something inside had been telling her not to bother. Defiantly deciding to make no more effort, she wrapped her hair up quickly in a towel and came out of the bathroom, pressing the entryphone button on the hallway wall without waiting to listen for his voice. She stood at the top of the stairs with her arms folded; although cross, a part of her was already pacified, already hearing the two of them laughing together later at this, at her standing there like Flo waiting for a recalcitrant Andy Capp. She could already feel a half-smirk at the thought lying in wait behind her face, twitching her mouth muscles. Control it, she thought, the expression I want to present is somewhere between distant and fucked-off – and so she looked down the stairs with that expression, or as near to it as she could manage, set hard into her face. She knew what his face would be like: ironic, apologetic only in a somewhat parodic way, lazily calm, not deeply bothered about her potential anger, deadpan, familiar; which made it all the more unsettling when the face looking back at her coming up the stairs was concerned, soft, earnest, serious, a little fearful, and Joe's.

Tess's living-room had a refined, classical air to it. The walls were painted that dark sand colour so prevalent in magazines like *Wallpaper** or *Interiors*. The furnishings – a low, ethnic, wooden table, a tight white sofa, minimal but not minimalist abstracts dotted around – could similarly have been laid out for a photo-shoot. Only the floor-to-ceiling windows lost the taste plot a little, forced as they were by the blaring proximity of Kennington Road to armour themselves with a metallic 1970s double-glaze. Joe sat on an armchair facing the sofa, waiting for Tess to come back from the kitchen with drinks; he had not been to her flat before, and found himself – despite everything else buzzing around in his mind – wondering if taste was now a gene, part of the physical evolution of women of Tess's age and class. He didn't think he knew a middle-class woman in her thirties who couldn't, if push came to shove, interior-design.

He was disturbed from contemplation of his surroundings by Tess, standing next to the armchair with whiskies for them both; he hadn't seen her come back in.

'Just with ice OK?' she said, handing him a glass.

'Fine, thanks . . .' Joe took a sip: Jack Daniel's, he guessed. He wasn't really much of a spirits drinker, preferring beer or wine; but Tess hadn't had any beer, and he had been a bit frightened of asking her for wine, for reasons he wasn't entirely clear about – something to do with her expertise. Besides, this was what people drank, wasn't it, when they had something momentous to say – whisky, or brandy maybe, to calm their nerves.

'Sorry it's so hot in here,' said Tess, sitting down on the sofa. 'When you turn on the hot water for a shower the radiators come on full blast too.'

'It's OK,' replied Joe, raising his eyebrows, indicating innocence, 'I hadn't noticed.' He hadn't; although now she mentioned it, he did notice that she was wearing, above long white trousers, only a loose black vest, and wondered if her remark was some kind of justification for this. He was happier, though, now she was dressed; he had wanted to leave immediately when he'd arrived and she'd been in a gown. It had made him too aware of his intrusiveness, and of their basic unfamiliarity with each other.

'So . . .' said Tess, after a short and somewhat awkward pause, 'how's Emma?'

Joe coughed, a half-laugh. 'Fine. She's fine.'

Tess nodded. The windows shook a little as a lorry went by. 'Vic's supposed to be here any minute – if . . .'

She trailed off, not wishing to appear rude, not wanting to suggest that Vic's presence could be the only reason Joe might have come round. Couples who hang out together rarely know each member of the other couple individually as well as they pretend to do when in a foursome; but this is a hidden truth – and the reference to Vic, the missing lubricant, only drew attention to it, making them feel even more like strangers.

The consequent awkwardness, however, spurred Joe on. He realised that with nothing else to say, he might as well begin.

'Tess . . .' he said, the use of the name immediately drawing a web of significance around them. Her eyes narrowed, with an intimation of bad news.

'Yes?' she said after a while.

'Look . . . the thing is . . . I know what's wrong. I know what the problem is.'

Tess blinked. A weight that had been suspended inside for some time fell to the ground of her, like a cartoon anvil.

'Right,' she said. Again, a silence. Joe grimaced internally. I'm not very good at this, he thought.

'Well – I just wanted to say – I'm here. You know. If you need – someone to talk to. I might be able to help.'

Tess put her whisky to her mouth. The tumbler covered her nose too, and for a while she left it there, trying to lose herself in the overpowering scent of alcohol. Then, she drank it down in one go.

'Did Vic tell you, then?' she said, leaning back, and speaking with a certain resigned grimness.

'Um . . . no.' Joe wasn't sure, at this stage, if he should tell her how he'd found out; he wasn't sure if it showed him in a very good light.

She looked up.

'No? So what – something you saw? Something you noticed?'

Joe nodded. Tess gave a short, melancholy laugh – just a breath out through her nose – and got up, returning a second later with a bottle of Jim Beam.

'Another one?' she said.

'Thanks.'

She filled his glass, a larger measure this time, and then her own, larger still.

'How have you been feeling?' said Joe.

Tess shook her head, and shrugged her shoulders.

'I dunno. Confused . . . tired . . . more depressed than usual . . .'

Joe nodded again, appreciatively. Tess stopped, and looked at him sharply.

'Why have you come here?' she said, frowning. 'Isn't that . . .' and here she laughed again, more bitterly, '. . . a *betrayal of trust*?'

Joe thought this was an odd way of putting it; but then he would expect a certain behavioural distortion, primarily in expression.

And, anyway, on a professional level, she was right.

'Well . . . yes. I suppose so. But seeing as you are . . .' he broke off, unsure how to pitch this; but then the whisky pushed him forward, '. . . someone I care about – you know – I just figured that was more important.'

Tess met his eyes: *someone I care about*. Really? she thought. She looked at him, quantitatively. Joe's physiognomy had always, to her, spoken of his sexlessness. It was all somewhats, Joe's face: a somewhat flat nose, somewhat blue eyes, somewhat firm chin, somewhat acne-scarred skin, somewhat high forehead – it had no extremes, and Tess liked extremes. Before Vic, she'd had a tendency to go out with ugly men, or at least, men who were deemed ugly because their faces were dominated by an extreme feature – a long nose, enormous eyes, an over-wide mouth. But they were men who wore this ugliness well; who by combining it with cool clothes and a confident attitude had managed to suggest, somehow, that their ugliness was attractive – a strategy that patriarchy has made open only to men. Joe's face, she thought, looked like it was missing something, like it was crying out for something; and once, in a passing glance,

173

it had come to her what it was: glasses. But now, readjusting her estimation of him – as we do when someone we've never thought about sexually before suddenly says something to us that could be interpreted as flirtatious – she wondered if that had been unfair; if it was just a thing she'd thought because she knew he was a scientist.

The phone rang, shaking her from her reverie. She knew straight away who it would be, and was surprised at how little she had been thinking about him in the past few minutes, as if Joe's visit had punctured her obsession.

'Hello? Well, well . . .' She looked at Joe significantly. He gestured towards the door, asking in mime whether he should leave. She shook her head.

'Has it now . . .' she said. 'What's the problem this time?' She looked out of the window, at the London Underground symbol on the station opposite, and remembered idly how as a young, bright child she'd thought of it as a cross-section of Saturn. 'So, what – you just going to stay home? OK. Yeah. Whatever.' Her eyes met Joe's again. 'No, nothing. No, I'm fine. Of course. As ever. Yeah, speak to you tomorrow. By-ee.' This last in a sardonic singsong. She replaced the receiver, deliberately.

'Guess who?'

Joe shrugged. He wondered if Tess had always been this sharp with him. He wouldn't have thought Vic could be fucked with the effort of a high-maintenance woman. But maybe she hadn't always been like this: it could be another symptom, aggression.

'Vic?' he said.

Tess nodded. 'Apparently, his bike's broken down again. He's only just got home and doesn't want to risk coming out again. Convenient, isn't it, that bike?' Joe shook his head, suggesting he didn't know. 'Someone in the street gave him a push. Yeah, right.'

'So – you've talked to Vic about . . . what's been happening?' Joe still couldn't quite bring himself to say the words.

174

'No! Well. Not really. I've tried to hint that something's wrong – that there's a problem – but he doesn't seem to take any notice.'

'Why don't you just come out with it?'

She clicked her tongue against the roof her mouth. 'I dunno. Frightened, maybe – frightened of the truth. Frightened that, basically, he's not that bothered about me anyway.'

Joe frowned. 'God, I know he can seem kind of . . . wrapped up in himself. But I'm sure – I know he loves you.' He didn't know that, but felt it was the right thing to say.

Tess sighed, and found herself again thinking like a woman. Only a man – she could hardly believe that she could ever think a sentence beginning with those words – only a man would think that it was possible to treat her as Vic clearly was treating her, and still be in love with her.

'Sorry,' said Joe, whose brow had been knitted for some short while, 'there's something here I don't quite understand.'

Tess did the laughy breath out through her nose again. 'Me too.'

'No, I mean – you asked me before . . . if I knew – y'know – what I know – because Vic had told me.'

'Yeah?'

'But . . . now you just said you haven't really spoken to him about it.'

Tess was feeling a bit tired of all this now. 'So?'

'Um . . . so how could he possibly have told me?'

Tess shook her head from side to side, slowly. 'What?'

'How could he have told me, if you haven't told him?'

Tess blinked at him. Why, she wondered, have I sometimes prided myself on thinking like a man? Clearly, they are all cretins. 'Because, Joe . . .' she said, her voice deeply sarcastic, mimicking the speech rhythms of a primary school teacher addressing the slowest pupil in the lowest stream, 'he's the one *causing the problem*. He's the one responsible. He's fucking *doing* it.'

175

Part of Joe thought that this might be more confusion: a not entirely unprecedented – he'd read about something similar in a neurological journal – tendency to blame someone close by for the onset of her condition. And another part of him thought he'd better just ask the obvious question.

'Doing . . . what exactly?'

Tess stared at him, sat back, and in the same movement drew her glass to her mouth again; then slowly, leadenly, shut her eyes. She took a deep breath, in and out. 'Fucking. Someone. Else,' she intoned, without opening her eyes.

Joe was glad her eyes were closed; he knew his face had flushed. 'Tess . . . I don't know anything about—'

'What have we been talking about?' Her eyes were open now, and if Joe hadn't been embarrassedly getting up, he might have noticed a hint of laughter in them.

'Look, maybe I'd better go.'

She put a restraining hand on his leg.

'Joe. Really. What is it that you came round here to tell me tonight?' His head was turning around in small, quick movements, like a chicken's. 'When you said "I know what's wrong",' she continued, 'what did you mean?'

He sat down again, puffing his cheeks out. 'Tess, I'm fucked if I know whether Vic's having an affair.'

'I gathered that.'

'I . . . Listen . . . have you had any tests recently?'

'Tests? What – like driving ones? Latin grammar ones?'

'No – more like medical ones.'

She screwed up her face, looking suddenly girlish. 'No,' she said, shaking her head. 'A check-up six months ago. That's it.'

Joe held his palms up to her. 'In that case, I've just made a really stupid mistake. Really. Let's forget this ever happened.'

'But why—'

'Your name came up on a computer at work, one that traces biopsy samples. For a malignant tumour. A *very* malignant tumour.'

Tess opened her eyes wide. 'Shit.'

'I say, your name – I mean, obviously, somebody with the same name: Tessa Carroll. It's just – well, the age was about right as well, and even the middle name . . .'

'Octavia?' said Tess, incredulously.

'Well, no, the computer just gave us the initial – O – but when I saw that I just got it into my head that it had to be you. I knew – ' his fingers swirled round and round, trying to express all the conditionals – 'I knew if it had've been you, you would've had the results back by now, and seeing as I know a thing or two about, y'know, all that, I thought I'd come round and see if I could help.' Joe's arms dropped to the side of the chair. 'Now I just feel like a complete berk.'

Tess, who had used the opportunity of the short pause to take another sip, felt the whisky go into her mouth, and at the same time her gullet start to tremble. She let her cheeks fill with the whisky, and looked at the ground.

'What?' said Joe. Tess put her hand out, palm upward. She was shaking. 'What is it?' he said, more insistently. She pointed at her mouth, and made over-elaborate arching gestures with her hand.

'Hmmm-mmmm! Hmmm!'

'*What?*'

Finally, she grabbed her glass, still half-full, and opened her mouth close to it. 'Paaaaa!' she said, as the brown oily liquid spilled back in. 'Oh! Hahahahaha! Haaaaa!'

Joe smiled gawkily, trying to look comfortable: hysterics are always awkward for the bemused onlooker. His earlobe was red raw.

'Haha – oh – I'm sorry Joe, I really am – ' She gulped the air, almost hiccuping, and half straightened. 'But – ah – it's been a long time since I've heard anyone unironically use the word "berk".' Joe nodded, happy enough to accept the buffoon's mantle. 'And – oh dear – ' she continued, wiping her eyes with her fingers, 'the thing is, the way you looked – so crestfallen – so *stuck* after all your seriousness – it was just such a perfect

177

description. You did seem like such a berrraahhahahhaha . . .'

This time, she let her body fall sideways on to the other end of the sofa. She's pissed, thought Joe, as Tess lay there, shivering. Arseholed. Childish self-pity welled up within him. I was only trying to do a good thing, he thought, and now look: laughed at. What's happened to me recently that women have got to treat me like such a . . . *berk*?

Perhaps that's why, after waiting for a momentary gap in her laughter, he said, for him, a cruel thing. 'So what makes you think Vic's having an affair?'

Tess didn't answer immediately, but gradually her body movement slowed, and the gasps and gulping punctuating her silent hysterics shrank away. For some time, she was motionless; long enough to worry Joe, who began looking at her upturned wrist, lying on the floor at the end of her floppily forgotten arm, with a view to feeling it for a pulse. Then her hand twisted around and flattened out, to push herself upwards. Joe, his senses heightened, felt he could feel the rough carpet graze her soft palm. She sat up at right angles and looked at him through screwed-up eyes, like a waking woman.

'How pissed are you?' she said.

Joe raised an eyebrow. 'Not as much as you.'

Tess's face remained impassive. 'Correct. But nonetheless . . .' she paused, '. . . somewhat?'

Joe smiled, and did two slow nods. 'Somewhat.'

Tess looked him up and down, and then looked to the window; rain had started to hit the outer glass, blurring the London Underground symbol, making it look even more like Saturn surrounded by a soft, gaseous blue ring.

'So looks like you won't be driving home, then,' she said, without looking back.

JOE

Sometimes you don't know how you ended up somewhere. Sometimes, you don't know it short-term: how you got home from the pub, how you made it through the turnstiles with five minutes to spare, how you finished up on the hard shoulder. And sometimes – less often – you don't know it long-term: how it happened that one minute you were a schoolkid, with a nose so runny, and socks falling into your shoes, and the next you're presenting spreadsheets on display boards and having affairs with women who wear blue dress-suits.

And sometimes you don't know it short-term *or* long-term: like how you ended up in bed with your best mate's girlfriend.

But Joe did know how it happened. He had been drunk, of course, but that was no excuse. A cliché, but true as well, in Joe's case: it was no excuse. People never completely lose themselves when they drink. People never completely lose themselves whatever they try to do to completely lose themselves – drink, or take drugs, or mentally break down: they do it on their own terms, in their own way. Vic on coke would be coked up in a Vic way, Emma's mum had Alzheimer's in an Emma's mum way, and Joe got drunk that night in a Joe way – that is, at no point was he unaware of what was going on, and he was never out of control. Part of him was always watching.

179

And if Joe – a puritan at heart, with all the masochism that implies – would not allow himself the get-out, the catch-all, of drunkenness, what excuses were left to him? He rifled his mind to find one, driving back towards Greenwich along the Old Kent Road, as dawn cracked over London.

He had, to be fair, remained frozen in his seat following Tess's comment about driving home: he had not, as some men would have on such an invitation, gone straight over to the sofa to cover her mouth with his. But then neither had he, as other men would have – the other men in whose Venn diagram Joe had always imagined himself centred – got up awkwardly, made some remark about catching a cab, and left hurriedly. Instead he had waited, waited while the world moved around him; waited, while Tess got up, took his hand and led him silently, solemnly, towards the bedroom.

Approaching Blackheath, he stopped by a pedestrian crossing. The lights were red, but there didn't seem to be anyone about to cross, just the system playing up, morning ghosts pressing silver buttons to light up green men. He waited for them to flash amber before pulling off; he was still operating within the law.

There was, he supposed, the dark excuse, the male cry *but my wife won't have sex with me any more*. Joe felt a bit more comfortable with this one, perhaps because, like all moralists, he was given to self-justification (paradoxically, despite the fact that they get up to much more in the way of wickedness, only the amoral feel no need to explain themselves). And, unquestionably, he had felt the first impact of Tess's nakedness, of her flesh on his, as something desperately needed, desperately missed. He had felt it, and was surprised, surprised by how much relief was generated, as when the intensity of relief felt by a junkie after a fix makes them recognise with a jolt how deeply they were in withdrawal.

But when he thought about that feeling, that moment of high relief, when he, in counsellor-speak, *unpacked* it, he realised that it happened, and it passed – leaving behind a deep trace of peace

– and then there was more: at which point Tess stopped being purely a substitute for Emma, a proxy filling her space within Joe's own yearning pit of desire, and became exactly the opposite – a site of *difference* from her. Not a site of comparison, because comparison implies judgement, and what Joe was after was pure difference: the good and the bad lay together unmarked in his apprehension of this. And so his thinking, his sexual thinking, as the night moved on, included no 'buts' or 'althoughs' – Tess's skin was harder and sandier than Emma's, her breasts were larger and more rounded, her pubes hairier and darker, her responses louder and more linguistic. All difference, for Joe, became a focus of excitement, as if he didn't care what the difference was, and the more extreme the difference, the more intense his excitement. He magnified them as if looking at slides of Tess and Emma through the *Grey Lady* – Tess's belly button pushed out instead of in, a whorl where Emma's was a dimple; her vagina had less symmetry to it, a rent in the earth of her, and filled his cupped hand more fully; she insisted on using condoms – as a matter of course, she said, she still used them with Vic – whereas Emma, drawn to myths of passion and immediacy, found them revolting; and where Emma's smell, even her close-up smell, was elusive, like a pastel colouring to the air, Tess's was so definite it felt like you could cut it into cubes around her – it had body and length and tar and pepper and all the things Joe thought she must talk about at her wine tastings. He wondered where he might have wanted difference to stop; if Tess had turned out to be a man, perhaps.

He realised, as he turned into Greenwich High Street, that he was no longer thinking of excuses at all; he was simply reliving, and re-relishing, the night. There were no excuses – only self-questioning and the muddying undertow of guilt. Guilt, unsurprisingly perhaps, began to prevail more as he approached their house; so much so that as he drove up to the front gate, there seemed nothing strange – it seemed only just and natural – about finding a police car waiting for him.

VIC

_____

Vic took off his clothes quietly, not wanting to wake up Tess. It was Wednesday morning. He had felt an unusual sharpness in Tess's attitude when he'd phoned to explain why he hadn't made it over last night, almost as if she hadn't believed his excuse about the Lambretta. As usual, he'd dismissed worrying about it soon after putting the phone down, but in the morning he woke early, obsessively wakeful, and thought he should maybe make a renewed effort with her. The thought of her brought relief, the sort of relief that comes when, after contemplating drastic change, you go back to what you know. After all, a chapter in his life was over now.

Not wishing to risk the bike, he'd taken the tube to Lambeth North. On the seats opposite him, amidst the rump of passengers left over from the rush hour, an old American couple, he bearded and overweight, she spectacled and overtanned, sat together; sharing their laps was an open tourist map, stuccoed with colourful drawings at the requisite co-ordinates – a smiling Beefeater, a jaunty Houses of Parliament, a deliberately out-of-scale St Paul's Cathedral. As they talked over their prospective day out in Tom and Jerry London, Vic felt a tug of sentiment, the compulsive philanderer's occasional attraction to the idea of monogamy. Knowing nothing of this couple, he felt sure

182

they must be like the aged twosomes who are interviewed documentary style in *When Harry Met Sally*, men and women who, long ago, resigned into each other, unfrightened of contentment, swimming side by side out into the still sea of peace.

He'd expected to find Tess up and working in her small study at the back of the flat, e-mailing to vineyards across the world, the window above her computer overlooking its view of wall; but after he'd let himself in – the doorbell having remained unanswered – he'd found her like this, still fast asleep in bed.

He put his clothes in a pile on the black wood of the floor, still keeping as quiet as possible; something about the idea of just slipping into bed with her without her knowing conformed well with his new-found monogamous resolve. Gingerly, he lifted the right half of her white duvet and got in, moving sideways along towards her. Vic's lanky thin body always fitted well around the long curve of Tess's, the two of them lying together on their sides like crafted parts of a kit. More's the pity that I can never lie like this all night, thought Vic, as he felt himself dock with her, his right hand snaking between her breasts to rest on her shoulder; perhaps I can now that I've managed it with – but it was best to avoid thinking about her. Tess moaned the moan of the barely woken, and threw an arm backwards to lie along his flank. Vic felt soothed, and in his mind he turned over this feeling, tasting it as Tess professionally tasted wine, over-tasting it, concentrating hard on its deliciousness, the deliciousness of an intimacy that allowed him to come round and get into bed with this woman without invitation. How lovely, he thought, that even in her sleep she knows who it is; such familiarity, such ease. Already, he assumed, her irritation of yesterday had dispersed.

On the other side of the bed, Tess's eyes opened wide, straight wide from closed, cutting out the mid-position of squint, despite the light breaking through her muslin curtains.

'Vic?' she said.

'Hmmm . . . ?'

183

She turned over. Her face and his had that closeness of lovers' faces in bed together, where the features of the other dilate enormously, like the heads on Easter Island. He kissed her, gently; her breath smelt musky, a mixture of sleep and, he guessed, drink from the night before.

'How long have you been here?'

'Five minutes . . .'

'Really . . . ?' She raised herself up to look over him, at the clock on the bedside table. 'Oh . . .' she said, touching her forehead, movement suddenly making her head ache.

'You OK?'

'Yeah . . .'

'Hungover?'

'Hmm. Possibly. What time is it?'

Vic turned and looked at the clock. '10.15.'

'Oh fuck—'

'It's OK,' said Vic, turning back, and encasing her in his arms. 'Stay in bed a bit.'

He had expected her to melt, but her body remained stiff in his arms.

'Vic. Let me just get up and get some Nurofen . . .'

He unlocked his hands from behind her back. She threw the duvet back and walked towards the door, grabbing a long white T-shirt and pulling it over her head as she went; the material covered the back of her in a swoop, coming down like the shutter in a Soho booth.

In the bathroom, Tess saw herself in the mirror, the same mirror that her self-image had crumbled in the night before. I look the same as yesterday, she thought. Things have changed, and yet I look the same. She scrutinised herself more intensely, bringing her face closer, seeking out changes. Perhaps, she thought, I could stop myself growing old by continually looking in the mirror. No one ever sees the ageing process, she reasoned. It only happens in jumps, in shocks – suddenly you notice a patch of grey hair; one day a wrinkle below the eye; in a moment, in a shop mirror, a stoop. So if, maybe, there was a way in which you could constantly look at yourself, perhaps you would never die.

She turned to the bathroom cabinet and saw another image of herself – still the same, she thought – which moved away as she opened it to take out a small bottle. She shut the cabinet. *Still the same.* She lifted a hand to her face, trying to smell herself, or rather, trying to smell if she smelt of someone else. Perhaps I should have a shower, she thought. But then she heard Vic say something.

'What?' she said, coming back into the bedroom, an enamel bathroom mug in her right hand and two red pills in her left. Vic had propped himself up on the headboard with her pillow.

'I said, since when do you get drunk on your own?'

She took the pills. Their sugar coating tasted sweet on her tongue, subduing the sour film left by drunken sleep. She downed the tap water, hungrily. 'Since you decided to fuck me off by standing me up on some stupid excuse,' she said, wiping her mouth.

'Oh *Tess* . . .'

'What?'

'I thought you'd forgiven me for that.'

'Did you. Why?'

'Because you seemed pleased when you realised I'd got into bed.'

Tess looked at him. I didn't realise it was you, she thought. Vic's remark, however, made her think twice about her annoyance, focusing the fact that she didn't hold all the high moral cards any more, and her next comment, though still argumentative, was said in a softer tone.

'Yes, well . . . I was half asleep. I'd forgotten about last night.'

Vic did his best approximation of shamefaced – a tough one, as shame was missing from his genetic starter pack.

'I'm sorry. I really am. But the bike really did go down on me.'

'Just the bike?' said Tess.

Vic frowned, questioningly, and remained silent, computing that this was most in line with the reaction of the genuinely innocent.

'Oh fuck off,' said Tess. 'Please don't give me that face. In fact, don't give me anything. I'm not really prepared to have this conversation.' She turned away towards the bedroom window, listlessly lifting one of the muslin curtains. Outside, London pulsed like her head. When the floorboards behind her creaked, she didn't turn round, although it could have meant Vic had gathered up his things and was leaving; but she guessed otherwise, and then couldn't help the wave of reassurance swelling inside her when she felt his hand on her hair.

She turned and immediately his lips met her lips, hard. She accepted them, and their mouths opened together into one of those kisses that are like a veto, designed to override problematic moments in a relationship. They held the kiss, for a long time, as if they didn't want to face what might lie on the other side of it.

Tess's eyes were the first to open on hearing the telephone ring. She watched Vic's lids rise, revealing his black pupils, a dark laughter swilling about in them. Too close to gesticulate facially, they tried to communicate purely through iridology, widening and contracting their eyes. Still with their mouths glued together, Vic shook his head, moving hers; but this made her start to laugh, breaking the fixed line of their kiss. She moved away, towards the phone on the bedside table. Vic clutched at her T-shirt, lifting it like a sail towards him, but she carried on, forcing it to drop away from his pinching fingers.

She sat down on the bed and reached for the receiver; before her hand could get it, Vic had dived on to the mattress behind her and grabbed it himself.

'The person you are trying to call is presently unavailable, or on another call,' he said, in a high polite feminine voice. Tess's eyes glowered, and she put her hand into a 'don't you dare' fist; he pushed her away with his palm, grinning. He would go through with this, and then take the phone off the hook, and she would forgive him for it. But, after a second, his grin tapered at the edges.

'. . . Joe?' he said. Tess felt her stomach dip.

'Yeah. No. Sorry, I was just pissing about. Are you OK?'

Oh Christ, thought Tess. He's phoned already. This is going to get complicated.

JEROME

London is more green than grey. There are more square miles of parkland in London than in any other city in the world. And so many park styles: the cropped, this-is-what-a-park-should-be precision of Regent's; the Northumbrian wilderness of Hampstead Heath; the flat plains of Battersea and Hyde; the eccentric safari of Richmond – as if, over the years, each generation of urban planners, driven to distraction by realising that the city they had created was gradually becoming a monster, was becoming the City, the archetype of the metropolis, had tried to do their bit to keep it in check by cramming it with countryside, every variety of countryside.

As a result of this neurosis, some parks have been built very close to the city. Not 'very close' in the sense of outside the city, but only just; 'very close' in the sense that some parks have only a tiny buffer between themselves and the roaring concrete: some parks have been built very close to the *road*. That's why they are products of neurosis. They shouldn't even be there. They're just there because the anxious urban planners saw a pygmy space between this corner of the conurbation and that, and said 'Oh! oh! yes! We can *just* fit in another park there!'

Gladstone Heath is one of those parks. It runs half the length of Denmark Hill on one side and Ferndene Road on the other.

These are not the quiet arterioles that surround, say, Regent's Park, cushioning it from Marylebone and Euston, and providing the park-leaver with a graduated walk-through back to urban life – these are big fuck-off thoroughfares, municipal freeways full of whiz-past traffic: these are *main* roads. Which is why Gladstone Heath has a tough time sustaining the 'you're in the countryside' illusion that is the duty of the park; and has been forced, for the sake of its joggers and bird-feeders and bench-sitters, to dampen down the city the only way it can, by erecting around most of its perimeter a ten-foot-high enclosing brick wall.

Jerome Abbott liked to sit most days on the third bench along from the Denmark Hill entrance, facing away from the wall. Some local people assumed he must be a loony, not for any of the usual reasons – he didn't wear a bobble hat and women's glasses, or shout at visions – but because he was so often in the same place. 'That bloke was in the park again, darling,' they might say to their loved ones on returning home, assuming that he must therefore be there every day, and not that serendipity might have led to him being there on exactly the same days as them, and he was presently at home saying precisely the same thing to *his* loved one about them. He wasn't, as it happened. He did use Gladstone Heath more often than most people, but would not have recognised others around him, as he found the park, and especially this bench, conducive to going into a trance-like state, in which nothing touched him. For Jerome, nothing touching him meant not only that he was undisturbed; it also meant that he was touched by nothing, as others might say that someone was touched by madness, that is, in the grip of madness. Jerome, in this park, on this bench, could find himself in the grip of nothing – possessed by the things he craved: silence, and blankness, and darkness. And besides, he didn't *have* a loved one; not any more.

Today had been a great success. He had been sitting on his bench for two hours now, keeping stuff out of his head. It was a two-pronged battle – he had to keep out the stuff outside his head – noises, light, voices – and he had to keep out the stuff inside his head – memories, feelings, voices. That was why he came to the park, because the stuff inside his head was too powerful when he stayed in his browning flat on Beckwith Road; but in the park the stuff outside his head was louder, and sharper, and itchier. He was winning, though. Inside, he had built the same kind of wall around himself that enclosed Gladstone Heath. He imagined looking at the scene from above and seeing the park and then his head as concentric circles of oases.

But just when he really thought he'd got there – when he was just about to hit the plateau of nothing – he was disturbed. First it was a sound, opening up his closed-down senses. He had no problem, usually, with the background blare of tyre and exhaust, but this was different, because it wasn't background. Background sound is characterised by monotone, by constancy of level. That's how you can relegate it to not existing at all, because you can trick the brain that it sounds like nothing, that it *is* nothing.

Jerome had so tricked his brain that he didn't notice the sound until quite late. At what point does background sound – in this case, traffic – become foreground sound? An engine revving, a rush of acceleration, two or three horns sounding together – none of these were enough to disturb him. These were under-the-line sounds, sounds that his consciousness did not have to process, everyday road rage easily dispersible in the melt of background sound. Then a screech of either tyres or brakes, like a car turning at right angles at speed. A *screech* – a sound made only by animals and the cars named after them – indicates alarm, enough for most people in the park to look round, registering something wrong, something coming out of the background; but still not enough to penetrate Jerome's inner ear. It didn't break his trance.

But the crash did. It broke through his wall even as it broke through the park's. Because all the revving and honking and screeching had stayed below the level of his perception, Jerome at first lacked a narrative for the crash sound, and therefore could not compute what it might be, thinking perhaps that a meteorite had landed, or that a terrorist bomb had gone off nearby. He felt he should get up and run, but couldn't work out in which direction, as he had no awareness that the crash had come from behind him, from the road. The sound itself provided no clue, as it appeared to be coming from all directions.

The crash was so loud he felt he might never be able to shut off his sense of sound again; the door to sound was a write-off for Jerome, hanging off its hinges. But before he had a chance to really worry about it, his other senses started over-responding, responding wildly to all these stimuli, as if he had had them turned down for too long. He felt himself showered in a cloud of heat and dust, the heat opening up his skin in blisters for the dust to settle in; his nose twitched to the burnt cake smell of the worsted fibres of his overcoat – or was it his own hair? – singeing.

By this time he'd worked out that the thing, whatever it was, was happening behind him. Don't turn round, he thought, through the pain. Don't. Jerome had smelt some bad smells, and heard some bad sounds, and felt some bad pains – taken together, the reason why he sat in this park every day playing Tommy – but he knew that sights were the worst. The bad sight was the thing outside your head that once you saw it – once you gave it access – stayed inside your head for a long long time, and he really wanted to avoid that. He could see a small crowd gathering about twenty yards in front of him, shielding their eyes and pointing beyond him; now that his ears were open, he could hear that some of them were crying, and one of them was trying to call an ambulance on a mobile phone. Don't turn round. A young man in tracksuit bottoms ran halfway towards him, gesturing, trying to get him to come away from the bench.

Slowly, he started to get up. He didn't have many dealings

with people any more, and it felt strange to be included, to be wooed like this to become part of a group. He felt beside him for his thermos, and then saw that it had fallen to the ground between the grass and the concrete of the jogging path. He bent down to pick it up. The cries of the crowd appeared to be getting louder. Don't turn round, they seemed to be saying to him too. But as he bent down, the corner of his upturned eye caught the bottom edge of the sight, a shaft of burning metal, a semicircle of shattered glass, many bricks, and, terribly, an arm, a bare arm with silver bangles on its wrist, lying on the ground. It was too late then. He knew that his mind, planted with nightmare, would take this bottom edge and build on it – it would grow from the bottom up like a figure energising in *Star Trek*, his favourite programme when he used to watch TV. The whole scene was already imprinting on his virtual memory. He might as well turn round.

He picked up the thermos and put it into his coat pocket. With a weighted air, and a sense of resignation – all those years turning his face from bad sights, to waste, to waste – he turned round. But what he saw – the caved-in remains of a burning Renault Clio, diagonally lifted on what was left of a section of a park wall, and the figure of a woman thrown a few yards from it, covered in glass like she was lying under a sheet of diamonds – he saw only for an infinitesimal moment, maybe not long enough for it to lodge for ever in his mind – maybe he was to be spared it after all – because next second there was a blinding flash, and after that Jerome Abbott saw only the darkness he'd always wanted.

JOE

Joe sat on the sofa for a long time after the police had gone
– long enough for the day to grow bright, and the house to
look strange from the outside with the curtains shut. Later he
realised he was exhausted, and thought about going upstairs to
bed, but still couldn't bring himself to move, having created by
non-movement a sense that he was in a dream, and knowing
that movement would make it clear he was not; so he took off
his clothes where he was, and lay on the sofa. But then he found
he couldn't sleep: and then, in contrast to his previous stasis, he
found himself restlessly moving, trying to bring all parts of his
body into contact with all parts of the sofa, trying to drown
himself in it – pushing his fingers down into the space between
the cushions, his face into the arms, his knees into the springs.
Somewhere in here was another space and time.

He didn't know how to feel. He didn't know how to feel,
not because that's what people say when faced with sudden
tragedy, but because he was faced with too many feelings, with
an overload of feelings, not all of them pointing the same way:
some seemed to cancel others out. Even the exhaustion was
confusing. An ordinary person, in stress, may feel tired, and
may finally succumb to sleep, as a way out; but Joe knew that
he wasn't exhausted because he was stressed – he was exhausted

because he'd spent the night with Tess, and now to succumb to that exhaustion felt evil.

Eventually, he sat back up again, thinking that he should go and see Jackson, who was asleep upstairs: he hadn't cried all morning, sleep and baby ignorance cocooning him from fact. The police had found Toni, already distraught at this new instance of Emma's lateness, alone in the house when they had arrived yesterday, and had sent her home soon after breaking the news; the policewoman, a mother of two, quickly reassuring her, in a businesslike no-nonsense fashion, that she would look after the baby. I must go and make sure he's OK, Joe thought. But then the idea of Jackson frightened him, he didn't know why – perhaps because of the flood of sadness that might flow out of him on seeing shards of Emma in Jackson's face, or perhaps because the sight of his baby brought with it an insight into his baby's future, rendered so uncertain now, so pregnant with potential damage. Or perhaps because at some level he still blamed Jackson for the problems between him and Emma, problems that might in some way have been responsible for her death.

Her death. The language the policeman and policewoman had used had whirled around the words – the policeman's formal, 'an accident', 'the impact', 'secondary explosion', 'a witness knocked unconscious', the policewoman's colloquial and concerned, 'tragedy', 'senseless waste', 'felt no pain' – but neither had actually said the sentence *your wife is dead*. Strangely, for such important news, it was something he had to garner, to piece together from hints and suggestions, so that the sentence formed slowly in his mind, like film titles, like white words which then dissolved in a black screen. Except in his mind the words were *my wife is dead*.

I shouldn't be on my own, he thought. But that was confused too. The last thing the policewoman had said was: 'Is there anyone you can call?' No, Joe said, he wanted, for the moment, to be alone. But he didn't really want to be alone; he said he did, because he didn't know who to call. He thought about calling Vic, his best friend, but he'd just spent the night with Tess and he felt guilt towards Vic about that. Guilt towards Vic? What about guilt towards Emma? That was guilt which now could never be assuaged. All through his drive, through his search for excuses, there'd been a background soundtrack in his head, and it had been the sound of his eventual confession to Emma, a confession he felt certain he would have to make at some stage. Now he would never make it. Or rather, he would always be making it: but never know whether or not she would grant him absolution.

He looked at the phone on the table beside the sofa, the old Bakelite number they had bought together at Greenwich Market one Sunday afternoon two years ago, after lying in late and teasing each other all morning about how they had vowed to go shopping today. For a while, Joe knew, every household item, every place he went, every person he saw, would carry this type of addendum, a footnote bursting out of the page of memory detailing Emma's involvement in it. For a while. Or maybe for longer than that.

He could see, through the crack in the curtains, that it was a glorious day. A glorious day: he realised that his life from now on would be like that of a lover on a solitary journey, who on seeing, through a train or plane window, a beautiful sight – the sea, a crimson sun, a heron – feels only melancholy at the absence of the loved one to share it with. He turned his eyes away from the hateful light, back towards the phone. The adjacent answerphone was blinking: two messages. One of them, he knew already. Fighting the weight that seemed to be hanging off it, he raised his arm over the edge of the sofa and pressed the quarter of the circular button at the bottom of the machine that said PLAY. 'Tuesday. 6.20 p.m.,' said the metallic woman who lived inside. Darting across his fear and suspense Joe felt a mundane thought – Toni must have failed to get it last night: probably upstairs looking after Jackson. The tape whirred on. He heard the click of their – his – phone pick up, and then the soft white noise wash of an open line with no one speaking; in the far background, traffic noise, in the foreground, perhaps, perhaps, someone breathing, still breathing. Please, he thought, if it is you, say something – just something, allow me to hear your voice one more time – but then – how unthinking the sound, so unaware of its cruelty in the face of the information brought by this new day – the tap of the receiver being replaced, and the needless four seconds of dial tone. 'Tuesday, 6.50 p.m.,' the woman said, and Joe, who knew what was coming, thought for a second that he could hear in her voice an element of reproach.

'Hi, darling – don't pick up – it's just me calling to say that I've got something I've got to do tonight – kind of a work thing . . . kind of.' He was on his mobile: in the background he could hear the Volvo's loud sensible chug. It must have been ten minutes before he got to Tess's flat. 'I'll explain when I get back. Might be late, I dunno.' Then, a pause; Joe remembered making the decision to say the next thing. 'Love you, 'bye.' Click, burr.

He hated that pause now, the fact that he'd had to think before telling her he loved her, and in such a small way, the way that husbands and wives on answerphones do. But that was what had given him pause: the feeling that 'Love you, 'bye' was meaningless – worse than meaningless – opposite almost, in its easy sayability, its reflexiveness, to a passionate, spontaneous declaration of love. He remembered Vic saying something about that once.

It was a very Joe sort of message, completely unredolent of deceit. He'd had no intention of ending up an adulterer when he'd left work last night, but he had decided not to tell Emma about his mercy mission to see Tess – not before speaking to Tess, or at least before finding out if the 'Tessa Carroll' on his computer was their friend. But despite having said the message in innocence, Joe felt now that he could hear in it, somewhere, bad intention; he felt he could hear his voice echoey, disguising within it a sneer and a laugh, like a stage villain's.

He looked at the machine, still flicking in twos and twos. On the drive home it had occurred to him more than once that he would have to explain this message when he got back, find a new explanation for what the 'kind of a work thing' was. How drastically have I been let off that hook, he thought grimly.

His hand wandered apathetically from the answerphone to the phone. His put his index finger in a random number hole, and pulled the dial forward. Why had they bought this old piece of shit, he suddenly thought angrily, so hard to work: his finger felt like it was about to break with the effort of heaving round the plastic disc. And then, as soon as it had come, the anger vanished, and Joe felt instantly alone, seriously alone, and knew that the policewoman had been right, that he had to call somebody. Who, though? He knew who he *wanted* to call. He wanted to call someone who would come round and give him comfort and reassurance and hold him until the shock and the fear and the guilt had gone: he wanted, in other words, to call Emma. And so perhaps it was not surprising that when he did, finally, dial a number, it was that of the person who already – when he had left her house the previous night – had begun to replace Emma in his subconscious.

Philosophers have often argued about which is the more powerful, eros or thanatos, sex or death. Clearly, on a simple level, sex wins hands down; at least, if we consider them, as Freud did, as two opposing instincts. As an instinct, death holds little pull; who feels the *instinct*, for example, to pop upstairs for a quick suicide (surely the closest thing in death's canon to masturbation)? Only adolescents, and even most of them are *mainly* indulging in the latter.

The scene in Joe's house after Vic and Tess arrived bears further witness to the power of sex over death. Sex, of course, will infiltrate the consciousness at all times, and at all levels. There is a tired old comedy trope about men trying to think of specifically unsexual things during sex in order to ward off orgasm; less spoken about, however, is the opposite – the tendency to think about sex during specifically unsexual things: for example funerals or, in this case, the immediate aftermath of death.

Now, to be fair to all the parties in this case, the encroachment of sex into their thoughts at this time should not be seen in the same light as that of a sexually incontinent teenager in the same situation. Sex could hardly not be in their thoughts. What was difficult, especially for Joe, was the weakness of death in the face of it. He had not expected Vic to be at Tess's when he called, and the thought of his presence – '*we'll* come round straight away,' he had said – troubled Joe when he put the phone down, but only for a second, because he assumed that seeing Tess and Vic together so soon after he'd slept with her wouldn't matter now, it wouldn't even occur to him.

But it did occur to him. Virtually as soon as they arrived, because the motions of comfort cut so confusingly across the plane of the motions of sex. Vic hugged Joe first, and even in that moment, even as he could hear Vic saying he was sorry, he was so so sorry, there was a problem – he couldn't dissolve completely in this, his friend's hug, because over Vic's shoulder he could see Tess standing on his doorstep, framed by the marbled blue of a flecked-with-clouds sky, and in her expression, amidst all the concern and care and sympathy, he recognised just an atom, ineradicable, imperceptible no doubt to Tess, of knowingness. And then *they* hugged, and that knowingness was there still, even without her expression, just in the quality of the touch; Joe could feel between them a recognition of the *irony* of this contact, so different in context, and yet so similar in the pure positioning of their bodies, to how they had aligned themselves in the night just gone.

And now they all sat together in the living-room, Vic and Tess on the sofa, and Joe on the armchair opposite, talking, over cups of hot sweet tea made by Tess, talking about the accident, about Emma, about what had to be done, about the unbelievability of it all, about care for Jackson, about how there could be no God, talking – and Joe didn't know whether it was just him, or whether they all felt it, but something was wrong. He wasn't completely *there*, none of them were: it wasn't what it should be, a space where pure feeling crashes from one commiserator to another, outpouring from one and rebounding off another like a stormy sea in a walled harbour. Another agenda, a cooler, more metropolitan agenda, blocked his way to that space, blocked it via the terrible tyranny of detail: detail that led elsewhere, that threw out arrows to hidden things. Early on it started, where it might be least expected, in the innuendo-less land of factual explanation:

'. . . so . . . the police were already here, when I came back last night . . .'

Came back from where? He could not say it without a flash-frame run through in his head of the naked Tess, circled around him in a hundred ways. And he so didn't want to see that now – he wanted it out of his head, to free it up for grief, for dissolution in tears, but still it would come.

And still it would not go.

'Where *was* she?' said Tess, after an interlude of silence, one of the many that punctuated this gathering. They had reached the point where inarticulate anger and sorrow was no longer appropriate; some sort of processing of the event had to begin. 'I mean, what was she doing in Denmark Hill?'

'I really don't know,' said Joe, heavily. 'Tuesdays were kind of *her* day – you know, her day off from Jackson and stuff – and so I never really knew what she did on them. I think she just went off places, saw friends . . . I dunno.'

He looked down, into his empty cup, a meniscus of brown liquid around the edges of the china circle. Tess glanced across at Vic, as if to say *help me, he's slipping away*, but he was looking down too. Eventually, she said:

'And the police said definitely – no other cars involved?'

Joe shook his head.

'God . . . that's weird. I mean, she was a good driver . . . wasn't she?'

Joe nodded. Speech seemed to be too effortful.

'Why should she just drive into the wall?'

But then he did speak.

'I think . . . I think she might have phoned.'

'When?'

'Last night. About half-six. There's a message on the machine.'

'What does it say?'

'Nothing. Just silence. And then it rings off.'

'Have you 1471'd it?' A look of gentle surprise crossed Joe's face at Tess's continued interrogation. 'Sorry, Joe . . . I don't mean . . .'

'That's OK.' He knew what Tess was doing, not wanting to let it go – continually asking questions to postpone finality, the finality of the single answer. 'No. I haven't. There's a message after it. From me.'

Another silence, another sense of coming to a dead conversational end.

'The thing I don't get,' said Joe, 'is the police said she wasn't wearing a seat belt.'

Vic looked up. Tess looked confused.

'She always wore a seat belt. *Always*. She used to get at me for being lazy about it.'

'How do they know?'

Joe looked her in the eye, and for a second there was nothing but this information between them.

'Because . . .' and here he could feel his imagination shut down, 'she was thrown clear of the car. Her body was found ten yards away.'

Tess hesitated before saying the next thing.

'I thought you said the car—'

'What was left of her body.'

Tess put her hand to her mouth, and Vic shut his eyes.

'The police were at great pains to convince me that she would have been already dead before the car exploded,' Joe continued grimly, the biochemist in him taking over.

'*Christ*,' said Vic, suddenly getting up. 'Let's not go over the details! She's dead. Does it matter exactly at what spot in that fucking park it happened? Or what she was doing half an hour before she died?'

'*Vic . . .*' said Tess.

'I mean, what are we going to find out! We *know* where and when she died! We know how long the three of us were carrying on our lives in blissful ignorance! What use is that to anyone!'

Vic stopped: he had found himself in the middle of the room, with Joe and Tess staring at him. Something about this outburst, Joe felt, was not natural – it didn't feel very Vic. But he ascribed it to the same condition he was in, where being natural seemed to have become an impossibility. Every response – the speeches, the facial expressions, the movement of head to hands – it all seemed acted in some way, learnt from other places, from books and films in which someone dies.

'Listen, maybe I should go,' said Tess, getting up.

'No . . .' said Joe.

'Well, you two are old friends, and I kind of feel . . . like I'm intruding—'

'No, I'm sorry,' said Vic, going over, his palms open in supplication. 'It's my fault.'

'Listen,' said Joe, 'why don't you both go?' They turned to him to protest. 'No, honestly, go . . . I think I want to be alone.' He meant it this time. He needed to feel pure, unadulterated loss, but the memory of last night *was* adulterating, was contaminating, and it was their presence here that was injecting the contaminating agent into his being.

Tess and Vic exchanged glances. Vic crouched down beside Joe, and took his hand. The third finger of his left hand was ringless, Tess noticed. Had he taken the ring off since he heard the news, in a sad overcast moment? Or had he taken it off last night before they'd got into bed together?

'OK . . . but if you change your mind – call us straight away,' Vic said. Joe nodded. 'And . . . look . . . maybe this is no comfort – and it's a bit of a cliché – but at least Emma died when she was at her best. I mean – when she was beautiful and bright and all the things she was. At least she's not going to end up like her mum, not knowing who she is, or where she is – just sitting out the last bit of her life next to a phone that never rings.'

Tess looked at the back of Vic's head, his black hair still messy from rushing out of bed – not that he ever combed it anyway – and felt her breath taken away by the brutality of this piece of supposed consolation. He's really misjudged it this time, she thought, as she watched Joe turn to face him, expecting any minute his features to contort with disgust; but instead, he sort of smiled, a costly, effortful smile.

'Yeah . . .' he said. Internally, Tess shook her head, flabbergasted. Vic got up, and, with a small flick of his head, gestured to her that they should leave now.

'Fuck . . .' said Joe as they were walking out. They turned to look at him sitting in the chair; his eyes were wide open in horror.

'*Sylvia* . . .' he said.

TESS

_____

'You were a bit quiet,' said Tess, as they found their way to
Sydenham blocked by a traffic jam along Dulwich Road. God:
we were there long enough for the rush hour to have started,
she thought. Although these days the rush hour in London lasts
all day; all hours are rush hour.

'Hello?' she said, when Vic didn't answer. He was looking
out of the window. Fuck: some music shop. So quickly lost to
himself and his concerns.

'Sorry?' he said, finally turning away from the window.

'I said, you were a bit quiet. Until you said that stuff at the
end about how great it is she's not going to end up like her
mother.'

He turned back to the window. 'Right . . .'

Tess clicked her tongue. The car in front, a Ford Mondeo,
moved off. Two seconds later, its red lights came on again.
Silence set in, broken only by the dry squeak of the windscreen
wipers, still going after rain. She turned them off.

'Well . . . I don't want to be mean, but at the end of the day,
Vic, you know – these aren't my friends. They're _your_ friends.
I mean – again, not wishing to sound like a hard-hearted bitch
but – basically, I hardly knew Emma. We never got close.'

'And Joe . . . ?' said Vic. Tess started inwardly: was that some kind of intimation? She looked askance at his turned-away face, but it was unreadable. She dismissed it. His bleakness of tone was no more than a mixture of depression, and weariness with this old couply issue – it always comes up in arguments, how much one partner has only been pretending to like the other's friends.

'Yeah, well . . . I like him. He's obviously a nice bloke. I feel . . . sorry for him.'

She was pleased that Vic continued to look away now, as she felt herself colouring slightly.

'All I'm saying is when an awful thing like this happens to people who are, essentially, your friends, I'd just rather not have to shoulder *all* of the emotional responsibility for it.' Twenty cars away, a traffic light changed from red to green, but such small movement as this created did not filter back to them.

'I mean, it seems clear to me. Joe is your best friend. So you've got to be there for him. It's a kind of privilege. Because it can be so difficult, you know – the etiquette of death. Especially when the person affected isn't a close friend. Or is like . . . a bit more than an acquaintance but still not a close friend. I had this once. You remember I told you about Gary, my friend from college?'

'The one who got AIDS,' said Vic flatly.

'Yes,' replied Tess, a little taken aback by the speediness of his response; she was surprised really that he was listening, and more surprised that he remembered. 'Well . . . he was like that. Well, actually, he used to be a close friend of mine, but after college we kind of lost contact. And then when I heard he had AIDS, the worst thing was . . . I didn't know how to position myself. If we'd still been close, I'd have been by his bedside; if we'd been passing acquaintances only, I'd maybe have sent a message saying how sorry I was. But I was kind of caught between two stools – I didn't want to appear heartless, but I also didn't want to be one of those people who suddenly crawls out of the woodwork from nowhere as soon as they hear somebody's terminally ill.'

She paused, wondering if she'd lost him again.

'I'm listening,' he said, but his face gave no impression of it.

'Well . . . anyway, I ended up seeing him a couple of times, and I wrote once. A difficult letter. And then about a year later I found out that he'd died.'

'Kind of . . . unsatisfactory.'

She looked at him. 'Yes. It was.' The traffic on the other side of the road moved off. Perhaps we should turn round and go another way, she thought. 'It's quite hard to imagine what it feels like. It's such a genuinely grey area. I suppose the same thing for you would have been if that bloke Ivan had died.'

Vic snorted, and turned to her at last. 'Ivan! Fuck, no. He's well below the passing acquaintance level.'

'Is he? Oh, I dunno. Who, then?'

Vic shrugged. 'I only have close friends. To me, everyone else is a cunt. Basically.'

'Charming.' She thought for a moment. 'Well – I don't know – Emma.'

Vic stared at her. 'What?'

'Don't look like that. I'm just making a point. Emma is – was – your mate's girlfriend. You weren't that close to *her*. Imagine if she didn't have anything to do with Joe, or maybe – yeah, if maybe she'd split up with Joe a few years ago – and then you'd heard that she'd died, or was dying.'

In front of her, the phalanx of cars began to move, in that occasionally inexplicable way that traffic has, when jams vanish for no apparent reason. She looked ahead to drive; they passed the traffic lights, turned right into Croxted Road, and were going steadily towards Sydenham before she turned back and noticed how tight-lipped and furious Vic was looking.

'What?' she said.

'Nothing.'

'Oh for fuck's sake, Vic – don't lie to yourself. Don't do that thing of when someone dies, suddenly pretending you were their best friend. That's just wallowing in it.'

Vic stared at her again. His brow furrowed, as if weighing something up. Then, looking out of the windscreen, his eyes blank as reflected sunglasses, he said: 'She was a sweet woman.'

'Yeah,' said Tess. 'She was. I really liked her. I just didn't *know* her very well.' He's being very odd, she thought. Perhaps he was closer to her than I realised. 'Actually it's strange, I was just thinking about Emma yesterday. When I was rushing home to meet you – more fool me, of course. She came into my head when I stopped for a moment on Parliament Bridge.'

'You really *were* rushing, then . . .'

She glanced over at him; at last, he was half smirking.

'Hm. Point taken. But . . . God, Vic it must have been about six . . . I remember now, 'cos I looked at my watch. 6.20.'

'So?'

'So that would have been . . . you know . . . almost exactly the moment when she—'

'OK. If I'm supposed not to lie to myself, can you spare us the psychic ability?'

She turned left on to Sydenham Hill, instinctively throwing her car, an unreconditioned Hillman Imp, into first. The engine roared with the effort of powering all that metal up the hill.

'In what way did she come into your head?' said Vic.

'I was just looking over London – over that view you get from the Thames. And it was really beautiful. It looked like – like you expect London to be, but so rarely is.' She paused; the masculine side of her felt a little uncomfortable with this kind of expressiveness. 'And then I remembered that Emma once told me that when she first came to London from Cork she wanted to visit places but was so poor she couldn't afford a guidebook, and so, instead, just used an old copy of the *A-Z*.'

'What do you mean, the *A-Z*? How?'

'She just used to look in the index for romantic-sounding street names. Lamb's Heart Yard. Old Seacoal Lane. Old Paradise Street. Golden Square. And then she'd go there, expecting, y'know, Dickensian gables and cobbled pavements, and, of

206

course, it would always be just streets full of offices and corporations and car parks. But she never quite gave up, apparently. Even now, she said, I'll still go on a diversion if someone giving me directions tells me a street name that sounds like William Blake might have walked there.'

She drew up to the kerb outside his building; the Imp shuddered and stopped. Without thinking, Tess undid her seat belt, opened the door and got out, reflexively, a mark of her grounded familiarity with Vic: they were well past the stage where she had to look at him and ask *shall I come in*? Which was perhaps useful for Vic, as had she stopped to do that, she would have seen how wet his face was with tears.

SYLVIA

———————

Sylvia O'Connell had been placed, by the Woolwich and District Community Services Residential Care Unit Assessment Office, in what is euphemistically known as sheltered accommodation: a series of glorified bedsits – glorified insofar as they were referred to by Park Lodge Residential Care, the company to whom this aspect of local borough health care had been tendered out, as 'units' – tiny brick bungalows clustered like prefabs, or ghost seaside-town chalets, around a central Warden Station, larger than any of the units and containing a complex switchboard ready to receive the innumerable panic button alarms and emergency messages sent out by the residents. Emma had been ambivalent about the placing, partly because Park Lodge was opposite the Harbridge Estate, where she had been convinced that, terrorising pensioners, and specifically, breaking into old ladies' premises, tying them up and stealing the £3.80 hidden under the tea-cosy, was, as it were, part of the syllabus; and also because the level of care at Park Lodge was, she sometimes felt, below that required by her mother, and Emma suspected that her placement there was just another of the cost-cutting measures on one of the council's million hidden agendas. Sometimes another part of her, the more romantic, actually *preferred* the lower level of care – Park Lodge units were self-catering, and residents had

208

their own keys and telephones – because it allowed her to believe that her mother was still capable of living her own life.

Which, in a manner of speaking, she was. Sylvia's Alzheimer's was characteristic of her. And Sylvia's principal characteristic, like many women of her generation, was common sense, or rather, a high and scathing awareness of her own common sense – her common sense was in fact, a sense of herself *as* a woman of common sense. A woman for whom 'no nonsense' was not so much a thing you occasionally said to children as a manifesto, a dictum for living. And so even now that, in truth, she made no sense – now that nonsense had taken revenge on her for banishing it for so long, by invading and possessing her entirely – her instinctive, fascistic ability to organise and control a domestic space had not entirely left her. She could still cook, and she could still clean: even if she could not remember whether her husband was still alive, she could remember where she kept the Pledge.

She was sitting in the middle of the living-room (a living-area, to be precise, with adjoining bed-area, bath-area and kitchen-area), wondering whether to dust again, but first whether she should perhaps phone someone to find out exactly where she was, when the doorbell rang.

'Now who on earth can that be?' she said, out loud, before getting up and checking her image in the mirror; it might be the priest, Mr Shaughnessy, who was always coming round these days to check on Jerry, since he was getting such a bad reputation in the town. She puffed up her hair at the back, and a little round the sides, and then sat down again: she knew there was something she was about to do, but for the life of her couldn't remember what it was. A little sit-down, and it'll come back to me, she thought. Seconds later, the doorbell went.

'I wonder who that might be at this time of day?' she said out loud. She got up and went straight for the door, wondering whether she should check what she looked like first, as it might be Mr Shaughnessy, or perhaps Jack O'Connell, the boy from Scull who everyone was saying had taken a fancy to her.

When she opened the door, though, it was a man she didn't recognise; a youngish man, in his thirties possibly, wearing clothes that, although quite smart, were lying untidily on him; he looked very tired in the face, and not a little ill. His eyes were bloodshot.

'Yes?' she said, somewhat haughtily.

'Mrs O'Connell,' said the man, and then, rather heavily, as if he really meant something by it, '*Sylvia* . . .'

'Yes?'

'Can I come in?'

Sylvia looked him up and down. Her eyes strayed off him to a sign on the wall next to the door, saying IN AN EMERGENCY. There was a red button beneath it. She didn't know how all that had got there, but she would use it if panicked.

'Who are you?' she said, eventually.

The man's face seemed to grow heavier and darker at her question, almost as if it caused him pain. He pulled at his left ear with his right hand.

'I'm Joe, Sylvia. *Joe*. Your . . .' he took a deep breath, and then let it out again '. . . daughter's husband.'

Sylvia frowned, and shook her head.

'I'm not with you . . .' she said.

The man sighed, reached into his coat pocket and took out a photograph. He showed it to her. In it was the man, standing in front of a Christmas tree, smiling, and looking much happier than he did now. He had his arms round a pretty young woman with ash-blonde hair, wearing dungarees; on her lap sat a lovely little baby. Something about this woman reminded Sylvia of someone; and something about her made her feel nice. Nice: reassured, comforted, familiar. The woman's eyes had gone red with the flash, but somehow Sylvia knew they were normally green.

Before she had a chance to look up, the man handed her

210

another photograph, just slipping it on top of the first one. In this one, the young woman was there again, but this time she had her arms round a much older lady. Now this lady Sylvia *knew* she recognised. In fact, she'd just seen her recently. Now when was it? The man's finger appeared above the old lady's grey head.

'That's you . . .' he said gently.

'Why of course it is!' said Sylvia, laughing. 'What an old silly I am!'

'And that,' he said, moving his finger along to the young woman, 'is your daughter Emma. My . . .' and again his voice changed slightly: this time it seemed to crack, '. . . wife.'

Sylvia looked up at him. She drew the two photos apart and compared them, and then looked up at him again.

'Well,' she said, 'you've lost weight. But you'd better come in, then.'

She withdrew back to the living-area. The man came in and paced around by the mantelpiece, looking a bit nervous; it reminded Sylvia of when Jack came to ask her father for her hand in marriage.

'Would you like a cup of tea?'

'No thank you.'

'I do a very good Earl Grey.'

'No, really.'

'Please yourself.'

'Sylvia . . .' he said, 'would you mind sitting down?'

'Well . . .' she said, feeling her haughtiness start to return – what right did this stranger have to tell her what to do in her own house? – but then she remembered he wasn't a stranger, was he.

'Please,' he said.

She made a face to indicate that, standing or sitting, it made no odds, and sat down. Rather boldly, he crouched down beside her.

'Sylvia . . .' he said, 'what I'm about to tell you is really, really

211

difficult. And I know you get a little bit confused sometimes these days, so I'd really like you to concentrate. Try hard.'

Again, she wasn't quite sure that she should be being talked to in this manner, but he seemed very urgent, so she just nodded. The man did that thing of breathing in quite deeply and breathing out again.

'Yesterday, there was a terrible accident. Emma was driving and . . . she crashed.'

Sylvia smiled sympathetically at him. 'Oh dear,' she said.

'She's dead.'

She nodded. There was a pause. 'Was anyone else hurt?' she said, eventually.

The man raised his eyes to heaven.

'No . . . not really . . . but that's not the point. She's dead, Mrs O'Connell. Emma, your daughter, is dead. That's what I've come to tell you.'

Sylvia pondered for a second, then laughed, the same, hearty, no-nonsense laugh she had given a minute earlier when she'd called herself an old silly. 'No! Of course she isn't. I remember now.' Then, enunciating carefully, as if speaking to a child. 'Emma went off to London to get married. That's all.' She put her hand on his cheek. 'You needn't worry. I know it's a long way away, but there's always the telephone.'

'No, Mrs O'Connell . . .'

'Be along with you, now.'

The man's face started to crumble. 'Please, Mrs O'Connell, I don't want to tell you again . . . I don't want to say it over and over . . . She's dead. Dead. Not even anything left of her because the car caught fire and exploded.' The man looked away from her and towards the window, his eyes filling up. 'Do you understand?'

'Of course I do, my dear.'

He looked back. 'Oh God. God. Why did I come here? What did I expect?' And then he laughed, a peculiar, heathen sort of laugh she didn't like one bit. 'It doesn't matter what I tell you, does it? I may as well tell you that I spent the night she died with my best friend's girlfriend, mightn't I? I did, Sylvia. I did that. And that now I can't get the guilt of that off me, I'll never get it off me. I can tell you that, or that Emma's dead, and you won't remember it tomorrow. You won't remember it five minutes from now. It's all gone. All gone.'

Sylvia couldn't follow him at all now, but still felt for some reason sympathetic towards him; he seemed so sad.

'You can tell me whatever you want, dear.'

'Can I? Oh Sylvia. I really loved her. I really, really loved her. Like a man is supposed to love his wife.' He stopped again, and this time his face went completely, all the parts of it turning downwards, like Jerry's always does when he grazes his knee.

'I was so . . . so *proud* of her,' he managed to say, before the tears came, full and flowing, like the river Lee bursting its banks. He buried his face in her long navy skirt, and shook. She stroked his head.

'There, there,' she said. 'There, there.' Now what could cheer this poor boy up, she thought. I know; what always cheers everyone up. What was that lovely one I heard the other day now?

Joe was crying properly now, his first real cry since Emma had died. Something about telling her mother about his guilt, even though he might as well tell it to the wind, felt cleansing; or maybe it was just her saying 'there, there' and stroking the back of his head, so long was it since he had been touched with affection. It was the type of crying he hadn't been able to do yesterday, assailed by the presence of Vic and Tess and all that brought with it: the type of crying where the soul pours out of the eyes.

That type of crying is quite destabilising – like orgasm, in the moment you can lose all sense of reality, existing only in evacuation, existing, literally, outside of yourself. And so, when she first started to sing it – beautifully, soulfully – Joe actually thought he might be having some sort of aural hallucination.

> *Looking out into the morning rain*
> *I used to feel so uninspired . . .*

In the folds of her slightly itchy navy skirt, Joe's face, even in the midst of tears, did a kind of double-take.

> *And when I knew I had to face another day*
> *Lord, it made me feel so tired*

Now he was actively staying down in the folds of her dress, surprise having stemmed his tears; the wipe-out effect of them gone, he began to notice how musty Sylvia's lap smelt.

> *Before the day I met you . . .*

He looked up, controlling an urge to go 'dadadadadadaaa . . .'

> *Life was so unkind . . .*

And then he knew what Sylvia was doing; he knew it from the blankness of her eyes. She was *repeating*. Someone had sung the song to her recently. It wasn't just fetched at random from the lucky dip of her musical unconscious. He knew it too from her voice: it wasn't really her own 'There Was a Girl from Galway Bay' vaudevillian twang. She was doing an impression. In it he could hear the voice he had so wanted to hear on the answerphone yesterday, the lost voice.

He would know for certain with the next line.

> *Your love is the key to my peace of mind . . .*

'Sylvia?' he said, but there was no stopping her.

> *'Cos you make me feel,*
> *Yeah, you make me feel . . .*

'Sylvia!' he said, putting both hands on her waving arms.

'Like a natural . . . natur . . .' said Sylvia, coming out of the trance. A moment of nothing, and then confusion widened her green eyes.

'Who are you?' she said, frightened. 'Why have you got your hands on me?'

'Sylvia, did Emma come here two days ago?'

'What?'

'Please, Sylvia, try and remember.'

'Stop shaking me! I'm phoning the police!'

Joe looked again into Sylvia's eyes and saw only terror and a flat, endless plain of emptiness: the moment was gone. He knew then that his questions were useless; but he also knew that Emma must have been in contact with her mother just before she died. There was no question that Carole King's version of *You Make Me Feel Like a Natural Woman* could have been in Sylvia's basic repertoire of tunes; it *must* have been sung to her by Emma. Sylvia would have retained it only for a short period, until now.

Joe could not process this. As he had said to Vic and Tess, he didn't really know what Emma did with her Tuesdays, but he knew they didn't involve going to see her mother – that was Friday nights – and anyway, she always used to tell him when she was going to see Sylvia, in case of emergencies.

A terrible thought, a thought that had dug a hole in Joe's subconscious ever since the police had told him about Emma not wearing a seat belt, emerged now like a twisting worm. Was it possible that Emma's death was not an accident? Was it possible that she had come to see her mother and tried to talk to her, one last time, because she was about to kill herself?

Joe's mind was twitching. She would have come here to talk to Sylvia. Meaningful communication would have failed, as ever:

so she would have sung to her. But why this? Why the song that was playing when he asked Emma to marry him?

His heart leapt at a possibility. He would never know whether or not this was true, but he wanted it to be; he so wanted it to be. Perhaps she had sung the song not for Sylvia, but for him. She would have known, after all, that Joe would come to see her mother just after she died; and she would have guessed that Sylvia would sing it to him. Emma was sending him a message . . . surely? She was telling him she still loved him, after all . . . wasn't she?

He was trying to fix on this possibility, trying to make it concrete in his mind, when his concentration was blown by a brazen klaxon tearing his reverie to shreds. When he looked round, Sylvia was standing at the door with her arms folded, next to the panic button. She looked just like Emma did when she was cross.

'Oh Sylvia . . .' he said, with a deep sigh.

'Don't come any closer. They'll be here any minute.'

Joe, still in a crouching position, looked at the space of brown carpet between his feet. Perhaps it was all rubbish. Perhaps she *had* heard the song before. Perhaps he was just lying to himself. He heard the door open, and looked up: the warden, a stocky Yorkshireman who wore a black jacket with a clip-on tie, because, or so Joe and Emma had thought, he would have liked the job to have come with a uniform, was strolling through the open door with little sense of emergency.

'Arrest this man!' said Sylvia, a dramatically straightened finger pointing towards Joe.

The warden looked at her laconically, and then at Joe. He pressed a button on some sort of remote control on his belt and the klaxon ceased, in a dying animal whine like the last note of an air-raid siren.

'Hello, Mr Serena,' he said.

'Hello,' said Joe, who had been told the warden's name more than once and really wished this time he could remember it.

'Everything all right?'

'Yes. Well, Sylvia's got a bit confused . . .'

'What are you waiting for?' she said.

The warden bent down towards her, and took her arm gently; his carefully plastered down side parting of black hair looked, from Joe's perspective, like the swirl of ink on the tip of a ball-point pen. He guided her to the centre of the room; passing Joe, he winked. 'Sylvia, why don't you sit down on the sofa here for a little bit, while we sort this out?'

'I was just leaving anyway,' said Joe, getting up. He didn't really like the warden's them-and-us attitude.

'OK, sir,' he answered, getting a bottle of pills out of his pocket.

'Um . . .' said Joe, hesitating. What was his fucking name? 'Excuse me . . . ?'

The warden looked up, an expression of polite inquiry on his face. Joe pumped up his courage.

'Did my . . . did my wife come here two days ago?'

The man frowned and, rather theatrically, scratched his head. 'Don't think so.'

'Please, it's important. Tuesday afternoon, or early evening?'

The warden's expression became a little colder. 'Yes, sir. As I say, I think not. *My* memory is perfectly adequate.'

'I wasn't suggesting—'

'Also, as you know, all visitors have to sign in at my office, and – we can go and check if you like – but I assure you we'll find from the logbook that Mrs Serena's last visit was . . .' he screwed up his eyes '. . . last week. Friday, I think you'll find.'

Joe's hopes sank; how terrible to have information this important relayed in the mechanical, unknowing tones of the jobsworth.

'All right,' he said. 'Thank you very much.'

Joe turned towards the door. He thought how stupid it was of him to have thought that Sylvia's singing was so significant. She might have heard Carole King's song on the radio in the

217

day-room, yesterday. Of course she might. And, inside, he was a little ashamed at his excitement – stumbling blindly towards the idea that Emma still loved him, forgetting that it was premised on the suggestion that she had committed suicide. One thought may be comforting and reassuring, but the other – the other led to a whole new arena of guilt and imagined responsibility.

'Told you she was coming here, did she?'

He turned back again. The warden had gone into the kitchen area; when he came out, holding a glass of water, his round red face was contorted into an approximation of a lascivious smirk. Joe followed his walk, holding his gaze. He thought about various options – saying 'I beg your pardon?' with emphasis, or 'what do you mean by that?', or just going over and punching him in his round red face. Instead, he said, expressionlessly, 'She's dead.'

His face drained of redness. It was good, after his experience here so far, Joe thought darkly, to see this information carry the power it should.

'Oh my God – Mr Serena – I'm sorry – I had no idea . . .'

Joe ignored him, and went across to Sylvia, who, he recognised, had switched off. He bent down and took her hand. He thought of Emma's hand stroking it.

'Goodbye, Sylvia . . . I'll come again soon,' he said.

She looked at him and nodded, and really looked like she understood. For that, at least, Joe was grateful, and bent down still further to kiss her parchment cheek. And then, looking at her as he withdrew, her hopeful face turned up to his, he saw a heartbreaking notepad by the phone on the table beside her, and something Vic had said came up like subtitles across his mind: *at least she's not going to end up like her mum . . . sitting out the last bit of her life next to a phone that never rings.*

A phone that never rings.

VIC

Vic wore contact lenses from the age of thirteen. He did wear glasses for a year before that, but the kind of teenager he was, they weren't really acceptable. He remembered first putting the lenses in (this was before the days when they could be made as thin as a single layer of eye-cells), the way the eye reacted so violently against an alien body being forced into it, how his eyelid would close involuntarily as his lens-bearing fingertip approached, the unbearable soapy tingling as plastic stuck to pupil, the lashings of tears. He also remembered how, when he first went out wearing the lenses, he couldn't get rid of the sensation that he was missing something. No matter how much he told himself that he no longer needed his glasses, he still felt that he'd forgotten them; his brain nagged at him, setting off its alarm systems, and underpinning his consciousness with a general sense of absence.

He had more acute moments of loss, but the chronic feeling since Emma died, the base one, was very similar: *I'm sure I'm missing something*, followed – hardly followed, in fact, rather felt simultaneously – by a keen awareness of what exactly was missing. He had it again now, as he drove the Lambretta through the gates of Blackheath Cemetery, cutting a surreal figure in his black suit – the only suit he had, from the desperate period towards the end of Pathology's career when they had attempted a change of image – and helmet. When someone dies, they are often spoken of as lost – *I lost my husband five years ago* – but Vic never realised before how this is not simply a euphemism, how you actually *lose* them, in the superficial, irritating sense: in the sense that you don't know where they've gone.

Tess had assumed they were going together to Emma's funeral, but Vic had put off making an arrangement to meet for so long that in the end she just said she'd see him there. He had been vague, which was nothing unusual, but he had been vague for a reason: he wasn't sure whether he should go. He was worried he wouldn't be able to deal with it. What if he started crying, for example, crying more than you would expect the friend of the deceased's husband to? It was possible; he had never cried so much as he had done in the last week. If he didn't go, however, as Joe's best friend and main comforter at this time, that would look peculiar too: questions would be asked. Everywhere he looked there were giveaways.

With fifteen minutes to go, he had decided to attend. He had spent the morning talking through reasons for his non-appearance, but the idea of Joe's hurt, and a potential inter-rogation on the subject from both him and Tess, was too much to bear. And, of course, he wanted to go. Vic had learnt a lot of stuff this week, a lot of stuff about death. Grief, he had learnt, despite all the talk in the press when someone famous dies about 'not wishing to intrude on private grief', was not really a private matter. Grief needs to be vocalised; the only way of lessening it is to express it, especially for someone for whom evacuation is a primary drive. But Vic's was grief which couldn't be expressed; it was illicit grief. It was made worse, if anything, by the small portion of acceptable grief he was allotted as Joe's friend, and someone who, apparently, knew Emma vaguely. But still, going to the funeral was an expression of grief, however disabled.

The cemetery path bent round from the gates to the right, towards a small chapel surrounded by greenery. He was late –

the rest of the funeral party had already gone inside – and so was forced to power the Lambretta round the corner towards it; as he bent his knee to the ground, he felt how unsuitable a place this was for Speedway-style antics. Passing graves at speed, one after another piling up quickly in his vision, he thought about this vast extent of the dead, and how many of them over the centuries have believed, fixedly and absolutely, in an afterlife, and now lie in their coffins, stumped, as it were, wondering what happened: the deadpan dead. At this moment, he too would have liked to believe in a life after death, but he couldn't; his own arguments played in his head. *How can there be a heaven*, he had often said, *when, for the people who come up with the idea of heaven, this world – with its soft mattresses, its antibiotics, its technology, its easy, guiltless sex, its bathrooms, its central heating – would be heaven. This is* heaven. Though the words sounded hollow today, when this world seemed so emptied of heaven, they still made too much sense to him: too much sad sense.

Driving up to the chapel, the bike seemed to be making even more noise than usual, although he told himself he was more aware of it because the surroundings were so silent. Stopping in front of the open oak door, however, he caught sight of the people at the back of the congregation turning round, and knew immediately how much its angry howl had crashed through the mood inside.

He hung around outside for half a minute, fidgeting with his helmet. The sun came out from behind a cloud, forcing him to squint, feeling, as he did so, tight lines forming around the corners of his eyes, the skin on his face dry from the wind against his visor-less features. He was putting off going inside, not wanting eyes to be upon him, feeling his complexities to be readable. But then the funeral came to him. The doors burst open and a priest appeared, soon followed by a coffin carried by Joe and some men Vic didn't know, but assumed to be members of Emma's extended Irish family. They were all ruddy, burly men, with too much hair for their side partings, and they all looked grumpy, rather than downcast. Vic remembered that there had been some attempt by Emma's family to reclaim her in death via a proper Catholic funeral, but this had been thwarted by the fact that there was no possibility of having a lying-in period: her body was too damaged.

As they approached, Joe threw him a look of anger, mixed with resignation at his lateness. Vic made an attempt at an apologetic face, but felt inwardly pleased that his established loucheness provided an inbuilt excuse for being late, pointing suspicion away from murkier reasons. The pleasure lasted only for a second, however, erased by the sheer presence of the coffin and the unyielding fact that Emma was dead inside it. His mind was blasted with the physical reality of death, like a child sees it, not as an absence of being, but as life inside the casket: a space of boundless claustrophobia, an infinity of breathless darkness. He couldn't escape it. Death had given him X-ray vision: his eyes seemed easily to pierce the thin piece of wood between himself and the encased-in-padding body of his lover. He couldn't escape it, because he wasn't presented with an abstract reality, here, death as it is so easily discussed by glib intellectuals straining to philosophise, but with someone who was still for him, in the purest sense, corporeal, someone whose physicality still existed live within him, her smell, her skin, her hair, her movement: someone he was fucking, for God's sake. He could not *not* imagine the actuality of Emma lying in the coffin, because he had not yet got out of the habit of imagining Emma all the time.

He was shaken out of this train of thought by seeing a small white piece of paper on top of the coffin, which, at first, he thought looked incongruously like a place setting at a dinner table. As it passed closer by, he could see that it was an envelope, a card-containing envelope, on which was written the word 'Mummy'. The shock of seeing it kept him by the side of the funeral procession, an onlooker, as other mourners emerged from the chapel, caught up with the coffin and threw flowers on it: tulips, roses, lilies, in bunches. No horses, no gun-carriage, no cameras raised above the heads of watching crowds, but still, he knew instantly what was happening. Joe was trying – too late, in so many respects, too late – to make amends. It occurred to Vic, grimly, to applaud.

His eye, finally moving from the incongruous scene, saw Tess, dressed spectacularly in a long black dress-coat and pillbox hat, at the back of the non-flower-throwing section of mourners. He couldn't see her eyes, because the hat included a veil, but her face was pointing in his direction, and he guessed they were reproachful. Flattening his expression, Vic hurried to join her and take his place amongst the sympathisers.

There was a wake. That much Joe had had to concede to Emma's family, although it was a customised wake, halfway between the solid binge of Irish proletarian mourning, and the restrained memorial services of modern middle-class bereavement. This being the Easter holidays, it was held in Maze Hill Primary, the school Joe and Emma had put Jackson down for on the day he was born.

As they entered the parquet-floored hall, gravedust still in their suit turn-ups, Emma's brothers and cousins headed straight for the makeshift bar set up at the back, paying little attention to the slide-show already playing on the screen on the stage in front. It was a montage of photos of Emma, backed by a tape of Gaelic harp music: child Emma, her hair in bunches and less blonde than Vic would've expected, student Emma, all eighties clothes and overdone eye-liner, bride Emma, smiling next to a shy but beaming Joe – a knowing smile, thought Vic, knowing like women sometimes are when they've mapped out their futures – mother Emma, laughing Emma, working Emma. Watching it through, Vic felt how little of Emma he knew, how little, at least, of the nuts and bolts of her life, the facts and figures, the map of her everyday history; and yet, how vital –

how unique to him, he told himself – the part of her he had known. As if to confirm this, the last photo in the sequence – socialite Emma, in conversation with friends at Sonia and Michelle's party – came up, and he felt the force – the thrill, almost – of his own reading of it, different from everyone else's in the room, because it was the only photo in the montage taken after their affair had begun.

It was Sonia who went up to the lectern in front of the screen as the images began to recycle. The Gaelic harp faded, and the slides paused at child Emma, her bunches visible above Sonia's austerely pulled back fringe. The final members of the Anglo-Saxon section of the funeral party took their seats along the stacking chairs lined in front of the stage.

'Ladies and gentlemen . . .' she said, and then coloured, perhaps feeling that such an introduction was a little showbiz: 'friends . . . we're here to celebrate the memory of Emma Serena, who died so tragically last Tuesday.'

The buzz of voices around the bar at the back picked up again, having died down for a second.

'And celebrate we shall. Everyone who knew Emma knows that she was someone who loved life – and she I'm sure would have wanted today to be as much about celebration as commemoration.'

And so it went on, speaker after speaker, reading prose, reading poetry. Vic sat next to Tess throughout, her face as impassive as if she had continued to wear her veil. He was aware, around him, of moist eyes and goose-pimpled flesh, even, periodically, of watery smiles, the happy sadness of an audience luxuriating in melancholy. He sank into semi-awareness, letting the memorial words wash over him: time, love, soul, life, friends, family, bird, fire, night, sea, beyond. Every so often he would tune in, and feel come over him a strange but familiar resentment, reminiscent of the days when Pathology were continually passed over for other bands. It reminded him of the one award ceremony they had been invited to. Nominated in three categories, they won none; and Vic remembered sitting amongst the round tables, watching as others went up to give thanks and take trophies, and thinking, even through his somewhat take-it-or-leave-it attitude to being in the band, *that should have been me*. He felt, now, as each new spokesperson for Emma's life took to the stage, that same sense of exclusion, of frustration at the ignorance of his peers. Listening to their résumés, oral versions of the slides of her, he was struck only by their shortfalls: by what could not be said, because only he could say it. Only he had the information. It was all he could do, at times, not to heckle.

The last person to speak was Joe. He had sat at one side of the stage throughout, with Sylvia, holding her hand, perhaps as a comfort, but more likely as a restraint. He had made a poor stab at a funeral outfit – his trousers, though black, didn't quite match his jacket, and underneath he had gone for a black polo neck rather than shirt and tie. Given his flat-tipped nose, this made him look, Vic thought, something like a cross between a member of the SAS and the Milk Tray man.

'I . . .' Joe began, looking down at the lectern, where he'd placed a sheet of A4, 'I . . .' He stopped and looked up. 'Sorry, I'm not really very good at public speaking. I had some things written down, but I think all that's been said better by others already.' Taking his hand from his ear, he folded up the paper, and neatly placed it in his inner jacket pocket. 'Um . . . although I did want to say thank you to Sonia for kind of hosting today, and helping to organise everything.'

There was a murmur of approval, and one person clapped, twice, before faltering. Joe appeared for a moment unsure whether to continue. His fingers flicked at his earlobe.

'I suppose one thing I wanted to say was . . . something about our marriage. It occurred to me just now, while I was listening, so forgive me if it maybe doesn't make much sense, or if it seems . . . inappropriate.' He took a deep breath. 'Um . . . this is kind of it. Some of our friends who have spoken today talked about how much me and Emma seemed to gel, how we were made for each other. The perfect couple, Nichole said. Which at one time, we were.'

There was a cough from the back; its echo zigzagged awkwardly around the hall.

'But I think at a time like this, it's important to tell the truth. Not just to paint the rosiest picture, so that we can all have the rosiest memories.' Joe put his hands on the lectern, like a preacher. 'That, I think, does . . .' his eyes closed '. . . *the deceased*, a disservice.'

He opened his eyes again; some of the audience glanced uneasily at their partners.

'In the first years of our marriage, and for the two years we went out with each other before that, we were without doubt very, very happy. Before I met Emma, I was always in relationships, some of them quite sustained. But I just took it for granted – that I had a girlfriend, I mean. It was only when I started going out with Emma that I realised what it was like to be made happy by your partner – to be constantly . . . uplifted by their presence, or by the thought of them.'

Vic felt himself begin to drift; his eyes moved along the row. Toni, cradling Jackson in a baby-sling, sat at the end of it. Despite himself, and castigating himself for it, he had a flash vision of her naked.

'But in the last year or so – by our standards, I suppose – things took a turn for the worse. I still don't know exactly why. Anyway, this isn't really the place to go into the details, but I mention it not . . . disrespectfully, but because, at the moment – and maybe this will go – the decline of our marriage is the context in which I see my wife's death.'

Vic turned back to look at his friend, noticing on the way that Tess's face had turned a little red. He would be surprised if she cried; she hadn't so far.

'What I'm trying to say is . . . it's a bit like people say after their parents die sometimes, if they had a major row with them, how they wish they'd sorted it out, or even – even if there was just stuff they left unsaid. How they wish they'd said it before they died.'

Vic glanced across at Sylvia. She was looking intently into the wings of the stage.

'But with your parents, past a certain age at least, you *know* that's something you have to do. Clear the decks.' He stopped speaking for a second; one of his hands left the lectern, and he pinched his eyes between thumb and forefinger. 'This was my *wife*,' he continued, forcing his eyes back open like an exhausted man, 'and so we let the situation go on, because, you know, there's always time. Isn't there? Always time.'

'Oh God . . .' said Tess, under her breath.

'It's advice, really,' said Joe, tears appearing at the corners of his eyes, 'yeah . . . advice. That's what I'm giving you. Banal, Christmas-cracker style advice. Be nice to the people you love. If there's trouble between you and them, find a way out of it. Sort it out. Today. Because . . .' And through the crumple of his face, his expression was still intent, it still said *do you understand*? '. . . they might die. They might fucking *die*. At any time. And then, it's all ruined. Even the thing death is supposed to leave you with – the one thing – memories, yeah . . .' he half laughed, in the way that people beset by crying sometimes do, ironising the next phrase '"memories of the good times" . . . they're wiped out – ' he raised a hand, cutting the air – '*wiped out*, by the knowledge that it all finished bad.' He broke off, and looked straight down, seeming to watch his own tears hitting the scratched floorboards. 'I – I'm sorry – I . . .'

'Joe,' said Vic, softly. He had walked onstage, and put a hand on his arm. Joe's flooded face came up to meet his. For a moment, they looked at each other, Joe clear in Vic's sight, Vic defocused and soft in Joe's; and then Joe's head flopped down, as if his neck was broken, on to his friend's shoulder. Vic led him offstage, creaking boards and sobbing the only sound left in the school hall now, Joe's speech having stopped even Emma's family from drinking, talking and threatening to sing.

In a storeroom behind the hall, strewn with school detritus – a rough book and chalk rubber sanctuary – Vic waited for Joe to speak. For ten minutes he had been sitting in silence on an H-backed chair in front of an old wooden desk, complete with tip-up lid and disused inkwell: he looked like an 11-plus examinee, having thought about a question for so long he'd grown old. Vic, his back bisecting the grey double-doors, looked about him for the hundredth time, wondering if this was where all the stuff that was made redundant when kids started learning with computers had been put out to graze. It was hot in there, and stuffy; on his upper left arm he felt his angel itch.

'Vic . . . ?' Joe said finally, although without looking at him; his gaze, as far as Vic could make out, had stayed fixed on a packet of coloured chalks on the ground.

'Yeah?' He was nonchalant, Vic, trying to suggest that nothing bad was going on, that the situation was not extreme.

'Can I ask you something?'

Joe finally looked up, away from the pastel spectrum. Vic nodded, although he hoped it wasn't going to be the question which leapt immediately to his mind.

'How well would you say you knew Emma?'

That was halfway towards that question. His answer was cautious, because he didn't know if it was a first step.

'Um . . . well, I don't know. She was kind of mysterious, from my point of view. Compared to your other girlfriends. You know, like with Deborah, you kind of got what you paid for.' Joe half smiled to himself, letting Vic feel that he was on safe ground after all, two blokes talking about women, even if one of them was dead.

'I mean,' continued Vic, 'Deborah wasn't someone who gave the impression that there was always something else you could discover about her. Em did. There always seemed to be more to her than she would reveal.'

He paused, not wanting to go too far; now was not the time to take the opportunity denied to him during the public eulogies.

'Why d'you ask?' he said, half as a brake to himself.

Joe coughed, raising a clenched fist to his mouth, something of a stage ahem.

'Would you say she was someone who could commit suicide?' he said.

Vic raised both his eyebrows in surprise, but, once the face was made, felt that it was contrived – that his look of surprise owed much to white clowns in pointed pom-pom hats. It was a thought that he too had not been able to suppress, although with greater reason than Joe.

'Why do you say that?'

Joe sighed. 'It's complicated. It's probably wrong. A strange thing happened when I went to tell Sylvia the news – made me think Em must have contacted her just before she died. *Knowing* she was about to.'

'What strange thing?'

'It doesn't matter. I'll explain another time. I just want to know whether you think she could do such a thing.'

Vic pushed his back off from the grey double-doors. He knew he wasn't a suspect, but felt inside the creeping hand of self-censorship, like when guilty men, caught near the scene of the crime, are questioned first of all as potential witnesses. Be careful what you say, they think.

'People don't commit suicide by driving their cars into park walls. Do they?'

Joe was silent for a second.

'Not all suicides are like Sylvia Plath's,' he said. Vic opened his hands, uncomprehendingly. 'They're not all planned and premeditated. Like you once said. Sometimes you're on top of a cliff – you suddenly get an urge to throw yourself off. Or, to put it another way: sometimes when you're driving, you suddenly think: why don't I just turn the steering-wheel sharply round this way . . .'

He mimed doing it as he spoke. Vic felt the disturbing disjunction between Joe the weeping widower and Joe the detective; but recognised somewhere in between the two the scientist, the man who drew conclusions from hypotheses. There was a flaw, however, in his reasoning.

'But if it was a sudden urge . . . how could she have spoken to her mum knowing she was going to die?'

Joe's hands, still frozen in their wheel, relaxed. 'I don't know. Maybe she'd made up her mind, but didn't know how she was going to do it. Maybe when she spoke to her mum, she was going to do it another . . .' he exhaled sharply, a savage half-laugh, '. . . *safer* way, and then got into the car, and just thought *fuck it.*' He stopped, and his voice became sodden with depression again, the excitement of conjecture quickly draining from him. 'I don't know.'

Vic folded his arms, and looked thoughtful; he felt the need to state a general position.

'I can't believe it,' he said. 'But I really didn't know her well enough to judge.'

Joe's face contracted sharply, and Vic thought he was about to burst into tears again; but instead he turned away, to sneeze.

'You OK?' said Vic.

'Yeah,' replied Joe, searching in his pockets for a handkerchief. 'It's just a bit dusty in here.' His right hand finally extracted a ball of compressed tissue from his right trouser pocket; bits of white came off it and stuck to the out-turned material because he'd washed these trousers without checking. Emma would have checked, he knew.

'I'd have thought you'd be the one to have problems . . .'

Vic looked blank.

'Allergic,' said Joe, dabbing at his nose.

'Oh. Yeah. I don't seem to be getting it this summer.'

'It's only April.'

'Yeah, but you're right, normally, I'd be getting hay fever by now, but I don't seem to be suffering from it so much this year, for some reason. I didn't feel it at all at the cemetery.'

Joe nodded distractedly, and scratched the surface of the school desk with his index fingernail, backwards and forwards.

'I never really told you, did I, that we'd gone downhill? I suppose I never really told anyone.' He pursed his lips into a tight-cornered smile. 'Now I've told everyone.'

'Don't worry about tha—'

'The thing is, the last few weeks, it was more than just the normal tension. She started behaving really weirdly. Really out of character. She was snappy with Jackson. Toni told me that one time she came back two hours later than normal, and said she'd got lost. Lost!' Joe slumped on the desk, like a schoolboy near a sunny window towards the end of a double period. 'Maybe something was really wrong . . .'

Vic looked back towards the doors. He felt a terrible drive in the pit of him to confess what he knew. And not just for his own sake; part of him desperately wanted to help, to lead his friend out of this awful maze.

'Listen, we'd better go back outside soon. People'll be worried,' he said.

Joe sat up out of his slump.

'It bothers me, Vic. It really bothers me. Because if she did, *why* did she? And how am I supposed not to think it was because of me? Because of what was going wrong between us?'

'Joe. It was an accident.'

'Was it?'

'Of course.'

'She wasn't wearing a seat belt.'

'Yeah, you said before. Look . . .' Vic said, and his stomach tightened against saying what he next had to, 'she loved you, and she loved Jackson. She wouldn't have just thrown all that away because your marriage was having a bit of a blip.'

Joe looked up at Vic: he had been using him so far as a foil, a sounding board for his dark imaginings. It could have been anyone, really. But suddenly he remembered who he was talking to, and was startled by the *earnestness* in those nearly-black eyes. It was the quality most foreign to Vic's personality; and it shook him from his solipsism, making him wonder if he wasn't just chasing his own paranoid tail.

'Perhaps,' he said, feeling like a bouncing ball slowly coming to rest, '. . . perhaps you're right.'

'I know I am,' said Vic. He gestured with his head in the direction of the outside world. Joe got up, and Vic led him, like a nurse leads a patient convalescing after a gruelling operation, towards the doors. Vic smiled at him, the mouth-shut smile that people call a brave smile, and tried to immerse himself in his helpmate role; but inside, his cogs were turning with congruencies between what Joe had been saying and his own extra information about Emma. Not the extra information he'd felt cheated in being unable to share during the service: his extra extra information, his very late news.

PART THREE

Summer 1998

Interviewer: Are you happy?
Prince Charles: Very happy.
Interviewer: And, of course . . . in love?
Lady Diana Spencer: Of course.
Prince Charles: Whatever love means . . .
BBC TV interview: Wednesday, 24 February 1981

FRANCIS

———————

Francis wondered sometimes why he bothered. Of course, he liked owning a music shop, even if, like most people involved in music who are not actually musicians, he would have preferred to have been a musician; and he made a pretty good living at it, what with Rock Stop being the only serious instrument and sheet music outlet – the only one the professionals use, he would tell people – this side of Camberwell. But sometimes, he thought, it just wasn't worth putting up with the wankers.

'The wankers' was his own term: Francis was not much concerned with originality of expression. They came in a variety of forms. First, obviously, there were the heavy metal kids, like the one playing 'Spirit of Radio' that day, smelling of virginity and managing to get everything – except, of course, the notes – slightly wrong, looking more like Brian May than Jeff Beck. Then there were the anoraks, as he liked to call them, who would come in and say something like – and Francis normally put this into a stage nasal voice when expounding to friends – 'you wouldn't by any chance have a Gretsch pre-EMI 1963 double-neck 12-string Fendercaster?' Actually, he didn't do that as much as he used to, after the time Perry, the barman at the George, had said 'I thought it was called a Stratocaster?' and Francis had had to explain that it was a joke, while Perry kept on giving him this sly look, as if he'd revealed himself to know nothing about his trade. Then there were the nutters, the ones who wanted a fucking lute, or a zither, or that bloke who asked him to mend his harmonica and then it turned out he'd spat a plum stone into it. And then there were the wankers who defied categorisation, who were just . . . wankers: like this fucking journalist cunt.

Actually, that wasn't true; he did fit into a wanker category. He fitted into the category of wanker who came into the shop and played every fucking instrument but never ever bought anything. It was just that he fitted into so many other categories as well.

'Um . . . bit on the trebly side, I think, Francis,' said Chris Moore, handing back the Les Paul. It was a gold sunburst Les Paul, 1967, and there was some, albeit flimsy, evidence that it had once belonged to Jerry Garcia. Trebly, my arse, thought Francis.

'What about . . . ?' said Chris Moore, from his sitting position on top of a Vox AC30 amplifier surveying like a lord the hanging 6- and 12-strings, '. . . ooh I don't know . . . that one.' He pointed at a Gretsch cherry-red semi-acoustic: £2,300. Francis could hardly bring himself to reach up for it; he knew Chris Moore would stumble his way through 'Teenage Kicks', and then say the pick-ups were too boomy. Why didn't he just save time and hand the bald twat one of the cheapo Jap copies?

'Didn't . . .' said Chris Moore, settling the beautiful instrument on his tight-trousered lap, '. . . Jeff Buckley play one of these?'

Francis raised his lower lip and shook his head, meaning *fucked if I know*. But he knew what was coming.

'He was a lovely bloke, Jeff. Really: like – ' Chris Moore twitched inverted comma fingers, ' – "a good person". Unusual in this business.'

Francis nodded, bracing himself for another round of deliberately obscure name-dropping. He imagined Chris Moore, as he sometimes did with customers, on an album cover, smiling under the title: *The Many Sides of Chris Moore . . .'s Wankiness.* Strum, strum, Chris Moore went, his right hand spacky against the strings: '*Every time she walks down the street . . .*'

'I remember going out with him and Moe when they were over here the one time . . .'

'Moe?'

'Moe Tucker. From the Velvet Underground.'

Francis nodded again, in his bones not bothered to find out how this personality configuration had occurred.

'And they're both, you know, rock and rollers, I mean by profession, but so *nice*, y'know, that I . . .' and here Chris Moore laughed the 'can you believe it?' laugh of the ostentatiously self-deprecating, '. . . I was the party animal. Of the three of us.'

Francis stifled a yawn. Outside, a group of young boys passed without even glancing into the window. I'm going to have to put in more bloody keyboards, he thought: sequencers and whatnot.

'Who did we go and see now? Oh yeah, I remember: Pathology!'

Francis looked round.

'Pathology? Vic Mullan's old band?'

'Yeah, remember them? At the Garage.' He stroked his chin. 'I think they were supporting the Cranes . . .'

'He rents the flat upstairs,' said Francis, with just a tiny element of trumping. Chris Moore looked up, sensing a contest.

'Really? Oh, right.' He searched his files. 'Yeah, actually, I was having a drink with him a few months ago.' Then he frowned, suspecting a lie to impress: he recognised such lies quickly, Chris Moore. 'What . . . he *lives* upstairs?'

'No, he just rents the flat. For occasional use.' He reddened slightly saying this awkward, estate-agency phrase. '*Very* occasional these days. I haven't seen him for ages.'

Chris Moore, feeling the balance of 'who knows the rock star better' going his way, nodded, and strummed more chords.

'Actually, if you know where he is, you could do me a favour,' said Francis.

'No problem.' Chris Moore said it breezily, but misgave a little, feeling his cover about to be blown: he had no idea where Vic was.

'There's all these letters keep on arriving for his girlfriend. Five or six of them piling up in my hallway. I think they might be important as well: they're all from some hospital or other . . .'

His girlfriend: wait a minute . . . I've still got that card somewhere, Chris Moore thought. A way out, and an implication that I know him well enough to know his girlfriend too.

'Oh yeah, Trish! She's great.'

'Tess, I think it is . . . or Tessa.'

'Right, right. Just give them to me and I'll pass them on.'

'Oh, OK.' Francis went out the back of the shop; rummaging in a swamp of mail in the side corridor, he could hear Chris Moore getting 'Femme Fatale' completely wrong. He came back inside, five official brown envelopes, the address TV-screened on the bottom left-hand side, in his hand. As Francis passed him the envelopes, Chris Moore passed him the guitar.

'Pick-ups. Bit boomy,' he said, his hand waggling, making the envelopes dance.

JOE

In the first months after Emma's death, Joe buried himself in work. Work provided – literally, in Joe's case – a sealed environment, cut off from people or objects that might cause him pain. He found, as well, that devoting himself to his research created its own inner sealant, because the concentration required excluded other areas of thought; the endless repetition of experimentation and conclusion and further experimentation was hypnotising, like a night motorway. Although his approach to work at this time was not, however, relaxed. The people underneath him talked in the canteens at Friedner about how Joe had started running the lab less like a benign professor and more like a crazed superchef. Utterly against the grain of his previous temperament, he would quickly and easily become exasperated by what he perceived as laziness or incompetence in his workers; as for his superiors, he would avoid seeing Jerry Bloom altogether, and always pretend to be too busy to take his calls, suspecting that he wanted to impose on the lab further diversions away from pure AIDS research. And his focus, more than ever before, was on discovering a cure: as if, at some level, his work was payback – a revenge against death.

This meant that his staff had to start compensating for him, getting some of the non-HIV work insisted upon in Jerry

239

Bloom's memos done when they could, almost behind Joe's back. Which is why Marian Foster had been surprised to find him one morning bent over the *Grey Lady*, because she had come in especially early that day to try to complete a series of spectrometer tests – on a new emollient cream – before he got in. Difficult, because he was getting in earlier and earlier these days, but 7.30 was early even for Joe.

'Hello?' she said, hanging up her civilian coat. He looked up; his eyes, as ever, adjusted to the light, but she noticed that they seemed more bloodshot than usual. He looked like a man waking from a dream and, following that cartoon, put his fists in his eyes and rubbed them.

'What are you doing back here?' he said, once his hands were down.

She laughed. 'What do you mean? I work here. That means I have to come back every day. More's the pity.'

Joe blinked at her, and looked 180 degrees around him, surveying this place that he knew very well as if he'd never seen it before. Outside the long window, the sky was i-Mac blue.

'What time is it?' he said, eventually.

She checked her watch, unnecessarily, as she had already done so on seeing him there. 'Just gone 7.30.'

His face seemed to shrug, although his shoulders remained motionless. He pushed the microscope aside. 'Hm. Could you do me a coffee?'

'Please?' she said, raising an eyebrow.

Joe inclined his head sideways. 'Please . . .' he said, mockingly, although not too mockingly: he still accepted Marian's licence to treat him with a certain levity.

'Better make it black . . .' he added, as she moved off towards the percolator in the corner of the lab.

'Out late last night?' she said, trying to maintain the jokey atmosphere: it was rare, things were tense in the lab so often these days. And she was interested: like many people who knew Joe, she was waiting the requisite respectful length of time before

240

thinking about introducing him to some single friends of hers. The broken heart, the young widower; the fact that he had a baby boy as well made it just perfect.

'You could say that . . .'

She spooned coffee into the open funnel, and set the machine bubbling, before retrieving her white coat from the hooks by the door. As she buttoned it up, Joe felt grateful for his, for the anonymous covering it provided; he couldn't be bothered with the anxiety he knew it might provoke if she noticed he'd got on exactly the same clothes as yesterday.

At the start of the summer he did, on the advice of his doctor, who he had only gone to see because of a persistent cough, start seeing a bereavement counsellor. Joe was someone who, before the needle of his life twitched violently into the red, had always been fairly scornful of therapy. Standard, middle-class malaise therapy, he reacted against. Even when he and Emma flew off the marriage run it never crossed his mind to go to joint counselling – although, looking back, he wondered why Emma never suggested it: she had other, compatible, new age faiths. Unsurprisingly, therefore, when he first went to see Charlene, a Bostonian with a terrifying shock of frizzy black hair and an accent so Anglo-American it seemed to force her mouth sideways, he would talk only about the process, not the problem.

'I mean, *bereavement counselling* . . .' he said, lying on the green couch in Charlene's book-lined room – Charlene special-ised in bereavement, but was, in her general psychoanalytic practice, a Freudian: 'the whole idea spells out to me what's wrong with therapy.'

'Uh-huh . . .' Her voice, through the metal of her accent, was mild, unreactive to Joe's aggression, making him more aware of it; since Emma's death he knew he had become more aggressive. Before he might at least have begun 'I don't mean to be rude but', but now, now it didn't seem to be worth the breath, or

241

more specifically, the time. 'I mean,' he said, and his tone did shift down a notch, 'therapy culture tries to give us the idea that all problems are solvable. Because they're all – ' he tapped his head, his neck supported by a green cushioned bump, ' – in here.' His arms reached up to make the next point. 'But they're not all in here. There are real problems out there.'

He halted. He didn't know the rhythms of therapy, how often to let her speak.

'Go on . . .'

'Well, bereavement counselling seems to me to be the top example of that. Almost a contradiction in terms. Because bereavement . . . *death* . . . there's nothing to counsel. It just is a terrible thing. The *worst* thing. And no amount of different ways of looking at it, or coming to terms with it – or whatever else you try and get people who've been through it to do – will change that.' A word came into his head, slightly surprising him; he had the scientist's distrust of language, feeling that it often betrayed him, slipping and sliding around the edges of meaning, but this time he felt his choice was correct. 'You can't *temper* death. With anything.'

In the silence following this little speech, he could hear Charlene breathing. She had a permanent minor wheeze, every exhalation producing a high soft whine. His eye roved along a row of books: *Freud*, *Understanding Freud*, *The Lacanian Unconscious*, *Death and the Ego*, *Speaking the Self*.

'I'm not sure therapy suggests that there are *no* problems out there. I think it suggests that all of us come into contact with very real problems, every day. But you would agree, wouldn't you, that all of us can deal with these problems in different ways?' He didn't answer; her voice reminded him of Loyd Grossman's. 'And that, therefore, there could be better ways of dealing with the problems, or worse ways – and my job, maybe, is just to help you find the better way.'

'But—'

'When someone dies,' she said, and Joe thought *surely it's a cardinal rule not to interrupt the client,* 'we sometimes don't want to do anything to minimise the grief. It feels maybe like some kind of betrayal – of the deceased. We berate ourselves – we feel that we let them down unless we remain completely stricken by their loss every minute of the day.'

'Look,' said Joe, swerving his feet off the couch and sitting up, 'this is exactly what I didn't want. Someone telling me what I feel.'

'I'm not *telling* you—'

'You *are* fucking telling me.' He angled his face to face hers. 'You're sounding just like I expected a therapist to sound.'

She looked at him, unmoved, although the quiet soprano note rode ever so slightly louder over the top of her breathing.

'Well,' she said, 'at the risk of sounding even more like a therapist . . . I think we're dealing with a lot of anger here.'

JESUS

Jesus's face was so cracked and lined that remaining impassive for him was almost impossible. Lines on the face are literally markers: like silent-film make-up, they accentuate every expression, drawing the gaze of the watcher like arrows to the eyes, the corners of the mouth, the nostrils – all the points on the face where the translation of emotion into expression is at its optimum. And Jesus, an old man now, who had lived most of his life outside, his skin under the cosh of an unscreened sun, had, as a result, no place to hide: the tiniest twitch of annoyance, the slightest purse of frustration, the merest eyebrow-jerk of impertinence – all these would be magnified a thousand times in his contours and crevices, and then in a domino effect of eddies and whirlpools around his face. So he tried hard – he actually focused and concentrated on keeping his face still – while Señorita Carroll drank from the first of the three bottles he had brought her from the new yield on the eastern side of the vineyard, where the amber plain slopes dustily down towards the Cap de Creus.

It was another fiercely hot day, although in August, in this part of Catalonia, such a description is virtually redundant. But the way the fat, overlapping sandstones of El Castillo de Santo Domingo bounced the light into the centre of the courtyard

244

doubled the intensity of the heat, like the stone ovens some
of the women in Peralada still used. Señor Corrego would not
have sat here to taste the wine, thought Jesus, he would have
realised how the heat confounds both it and the head of the
taster – but then tried to banish the thought as fast as it had
come, knowing it would be born again in his face. He must
suppress what he felt about her – his sense that it was wrong,
this woman doing a man's job, an English woman as well; what
could she possibly know about wine, especially Priorato? All
that must be buried lower in his soul than the roots of the
vines he planted year after year are buried in the soil, because
if she saw such thoughts in his face she would tell him that the
wine wasn't good enough out of spite – women acted on such
impulses, he hadn't lived sixty-eight years in their company not
to know that – and then he would have to go back to the fields,
and replant, and refine, and all he wanted to do was switch the
taps off on the barrels and go home. Besides, there was talk,
since she had come, of new methods – of *filtration*, and *acidic
regulation*, and *chaptalisation*, whatever that was – and Jesus
didn't want anything he did to put her off tasting these three
bottles and realising that none of this was necessary, that the
wines they had made at Santo Domingo for over sixty years –
wines that El Generalissimo himself had once ordered directly
from the Castillo, although some said that he drank it only to
humiliate the Separatists – were fine as they were.

Señorita Carroll poured the wine from the first bottle into
her smoked-green glass goblet.

'Tempranillo . . .' said Jesus. Señorita Carroll, lifting the glass
to her lips, paused; under the dark sheen of her sunglasses,
her eyes stared into the middle distance for a second before
closing.

'*Gracias*, Jesus,' she said, and continued the upward movement of her glass. Jesus, she called him, like the English say it,
Ciiesos, and something about the flat way she always said it
made Jesus suspect it was a joke at his expense. He wondered

whether or not to tell her again how to say it in Spanish – Jesus, with a guttural *Ch*, and swooping *sus* – but once again recalled the importance of the moment and felt that now was not the time.

Señorita Carroll swallowed the wine. Jesus could not understand this: he had never seen it before in any of the people whose job involved tasting – not the ones who came from Barcelona to buy and certainly none of the other managers of the Castillo before her. Señor Corrego, in particular, used to enjoy the spit: over the years, Jesus had come to know instantly what he felt about the wine from the way he would spit it out. In fact, the moment that Corrego had really found a place in Jesus's heart had been when, on tasting a bottle of Txacoli, the grape at the centre of what Jesus considered to be the Santo Domingo spirit, the truly *Basque* grape, he had spat the wine out into the silver bucket that Jesus held for him with such vehemence, with such a resounding 'pah!' that Jesus thought it must have been corked; but instead, Señor Corrego had wiped his mouth in a single movement with the silk handkerchief he kept in his top pocket, and, looking at him, eyes burning with indignation, said: 'This wine tastes of *Spain*.' And then Jesus had been happy to pour the barrels down the drain, and start again, knowing that the man he was working for was his brother.

She took another sip of the wine, and wrote something down on the electronic notepad in front of her. Jesus could not see what it was, and anyway his grasp of English was poor. He felt alienated, like a child watching a teacher write a letter to its parents that the child itself is not allowed to read; why could she not just tell him what she thought of the wine?

'OK . . .' she said, clicking off the notepad. '*Bueno*. I'll talk to Vaquero about it. How many barrels have we produced so far?'

'*Ocho*. Eight.'

'Right. Hold production there. I'll speak to him tonight and then tomorrow let you know how much more of that I want the estate to produce this season. OK?'

Jesus stood there for a while, not sure what to say. Señorita Carroll checked her watch, then lifted her head, as if listening for something.

'Sorry, Jesus, is there something else?' she said, as if she had just realised he was still there.

'*Si, señorita.*' He struggled for a second with what he was trying to say next, and not just because of the language. 'I bring you three bottles. It is best to try the vino from all three bottles.'

Señorita Carroll pushed her sunglasses on top of her forehead, forcing strands of her hair up and over the lenses.

'It's all from the same barrel. Isn't it?'

'*Si, señorita*. But I leave the wine for a while in the bottles. Because every bottle – ' he tapped at the first one, standing three-quarters full on the black wrought-iron table ' – is different. Even the glass.' He raised a hand to his chin, defensively. 'It . . . *como se dice* . . . affects?' he looked to her; she nodded, '. . . affects the wine differently.'

In the distance, the sound of a car approaching could be heard. Señorita Carroll blinked quickly, and put her sunglasses back in front of her eyes. 'OK, Jesus. I'll try a glass from all three bottles. Just in case the contact that – ' she raised her glass – '*this* one has had with the glass from *this* bottle means that it tastes really different from all the other Tempranillo from the same barrel.'

Jesus smiled, and nodded, although he wasn't sure again about her tone; it was the same way that she said his name, like she meant something else by it.

The car noise became louder. Señorita Carroll got up and walked out of the courtyard towards the baking ground of the approach road. Jesus surmised that the tasting, or at least his role in it, was over; he arranged and rearranged the line of the three bottles for a pointless minute, before turning to go out of the courtyard himself. Through the white arch, he saw in the distance a Fiat Panda draw up at the front gate, and a man,

247

also in shades – clearly an Englishman: only they had such bloodless, doughy skin – get out. From his view, Señorita Carroll then appeared as if from stage left, walking towards him. Jesus expected her to hug the man excitedly – presumably it was some old friend she hadn't seen for ages, or possibly even an ex-lover, although he felt slightly ashamed for wondering about that – but instead she stopped about a foot away, and just took his hand briefly. The English, thought Jesus, as he went through the arch and away towards the bottling plant in the north wing; so passionless.

TESS

In the cool interior of the Castillo drawing-room, cool the way that these rooms are designed to be, marble working like medieval air conditioning, Tess handed Joe a glass of Txacoli.

'I thought you didn't like white wine?' he said.

She shrugged, pouring herself a glass. 'Don't have that much choice here. The estate makes three reds, which I'm doing my best to work up, but this is the speciality of the region. Txacoli. Sounds like something Scottish pensioners get every time they eat a bit of off meat.'

Joe sipped: the wine was tart and cold, and reminded him a little of Strongbow, but he kept that to himself.

'I don't remember telling you that . . .'

Joe looked across at her: it felt so incongruous, sitting here on these chairs, all red velvet and gold curls, whilst above them angels and bearded men fought over some crack in the sky. They were from South London, for goodness sake.

'About white wine.'

Joe put his glass on the marble table between them.

'Yeah. I think Vic told me once,' he said, keeping his voice straight, knowing it was the first mention of him. She nodded, and pulled her loose white top slightly away from her skin, as if the coolness of the room hadn't quite got through yet.

249

'Nice tan . . .' said Joe, feeling that they were still within the margin of small talk.

'Thanks.' She looked him up and down; spots of red appeared on his skin in places where, with no woman to do it for him, he had failed to properly apply sunblock. 'Have you lost weight?'

Joe smiled, internally as well. 'I have, actually. So . . . what the fuck are you doing here?'

'I think I should be asking *you* that, shouldn't I?'

He smiled again, a little nervously, though, because he wasn't yet clear about how he would answer that when the time came.

'You first . . .'

Tess exhaled, puffing her lips out as she did.

'This place is owned by the Vaqueros, a big Catalan wine-making family. Has been for years. But they just basically produced for the local area. And then, two months ago, Old Mr Vaquero kicks the bucket, and his son—'

'Young Mr Vaquero . . .'

'Yeah. Although young like Young Mr Grace was in *Are You Being Served?* He's about seventy-one . . . Anyway, he takes over, and, bless him, he feels that it's time for El Castillo de Santo Domingo to become a bit more of a player in the international wine market.'

'So he brings you in.'

'Yeah. Although, to be honest, I'm not sure whether that's because he thinks I'd be a hot shot at running the estate or because when he met me at a tasting two years ago, his grey old hormones took a fancy to me.' She swallowed some more wine. 'I've always been a bit of a babe for the old buffers in the wine world.'

Joe nodded, but blushed a little, this direct mention of her own attractiveness brushing at the locks of the emotional baggage he'd brought with him for this trip.

'But are you happy . . .' he said, preferring to keep the conversation, for the moment, in a safer haven, '. . . working for someone after being freelance for so long?' He felt a little bit stilted saying it, like a 1930s interviewer.

'Well, it's got its drawbacks. The old geezer who's in charge of the actual day-to-day wine-making – he hates me. Clearly doesn't like a woman being his boss.' She shrugged. 'But I can live with that. The money's good. The weather's fantastic. I've already done three months of a two-year contract, after which I can go back to buying and selling for myself, if I want to.' She paused. 'And I wanted to get out of London . . .'

Joe hesitated, but her reference was clear: the door was now open for him to ask.

'So why did you split up with Vic?' he said.

She finished the remaining wine in her glass.

'He didn't tell you?'

'No . . .'

She breathed in, slowly, through her steep nose; her eyes squinted a little.

'You hungry?' she said.

They drove, in the Panda, to a place called the Restaurant at the End of the World. This is a hippie outpost, a lone shack in the middle of the treeless tundra that is the Cap de Creus. There are a few landscapes on this planet that look very much like they belong on another: the rock-mushroom fields of Cappadocia in Turkey, carved from the hard land as shelters by troglodytes in the fourteenth century, the desert valley of Soussesvlei in the Namibia, bordered on all sides by sunburnt red dunes higher than mountains. And in Europe, here, where the Pyrenees crumble down to meet the Mediterranean, in a series of lichen and brush-covered promontories, like huge rock hands splayed out into the water.

They drove north along the Costa Brava, past Cadaques and Port Lligat, where Dali lived and worked; looking out the car window, Joe, who knew little about art, thought that he could see here how his landscapes made sense, how they deserved more than their tapestries-for-sixth-formers'-bedroom-walls fate. During the journey he talked of his hotel in Barcelona, of his fears of leaving Jackson with Toni for a whole weekend, of upgrading the hire car to a convertible; she of life amongst the locals, and plans for extending the estate. Conversation stayed in the same zone in which they had left it at the Castillo, as if she was suspending time until the moment was right to answer his question.

'It's a bit of a naff, grungy place, this,' said Tess, once they could drive no further and had begun step-climbing their way towards the Restaurant. They could see it in the distance, centred in the rock plain and backed by the sea, the only man-made thing for miles, like a house in a dream that might be a nightmare. 'Run by pikey traveller types. But it's worth it for the situation.'

Joe nodded, but wondered *what* was worth it; now they were nearly there, he was becoming tense again at the thought of all that still needed to be said, and felt that he'd rather have got it over with at the Castillo.

'It *is* an incredible place,' he said, trying to sound grateful for being brought here. He had to raise his voice now against the wind. 'It reminds me of the Thing.'

'What thing?'

'No, *the* Thing. He was a guy – a superhero – in The Fantastic Four. A Marvel comic.'

'And . . . ?' she shouted back to him, without turning round. She was getting ahead of him; more used to the landscape, it seemed easier for her, even though she only wore sandals, to hop through the cracks in the rock. He wouldn't have thought of her as so outdoors, in London.

'Well, he was this bloke who because of . . . I can't remember why, but his body gets covered in rocks. That's what he looks like, sort of the Incredible Hulk, but covered in cracked, red rocks.' Now the sound of the wind was boosted by the sound of the sea, crashing so loudly against the craggy edges of the

Cap that their distance above the water seemed smaller than it was. In his mind's eye, he saw the curves of the waves as they hit the rocks and splintered into foam. 'That's what this feels like. Like we're walking over a giant version of the Thing.'

Reaching the Restaurant, she stopped and turned. Joe approached her, smiling somewhat apologetically, in part for his out-of-puffness, in part for his simile. He expected her to lead the way in, but she stopped, looking out towards the beachless cliffs. The wind threw her long black hair across the lower half of her face, like a yashmak.

'You know, Joe, I used to think – for a long time, I used to think that I had sort of a man's brain. That I thought more like a man than a woman.' He nodded. 'But now I've come to realise that whatever it is I do think like, it's not like men; because men don't really think like men.' She shook her head. 'They think like boys.'

Joe felt a little abashed, but she turned back to him with a resigned but affectionate look, indicating that she wasn't really being critical: and so he felt all right again, at least for a moment.

They were the only people in the Restaurant. A young man of indeterminate nationality with blond dreadlocks thicker than rope served them octopus in terracotta bowls. The glass in the window next to their table clacked with the wind: now inside, Joe felt the landscape to be even more hostile, the thinness of their shelter bringing home to him the power of the forces outside, how they could if they wanted spin this shack easily up into the air, or collapse it into the sea. Around them, the unsteady walls were hung with reproductions of Dali's unsteady visions of Catalan nature.

'So . . .' said Tess, pushing her plate away – Joe noticed that she had finished in the time it had taken him to have three mouthfuls – 'to answer your question: he started talking about children.'

Joe almost comically spat out his octopus, like Terry would his tea when June told him the vicar was coming round.

'Vic? Children? Are you sure?'

'Yes, well that was my reaction. That's why I knew something had gone terribly wrong. This is the man who used to say that babies were poofs.'

'Poofs?'

'Yeah. Because they could die from *being in a cot*. They weren't even hard enough to live through some blankets and a nice lie-down.' Joe smiled; she wiped her hands on the tablecloth, snapping out of nostalgia. 'I mean, it wasn't just him suddenly wanting children. There is a version of me that would have liked that: I don't mean children *per se* – but a man like Vic changing enough because of me to want children . . .' Her face became complacently honest: 'That's something of a triumph.'

'So . . . ?'

She shook her head. 'It wasn't because of me. I don't really know what it was. But it wasn't because of me.' She looked out of the shaking window at the sea, and then back to Joe, fixedly. 'You know, of course, that there was a time when I thought he was having an affair.' Joe nodded; he did, of course, know that. 'He never admitted it. And I think it stopped, anyway. But I got the feeling after that that he was trying to make our relationship something it wasn't. You know, suddenly he wanted to be all couply, and domestic, and stuff: and the kids thing was like the last straw.' She swirled a piece of bread round and round the base of her bowl. 'I mean, I'm not stupidly against domesticity. It might have been quite nice. But I felt . . .' she tutted, 'I *knew* – that it all came from somewhere else. From this other relationship. Whatever it was, he was trying to rebuild it with me.' Still she swirled, as if her thoughts were on the plate. 'You know, an affair is supposed to be the wild thing: but I reckon that actually, Vic was having an affair with someone who was giving him . . . y'know, the opposite – stability, and cosiness, and security . . . whatever.' She looked at her piece of bread, sodden brown, and then dropped it back in her bowl. 'I suppose when you go elsewhere, it's always for what you haven't got.'

Joe nodded, but felt now that she wasn't really talking to him at all.

'So when he suggested kids . . . I returned Young Mr Vaquero's calls.'

'Don't you miss him?'

'Yes,' she said instantly. And then: 'No.' She paused, wanting to get this right. 'I miss the person I first started going out with,' she said firmly. She adopted an ironic earnestness. 'The real Vic, as I like to think of him.'

'Anything else for you guys?'

They looked up at the dreadlocked waiter/manager speaking the Euro-American of the MTV VJ.

'Espresso?' said Tess.

'Can I have a Crema Catalana?' said Joe.

He nodded and walked off.

'You'll put that weight back on. Those things are lethal. Five-foot wide *Crèmes Brûlées* . . .'

'Yeah, but I'm working out now.'

'Really?' She moved her eyes from his face to his shoulders and arms. 'I thought you looked a bit muscle-bound.'

'Yeah. I did lose a lot of weight – after Emma died.' This first mention of it passed between them electrically. 'But I've been seeing a bereavement counsellor . . .'

'Have you?'

'Yeah. And one of the things she suggested – sounds sort of crap, I know – is physical exercise. Apparently, it staves off depression.'

Tess did a facial shrug. 'No, I can see that . . .'

'Yeah, well, I've been on this antidepressant – paroxetine, it's called, some kind of Prozac derivative – for a couple of months. And I don't really like being on it. I mean, it does keep the depression down – that's what it does, it keeps it down, sort

255

of mutes it, it doesn't make it go away, but I don't like it.' He coughed again. 'It disorientates you – it makes you distrust your own feelings, the good ones as well as the bad ones. Like for a second you might feel happy, and then a second later you're thinking, am I happy? Or is it just the drug?'

'Yes,' said Tess, feeling she was not the first person to whom Joe had said this; he was speaking like other people she knew who were in therapy, over-expressively.

'And at some level, the bad feelings – I'd rather feel them anyway. I'd rather go through them. Cleanly . . .' He paused. 'Knowing exactly what it's doing to my brain doesn't help either. And so, on Charlene's suggestion—'

'She's American?'

'Yes – I'm at the gym all weekend.'

'Can't you go before work?'

He shook his head. 'No,' he said firmly. 'I haven't got time. I think we might be on the verge of a breakthrough.'

'That's fantastic!' said Tess, genuinely pleased.

'Yeah,' said Joe, half-heartedly. He was surprised, after all his effort, to find himself unable to respond in kind – as if he knew that it was, but could no longer tune himself into the wavelength *fantastic*; and perhaps also because he knew that beyond his breakthrough, he would have to find a new reason for living.

Neither of them spoke for a second; outside, rushing sounds continued, a mix of sea and air. Eventually, Tess asked a plain question.

'How are you coping with life without Emma?'

He looked up; the hollows in his previously full cheeks made him look for a second not fit but old.

'I don't know,' he said, sighing. 'I don't know what would be considered coping.' He swallowed. Tess noticed how the loss of weight made the movement of his Adam's apple more intrusive, a dumb waiter in his throat. 'Looking after Jackson by myself is tough.'

'Where is he now?'

'With my parents.' Tess remembered Joe's parents from Emma's funeral, a stooped, whiskery man, his face jowly to the point of genital, held at the elbow by a round-shouldered woman wearing an inappropriately flowery hat. She wondered if Jackson might find them frightening. 'I mean, not just tough because of time and tiredness. Tough because bringing up a kid – there's a hundred decisions to make every day, big ones, small ones. Now I've got to make all those decisions on my own – or at least, hoping that what I decide is what she would have wanted.' His features became apologetic in advance. 'That the voice I hear in my head before I make those decisions is really hers.' Tess smiled, reflexively forgiving him the sentimentality. He smiled back. 'Although it's also made me realise how much time we used to spend discussing those decisions.'

He leant back, tilting his chair slightly away from the dark timber table, with an expansive air, as if he was really getting into the subject now.

'So many things you don't know,' he said. 'About death. About how it really affects you. Like . . . I thought it would be linear. My recovery. I thought it would be terrible at first but then gradually get better?' His voice went up at the end of the sentence, like an American. Charlene, thought Tess. 'But in fact you just go through different types of pain. Now – now I just feel how she isn't there. Like yesterday – I was in Barcelona, and I went to see the Sagrada Familia – y'know Gaudi's cathedral, the melting one . . .'

'Yes,' she said, smiling at the resolute Anglo-Saxonness of his pronunciation.

'And afterwards, I just wanted to phone her and tell her about it. Not like a big thing, not like – here's all the things I ever wanted to say. Just to tell her how amazing this building was.' He stopped, a small 'v' knitting his eyebrows together, like a child trying to work something out. 'After a while, the shock goes, but the bit of my brain that used to refer everything to her

– that's still there. It still prompts me to . . . to look for her first.'
He broke off again. 'Because nothing I think seems to have any
meaning without knowing what she thinks about it.'

'Have you thought about starting to see someone else? Or . . .'
she hesitated, but then her directness surfaced, 'are you too
worried about what she'd think about *that*.'

His head moved from side to side and the corners of his mouth
turned downwards, one corner pointing to a shaving nick on the
left-hand side of his chin. 'I've *thought* about it.'

'Good. Although . . .' Tess sucked in the air through her teeth,
'. . . it's a tough gig.'

'What is?'

'Going out with someone whose partner's died. I almost had
an affair with a widower once.'

'Did you?'

'Yeah. A fifty-year-old wine buff. Nice-looking, in a Robert
Kilroy-Silk sort of way. But, you know, I – like most women
– like most *people* – like to have a bit of a head start on my
partner's ex. I like to be able to slag them off if I want to.' She
shook her head. 'Death puts them beyond that. *Way* beyond
that. It's probably the only way of forcing your new girlfriend
to be nice about your last one.'

She smiled at him, hoping that her tone hadn't come across
as too breezy. He smiled back, but fleetingly, wanting to stay
serious.

'So anyway,' he said, with an air of moment, 'the other thing
Charlene suggested . . .' He stopped, and looked directly at her;
she raised her eyebrows expectantly, and then, it coming to
her, said, through one long nod, 'Was that you come and
see me.'

'Yes.'

'Hm.' She looked at her hands, wondering how Charlene
would have put it: *you have to find a way to absorb the guilt/
accept the reality of what happened that night*. Something like
that. 'Does the cost of the trip come off her price?'

'No,' said Joe, half smiling. 'She thought a holiday might be a good idea for me, anyway.'

His dessert and her coffee arrived. He stabbed his spoon through the brown-sugar covering: it broke in triangles.

'I should have come to talk to you before – when you were still in London – but I . . .'

'You couldn't face it,' she said, matter-of-factly. 'That's reasonable.' She filled her tiny cup with powder from lilac Sweet n' Los. 'So what is there to say now?'

'Well . . .' He trailed off. Tess opened her hands, waiting. Joe ate a couple of mouthfuls of Crema Catalana, the sweetness as he wanted it, almost unbearable.

'OK,' she said, when he put his spoon down and looked away through the window. 'Looks like it's incumbent upon me to speak.' She drank her espresso in one, then pushed the cup away. 'I know that sometimes I come across as a bit . . . hard. Most of the time I don't mean to. And certainly, now, I don't mean to. You've been through something terrible, and you deserve – ' he looked back at her, clearly wondering what it was he deserved, ' – to be treated with gentleness.' His face started to go at this; through the paroxetine mufflers, he felt once more his own sea begin to heave and roll. 'But what there is to say is simple. So my instinct is to say it quickly. Please understand, Joe, I'm being quick – that doesn't mean I'm being cruel.' He nodded, ready to assent to anything; she girded herself to say long-thought things. 'You can't blame yourself. You had no idea what was going to happen the night we slept together. It may have been wrong in itself, but the fact that it looks so much more wrong in hindsight – that's bollocks. Hindsight is bollocks.'

'I know . . .' he said, 'but that's the problem. When your wife dies, right, people all over the place comfort you. And that speech I did at the funeral? That's just made it worse. Endlessly, friends ringing me up, saying what you just said: "You mustn't blame yourself. You didn't do anything wrong."

And I want to tell them, I really want to tell them: I did. I did do something wrong.' Tess raised a hand to correct him, but he waved it away. 'I can't even *blame* myself normally. Some people in my situation, they think, y'know, if only I'd been there, if only I'd been with her. I can't even think that – because it leads me straight to *where I was.*'

'Joe . . .' she said, wanting to do something, touch his cheek with affection, but unsure, knowing that the action of her touching him might reverberate through his pain, 'if you want . . . blame me? OK? It was my fault. You didn't come round that night to go to bed with me. Did you?' He was looking away, trying not to break down. 'So it was me. *I* made the first move. *I* was fucked off with Vic.' Her face went hard again, but her hardness here was harnessed to doing a soft thing. 'Think of me as a fucking whore, Joe. Think of me as a fucking old whore who seduced you against your will.'

Joe carried on looking out of the window; he was shaking now too, his heart flapping like the glass in the frame. A small time passed, during which Tess sat back, feeling excavated, all that she could bring to the table laid out like paschal lambs and other sacrifices in front of him; and then he turned back to her and she realised her offer had been accepted: unable to speak, his face, though streaked with tears, was etched with thanks.

'Do you think that'll do for Charlene?' said Tess, softly. A laugh burst from Joe's quivering lips; he nodded, again and again, the motion of his head seeming to throw the tears out of his eyes.

'Oh Joe,' she said, reaching over to touch his cheek, 'you'll always find some woman somewhere to be your guide.'

Just before Joe shut the door of the Panda, Tess said, 'How did you find me, by the way?'

She stood underneath the elaborate portal of the Castillo, which was adorned with the Santo Domingo crest, two unicorns leaping over a fire. Joe looked up at her: tall though she was, over her shoulder he could see the sun, poised halfway between the curve of the arch and the roof of the Castillo beyond. It had already turned gold, in preparation for setting.

'Not easily,' he said, folding up his road map of northern Spain, or at least trying to – road maps, once opened, he could never seem to fold back to how they were. 'Seeing as you didn't leave anyone a contact address.'

'No.' She smiled. 'I'm a clean-break type of woman.'

'Right. So I got it through an organisation called the Wine Traders' Guild.' Tess laughed with recognition. 'I had to pretend to be interested in buying at least twenty crates of Rioja.'

'We don't make Rioja. That's 100 kilometres inland.'

'They don't seem to know that at the Wine Traders' Guild. And, luckily, you're the only Tessa Carroll on their register.'

'Strange, that . . .' said Tess, with a mild glint in her eyes; 'it's not an uncommon name.'

Joe shifted in his seat, but nodded, both in recognition and acceptance of the reference. Together, they had moved to a place of some acknowledgement.

'Which reminds me . . .' she continued. 'The Tessa Carroll who had a brain tumour . . .'

'Yes?'

'Did you ever find out who she was?'

He frowned. 'No . . .' She nodded, with a *no matter* air. 'Why d'you ask?'

'Oh, nothing. A weird thing happened just before I left London. I got a bundle of mail sent on from somewhere – I presume where she used to live – which must have been for her.'

Joe raised his eyebrows. 'Really? That's peculiar.'

'Yeah . . .'

'How did you know it was her? I mean – the woman with the brain tumour?'

'Because they were all from the Royal Brompton Hospital. And I opened them – I mean, why not, I thought they were

261

for me at first. I was petrified ... anyway, they were all quite scary. Increasingly scary, in fact – going on about why hadn't she confirmed any appointments and how important the treatment was that she was missing – and they were all from some neurologist, so you know, I guessed it must have been a Tessa Carroll who had a brain tumour.' She paused. 'And how many of them can there be in London?'

Joe coughed, quite badly this time.

'Do you want me to get you some water?'

'No, it's OK.' He recovered, taking a deep breath, his lungs filling with the sunburnt air. 'That's really strange. Even if she didn't live where she used to, why should they get sent on to you? I don't understand.'

'Neither do I.' She shrugged, and dug her hands in her pockets. Over the car roof, she could see Jesus and two of his men walking up from the lower vineyards, laughing. Jesus nodded towards her, and their smiles faded.

'What did you do with the letters?'

'Sent them back to the hospital, marked "Not Known at this Address".'

He nodded, then leant back in the car seat, processing the information. 'Listen,' he said, intently, 'can you remember the name of the neurologist?'

She put a hand to her mouth. 'Um ... difficult. Is it important?'

'Well, it's just that that particular biopsy – the tissue sample was really interesting. From my point of view. The stage I'm at with my research it'd be useful to know more about the patient.'

'She might be dead by now.'

He shook his head quickly. 'Doesn't matter. They'll still have useful data. Maybe some sort of autopsy report.'

'Well ... Joe – you're asking me to remember the name of someone from some letters I read two months ago. Which weren't even for me.'

'Try.'

She looked at him: his eyes were dilated palest blue against the setting sun.

'Professor . . . Dwyer? Dwight? Dinkins?' She opened her palms, apologetically. 'Sorry.'

'Well, look – if I e-mail you a list of the neurologists at the Royal Brompton, one of them'll jog your memory, won't it . . . ?'

She looked down at him, and wondered for a second if this was all a ruse – at least on a subconscious level – to stay in contact. It had crossed her mind when he'd first phoned to say he was coming that his purpose might be romantic; that perhaps, having got over the initial pain of losing Emma, he was thinking of picking up from where they had left off the night of her death.

'Yeah,' she said, dismissing the thought. 'Fine.' From her loose white cotton trousers, she fished out a card: not unlike the one still in Chris Moore's wallet, only now remade with the Santo Domingo crest. Joe pocketed it, and smiled.

'I'll be in touch.'

'Do that.'

He drew his shades down to his eyes and his seat belt across his chest.

'Joe . . .' she said, as he grasped the door handle once more: he stopped and looked up, thinking maybe she'd remembered already. But she bent down and kissed him, gently, on the forehead; it occurred to her as she did so that it was, of all things, a *maternal* action. His face as she drew hers back was warm and grateful.

'Look after yourself,' she said.

'I will,' he said, and shut the door. As the car sped away, dust clouds shooting from its back wheels, Tess felt a little troubled. Joe had clearly come here with unfinished business, and in the Restaurant at the End of the World she thought maybe she'd helped him finish it, to achieve what she imagined Charlene

263

would refer to as closure. But something about their parting exchange here made her sense that she'd only helped him so far, and no more; that she'd only closed one of the doors in the house of Joe's soul, and that others were still wide open, wide open and banging in the Cap de Creus-like wind.

PROFESSOR DEWAR

Professor Anton Dewar was of that rank of eminence in the medical profession which meant that, even when working in hospital, he didn't have to wear a white coat. Instead, of course, he had to wear a blue pin-striped suit. As a biochemist, Joe – sitting opposite him now in his private consulting room in Harley Street – could never understand this: he tried to imagine how seniority in his own field could be sartorially marked, but knew that scientists, however distinguished, would always wear the white coat. As Professor Dewar bustled clips and paperweights and papers around on his desk, Joe drifted off slightly, imagining a coat becoming incrementally more white with every achievement, ending up for a Nobel Prize winner's as whiter than white, glaring with whiteness, hired out to Persil for corporate events: the antithesis of the biblical Joseph's, a coat of single shining colourlessness.

'So sorry again you had to come all the way over from the Brompton,' said Professor Dewar with a smile, having settled his desk into a pattern no more ordered than before. Professor Dewar was one of those people who smiled at all times. Not a big grin, more a sort of shared-assumption smirk; his mouth for every utterance retained a background shape of half-moon, as if always inviting the listener to share the joke, to join hands with him in a 'you-know-how-it-is' wryness. Joe wondered how he told people they had cancer.

'That's OK,' said Joe. He had arranged with the Royal Brompton to meet Professor Dewar in his room at the Neurology Department, but once there had been told by an overstressed receptionist that the professor was always at his private practice on Thursdays and she didn't know anything about it. When Joe rang the number she gave him, the man himself had answered, and – although Joe had a sneaking suspicion that Professor Dewar had no idea who he was – the rich Scottish voice at the other end had apologised incessantly and insisted that Joe come to Harley Street as soon as was convenient – which turned out to be later the same afternoon. 'I had a slight problem because there's another Dr Dewar who works in immunology.'

'Marcus! At the allergy clinic! Yes!' Professor Dewar's eyes twinkled as if he was pouring a malt whisky into a satisfyingly large glass. 'Often confused. And he's not even a proper Scot!'

'The allergy clinic?'

'The pride of the Immunology Department. Great success in reducing allergic reactions by injecting sufferers with steadily increasing dosages of the allergen – hay fever people with pollen, and so on.' Professor Dewar's smile magnified. ''Course if you ask Marcus how it actually works, he hasn't a clue. Not a clue! The immune system's such a mystery. Which . . .' he said, producing from amongst the papers on his desk a copy of Joe's letter, on Friedner-headed notepaper '. . . brings us to neatly to your own area of interest, does it not?'

'Yes,' said Joe, relieved that the professor had – even if it was only this afternoon – established who he was. 'As I think it says there, I run a research lab for Friedner. Working towards an HIV vaccine. And, of course, drugs for presently infected patients.'

'Right, right, of course. Yes.' Professor Dewar frowned a little, his eyebrows, grown bushy with greyness as eyebrows sometimes appear to do, meeting in the middle, and point-ing diagonally up at either end, like a werewolf's; but, even though the effect was to exaggerate the frown, his predominant expression still seemed to be smiling. Above his eyebrows, his skin peeled away into acres of shiny bald scalp. 'Didn't I read in the *Lancet* something about Friedner diverting funds away from HIV research? They were originally one of the main commercial funders of AZT, weren't they?'

Joe put a flat hand up to his temple and sank his face into it; this information made him feel tired, although at the same time impressed by Professor Dewar's up-to-dateness, at least in medical terms. He imagined that in all other respects he was one of those people whose contact with the world extends no further than the wavelength of Radio 4.

'Yes. But we've managed to keep things going, just about.'

'Splendid! So you think you might be on to something?' He said it as a bumptious detective inspector might say it to Sherlock Holmes.

'I don't know. Maybe.'

A silence set in – a deep silence, protected by the thick layers of panelling that enclosed the room on three sides; a silence not contaminated, as it would have been at the hospital, by generator hum, trolley roll, double-door crashing, medicine calls and the distant bleeps of electronic heart-meters. It is the silence of wealth – the sort of silence that is enhanced only by the slow ticking of a grandfather clock; there was none in the room, but Joe felt he could hear one anyway.

Professor Dewar continued to look eager and enquiring despite the silence. The research bulletin he clearly expected not being forthcoming, however, he said, 'Mm-mm. So how can I help?'

'About six months ago, you had a patient called Tessa Carroll. She would have come in with symptoms suggesting a possible tumour of one of her frontal lobes. She had a lymph node biopsy performed at the Brompton . . .'

Joe trailed off. Professor Dewar assumed an air of polite interest.

'As I said before, how can I . . . ?' he said, eventually, lifting a hand up sideways as a substitute for repeating the word 'help'.

'Well, I was wondering if you could give me any information about her.'

Professor Dewar held his smile. 'And your relationship to Ms Carroll is . . . ?'

Joe's innards felt weighted down; what else had he expected?

'I don't know her.'

Blasted, suddenly, with depression, he couldn't be bothered to continue; he had no ideas about how to scale the confidentiality wall.

'So . . . how do you know *of* her?'

Joe coughed.

'You want to get that seen to,' said Professor Dewar. Joe nodded, wearily, and then made a decision just to go for honesty. He had invented some stories on the way here, but they faltered on his tongue faced with the overweening teacherliness of Professor Dewar.

'My lab is one of those that the NHS tenders work out to. The biopsy was sent there for carcinomatic analysis.'

Professor Dewar frowned again. 'The biopsy was sent out under her *name*?'

Joe sighed. 'No. I found that by hacking into the mainframe of the hospital computer.'

For the first time, Professor Dewar's smile seemed to be under pressure; at least, it seemed suddenly frozen. But then he took out a fat gold pen from the inner lining of his jacket, and, on a notepad in front of him, wrote the words 'Tessa Carroll' in capitals and underlined them. He underlined them again. Without looking up, he said: 'It was positive, was it not?'

'Yes.' Joe felt a sense of now or never come upon him. 'But beyond that – it interested me. The tissue I saw looked very like it came from a particularly virulent non-Hodgkin's lymphoma. I've seen cases like it – rarely – but I have seen it in my research. Particularly with advanced T-cell diminishment.'

'Are you suggesting this woman might have had AIDS?'

Joe nodded.

'And this tumour appeared as a consequence?'

'Yes. Would you have tested for HIV?'

Professor Dewar shook his head. 'Not at that stage. We would—'

Joe raised his hand to interrupt. 'What stage?'

'Well, the stage we got to with this patient.'

'How do you mean?'

'If my memory serves me correctly . . .' He stood up, revealing the oxblood diamonds of his armchair; a broad-shouldered man, whom age had not yet narrowed, Professor Dewar went over to the thick oak shelves lining the far wall, packed neatly with fat black clip-files, and picked out one embossed – *fucking embossed*, thought Joe – with the letters A–D. He moistened his index finger with two fastidious licks, and flicked the crêpe-like pages.

'. . . yes: Tessa Carroll came to see me twice: once at the Royal Brompton, in March – when we did some X-rays, excised the tissue and performed an MRI brain scan – and then here a week later for the results, which as you say were, unfortunately, positive.' He shut the file. 'We did of course take a preliminary blood test the first time she came, but would not at that point have tested for HIV.'

'And after that . . . ?'

Professor Dewar came back round to his chair. Settling, he said, 'There is no after that, I'm afraid. After I gave her the results, I never saw her again.' Joe started. 'I outlined the possible courses of treatment and I think she was booked in immediately for radiotherapy, but she never came back. I wrote to her five or six times, but to no avail.'

Joe leant back; behind Professor Dewar, a window gave out on to a less-salubrious-than-you-might-expect view of fire escapes and concrete courtyards, lit grey by the sky of a poor English summer, a summer that really let the country down.

'To be honest with you, Mr Serena, that is why I've been prepared to share this information with you – somewhat unethical though doing so is. I would very much like to know what became of Tessa Carroll.' Even this he said with a smile, as if the remark was less one of sadness at his patient's uncertain destiny and more one of self-deprecation at this new example of his own inimitable curiosity. 'But it seems to me that our knowledge of her is about equal.' He held his hands up at right angles to his chest. 'That she is a young woman with cancer.'

'Or was . . .'

Professor Dewar shook his head. 'I doubt it. Even if the cancer was multiplying at the rate you suggest, I don't imagine that she would be dead in six months. And . . .' He stood, with enough of an air of winding up to make Joe stand too, '. . . for all I know, she just decided to get treated elsewhere, and is now in remission.'

They made their way across a Persian rug so thick Joe felt his shoes had been given an extra sole, to the heavy oak door. Professor Dewar opened it, into the unpanelled, uncarpeted corridor.

'I'm sorry I couldn't be of more help . . .'

Joe made a resigned face. 'You sure there's nothing else you can remember about her that may be of use . . .'

'Not really. A great shame, of course. Pretty girl. Family, I believe.'

'But medically . . .' said Joe, pressing gently.

'I don't think so.' But then his smile moved from its base position to one of actually smiling, with memory. 'No, wait a minute. It's a very minor point, but . . .'

'Go on.'

'Well, I made a routine inspection of her scalp, obviously. And I noticed that the area around her crown had gone slightly bald.'

'Bald?'

'Yes.'

'You think she may already have had chemotherapy?'

He shook his head. 'No. I wondered if it was some unusual symptom of frontal lobe swelling, but when she came back for the results I realised what it was.'

The smile was really quite big now, almost Joker-like; he was enjoying this medical anomaly. Joe made a hand movement to indicate that the professor should continue.

'Well, obviously, she was very nervous. And I noticed that, when nervous, she had a habit of unconsciously pulling at the hair on the top of her head. She would even pull single hairs out, and play with them across her hands without, as far as I could make out, quite realising she was doing it. It's a condition called, something or other . . . what is it now . . .' He put his hand across his eyes.

'Trichotillomania,' said Joe.

'That's it!' said the professor, lifting his hand away, smiling as broadly as he had ever done. He kept the smile there, as he always did, although internally he was really quite shocked at how unsmiling – indeed, almost thunderous – the face of the odd little biochemist was in response.

VIC

Vic sat in his living-room all day, waiting for the naked old woman to come out on to her balcony. Every day she would come out, normally round about two o'clock, although sometimes as early as twelve, other days as late as half-past five. She was always naked. At first, Vic thought she might just have been topless, as her lower half was hidden by the balustrade, but lately he had caught sight of her parallelogrammatic buttocks walking back into her darkening corridor, and she was naked. She would come out as if preparing to hang clothes, but she never had any clothes. Her breasts were enormous and low-slung, breasts that Western man only sees these days on famine appeals or extremely remote sections of the World Wide Web.

Actually, 'waiting' isn't quite the word. 'Waiting' implies expectation, and perhaps in this case might suggest some form of perverse salaciousness, but that would be wrong. Vic was sitting facing the window in his living-room, from where he could see her balcony, but he wasn't really waiting for her to come out, he was just marking time, staring at the off-white walls of the flats opposite, deeply doing nothing, and the only thing that would mark one moment from the next and define movement in time would be the appearance of the old woman. It would break the trance.

By a quarter to seven, it was starting to get dark. Not coming, he thought, eventually. Gone: just like all the other women in my life. He thought about getting up, but then wondered where he would go once he did. No reason to go to the kitchen, he thought: there was no food in it, and he was not hungry – he hadn't been hungry, it seemed, for weeks. No reason to go to the bedroom – it was too early to sleep, and anyway, sleep was much like food now, something he couldn't get but didn't really want anyway. Last time he had slept, he had dreamt he was lost at sea and dying of thirst, so he cried and tried to drink his own tears, but realised he couldn't because they too were salt water. No reason to go over to the TV and switch it on – it would be the news soon, and he had never had much interest in the world outside, and now none. No reason to go to the bathroom – he had no one to keep himself clean for. A couple of weeks ago, or maybe it was yesterday, he'd had a bath, and had tried to read a book in it, but, listlessly, the book had fallen from his hands into the water, and when he saw it now, its pages stuck together on the tiled floor, it only made him feel more deeply the no-going-backness of accident, how irreparable damage can be. The only place that seemed worth going to was the toilet, although then again he could always just stay here and soil himself. Maybe, he thought, if I don't eat or drink again, soon I won't even have to do that, and then I can just stay sat here for ever.

However obvious the diagnosis might seem, Vic didn't know he was depressed. He knew of course that he was sad, and still often cried about Emma, and, in a different emotional compartment, missed Tess, but he was so used to hard-core laziness that the main symptom of depression (which people who have never been depressed do not know, thinking that depression means that you just feel somewhat joyless) – the inability to move – felt not dissimilar enough from his normal disinclination to movement to inspire in him a recognition of his condition, or that he even had a condition. Depression, though, is actually just that, a sense of being pressed down, and the other words for it – feeling downcast, or low, crestfallen, crushed, heavy at heart – taken literally, all convey equally well Vic's state of being: he felt as if the air pressure around him was much higher than it ought to be, or as if he was far, far underwater, or as if – and sometimes you just have to use the stock phrase, because sometimes it is indeed the correct description – as if a great weight had been placed on his shoulders. Sitting there, as he had done for days, he liked to picture this weight as an anvil, or possibly a comedy ten-ton ballast, sculpted in its lower section perfectly to fit his upper body, such that when he did get up it rose with him, as it were, easily – that is, with enormous physical effort on his part, but without threatening to throw him off balance, thus allowing him, when walking around, to still feel at all times intensely freighted.

And yet, it didn't feel that different from how he often felt, once he had got comfortable.

Much later, although as far as Vic could tell it might have been only five minutes, he noticed that he had changed his trousers. Not that he had changed his trousers in the time between waiting for the naked old woman to come out and now, but that he had changed his trousers *today*. When he realised this, he also realised that he couldn't remember how long he'd been wearing the same clothes, but that was hardly surprising since he wasn't, at the present time, taking them off to go to bed. But he knew that last night he'd been wearing the black jeans, and now he was wearing blue ones.

He couldn't remember taking off the black jeans, but surmised that he might have stepped out of them when he went to the toilet this morning, or rather, that they might have stepped out of him, floating free of his feet into a crumpled heap around the china base. Following this train of thought – improvising it, rather than remembering it – Vic guessed that he had probably wandered around in his pants and socks for some time, and then noticed that his legs were bare, and then put on a new pair of trousers.

This awareness – that he had different trousers on – did, at least, provide the mark, the point in the day which denoted movement in time, missed by the non-appearance of the naked old woman. Without such marks, Vic noticed, time lost all its linearity, and consciousness became no longer a continuum, calibrated by new or recurring experiences, but rather a black hole, a thing without chronology: whole days would go by in a state of such narrative collapse.

It spurred him on to activity. Not much activity, by ordinary people's standards – not even by Vic's own usual standards – but, considering he literally hadn't moved all day, something of a herculean leap. He put his hands in his pockets. Even this proved more difficult than expected – the denim, as his skin slid slowly across it, felt like glue, and the entrance to the pockets so tight he thought for a moment that they must have been stitched up. Once inside, his hands felt trapped, snared in two cloth vices, and he panicked a little, thinking he would never get them out. There was something else in the right-hand pocket, as well, that was making it still harder for him to put his hand there – for that was his project, just putting his hands in his pockets (characteristically, the one activity he had chosen for himself today was designed to enhance his inactivity) – and it was a surprise to discover that there was actually something in his pockets: he had not really considered the idea that putting your hands in your pockets might be motivated by looking for things within, rather than simply to provide hammocks for the hands.

It was something hard and cold. He left his fingers touching it for a while, interested in the sensation: it felt like some time since his fingertips had been in contact with anything but air. Then, impinging no more than the almost inaudible drone of an insect under an enormous rock, he became aware of another sensation long unencountered: a stirring of interest.

He wondered what it was, this thing in his pocket. He could even guess what it was.

Summoning up every reserve of strength he had – or so it felt – he pushed his hand deeper still into his pocket, and allowed his fingers to fold over the hard cold thing. He could tell now that it was also thin, and some of it was jagged. He knew now what it was; he didn't know whether or not to pull it out. He thought about this for two or three minutes, because the only point of taking it out was to use it, and he didn't know what the point of *that* would be; but he did know that, for the first time for many months, something he had done – putting his hands in his pockets – turned out at least, and even though by accident, to *have* a point, to lead somewhere: he felt, therefore, that he should follow it through. He steeled himself, thinking that this was going to take more effort than he could bear, but actually it was easy: he just took it out of his pocket like a man taking something out of his pocket. What made it easy, had Vic but known it, was the re-entry of narrative into his life, action restarting action: all we need to reverse inertia is some sense of consequence – even bad consequence – some sense that beyond this occurrence there is another, and that they are linked, some sense that life has chapters. But he didn't have time to think about all that, really, because almost as soon as he'd held it up to the dim light coming through his curtainless window from the flats opposite, he'd got up, picked his leather jacket off the floor and gone out, holding like an arrow in front of him the key to the flat above Rock Stop.

He parked the Lambretta up on the pavement outside the side door of the shop. It was raining: it was impossible to read the prices of the guitars through the drip-spattered pane. The weather this summer had contributed to Vic's malaise, because the seasons didn't seem to be passing in the way they should – instead, this summer was all mixed up with bits of winter, autumn and spring, consolidating his sense that time had turned in on itself. Everything about the Lambretta was more difficult when it was raining – it started less easily, you got soaked riding it, the parts gathered more rust – and on the way there, Vic had got pissed off (something you can still be – or not – when you are depressed), and thought about turning back. He didn't – the power of finding the key drove him on – but, as he slipped trying to heave the dinosaur of a moped backwards on to its stand, scraping his shin, he felt frustrated, his sense of fate and direction subverted by banalities – the frustration of the man who, having thought himself following his destiny, finds he is actually on the A318 to New Malden.

Inside the flat itself it was darker than he remembered; but then, he'd never been there this late before, except once, and then he was asleep. When he switched the light on it burnt his eyes, leaving a smattering of naked light bulbs across his field of vision.

Not much had changed, although without the ameliorating effects of secret love, the full skankiness of the place was revealed: the sofa-bed was smaller, the sheets greasier, the wallpaper more mouldy, and the dust on all surfaces thicker than he had, in his mental re-creations, pictured. A few things appeared completely new, or rather, seemed to have escaped his notice before – he'd had no sense that the floor had been covered in black, scratched lino, nor that the sink next to the bed had a depressing bottle of hand-soap hanging above it. He pushed the funnel-gun in: a trickle of old clear liquid oozed out of the tip, hung there for a second, and then dropped, uncaught, into the plughole. In the corner of the sink, held by white cakey flakes atop an indentation too small for it, designed presumably for those thin cream Milky Bar tablets from the days of rationing, lay the reason why he'd forgotten the hand-soap bottle: a bar imprinted with the word DOVE, that he now recalled Emma bringing on their second liaison here. He remembered her opening the blue and white box, and setting the bar down on the sink. He had at the time wondered

277

whether her instinct in doing so had been sweet – to make the space, in a small way, wholesome – or sour – to provide them, pragmatically, with the means of cleansing their bodies of each other's juices before returning to their rightful partners – but now he realised that it was neither one thing nor the other: that buying soap for an illicit love nest is an action perfectly poised halfway between home-making and home-wrecking.

In the poor light of the bedroom, he thought he could make out some fingerprints still on it. They looked too small to be his. He spread his three middle right-hand fingers and placed them gently on the prints. Gently: trying just to touch where her fingers had touched, trying just to touch his fingertips to hers, this mould of hers, but the bar had grown soft and pappy with age and water, and the white surface gave way, implanting his nails in the O and the V.

He washed his hands and wandered through to the other room. Flicking the light switch, he realised that the bulb had gone, but he knew his way around: even in the dimness he could recognise the shapes and outlines well. He'd been expecting, for some reason, the furniture and the scattered instruments to be covered in enormous white drapes, like they always are in the rooms and hallways of revisited houses in films, but they weren't. It brought home to him how much this place was and always would be primarily a storeroom, somewhere where things are kept. Not a storeroom for an especially successful business, he thought, noticing, as he walked between the cases, that virtually all the instruments that had been there on his last visit six months previously were still here.

Except, where the harp had stood, in the middle of the room, sat a large wooden crate. On the side facing Vic was a piece of A4 paper, stuck to the wooden panel by a diagonal strip of Sellotape; squinting, he read: 'Deliv: Mr P. Drake, 5 Wolleston Gardens, SE2'. Suddenly getting an urge to see the harp, he tried to pull the panels off the crate, but even with his hard-as-nails nails, he couldn't get any purchase on the squares of the wood and succeeded only in giving himself a splinter in one of his still slightly soapy fingertips. He sat down on top of a black guitar case opposite that was lying up on its side; he sat in the dip of its top curve. He stared at the crate for some time, wondering what to do. He wondered what the time was, but didn't have a watch on. He wondered if this was what he'd come here for.

After some time he recognised the case he was sitting on. He got up and carefully pushed it backwards, laying it flat on the floor. He flipped the gold buckles upwards: inside, lying like an embryo in a kitsch womb, was the Gretsch Chet Akins 1600: the mother-of-pearl inlays on its neck glinted milkily in the light limping in from the other room. Gorgeous, even in the dark. He picked it up and played a G chord, followed by an A minor and then a D seventh: the opening of 'Shop Girl Queen'. Like all semi-acoustics, the word 'semi' was an exaggeration, and the strings sounded as tinny and thin as he knew they would have sounded rich and complex when amplified. He let the sine wave body fall from his hips, holding on to the neck with his left hand. He looked at the guitar for a few seconds and felt, unreduced, even through the heavy sense-blanket of depression, the sharp purity of his admiration; and then he joined his left hand to his right, curving both sets of fingers round the top of the neck, and swung it over his head, to come crashing down on to the top of the crate.

The white scratchplate flew off immediately, and a section of the body around the lower f-hole cracked; but, spurred on by noticing he'd made a sizeable dent in the top of the box, he swung it again, the same way, remembering how as a kid in love with guitars he'd always hated Pete Townshend for doing this. This time, both pick-ups came loose from their holsters like a pair of comedy eyes on springs, and the silver engraved tremolo spun off in fast circles like a knife from a circus thrower. He knew he might only have one more really good shot left, and so brought the guitar all the way back behind his head this time – he could feel its rump touching his own – and then flew it, in

279

an outrageous arc, all the way over himself, jumping as he did so to try to add weight to the contact. Wood shattered, he wasn't sure where: an explosion of wood. When he recovered his balance, he was holding the neck of the beautiful guitar; the body had come off and was stuck in the top of the crate, its upper curves still visible above the fractured panel. It looked like the cover of a 1970s album, designed by Hipgnosis for Yes or Gentle Giant or someone, an image of a guitar rising up from burial alive.

Vic raised himself up to his full height and dug his fingers into either side of the rent made by the guitar in the crate. He pulled at the wood, which, weakened by impact, came away in shards in his hands. He threw them over his shoulder, creating a pile behind him that grew steadily into an unlit pyre.

Let me see it, he found himself saying out loud, *let me see it*, knowing full well what the symbolism was, it wasn't complicated. Eventually, most of the top section of the crate had gone: underneath he could feel an ocean of bubble-wrap. Holding gently on to the top of the bubble-wrap, he tipped the crate up, laying the front panel down; then, going round to the hole that had been the top, he pulled the instrument out from within. Breathing heavily, he stood it up – it was lighter than he expected; it sat in the centre of the room, in a misshapen clump of pocked polythene, like an enormous bust of John Merrick's head. He tore at this, an easier ripping, although every so often he would come across a section held together by hard brown gaffer-tape, and would have to go at this with his teeth. Finally it yielded, coming apart and falling like an unzipped dress.

Vic looked at his prize: and then with a quiet cry, down. In his hand he held a ball of bubble-wrap; it unfurled as he looked at it, the bubbles held tight in their lines, not floating away, not floating away. In front of him stood a Roland G300, one of the best electronic keyboards on the market. Vic knew this, because on his last job, for Iceland, the keyboard player had gone on about it, particularly how great it was for sampling other instruments. Oh, he thought, oh *good*: so I could probably get a fantastic Gaelic harp *sound* out of it. That was his last thought, before the phone rang.

It *is* connected, was his first next thought. Then he wished he did have some idea of what the time was. Not that it would have made that much difference to the mystery of who could be calling, since no one had ever called the flat before in the day either, but he did it instinctively, as you do when the phone rings at night: look to the clock, and past a certain time, different for different people, think about not picking it up, because it can only be something you don't want to hear. It rang still, now on its fifth pair of bells; Vic wondered why Britain insisted on that, the double-bell, when everywhere else it was single. He went through to the bedroom, and thought he could see the beige dumbbells of the receiver shaking with each ring, like a cartoon phone.

Vic wanted to know if this was it, then, his destiny. He was starting to get fed up with stuff not being his destiny. Coming here, he'd thought was, but then it rained and he hurt his shin, which didn't fit at all; then the harp was gone, replaced by a keyboard – that too felt all wrong. That's why he hesitated about picking up the phone. He didn't think he could bear a new banality. The worst thing – worse than it being the Angel of Death on the line, much worse – would be that it was just a wrong number, a cross fast voice saying 'Is Jimbal there?' That's the thing about your destiny: how are you supposed to know it when it arrives? How are you supposed to recognise it from the random life?

His hand rested in the air just above the receiver: he felt he could feel an air cushion between his palm and the plastic. He'd lost count of the rings by now, but knew at least it was someone on a mission, someone who wanted an answer.

He picked it up. For a moment he forgot who it was in this

set-up who was supposed to speak first, the power seemed so much all on the other end of the line.

'Hello?' he said at last, something in him declining to say 'Vic here'. Once said, though, 'Hello?' actually felt *more* vulnerable, because it was a question, a cry in the dark like 'Who's there?' It somehow opened him up more then just the flat saying of his name. Nothing: although the very faint sound of breathing was definitely audible. 'Hello?' he said again, a little more insistently. Still no reply; the breathing was constant, soft and unobscene. His stomach filled with lead at the thought that it was indeed a wrong number, and he waited for the dumb query or, more likely, the click as the caller just put the phone down.

But before the click came, he did hear a distinct sound, a sound not that different from the breathing he could hear anyway – a sound that is in fact just a different form of breathing, just breath forced out of lungs a little quicker than usual – but for Vic the difference was significant. He heard a cough.

He hadn't seen him for some time, but he knew he had a cough.

'Joe?' he said, but the click had come now, leaving his ear only with the half-silence of the unrequited line. He listened to it for some time, the quiet crackle of electricity along the dark pylons, before thinking: I suppose that's probably it, then. My destiny.

VIC AND JOE

Vic didn't have to wait long for it to play itself out. He went back to his own flat in Sydenham, and was sitting again in the living-room when the doorbell rang. This time he had access to a clock, an old-style station one Tess had bought for him: 2.16. The lateness didn't concern him. He went down the communal stairs of his building, not bothering with the entryphone. Opening the front door, he saw, as he expected, Joe, in a light grey mac, scant cover for the pouring rain. His hair was matted down over his forehead, making him look, Vic thought, younger.

'Hello,' said Vic, and then, genuinely, 'have you lost weight?'

As if in answer, Joe hit him – with all of it – full in the face.

The first thing Vic saw on coming round was white: pure, bright white, and it made him wonder if he was dead, or in hospital, or if perhaps he'd gone blind, because he'd once read somewhere that what blind people see is not necessarily black. The white appeared to be moving, however, in planes – in front of him there was one plane of bright white and behind that another. A new plane of white then appeared, much closer to him, directly in front of his left eye. This one was less brilliant, and bobbled: it closed on to his eye, forcing

283

him to see a two-tone world, black in that eye and white in the other.

He looked up with the open eye. Joe, in his white coat, was moving around to his side.

'Just sit still,' he said, and unfurled a further section of bandage from the roll, walking around behind Vic in order to wind it round his head.

'Right,' said Vic. The realisation that he was being bandaged clarified for him why both his nose and left eye ached. He looked, as far as he was able, about him. He was sitting in a black leather swivel-seat, and, now his vision had cleared, he could guess where they were.

'This where you work?' he said.

'Uh-huh,' said Joe, a phrase he had picked up from Charlene.

'Nice.'

'Thanks.'

'Although if you wanted to have a boys-together chat, surely we should have done it at the Spice of Sydenham.'

Joe stopped his bandaging for a second, looking down at him.

'We stopped going there, though, didn't we? Soon after I got married. In fact . . .' and he seemed to tighten the bandage a little here, '. . . soon after I *told* you I was going to get married.'

Vic nodded, a little queasily, feeling the time had come to change the subject. 'What's that?' he said, pointing at a large square of grey machinery in the corner.

'An electron microscope.'

Vic squinted at it. There were similar-looking machines all over the long, wide room. He was surprised: he expected, these days, all technology to be small, but most of the devices he could see here wouldn't have looked out of place in *The Forbin Project*. Where, he wondered, was the wall of computers with the reel-to-reel tape-wheels, the ones that said *I have been programmed to prevent war*?

'You're pretty good at this,' he said, as Joe fastened the bandage together at his temples.

Joe's fingers carried on working. 'Yes. Well, I'm sort of half a doctor.'

Vic considered his situation for a moment. 'You know you could have saved yourself a lot of trouble by – how can I put this – *not* hitting me?'

Joe nodded. 'I suppose the other half of me did that, though,' he said.

'The Non-Doctor.'

Joe paused. 'That's a name for a vibrator, isn't it?'

'Yes,' said Vic, and felt instantly embarrassed, his wit never feeling so out of place. 'I thought you worked in Kent somewhere,' he continued quickly.

'I do.'

Vic's composure trembled. 'How long have I been out?'

'About two hours.'

Joe walked backwards, surveying the bandage carefully; then sat, with his arms behind him and his legs still on the floor, on a long work-desk about five yards away. To his left side, Vic noticed, there were two glass cages, one containing what looked like rats, the other mice. They, too, were white.

'You must have hit me quite hard.'

'I think I probably did.'

'And then carried me up here?'

'I've been working out.' He flexed his shoulders. 'And besides, you've always been absurdly thin.'

Vic nodded, easily, this talk of established truths between them creating a bizarre atmosphere of normality.

'Don't they have a security guard here?'

'Yes. He let my car through the gate. I'm always coming here, all times of the day and night.' Joe's blue eyes remained impassive. 'He didn't bother to check the back seat. Why should he?'

'Right.' Vic looked at him; he was impossible to gauge. 'So . . . didn't you have a bandage at home?'

Joe shook his head.

'No 7-11s open?'

Joe folded his arms. 'I didn't intend to bring you here. When I went round to your flat.'

'What did you intend?'

'I had no idea. But then when you opened the door, punching you seemed the logical thing to do.' Joe stroked the knuckles of his right hand with the fingers of his left. 'I've never punched anyone before.'

'Is it satisfying?'

'Yes. Hurts, though.'

'Oh does it.' Vic looked him up and down. 'So I suppose it's safe to assume it was you on the phone?'

'It was.'

Vic held his gaze. Joe's calmness was starting to get on his nerves, although he knew his own attitude was similar: but he felt Joe's to be more studied.

'How did you get the number?' *Did she write it down somewhere?* he wanted to say, but didn't want to refer to Emma, even though he knew that whatever the other reasons involved in Joe bringing him here might be, she was the basic one. Joe levered himself off the work-desk and from something like a tissue box attached to its underside, he pulled a pair of limp white surgical gloves.

'I got it off Sylvia,' he said.

Vic half gasped, half laughed. 'What?'

'Yeah,' he said, pulling the fingers of each glove long, and expertly snapping his own fingers within. 'You remember I told you at the funeral that I thought Emma must have been in contact with her just before she died?'

He said it so coolly, so straightforwardly – as if he were asking Vic if he remembered a pair of trousers he'd recently bought – that Vic began to wonder if he was right about Joe's attitude being studied. To mention her name, and her death, now, knowing what he must, and not shake, for his voice not to tremble – it slightly frightened him.

'Yes.'

'I was right. But she didn't go and see her. She *phoned* her.'

This was news to Vic. 'Oh . . .' he said, weakly.

'I 1471'd Sylvia's phone when I went to see her. A day and a half later, but luckily – as you sort of pointed out when you came round the day after Emma's death – no one else would ever have phoned Sylvia. It gave me a day and a time *twenty minutes before the crash*.' For the first time Joe's neutral, almost chipper tone seemed to harden; then it flipped back. 'And, of course, a number. Which I've been ringing periodically ever since.'

Vic's thoughts whirled. 'How periodically?'

'Every night. Before I go to sleep. And when I wake up during the night. Which is a lot, these days.'

Saying this, he walked five or six paces towards a filing cabinet next to the window speckled with globules of rain.

'It was very exciting when it got picked up. Can you imagine, ringing a number every night for – ' he lifted his eyebrows – 'well, over six months now. And then finally, the phone's answered! But then, for some reason . . .' he said, opening the top drawer, '. . . it was really *un*surprising to hear *your* voice.'

Vic wondered if there was an opening to lie about how he came to answer that call; but he didn't know where to start, and besides, something about Joe's attitude suggested that he had other information at his disposal.

'Joe . . .' he began instead, 'I'm so sorry . . . I—'

'Where is it?'

'What?'

'The number. Dulwich, or something isn't it?'

Vic looked at him open-mouthed. 'Herne Hill. It's a flat in Herne Hill.' Joe nodded. He took a folder out of the cabinet. It was one of those polythene folders divided into several separate sealed pockets; in each lay a microscope slide with some form of blood, culture or tissue on it. He held the folder up to the tubular neon light.

Vic thought that perhaps, if he was going to apologise, he

287

should go over to him – offer an embrace, even. He made to get up, but had to sit down again immediately, a sharp burst of pain imploding around his nose and eye.

'I wouldn't do that, for a little while,' said Joe, removing a slide from the folder. 'I gave you some Bulatol while you were out, which should have dulled the pain a bit, but you'll still feel dizzy if you try and get up too fast.'

'Bulatol?'

'It's a painkiller. And . . .' He coughed again. 'Sorry . . . a sedative.'

Vic stared at him, feeling suddenly tired of all this. He had been *sedated*?

'Joe. Let's stop pretending we're in a James Bond film, OK?' He rubbed his bandaged face. 'Why the fuck have you brought me here?'

Joe finally took his eyes from the slide, and let them rest on Vic. 'When I hit you, you bled,' he said.

'Right. An expert in biochemistry and you couldn't work that one out *theoretically*? You had to do the practical?' Joe said nothing. 'And so you took me all the way to Kent to bandage me up?'

'No. It made me wonder something.' He drew a microscope – a more recognisable version of one than the machine in the corner – towards him along the work-desk. 'Does it not surprise you that you haven't got hay fever this year?'

Vic started, his head moving back on his neck. 'Yes. Of course. But I haven't given it much thought. Something to do with the shit summer, I assumed.'

Joe shook his head. 'No. Pollen counts are higher than ever.' He sniffed. 'Even I'm suffering a bit, and I hardly ever get it.'

'So?'

'So . . .' said Joe, looking for a second as if he could do with a flip-chart and a pointer, 'let me explain something to you about hay fever. Basically, you – as a sufferer – have cells in your body covered in a chemical called IgE. This reacts to pollen, thinking that it's an invading body, and sets off antibodies to fight it, which are then carried around in the blood by T-cells. The antibodies cause mast cells to give off histamines and leukotrienes, which are what causes – but I can see I'm boring you.'

Vic looked round. He had been, of course; Vic had found himself watching the twitching nose of one of the rats, visible in its cage above what he presumed to be the legal minimum amount of straw, almost as soon as Joe had named the first chemical.

'No, not a bit.'

'Well, anyway, my point is: hay fever is an autoimmune response. It's basically a product of an *overactive* immune system. An immune system which goes crazy the minute it thinks it's under attack.'

'Right . . .' Vic felt a yawn coming on.

'Now: for you not to have hay fever, suddenly, and without reason . . .' Joe put the slide he had been holding in the microscope clips, delicately, '. . . your immune system would have had to become *significantly* less active.'

Vic's yawn got swallowed somewhere in his chest. 'What are you saying?'

'I'm saying that you were lying on the floor in your flat, bleeding, I touched your face and your blood got on my fingers. And for some reason, before I'd even formulated the thought in my head, I wanted to wash the blood off. Quickly. Then I remembered what you said about not having hay fever this year, and I thought . . . I thought a blood test might be a good idea.'

Vic sat back in his seat. 'A blood test.'

'Yes. Have you had one recently?'

Vic smiled sourly, sarcastically. 'No.'

Joe walked round the other side of the desk, and bent his eyes to the microscope. Vic wasn't prepared, as yet, to give in to his logic: he felt bullish, resistant.

289

'So just that then, me not having hay fever this year made you think you should kidnap me and force me to have a blood test?'

'No,' Joe replied, without looking up, 'that was just one of a number of pointers. You know, of course, that Emma was suffering from a brain tumour?'

Again, the shockingly calm voice. Joe was so removed, removed from the situation, removed from himself – a man who events have pushed through and then beyond the normal play of emotions, to the numbest place.

'Of course,' said Vic, trying to reply in kind, although baffled as to how Joe had found this out.

Joe adjusted his ratchets quickly, in large movements. 'Cells from her tumour were actually examined in this laboratory.' The pace of his adjustments slowed. 'I saw it.'

'God . . .' said Vic, not able to imagine this experience.

'I didn't know it was hers at the time.' He looked up. 'She used Tessa's name when she went in for tests.'

Vic breathed in. 'I know.'

Joe nodded, as if this was already a past issue, already discussed.

'The tumour was of a kind that I've seen from time to time in my research – similar to something called a non-Hodgkin's lymphoma in size and shape – and looked like it had been multiplying at great speed, which would be indicative – again – of a collapsed, or much diminished, immune system in the patient.' He put his eyes back to the two black tubes. 'You see tumours like it *only* in my field of research. You know what my field of research is, don't you?'

'Joe,' said Vic, getting up now through the pain, 'fucking stop it, all right? This is me. It's Vic.' He pointed to himself. '*Vic*.'

Joe looked up again, meeting Vic's eyes, which were frantic and normal at the same time, or rather, frantically trying to be normal. *I know who you are*, the calmness in Joe's seemed to say. *That's why I'm doing this.*

'Why should my wife have had a tumour like this? And why should *you* not have hay fever suddenly this year? Those are two questions which appeared unrelated . . .' and here his blue eyes seemed almost to smile, not a laughing smile, but one like Professor Dewar's, symptomatic of the scientist's pure pleasure at finding the key, '. . . until you picked up the phone.'

Vic held his gaze for a second, with his single eye.

'Joe. Please will you stop pissing about and just say what you fucking mean,' he said, intoning each syllable of each word.

Joe scratched his nose.

'You've still never had an AIDS test, have you? Except for the one I've just given you.'

Vic's insides balked. It was true. Even though he was older, and less likely to shoot his mouth off just to break taboos, he still basically believed the speech about heterosexual transmission he'd given in the Spice of Sydenham almost a decade ago now. He looked at Joe, amazed, and realised that he was waiting for him to say it, that these were his lines in Joe's personal drama.

'You're saying Emma's tumour was AIDS-related? That I gave it to her?'

Joe nodded, his unchanging face disappearing from view for a second and then resurfacing.

'And therefore – please, let's be clear about this – that I have AIDS?'

'You're HIV positive,' said Joe, firmly. 'On the cusp of having AIDS. Enough on the cusp for – as I say – your immune system already not to be functioning at its highest level.' He paused. 'It's possible, actually, that as you go on to develop fully blown AIDS your allergy will return. I did some investigation into the relationship between AIDS and allergic reaction – not a very studied area, unfortunately – and it seems that AIDS sufferers with previous allergies which had gone away tend, in the late stages of the disease, to get them back, much much worse. No one knows why.'

In the silence following this speech, Vic could hear the unidentifiable hum that buildings like this always make. He looked out of the window, although there was nothing much to see; this type of countryside is very dark at night, since the only buildings are working ones, where people only come during the day. A small battle raged inside him, his instinct for survival kicking against the weight of his depression, whirling back to him now, triply heavy, telling him just to lie down and accept it, it didn't matter. Nothing mattered.

'I don't believe you,' he said at last.

'See for yourself.'

He turned round. Joe had his palms held out towards the *Grey Lady*.

'That's a sample of your blood under there. I took it while you were unconscious.'

Vic stared at him, all thoughts of apology gone.

'Really,' Joe said. 'This is my own microscope. Using this one you can actually see the virus itself.'

He said it obligingly, accommodatingly, as if it might perk Vic up a bit. Vic walked over, feeling stiff and robotic, aware of his movements, of the weight of his soles on the floor and the breath in his nostrils, the possibility of illness making him suddenly take none of these things for granted. He didn't look at Joe, instead putting his eyes straight to the lenses. As the initial binocular shape melted into one, he could see, through the colour filter, a series of greenish blue plasmas, swimming around three larger cellular structures; these larger structures contained within them tens of tiny misshapen red balls. Inside most of the balls, although not all, there was a single black dot, of varying size. The whole thing looked like three transparent bags, loosely stuffed with red eyes, afloat in algae.

'Those black particles in the nuclei of your blood cells are called RNA: the HIV gene.' Joe's tone was helpful, instructive. Vic moved his head backwards from the microscope.

'And that's definitely my blood?' he said, pointing at the slide.

Joe nodded. Vic walked slowly back to his seat. He had felt, a little ironically before, something of a captive there when he'd first woken up; now he felt a captive everywhere, and not ironically.

'How long have I had it?'

'Impossible to tell. As you probably know, the virus can lie dormant for years. All we know is that there has been some replication fairly recently, because that's what's had the effect on your hay fever.' Joe glanced back down the lens, but didn't put his eyes right up to them. 'Your T-cell count looks lower than it should be already. And they're what carry histamines around.'

Stop talking about fucking hay fever, thought Vic; *stop going on as if I should be pleased – like, hey, I've got a terminal disease, but it's OK, a side-effect means I'm not going to sniffle so much in the fields.* But he couldn't find the energy to be aggressive. Instead, he said, as if he was speaking to his doctor, 'How long before it develops fully into AIDS?' In his mind, he scanned the tapestry of his sexual history, but it was long and involved, it was like Bayeux; in the Pathology years, there were encounters he couldn't even remember. And, on a few occasions during that time he had injected heroin, not enough to become addicted, although he had toyed with it – he remembered thinking about systematically choosing to become addicted because of the wondrous relief fixes would then afford.

'That's difficult to tell as well, especially without knowing when you were infected. It's possible that it still won't, for years.' Joe raised a considering finger to his lips. 'It's even possible that you'll never develop it fully. Although, looking at this, you're on your way. But there are people who remain, for their whole lives . . .' and here he paused, weighting the word, '. . . carriers.'

Vic looked down. He wasn't really listening. He was thinking about how much he had loved life, or at least, the memory of life,

293

as he had lived it before Emma died, scooping out the corners of experience, so that when his soul was switched off he could say he'd watched all the channels – satellite, cable, oh yes: he'd had a 94-stationed evening in. And yet now none of it seemed palpable, none of it touchable within him as consolation, as the myth of *oh well, I had a good crack of the whip*: he realised that all that pleasure had just passed through him, only there for as long as it was there, and then gone, like candy floss in the mouth. To think of it only gave him pain; living life that intensely had brought him not peace in the end, but simply a clearer sense of what he would now be missing. His good crack of the whip was landing squarely on his back.

'Basically, the rate at which HIV develops into AIDS varies enormously from individual to individual,' Vic heard Joe say. 'I've seen cases as low as three to four months.' He stopped then, and when Vic looked up at him, he realised that Joe had been waiting for him to do so. 'I don't know how long your affair lasted – six months? A year?' Vic didn't answer: he didn't want to, but also felt he didn't have to – Joe's tone was virtually rhetorical. Joe closed his eyes, and then opened them again, as if to let Vic's silence pass. 'In any case, for my wife to have developed AIDS so quickly is unusual. Not unprecedented, but unusual.' Now Joe looked down. 'If you *are* a carrier . . .' and then back up, his eyes blue like gas flames '. . . it's a very virulent strain.'

'Well,' said Vic bitterly, fed up now with Joe's edge of melodrama, his Jacobean overtones '. . . congratulations.'

'For what?'

'For working it all out so cleverly.'

Joe coughed. He didn't put his hand up to his mouth. 'Yes. Thank you,' he said, coldly. 'I am still confused about one thing, though. Which I would like to know.'

Vic kept his eyes on the floor. Knowledge, he felt now, was a bad thing.

'I'm still not entirely clear whether or not my wife did, in fact, commit suicide.'

'And that's something that you must know. For your own what, Joe? Peace of mind, is it?'

A minor tremor seemed to cross Joe's blue eyes, a tiny hint of weakness in the face of aggression, something of a throwback to his old self. His right hand twitched upwards, perhaps feeling impelled towards his earlobe, but then came squarely back down on to the worktop surface, his fingers curled into a fist.

'Yes. I suppose. Or at least – one day, some time in the future,' he said, 'I would like to be able to pass flower stalls by the side of the road and not wonder, first of all, before I've realised my mistake, who it was that crashed there.'

He said it with that element of resignation that lies on the far side of pain. Those who have been there know that violent responses – tears, despair, suicidal urges – they go in time, replaced by the simple acceptance that from now on, life operates from a base-line of sadness. It was the nearest Joe had come so far to vulnerability, and it made Vic want to cry.

There was a pause, filled not really with tension: too much had passed between these two for tension, and anyway, tension is a function of linguistic pregnancy, of things that might be said, and nothing – surely – was unsayable now. Was it?

'I think perhaps knowing whether my wife's crash was an accident will help that,' said Joe, eventually. 'And there are things you must know that I don't. Were, for example – ' he coughed – 'were you with my wife just before she died?'

Vic looked up. He wondered if, really, he should spare Joe this information. But what information had Joe spared him?

EMMA

Emma drove back from Harley Street to Herne Hill hardly noticing the great swathe of London this journey represents. Or at least, not noticing it as space – she noticed it only as time, as London time, a series of waits – late on this Tuesday afternoon, one of those when London chooses a random day of the week for a *showcase* rush hour, confounding the sense that this should only happen on Friday night and Monday morning. And so she waited – at lights where the green illuminated for only a single car flash, before amber-switching back to the endless red; deep in cone jungles, strung along sections of the south so dug up the sign ROADWORKS seems like a cruel joke, because these roads will never work; behind other drivers snailing along the road looking for numbers, listening to the numbingly cheerful intonation of radio traffic reporters as they spin out the usual black spots, the Gyratory, the Tunnel, the blocked Ms and the blocked As, closing down the options one by one until she wanted to scream *'There's nothing left! There are no other ways!'*

She was crying, but she was crying at the traffic, or so she told herself: with frustration at not being where she wanted to be. She tried hard to stop herself building on this basic frustration, to stop herself thinking how unfair it was that the traffic should

296

be so bad at this particular time. Her mother always used to do that when she misbehaved as a child, always compounded her guilt by bringing into play some previously unknown – and Emma now suspected, made-up – information about the day on which it occurred: *And on this day of all days*, she always used to say. It was hard, though – hard not to delve into self-pity, to think 'Why can't the traffic be OK, just this once?' – hard to drive so slowly through London's thickset obliviousness.

When faced with news such as Professor Dewar had just told her, people tend to talk about having too many thoughts, or conversely, not knowing what to think. Not so with Emma. She knew, rather, what she *ought* to be thinking about. About Jackson, primarily, a mother's first duty: every cancer columnist she'd ever read wrote of the sharpest loss being that of involvement in their children's future, how that represents the real jewel in the treasure of life slipping through their hands with every passing day. About Joe, her husband, and the prospect, considered before but now definite, of not growing old with him; or about his predictable devotion to her in the face of this, the ideal partner at a time of crisis; possibly even how they could have one of those marriages that rebuilds around one of the partners becoming ill. About her mum, how on earth she would survive without her, or, on the other hand, about how it was perhaps a blessing that she was too detached from reality to understand the idea that her child was now likely to die before her. And about herself, about all the life she was going to miss, the music which would raise no hairs on her neck, the jokes that would not make her laugh, the hot days on which water would not cool her skin.

She did think about these things, but through a prism of self-consciousness. Their presence in her mind felt not like the product of immediate, instinctive reaction, but, rather, of a scan, a search-engine plugged into her life with the key-word IMPORTANT. She felt disturbed by this detachment from herself, and wondered if it was another by-product of her illness; she was already disowning every mood, every judgement, every anxiety and virtually every physical feeling, as corrupted, as coloured, grey and black, by her tumour. Nothing that came into her mind might have come there naturally. It was all possibly the result of the pressure of tumour on tissue.

The only person she felt certain she wanted to think about was Vic. It was easier, at some level, to do so, because it was more immediate – she was going to see him now, and the managing side of her felt it was best just to think about that. She filled the time, in the long static spaces, by framing the words she would have to say when she got there, as if on her way to an interview, or a first date. It provided her with a means of ordering her wordless, rushing panic, by forcing it into language. 'Vic . . . I don't know how to say this . . . but the tests were positive,' came first, but felt too *ER*, and not expressive of how she actually felt. She considered a doomed romantic note – 'Darling, I think we may not have that much more time to spend together' – but felt sick as soon as she'd thought of it: despite the fact that death often crops up in romantic narratives, its appearance in actuality leaves one with little heart for brave sentiment. She could, she thought, perhaps just repeat Professor Dewar's method, which had been to quickly say, 'It's not the best news, I'm afraid', go on to speak some sentences containing the word *malignant* and then talk in detail about the efficacy of treatment these days, but then, she and Professor Dewar were not locked together in love. The only thing that felt real, that actually matched what was going on in her head, was to repeat 'I've got a brain tumour, I've got a brain tumour', over and over again; but when she thought of saying it, it felt too much like what was in her head, and she didn't want Vic to see inside her head, not now it was full of dark ugly shadows.

She had seen them herself, these shadows, on the X-rays lit up against white which Professor Dewar had shown her on the previous visit, at the Royal Brompton – when he'd assured her that the dark spot towards the front of her skull was almost certainly benign. These photographs came back to her now, with menaces; already, she felt she had been forced, just in the process of diagnosis, to see herself as the worms would. Glancing at the wing mirror, she thought she could see her X-ray image superimposed on her reflection, the misty outline of tissue and bone sliding over her profile. She shook it off, turning back to the non-moving bumper of the car in front, but still felt desperately aware of the inside of her head. You can feel aware of your head, of course, at any time, more than any other part of your body – you can feel yourself to be inside your own head in a way that you can't, really, feel yourself to be inside your own knee or your own wrist or, unless you're very gifted, your own mouth. But she felt it physically, like sometimes you do during a particularly bad hangover, where the brain is so dehydrated it seems to scrape on every movement against the inside of the skull. She was sure she could feel her brain: as if she had another hand inside her head, running its fingers over her grey mushy contours, like a blind person checking a cauliflower.

And she was sure she could feel the lump, pressing against her skull. It was in her frontal lobe, Professor Dewar had said and had given her a vague sense of the area, just above and to the right of her forehead. She found her eyes straying to the rearview mirror, not to look for traffic behind, which was moving too slowly to be worth checking, but to see if her scalp in this area was not rising to a point, a comic-book-style bump, forced up by the frenetic growth inside. It seemed to itch, this point, although not in a normal surface way, a result of unwashed hair or nits. The itch was inside her head. She wished the hand inside would scratch it, manically, as if the tumour were a scab, scratch it till it bled.

Towards the end of her journey she heard on the traffic report that Dulwich Road was end-to-end: *avoid if possible*. It felt like the last blow. She didn't know another way there, and besides, she wasn't confident about going off-route, and not just because of her previous experience of getting lost:

299

her new-found distrust of her body extended to whole areas of consciousness, of which sense of direction was one. The orange and yellow configurations of the *A-Z* open on the passenger seat bounced off her eyes, like words in a book too complicated to understand. It wasn't possible. She accepted the inevitability of the jam, turning into Dulwich Road from Herne Hill resigned to despair: and then, miraculously, the traffic report being wrong or late, was able to put her unshod foot down, pleased, before she felt the greater pleasure of speeding down the comparatively free road, that her nerve centres were still working enough to feel the touch of the accelerator circles through her tights. She had worn a dress-suit to go to see Professor Dewar, thinking it more appropriate than her usual jeans or dungarees; and, heartbreakingly, although she would never have admitted this, because she thought it might somehow improve her chances.

Her spirits rose disproportionately at this tiny change of fortune. It may seem odd that being prevented from getting where she wanted to go had caused her such grief; it is arguable that being stuck in traffic, or anywhere for that matter, is only frustrating if you're on your way to a place of potential joy – a concert, a match, a sexual encounter – and the frustration is but an expression of time lost, time that would otherwise have been spent in delight. It may seem odd, because she was not on her way to a place of potential joy. She was on her way to tell her lover that she had cancer. But, as she drew up to the kerb and parked uncaringly on the single yellow line outside Rock Stop, she could still feel, battling against the oncoming dread of what she now had to face, the uplift of having at last made it here, a feeling that intensified when she saw Vic's Lambretta parked up by the side door. She hadn't arrived at a place of joy, but, at least, or so she thought, a place of some relief.

As it was, she didn't have to say the words anyway. When she came through the door of the flat, Vic was replacing that red guitar he really liked into its case; even with all the other things racing through her head, she felt a stab of affection at the thought of him sitting here by himself, trying to cram all his anxiety into music. He looked up, his dark shaggy features framed, somewhat obviously – as if he'd been practising this face for some time, just as she had her words – into an expression of complete happy confidence. It was so desperately convinced, his face, that it was the more upsetting to see it melt away, like someone taking off a mask, as she began to cry again.

'Oh Emma . . .' he said, and rushed to hold her.

'I'm sorry I'm so late,' she said, her voice on the edge of hysteria, almost singing. 'The traffic was so bad. It was terrible. Everywhere was blocked.'

'It's OK,' he said, stroking her hair, one hand after another, down, down, wishing what she was saying was the real reason she was upset. 'It's OK.'

She buried herself in his hug, trying to lose herself in him, or rather, trying to lose her present self and find again, somewhere in the weave of his black jumper, in the warmth of his body, warmth that seemed to her a direct product of its pure, unalloyed health, her old self, the unmutated one.

'You smell smoky,' she said, her voice muffled in his chest.

'Yes,' he said, through broken breath, 'I came straight from the studio. Where we're doing the Thomson Holidays song.' They laughed a few sobbing laughs at the incongruity of this information, now. 'And the keyboard player was smoking and because I was so nervous, I had two fags.' He cupped her chin in his right hand, and lifted her face. 'Sorry.'

She kissed him, slipping her tongue into his mouth to indicate how little she cared. Their tongues lapped at each other. She opened her mouth wider, wide enough for her jaw to ache, trying to fit her whole mouth into his, pursing her lips inside to suck his tongue – but suddenly, he backed away.

'Em,' he said, sitting back on a flight case. 'Please. I can't – we have to talk.'

The room fell silent, or as silent as the unglazed windows on to Dulwich Road would allow. Emma felt rather taken aback – Vic had never interrupted proceedings that might lead to lovemaking before – but she composed herself, telling herself that he was right, they did have to talk. She went and sat by the harp, her legs on either side of it.

'I don't know what to say, Vic.' She hit the strings on one side with her fist, although not very violently, a slightly half-hearted bit of anger; they made a chromatic chime. 'I don't know what we're going to do.'

Neither did Vic. He didn't understand how this kind of situation might work; it had, he felt, no precedents. Sex – he understood how that could be conducted in secret. But caring for someone who was seriously ill – proper caring, the sort of caring he would want to do, rather than just the odd visit in his official capacity as Joe's friend – he had no idea how to do that in secret. He saw, a few months down the line, the two of them making covert assignations to meet here, just as they always had, except this time so that he could mop her brow and hold her hand while she lay in bed.

'How . . .' He faltered. He couldn't bring himself to say it, and not just because it was painful: it was so *tired*. Sometimes, in the past, women had asked him to talk sexily to them, and he found it difficult, not because he was embarrassed, but because all the phrases felt so over-used – he was amazed at the thought that anyone could be turned on by them, they felt so deactivated by time. He had a similar feeling now, faced with the lexicon of death. 'How . . . long?'

It sounded, he thought, a stupid question.

She rested her face against the strings, feeling them cut slightly into her cheeks: her head like an egg, she thought, against one of those salad slicers.

'They don't know. I have to go back for more tests. My neurologist was very positive, but they always are, aren't they? That's their approach.'

'You still haven't told Joe?'

Emma shook her head. 'I couldn't bear it. And I didn't think there was any point, while I didn't know.'

'You couldn't bear it because ... you couldn't bear his sympathy? Or you couldn't bear his pain?'

Emma stared at Vic, his face on the other side of the strings as if behind bars. 'Does that matter?' She felt the tears welling up again inside her, somehow from her stomach rather than from her eyes. Why was he being like this? *And on this day of all days* ...

'No, no,' he said, aware that his tone might have been inappropriate. 'I suppose not.' He hesitated, trying to pre-adjust his voice, stretching his fingers slowly into the softest of kid gloves. 'Emma ...' She hadn't taken her eyes off him. 'What's this?' he said, picking up a brown ripped-open envelope from beside him.

She squinted slightly at it; and, like a child when confronted with wrongdoing, focused on what she knew full well was not the issue. 'It's from the hospital. It was their last letter. About the appointment today.'

He paused again, wondering how to do this, how to avoid sounding like he was telling her off.

'It's got Tess's name on it.'

Emma felt for a second like saying 'Has it? How odd,' but then the adult in her took over. It becomes more difficult to be childlike as you get older; and if the time between you and death is suddenly elided, you are, effectively, without having actually aged, much older.

'Yes. I forgot to throw it away.'

He put it down. 'I don't understand.'

She closed her eyes, and wiped her face with her hand, as if it were wet. She knew that she should explain herself, but felt that she shouldn't have to right now.

'When I went in for my first appointment at the Royal Brompton, the receptionist at Oncology had managed to lose

303

my files,' she intoned, colourlessly. 'She couldn't find my GP's letter of referral, nothing. It made me feel really shit – like something so important, and they've got it all wrong. Anyway, she let me have the appointment anyway, by getting me to fill out a form. Which I filled out properly. I did. Except when it came to my name and address . . .' She hesitated.

'You put down Tess's name and this address.'

'Yes.' This defiantly; she looked at him. 'Oh for fuck's sake, Vic, don't look so appalled. I didn't want Joe to know about the tests. So I couldn't have letters from the hospital turning up at our house. And then, I didn't like the idea of my name being on the mail here, for Francis and all that lot to see.'

Vic's face went dry and sulky. 'Is that it?'

She pushed the harp away; its wooden platform screeched on the lino. 'Yes!' And then, coming closer to him, 'No. I don't know. What do you want to hear? I did it because I didn't want it to be happening to me, all right? I was projecting.' Her voice went sardonic, singsong quoting: 'Projecting my pain on to someone else.'

He wouldn't look at her. 'But why Tess?'

'Because I wanted *her* to die!' shouted Emma, all her anger at what was happening to her coming to a focus. 'I wanted *her* to have fucking cancer! I would rather it happened to my lover's girlfriend! That's how fucking shallow I am! All right?' She turned away from him, holding herself in her arms, for lack of his. The dwindling light from the window lit her in profile: she felt awkward presenting the side of her head to him, like she did early on her naked back, worried about him seeing cellulite or some such other flaw on the back of her legs. She thought of him imagining the unquiet thing inside. The sound of a distorted guitar playing 'Bad Moon Rising' started up through the floor, underscoring her sobs. When she spoke again, still facing the opposite wall, she had stopped shouting. 'So there you are, you see.' Her voice was straining, trying to get through the lump again, as on that first day. 'I'm not the fucking . . .'

and here, searching for the right words, the phrase *Queen of Hearts* flew into her mind, strangely, as she, like everyone else, had stopped thinking in that vocabulary a long time ago; she let it fall, floating to the floor, like the card in the pack it was, '. . . *goddess* you always thought I was.'

'Really?' said Vic after a short while, his voice thin and stretched, as if his throat was closing too, but it didn't matter – she could hear him easily, because his mouth was next to her ear. His arms closed around her from behind, the reassuring rucksack of love. She put her hand up to them, crooked across her, feeling for the top of his left arm, feeling for his angel.

'I'm sorry,' she said, turning, 'I didn't mean it. I didn't mean anything terrible by it.'

'Shush,' he said, kissing her neck.

'I don't really know why I did it. Now I've said it, I don't even know if it's true. Maybe I didn't want her to die. Maybe the opposite. Maybe I wanted to *be* her. Or, at least, be your girlfriend, living with you here . . .'

He kissed her face, lightly, in a hundred places. She let him do it, but her thoughts were elsewhere.

'Maybe it was the . . . tumour,' she said, getting the word out somehow. 'You know: it causes personality changes. Makes you do mad things. Oh Vic . . .' She pushed his face away a little, to look into his eyes. 'You will tell me. If I go mad. If I start doing things that are really out of character.'

He shook his head. 'It's not going to happen.'

'Because you're the only one who could tell me,' she said, ignoring his blithe reassurance. 'No one else knows me now. Not completely. Not everything about me. You're the only one.' Her eyes were touched suddenly by a different sadness. 'That's what happens when you start to have secrets.' She looked back up at him, putting her delicate harpist hand up to stroke his emery cheek. 'You do know me, darling, don't you?' He nodded. 'And I know you. We have no secrets. Do we?' He shook his head.

There was the longest pause. 'Bad Moon Rising' stopped.

Their hands snaked together. Outside, an urban seagull cried, searching for the sea. So lost: such a long way off.

'I'm so scared, Vic,' she said, eventually, breaking the silence-inspired dream-state. 'Really scared.'

He nodded, trying to fill his eyes with sympathy. 'What can I do?' he said.

She looked back at him, knowing that the answer really was nothing, that they had reached the limits of what love can do, in its ongoing battle with its opposite.

'Fuck me,' she said.

VIC AND JOE

'No,' said Vic. 'I wasn't.'

'You weren't at the flat with her?'

'No. We'd arranged to meet, but I couldn't make it.' He paused. 'The bike broke down.'

Joe raised an eyebrow. 'Right . . .' He took off one of his white gloves, stretching the fingers one by one.

'You don't believe me?' Joe didn't reply. Vic got up and came close to him; it occurred to him for a second to grab the lapels of Joe's white coat. 'OK, don't believe me. Why should I fucking believe you?'

'You've seen your blood—'

'Fuck my blood!' shouted Vic. 'You could be talking bollocks for all I know. I've never heard this shit about people with AIDS not having allergies! I don't know if you're telling me the truth about Emma's tumour!' Despite the bright laboratory light, his pupils were massive, black and engorged. 'I don't know what you did while I was out cold. You must have samples of the virus here. Maybe you fucking injected me with it.'

He searched desperately, but could see no sign of guilt in Joe's eyes. Instead, calmly, Joe snapped off the other glove.

'I guess that's something you'll never really know,' he said, his expression the deepest shade of neutral.

Suddenly, Vic's anger threw off the dark weights of his depression; anger, not so much at what he'd been told, as at the manner of the telling. It needed an outlet; it found one in front of him. He picked up the *Grey Lady* with both hands and, summoning up all his strength, threw it, in an overhead, from-the-touchline manner, towards the window. It revolved in the air quite slowly, like a cog in a machine from a futuristic silent film; drips of his blood came off it from the clipped-in slide, making a trail on the floor. And then it went through the long dark glass – reinforced glass because Friedner had had their fair share of threats from Animal Liberationists – with an almighty crash, splitting the rolling silence of the Kent night. In the shattering, the glass seemed not so much to fracture as to disintegrate, to *powderise*, falling from its vertical plane in a million flakes, as, Vic thought – knowing why he was thinking it – a windscreen does.

'Oh,' said Joe, blinking, 'that's a pity.' He shook his head. 'There goes your best chance of a cure.'

Vic breathed: something about this clumsy sneering made him feel oddly sorry for Joe. He had lost himself. The Cold Revenger, it wasn't him at all; just a voice and a face he was using because his own – benign, assiduous, unreactive – had been scoured away by events. It was fine for now, but what would he do tomorrow? What would he do for his daily purpose?

Vic's sympathy passed. He looked around him for another weapon, something else to throw in the air, but found one instead in his mind.

'Tess!'

'What about her?'

'If what you're saying is true, *she* would be HIV positive. And she isn't.'

'How do you know?'

'Because she had to have a test. Before she got her new job abroad. And it was negative.' He remembered her telling him it, the good news before the bad, that she was leaving.

A look passed across Joe's face, a look Vic couldn't deci-
pher.

'I believe,' he said, taking off his white coat and going over to
the hooks by the door, 'that Tess has always insisted on using
condoms . . . hasn't she?'

Vic blinked, the full scale of his defeat coming to him. 'I don't
remember telling you that . . .'

Joe shrugged. 'Fancy a lift?' he said.

Vic looked away, through the glassless window; it looked
almost exactly as it had done before it was broken, except
that the blurry reflection of the two of them facing each other
had vanished, like a dream from the memory. His arsenal was
empty. He had only one thing left, one possibility of denting
Joe's infuriating composure. He could tell him the truth.

He could tell him how he had indeed been with Emma. How it
hadn't ended as it should, as history and mythology would have
hoped, in romance, in passionate sexual defiance. How they
had gone to bed, and how it had been all right at first, their
torturous circumstances spurring them on, as if sex itself could
be healing, all that tabloid talk of it being good for your health
taken seriously for once, his hands full of vitamins, his tongue
a transplant, his penis a chemotherapy needle. And how that's
where it went wrong, because once it started, he couldn't shake
such imagery from his mind, it stopped him being taken over by
the sexual trance – and then how suddenly, all he could feel was
lumps: her body felt like the surface of another planet. Every
part of her reminded him of cancer, especially the sexual parts.
Her breasts seemed two black growths; her buttocks, the bald
heads of children; her vagina, a surgeon's incision. And how,
when those thoughts had taken their inevitable toll, and she
had said, finally, his limpness in her hand, 'What's the matter?'
he hadn't been able to tell her – oh God, what was he supposed
to have said; what on heaven and earth? Instead, he had run. He
had got up and grabbed his clothes and, without another word,
rushed out, scrabbling them on as he went. And how the next

time – the last time – he had seen her, he was looking round from his scooter, smiling and doing a thumbs-up towards an attractive woman who had given him a push.

He could tell him all that, how in the end death had won, really really won, a victory without measure: death had *whitewashed* it. He could tell him how, given what Joe had now told him, he'd killed her twice it seemed – once by fucking her, and once by not fucking her. He could; but he was just too ashamed. He would always be just too ashamed.

'Yes,' he said, not knowing how else he would get home.

ACKNOWLEDGEMENTS

I would like to thank: Dr Caroline Hill, Dr Jane Anderson and Samantha Walker at the Allergy Clinic of The Royal Brompton Hospital for scientific information; Tracey Macleod, Peter Bradshaw, Sarah Bowden, Michael Marshall Smith, Janine Kaufman, Sarah Shrubb and Alan Samson at Little, Brown for editorial advice; Alison Sweatman and Jon Thoday for doing what they do; and for help beyond categorisation, Morwenna Banks.